The Masterworks of Literature Series

Sylvia E. Bowman, *Editor*

Indiana University

D1637426

The Story of Kennett

The Story of Kennett

by BAYARD TAYLOR

Edited for the Modern Reader by
C. W. La Salle II

COLLEGE & UNIVERSITY PRESS · *Publishers*

NEW HAVEN, CONN.

New Material, Introduction and Notes
by C. W. La Salle II

MANUFACTURED IN THE UNITED STATES OF AMERICA BY
UNITED PRINTING SERVICES, INC.
NEW HAVEN, CONNECTICUT

Contents

Introduction

One hundred years ago, few serious readers in America would have thought it possible that Bayard Taylor would someday be an almost forgotten author, for he was one of the better-known writers of his period. Taylor's fate serves to remind us that two very different literatures were being written in the 1850's and 1860's. Among Taylor's contemporaries were Nathaniel Hawthorne, Herman Melville, Ralph Waldo Emerson, Henry David Thoreau, and Walt Whitman; but from another angle, the literary life was dominated by Henry Wadsworth Longfellow, James Russell Lowell, and John Greenleaf Whittier. The general devaluation of the "Genteel writers" of New England has consigned to obscurity such members of that tradition as Taylor, Thomas B. Aldrich, R. H. Stoddard, and George Henry Boker. Only by recalling the work of a writer such as Taylor, however, can the modern reader acquire a complete picture of American literature of the mid-nineteenth century.

I

Taylor's America was a country in flux. "Manifest destiny" was a popular doctrine, and the geography of America was being radically altered during Taylor's young manhood. While he was on his first voyage to Europe, the annexation of Texas took place. Within the next decade, that state's territory was substantially expanded, the territories of California and New Mexico were acquired, the border of Oregon was fixed along the forty-ninth parallel, and the Gadsden purchase was accomplished. This expansion accelerated the western drift of the population in the United States, and the census of 1850 revealed that fully forty-five per cent of the population resided west of the Alleghenies.

More than most of his contemporaries, Taylor must have been conscious of this vast "other" America, for he made a trip to California in 1849 for Horace Greeley's newspaper, the *New-York Tribune*. The new literary market was one which Taylor would try repeatedly to tap on the lecture circuit tours of his middle years, although without complete success. This enlarged America would ultimately subscribe to values different from those associated with the New England literary establishment and with its heirs.

The other major historical event of Taylor's lifetime was, of course, the Civil War. For whatever reasons, Taylor himself did not go to war; but he secured a commission for his brother, gave speeches supporting the Northern cause, and was for a time a war correspondent for the *Tribune*. At the war's end, America was a country at once politically one and yet simultaneously ever more conscious of its cultural multiplicity. This heightened awareness of sectional peculiarities found expression in the "local color" movement in literature.

These historical occurrences encouraged the growth of a realistic, empirical American literature (as opposed to an idealistic one). And because of his involvement in these events, one could have expected Taylor to be a part of that development. Officially, he was not. It would remain for the next generation of American fiction writers—Bret Harte, Edward Eggleston, Mark Twain, William Dean Howells—to reflect the new modes of life to be seen in this enlarged America, and the ways in which the values of the new territories would conflict with those of the more traditional East. Only Whitman, at the time of Bayard Taylor's literary successes, was dealing with the expanded America as subject matter.

Despite Taylor's apprenticeship in journalism, much of his literature did not reflect his observations of the world about him; instead, it illustrated his commitment to the Genteel Tradition—the literary Establishment of his day. *The Literary History of the United States* (1948) phrases the problem tersely, as it identifies the choice which Taylor and his cohorts made: "The securities of Concord and Cambridge were gone, even though Longfellow and Lowell, Holmes and Emerson lived on. . . . The issue was sharply drawn: if one wished to write, one must choose to defend the old order or to throw in one's lot with the new. There was no easy blending of ideality with reality in these uncertain times .... resentful of the claims of the realists, [Boker, Stoddard, Taylor, Aldrich, and Stedman] self-consciously proclaimed themselves the champions of Ideality in literature" (809).

What were the intellectual values of this tradition to which Taylor had bound himself? Its assumptions can be briefly summarized: that there was an "ideal" order which it was the writer's duty to express; that moral codes were of higher importance than, say, esthetic ones; that man was capable of virtually endless self-improvement in the ethical and cultural spheres; and that it was the social responsibility of literature to encourage this perfectibility. To be a useful, moral document, art should present a very disciplined experience, and call the reader's attention to the ideal, universal aspects of a present, specific situation.

V. L. Parrington in Volume II of his *Main Currents in American Thought* (1927-30) observes: "The essence of the Genteel Tradition was a refined ethicism, that professed to discover the highest virtue in shutting one's eyes to disagreeable fact, and the highest law in the law of convention .... The first of literary commandments was the commandment of reticence .... Any venture into realism was likely to prove libidinous, and sure to be common" (436). To take one specific example, the Genteel writers usually represented the "common man" in an idealized fashion, often in a semi-pastoral setting. For such a figure, contentment with one's social lot was a highly regarded virtue, although a certain measure of material ambition was acceptable. Sustained vernacular expression, physicality, and controversial ideas were avoided. Plot, in the mechanical sense, was an important element. The ideas which that plot projected were designed to flatter the social and moral preconceptions of the largest number of readers.

Ultimately, it is not surprising that the writers of the Genteel Tradition devoted an inordinate amount of attention to such minor literary forms as the more impressionistic kind of "local color" story, the historical romance, travel writing, and children's literature. It is of particular significance, however, that the tradition produced no major novelists, perhaps because the novel, more than other genres, has historically had social change as one of its basic subjects. The Genteel writers, in declining to have their work reflect the turmoils of their world, were really turning away from the major line of development of narrative fiction. Thus the writers of the Genteel tradition are usually remembered as poets or essayists rather than as novelists. Actually, they produced an appreciable amount of work more or less in that genre: Longfellow wrote two volumes of narrative fiction, Whittier one, Holmes three, Aldrich three, Taylor four. But—as Taylor undoubtedly noticed—most of the Genteel writers never achieved the popular success in the novel that they had enjoyed in other forms.

Such novelists of the period as Susan Warner, Maria Cummins, and Augusta Jane Evans Wilson were reaping financial rewards with a somewhat different kind of book. Alexander Cowie in *The Rise of the American Novel* (1948) comments that "When Holmes published *Elsie Venner* in 1861, the vogue of the historical romance and the Gothic tale was largely over or in abeyance, and the novel of domestic life was in ascendancy" (495). He defines the latter as "an extended prose tale composed chiefly of commonplace household incidents and episodes casually worked into a trite plot which involves the fortunes of characters who exist less as individuals than as carriers of moral or religious sentiment. The thesis of such a book is that true happiness comes from submission to suffering" (413). Virtually none of the practitioners of the "domestic novel" were considered serious writers by Taylor and his contemporaries, and he was certainly trying to go beyond the obvious limitations of such writing. Yet *The Story of Kennett* seems related to the "domestic novel" as it is defined by Cowley.

Kennett serves to remind us that the tradition of Melville and Hawthorne was not so dominant in the latter half of the nineteenth century as it is today. The decade of the 1850's had seen the publication of Melville's monumental *Moby Dick* and of Hawthorne's *The Scarlet Letter* and *The Blithedale Romance.* Hawthorne's *The Marble Faun* inaugurated the next decade in fiction, but no works in what might be called the Symbolist tradition followed it. To consider the American novel at its best in the 1860's is to be concerned with such Genteel items as Oliver Wendell Holmes's *Elsie Venner* and *The Guardian Angel*, Sidney Lanier's *Tiger Lilies*, Louisa May Alcott's *Little Women*—and the novels of Bayard Taylor.

The directions taken by the novel in the twentieth century allow us to forget the existence of Genteel narrative fiction. The modern American novel, as well as the tradition of American Realism in general, descended at least in part from the symbolic and allegorical interpretations of America written by Melville and Hawthorne; but it owes relatively little to the idealized depictions of the Genteel writers. The consequence is that Genteel novels have almost disappeared from the histories of American literature. Nevertheless, they are a part of America's literary history, and the present reprinting of a novel by Bayard Taylor will permit the examination of this sub-genre by a new generation of readers.

II

Richmond Croom Beatty's definitive *Bayard Taylor, Laureate of the Gilded Age* (1936) portrays the writer as one who embraced social and cultural values which led him to substitute activity for substantial achievement. Taylor was born in Kennett Square, Pennsylvania, in 1825. His formal education ended in his sixteenth year; an apprenticeship with a printer and newspaper publisher provided his introduction to writing as a profession. His first poem was published in the *Saturday Evening Post* in 1841, and his first volume of poetry, *Ximena*, appeared in February, 1844, under the name of "James Bayard Taylor." Shortly thereafter, he departed for a walking tour of Europe which lasted almost two years. His travel letters, originally sent back to Philadelphia magazines, were published as *Views Afoot* (1846). The activities which were to claim the largest part of Taylor's attention—newspaper work, poetry, travel writing—were begun, therefore, by the age of twenty-two.

Taylor recommenced newspaper work upon his return from Europe, first in Phoenixville, Pennsylvania, and later in New York. Out of the already mentioned trip to the California gold fields came more travel letters (for the *New-York Tribune*), and an impressionistic book called *Eldorado* in 1850. Although Taylor had married that same year, his wife's death a few months later led him to embark on additional travels. He sailed for Africa in 1851, shortly before his first major volume of poetry, *A Book of Romances, Lyrics, and Songs*, was published. The trip through Egypt, Ethiopia, Turkey, and Palestine was extended, at Greeley's order, by a trek through India en route to Hong Kong, where Taylor joined Commodore Perry's expedition.

Thus Taylor also visited Japan before returning to America at the end of 1853. His adventures were then recounted for an eager public in a series of travel books: *A Journey to Central Africa* (1854); *The Lands of The Saracen* (1854); *A Visit to India, China and Japan in the year 1853* (1855). *Poems of the Orient*, with "exotic" themes, was published in 1854.

In that same year, and in addition to performing miscellaneous editorial chores and preparing another volume of poems, Taylor entered the Lyceum circuit. He returned to Europe in 1865, and by the end of the year had made an extensive tour of Scandinavia; the resulting book was *Northern Travel* (1857). He remarried while abroad, and his growing responsibilities encouraged even more furious activity. Two books of miscellaneous essays, *At Home and Abroad*, were published in 1859 and 1862. *The Poet's Journal* appeared in 1862, and a collected edition of his poems in 1864. By this time, he had embarked on a new career in novel writing.

Taylor began his first novel, *Hannah Thurston*, while acting first as secretary, then as chargé d'affaires at the United States Embassy in St. Petersburg. This book, which dealt with his birthplace under the thin disguise of "Ptolemy, New York," and sold fifteen thousand copies within a few months of its publication in 1863, was soon issued in London, and later was translated into German and Russian. Its success led Taylor to work immediatcly on a second novel, *John Godfrey's Fortunes*, which appeared in England and in America in 1864. A first-person narrative, it is a satire on the literary life in New York City. *The Story of Kennett*, usually considered Taylor's most successful novel, was published in 1866.

III

Taylor's correspondence during the composition of this third novel (as quoted in Marie Hansen-Taylor and Howard E. Scudder's *Life and Letters of Bayard Taylor* [1884]) is interesting for what it reveals about the author's attitude toward the novel as a form. In a letter of January 6, 1866, to a Kennett Square friend, Taylor called the book his "pet novel," and described it as "totally different from the others—altogether objective in subject and treatment—" (451). By April, Taylor was anticipating good fortune: "My new novel ... promises to be a marked success, so far as present indications go. Although the publishing business is as flat as possible, more than six thousand copies have been ordered in advance of publication, and the few who have read the book are unanimous as to its interest . . . . I . . . am entirely satisfied . . . with the experiment of writing three novels and am now sure that I can write a good and characteristic American Novel" (453). The two interesting implications in this letter are, first, that Taylor's measure of his novel's achievement was clearly a commercial one; secondly, in his view, the "characteristic American novel" would be something on the order of *Kennett*—an idealized romance with a historical background and some Genteelly treated "local color" material.

Another letter, from the same volume, shows Taylor's concern with character psychology. When he replied to a protest about the impropriety of the funeral scene—a scene that is one of the best in the novel—he justified Mary Potter's actions in terms of logical character projection, not ideality or historical accuracy: "What you say of the order of the funeral in Kennett is quite true. Such an incident as I have described probably never occurred, but that makes no difference whatever. It is natural for Mary to do it; there could be no other culmination to her history. I was a year studying out the plot before I began to write, and the idea of the *denouement* at the funeral came to me like an inspiration" (456). He was not consistent, however. In too many other instances he imposed authorial values on his figures, rather than dramatizing those of the characters themselves.

Taylor's pleasure in the public acceptance of the book was expressed in a letter to Thomas Bailey Aldrich on April 16, 1866: "I had bestowed much preliminary thought upon the book, and I worked out the idea with the most conscientious care, hoping to make a stride in advance. It is a great joy and a great encouragement to be so unanimously assured that I have not failed in my aim. The moral is that labor pays, in a literary sense" (458).

Clearly, Taylor had high ambitions for *The Story of Kennett*; however, he also wanted a popular success. Thus he attempted in a single work to blend together several things: the material, settings, and melodramatic action associated with the historical romance; the theme of "patient suffering" and the housewifery of the domestic novel; and the didactic morality of the Genteel tradition.

The reader of *Kennett* is kept aware of the historical frame-work by a series of references to the Tories and their suspected sympathizers, one of whom is Old Man Barton. When Gilbert is being given advice on reporting his robbery to the proper authorities, one suggestion is that he write to General Washington demanding protection, " 'and say the Tory farmers' houses ought to be searched' " (Chapter XXI). There are references to such local places and events as "Chadd's Ford," "the Hessian Burying Ground," and the " 'Lammas flood o' '68' " (Chapter XXI). Gilbert's problem in borrowing money to pay off his farm's mortgage is explained in terms of the historical period: "In ordinary times he would have had no difficulty; but, as Mr. Trainer had written, the speculation in western lands had seized upon capitalists, and the amount of money for permanent investment was already greatly diminished" (Chapter XXVI). Finally, Taylor provides for us that standard figure of the historical melodrama, "Sandy Flash"—a flamboyant highwayman with overtones of Robin Hood.

A counterpart to the above is the love story of Gilbert and Martha, designed to attract the feminine audience. The tale is a conventional one: the young man of uncertain birth is inspired by his fair maid to triumph over his difficulties. A good deal of attention is devoted to various domestic arrangements and, in particular, to descriptions of the clothes worn by the female characters. This detail occurs throughout, but is particularly obvious in the descriptions of the wedding party in Chapter XXXIV. And Mary Potter, it should be noticed, is the perfect exemplification of the "domestic novel" heroine, as defined above.

But the book also exhibits the stylistic and intellectual characteristics of the Genteel literary tradition. Gilbert Potter, the "common man" protagonist, is heavily idealized—in his character and actions, as well as in his grammar. The heroine, Martha Deane, is without a single humanizing flaw. The plot is tightly constructed in a very mechanical way, and the suspense is situational rather than psychological. There is a clear implication that life in the past must have somehow been more pleasant, more meaningful than it was in Taylor's present. Vice and virtue are rather rigidly separated. The moral of *The Story of Kennett*, heavily underlined, is that the virtuous will always triumph—with patience—over their adversaries.

Taylor's novel is interesting, therefore, partly because it provides a sort of summary of trends current in American writing during the third quarter of the nineteenth century. Yet *Kennett* seems also to go beyond some of the contemporary Genteel literature; surprisingly, the movement is in the direction of greater realism and a more critical view of the society. For one thing, the reader is often given the sense of a dense cultural fabric such as one expects to find in the "novel of manners." The differences between the architectural styles of the Deane, Barton, and Potter homes are carefully rendered, for example; and the domicile is suggestive of the character within. The set-piece descriptions of fox hunt, barn raising, Quaker meeting, and country wedding correspond to the traditional "social gathering" scenes of that sub-genre. Even more striking is Taylor's attempt to render the intellectual, as well as the physical, landscape.

In his Prologue, the author calls attention to the fact that "the conservative influence of the Quakers was so powerful that it continued to shape the habits even of communities whose religious sentiment it failed to reach." Among the major characters, the only practicing Quaker is Dr. Deane, and his portrait is far from flattering. Taylor sees him as a humorous rather than a wicked villain, but the hypocrisy of his "plainness" is insisted upon. A similar irony is suggested by Taylor's rather rich vocabulary in his description of the Quaker meeting in Chapter VII. Again and again—through the figure of Martha Deane, for example—Taylor ironically ascribes the virtues associated with Quakerism to non-members of the sect.

The Quaker physician serves to introduce the question of "public opinion." Dr. Deane's concern for his reputation among the members of his sect also allows one to observe the extent to which the society is class-conscious. Gilbert Potter is constantly made aware of the gradations of a system which is prepared to make distinctions between "legitimate" and "illegitimate" human beings. For Gilbert, a great passion is the only excuse for his presumption in courting Martha Deane: " 'It might seen like looking too high, Mother, but I couldn't help it' " (Chapter XII). Viewed from this angle, Gilbert's real problem is with the caste system of his culture.

A third element is that, as rendered by Taylor, much of the society of rural Pennyslvania in the eighteenth century is money-fixated. Dr. Deane's criterion for a future son-in-law is largely financial, Alfred Barton's relationship with his father is totally governed by his anticipation of future inheritance, and Mary Potter confesses that it was Barton's prospects that led her to agree to their secret marriage. Even Gilbert Potter reacts to the symbolic value which money has taken on in his culture: "When Gilbert had delivered the last barrels at Newport and slowly cheered homewards his weary team, he was nearly two hundred dollars richer than when he started, and—if we must confess a universal if somewhat humiliating truth—so much the more a man in courage and determination" (Chapter IX).

Hypocrisy, snobbery, materialism—these are the values which Taylor seems to be ascribing to rural Pennsylvania in the eighteenth century. They are not the qualities which we immediately associate with that time and place; but they are exactly those that a writer like Mark Twain has taught us to associate with his—and Taylor's—nineteenth-century America.

It becomes important to realize that Taylor's knowledge of his own century did, in fact, surreptitiously enter the narrative. Albert H. Smyth in his biography (*Bayard Taylor* [1896]) assures us that the author based several of his eighteenth-century characters on people of his own day, some of whom he had known personally. Sandy Flash was based on an actual nineteenth-century highwayman; Gilbert Potter, Deb. Smith, Martha Deane, the farmer Fairthorne, and the boys Joe and Jake are modeled on people from Taylor's own period (167-73). Knowing this raises the possibility that Taylor was using his historical setting as a screen for critical comments about a culture which he knew at first hand.

But Taylor could not bring himself—or his protagonist, Gilbert Potter—to deal directly with the issues that he had raised. Both Gilbert and his friends plainly prefer to accept their society's values rather than question them. Only once in the narrative does Taylor have Gilbert come close to a critical look at the way in which his society operates—when the protagonist senses the analogy between his position and that of Deb. Smith:

> ... her words hinted at an inward experience in some respects so surprisingly like his own, that Gilbert was startled. He knew the reputation of the woman, though he would have found it difficult to tell whereupon it was based. Everybody said she was bad, and nobody knew particularly why .... The world, he had recently learned, was wrong in his case; might it not also be doing her injustice? Her

pride, in its coarse way, was his also, and his life, perhaps, had only unfolded into honorable success through a mother's ever-watchful care and never-wearied toil (Chapter VI).

Gilbert could have turned at this point to questioning the moral and social bases of his society—as Huckleberry Finn would do a few years later. From this possibility, Taylor felt it necessary to retreat. And the Genteel Tradition provided him with an easy escape route, through the sentimentality of the last sentence in the paragraph quoted above.

Perhaps because he sensed that prose fiction was a dangerous tool, Taylor wrote only one other novel: *Joseph and His Friend* (1870), his least interesting work in that genre. Taylor's real love was poetry, and he perhaps viewed his novels as distractions from what he considered his more serious work; indeed, he had stopped in the middle of writing *Kennett* to compose a long poem which he believed to be his masterpiece: *The Picture of St. John*, a narrative poem running to thirty-two hundred lines that appeared in 1866. His next major work was his translation of *Faust*, published in two parts in 1870 and 1871. Taylor's great feat was to render the poem in its original meter, and his translation is still admired. Various poems, stories, essays, editions, and travel books followed. Another long poem—*Lars: A Pastoral of Norway*—and two plays—*The Prophet* and *Prince Deukalion*—appeared between 1873 and 1878.

Public honors rewarded such prodigious activity. Taylor was invited to write and deliver the "Ode" at the Centennial Celebration in Philadelphia in 1876, and in 1878 he was named United States Minister to Germany. His death came less than a year after accepting that post. In the next two years, two collections of his work were published, and by the end of the century, three biographical studies had appeared: the previously cited Hansen-Taylor and Scudder volume, Smythe's work, and Russell H. Conwell's *The Life, Travels, and Literary Career of Bayard Taylor* (1884). To his large public, Bayard Taylor's literary reputation must have seemed firmly established.

IV

Taylor's letters and the magazine reviews show that *The Story of Kennett* was, in general, well received. Taylor summarized some of the praise in a letter to E. C. Stedman on April 15, 1866: "Whittier is enthusiastic about 'Kennett,' ditto Howells. The former says it contains 'as good things as there are in the English language;' the latter, 'it is the best historical (historical in the sense of retrospective) novel ever written in America.' [George W.] Curtis said very nearly the same thing to me at our dinner. So, you see, my hope and your prophecy are in a way to be fulfilled. The people in this country are buying it like mad" (Hansen-Taylor and Scudder, 457).

In the literary journals, none of the anonymous reviewers found the plot of the book its most engaging aspect, nor the attempts at humor very telling. Most praised the portrayal of individual incidents and the characterizations to be found in Taylor's work. All seemed to accept the book as Taylor's attempt to depict the Quaker character within the framework of a regional portrait. The *Nation* (April 19, 1866) offered an unfavorable comparison to J. T. Trowbridge's New England novel, *Lucy Arlyn* (1866). The reviewer, who complained that Taylor's was not really a historical novel since it merely dressed contemporary events in the clothing of 1796, was particularly offended by the presentation of the Quakers: "We do not see real Friends. Perhaps we do see *Quakers*. Quakers are the sect beheld from the outside; but the Society of Friends can be known only by the most delicate interior affiliation, by spiritual rapport, or by the highest refinement of appreciation."

The reviewer concluded that the novelist simply did not comprehend the "inner life" of the Quakers—not allowing for the possibility that Taylor consciously might have chosen to concentrate on the sect's public aspect. A letter which Taylor wrote to Aldrich suggests that personal animus may have been involved: "Both the 'Round Table' and the 'Nation' seem to have a spite at me, altho' the managers of both papers want me to write for them" (Richard Cary, *The Genteel Circle: Bayard Taylor and His Friends* [1952], 33).

Interestingly, the reviewer for *The Athenaeum* of London (May 12, 1866) praises those elements which had offended the *Nation*: "Much of the population of Kennett is Quaker; and we can vouch for the fidelity of Mr. Bayard Taylor's portraits of Quakers at meeting or in their own houses."

A much more perceptive review was the unsigned one by William Dean Howells which appeared in the *Atlantic Monthly*

(June, 1866). Significantly, the critic praised Taylor for the specificity of his material: "There is such a shyness among American novelists ... in regard to dates, names, and localities, that we are glad to have a book in which there is great courage in this respect." The reviewer grasped the point that what other commentators had seen as a lapse of taste on Taylor's part in the funeral scene was actually a bit of psychological verisimilitude: "Considering her [Mary Potter's] character and history, it is natural that she should seek to make her justification as signal and public as possible."

Howells also held that the actions of Dr. Deane and Martha were intended by Taylor to represent opposite sides of the single coin of Quakerism: "In the sweet and unselfish spirit of Martha, the theories of individual action under special inspiration have created self-reliance, and calm fearless humility, sustaining her even in her struggle against the will of her father, and even against the sect to whose teachings she owes them .... [Dr. Deane] is the most odious character in the book, what is bad in him being separated by such fine differences from what is very good in others."

This point is a valid one. Whether Taylor's presentation of the religious sect is historically accurate, or even fair, is one question; whether or not the author has created believable psychological relations between his characters is quite another. What is worth noting is that the opposing characters of Dr. Deane and his daughter Martha are so created as to have additional meaning because of their contrast.

More recent critics have given Taylor's work in general, and his novels in particular, only passing reference. *The Literary History of the United States* comments tersely that he wrote "three creditable novels on social themes" (810). Arthur Hobson Quinn says in *The Literature of the American People* (1951) that "in *The Story of Kennett* (1866) ... Taylor created a masterpiece." This surely overgenerous evaluation was made on the basis that Taylor wrote with affection of an era he knew well, that several characters were based on "real people," and that the novel has become a part of the "local life" (357).

Carl Van Doren in *The American Novel, 1789-1939* (1940) regards Taylor's work as an example of those sentimental narratives of the mid-nineteenth century which also reflected the rising interest in realistic literature: "During the sixties realism hovered in the air without definitely alighting. Oliver Wendell Holmes, for instance, in *Elsie Venner* (1861) worked his romantic problem of heredity upon a ground of shrewd realistic observation; Bayard Taylor employed a similar composition of elements" (177).

But only Alexander Cowie in *The Rise of the American Novel* (1948) attempts to define fully Taylor's place in the history of fiction in the United States. He describes Taylor's four novels as "useful links in any study of the evolution of fiction before the dawn of Howellsian realism" (475). Although he doubts that *The Story of Kennett* can accurately be called a "historical novel," the author's use of factual material "makes for authenticity in atmosphere and episode . . . . There are many homely illustrations of the quiet (Quaker) life of Kennett Square—social, religious, industrial—that ring true and that seem to be integral parts of the story . . . . " Taylor was "on the whole . . . on the side of realism in fiction" and "anticipates Howells in protesting against the morbid tone of many novels of the 1850s and 1860s, but it remained for Howells to inaugurate a new regime in novel-writing" (481-86).

While Taylor's verse today seems irrelevant to the development of American poetry, *The Story of Kennett* appears to have been part of a growing realism in the American novel. In this novel about his birthplace, Taylor seems to be part of a tradition in the American novel of manners—one with James Fenimore Cooper for an ancestor, and George Washington Cable for a descendant. If Taylor sometimes relied on plot contrivances, idealized love stories, and melodramatic adventures, he differed from both his predecessors and some of his followers more in degree than in kind.

Much more than he seems to have done in his poetry, Taylor in *The Story of Kennett* was dealing with material which he knew in depth (even if he chose sometimes to concentrate on its superficial aspects). And he goes somewhat beyond a mere surface realism. The Quaker beliefs as a social force, the importance of money to one's status in the emerging American community, the tyranny of public opinion—all of these things are described and sorted out with the care, if not always the emphases, of the social historian.

Beatty comments "In his fiction, as in his other prose, he [Taylor] remained fundamentally a reporter" (238). The reporter and the romancer have an uneasy coexistence in *The Story of Kennett*. What one misses is the insistence on the inter-relationships within the social fabric which one gets on occasion from the novels of Cooper, and more certainly from a work like Cable's *The Grandissimes*. Some of the most interesting aspects of Taylor's novel for the modern reader are things which are only hinted at by the author—for example, the connections among the economic, social, and religious life in this small, culturally unified community. Why, one wonders, did he stop with these veiled suggestions? The answer lies in Taylor's relationship to the values of his own culture. Both in its achievements and in its limitations, *The Story of Kennett* is a document which implicitly defines the Genteel Tradition.

A Note on the Text

The first edition of *The Story of Kennett* was published in New York by G. P. Putnam, and in London by Sampson Low, Son and Company, in March, 1866. It was reissued by Putnam in 1867, in the "Household edition" of 1882, and in the "Cedarcroft edition" of 1903. The present text is based upon the first edition, but spelling and punctuation have been modernized, and a few emendations by the present editor have been inserted within square brackets. Notes added for this printing are marked (ed.) to distinguish them from Taylor's own footnotes, all of which have been retained.

Fordham University   C. W. La Salle II

Prologue

To My Friends and Neighbors of Kennett:

I wish to dedicate this story to you, not only because some of you inhabit the very houses and till the very fields which I have given to the actors in it, but also because many of you will recognize certain of the latter, and are therefore able to judge whether they are drawn with the simple truth at which I have aimed. You are, naturally, the critics whom I have most cause to fear; but I do not inscribe these pages to you with the design of purchasing your favor. I beg you all to accept the fact as an acknowledgment of the many quiet and happy years I have spent among you; of the genial and pleasant relations into which I was born, and which have never diminished, even when I have returned to you from the farthest ends of the earth; and of the use (often unconsciously to you, I confess) which I have drawn from your memories of former days, your habits of thought and of life.

I am aware that truth and fiction are so carefully woven together in this story of Kennett, that you will sometimes be at a loss to disentangle them. The lovely pastoral landscapes, which I know by heart, have been copied, field for field and tree for tree, and these you will immediately recognize. Many of you will have no difficulty in detecting the originals of Sandy Flash and Deb. Smith; a few will remember the noble horse which performed the service I have ascribed to Roger; and the descendants of a certain family will not have forgotten some of the pranks of Joe and Jake Fairthorn. Many more than these particulars are drawn from actual sources; but as I have employed them with a strict regard to the purposes of the story, transferring dates and characters at my pleasure, you will often, I doubt not, attribute to invention that which I owe to family tradition. Herein, I must request that you will allow me to keep my own counsel; for the processes which led to the completed work extend through many previous years, and cannot readily be revealed. I will only say that every custom I have described is true to the time, though some of them are now obsolete; that I have used no peculiar word or phrase of the common dialect of the country which I have not myself heard; and further, that I owe the chief incidents of the last chapter, given to me on her deathbed, to the dear and noble woman whose character (not the cirucmstances of her life) I have endeavored to reproduce in that of Martha Deane.

The country life of our part of Pennsylvania retains more elements of its English origin than that of New England or Virginia. Until within a few years, the conservative influence of the Quakers was so powerful that it continued to shape the habits even of communities whose religious sentiment it failed to reach. Hence, whatever might be selected as incorrect of American life, in its broader sense, in these pages, is nevertheless locally true; and to this, at least, all of you, my friends and neighbors, can testify. In these days, when fiction prefers to deal with abnormal characters and psychological problems more or less exceptional or morbid, the attempt to represent the elements of life in a simple, healthy, pastoral community has been to me a source of uninterrupted enjoyment. May you read it with half the interest I have felt in writing it!

BAYARD TAYLOR

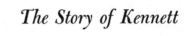
The Story of Kennett

CHAPTER *1*

The Chase

At noon, on the first Saturday of March, 1796, there was an unusual stir at the old Barton farmhouse, just across the creek to the eastward, as you leave Kennett Square by the Philadelphia stage-road. Any gathering of the people at Barton's was a most rare occurrence; yet, on that day and at that hour, whoever stood upon the porch of the corner house in the village could see horsemen approaching by all the four roads which there met. Some five or six had already dismounted at the Unicorn Tavern, and were refreshing themselves with stout glasses of "Old Rye," while their horses, tethered side by side to the pegs in the long hitching-bar, pawed and stamped impatiently. An eye familiar with the ways of the neighborhood might have surmised the nature of the occasion which called so many together, from the appearance and equipment of these horses. They were not heavy animals, with the marks of plow-collars on their broad shoulders, or the hair worn off their rumps by huge breech-straps; but light and clean-limbed, one or two of them showing signs of good blood, and all more carefully groomed than usual.

Evidently, there was no "vendue"* at the Barton farmhouse; neither a funeral, nor a wedding, since male guests seemed to have been exclusively bidden. To be sure, Miss Betsy Lavender had been observed to issue from Dr. Deane's door, on the opposite side of the way, and turn into the path beyond the blacksmith's, which led down through the wood and over the creek to Barton's; but then, Miss Lavender was known to be handy at all times, and capable of doing all things, from laying out a corpse to spicing a wedding cake. Often self-invited, but always welcome, very few social or domestic events could occur in four townships (East Marlborough, Kennett, Pennsbury, and New-

*A public auction or sale (ed.).

Garden) without her presence; while her knowledge of farms, families, and genealogies extended up to Fallowfield on one side, and over to Birmingham on the other.

It was, therefore, a matter of course, whatever the present occasion might be, that Miss Lavender put on her broad gray beaver hat, and brown stuff cloak, and took the way to Barton's. The distance could easily be walked in five minutes, and the day was remarkably pleasant for the season. A fortnight of warm, clear weather had extracted the last fang of frost, and there was already green grass in the damp hollows. Bluebirds picked the last year's berries from the cedar trees; buds were bursting on the swamp-willows; the alders were hung with tassels, and a powdery crimson bloom began to dust the bare twigs of the maple trees. All these signs of an early spring Miss Lavender noted as she picked her way down the wooded bank. Once, indeed, she stopped, wet her forefinger with her tongue, and held it pointed in the air. There was very little breeze, but this natural weathercock revealed from what direction it came.

"Southwest!" she said, nodding her head—"Lucky!"

Having crossed the creek on the flat log, secured with stakes at either end, a few more paces brought her to the warm, gentle knoll, upon which stood the farmhouse. Here the wood ceased, and the creek, sweeping around to the eastward, embraced a quarter of a mile of rich bottomland, before entering the rocky dell below. It was a pleasant seat, and the age of the house denoted that one of the earliest settlers had been quick to perceive its advantages. A hundred years had already elapsed since the masons had run up those walls of rusty hornblende rock, and it was even said that the leaden window sashes, with their diamond-shaped panes of greenish glass, had been brought over from England, in the days of William Penn. In fact, the ancient aspect of the place—the tall, massive chimney at the gable, the heavy, projecting eaves, and the holly bush in a warm nook beside the front porch, had, nineteen years before, so forcibly reminded one of Howe's soldiers of his father's homestead in mid-England, that he was numbered among the missing after the Brandywine battle, and presently turned up as a hired hand on the Barton farm, where he still lived, year in and year out.

An open, grassy space, a hundred yards in breadth, intervened between the house and the barn, which was built against the slope of the knoll, so that the bridge to the threshing-floor was nearly level, and the stables below were sheltered from the north winds, and open to the winter sun. On the other side of the lane leading from the highroad stood a wagon-house and corn crib—the latter empty, yet evidently, in spite of its emptiness, the principal source of attraction to the visitors. A score of men and boys peeped between the upright laths, and a dozen dogs howled and sprang around the smooth corner-posts upon which the structure rested. At the door stood old Giles, the military straggler already mentioned—now a grizzly, weatherbeaten man of fifty—with a jolly grin on his face, and a short leather whip in his hand.

"Want to see him, Miss Betsy?" he asked, touching his mink-skin cap, as Miss Lavender crawled through the nearest panel of the lofty picket fence.

"See him?" she repeated. "Don't care if I do, afore goin' into th' house."

"Come up, then; out o' the way, Cato! Fan, take that, you slut! Don't be afeard, Miss Betsy; if folks kept 'em in the leash, as had ought to be done, I'd have less trouble. They're mortal eager, and no wonder. There!—a'n't he a sly-lookin' divel? If I'd a hoss, Miss Betsy, I'd foller with the best of 'em, and maybe you wouldn't have the brush?"

"Have the brush. Go along, Giles! He's an old one, and knows how to take care of it. Do keep off the dreadful dogs, and let me git down!" cried Miss Lavender, gathering her narrow petticoats about her legs, and surveying the struggling animals before her with some dismay.

Giles's whip only reached the nearest, and the excited pack rushed forward again after every repulse; but at this juncture a tall, smartly dressed man came across the lane, kicked the hounds out of the way, and extended a helping hand to the lady.

"Ho, Mr. Alfred!" said she; "Much obliged. Miss Ann's havin' her hands full, I reckon?"

Without waiting for an answer, she slipped into the yard and along the front of the house, to the kitchen entrance, at the eastern end. There we will leave her, and return to the group of gentlemen.

Anyone could see at a glance that Mr. Alfred Barton was the most important person present. His character of host gave him, of course, the right to control the order of the coming chase, but his size and swaggering air of strength, his new style of hat, the gloss of his blue coat, the cut of his buckskin breeches, and above all, the splendor of his tasselled top boots, distinguished him from his more homely apparelled guests. His features were large and heavy: the full, wide lips betrayed a fondness for indulgence, and the small, uneasy eyes a capacity for concealing this and any other quality which needed concealment. They were hard and cold, generally more than half hidden under thick lids, and avoided, rather than sought, the glance of the man to whom he spoke. His hair, a mixture of red-brown and gray, descended, without a break, into bushy whiskers of the same color, and was cut shorter at the back of the head than was then customary. Something coarse and vulgar in his nature exhaled, like a powerful odor, through the assumed shell of a gentleman which he tried to wear, and rendered the assumption useless.

A few guests, who had come from a distance, had just finished their dinner in the farmhouse. Owing to causes which will hereafter be explained, they exhibited less than the usual plethoric satisfaction after the hospitality of the country, and were the first to welcome the appearance of a square black bottle, which went the rounds, with the observation: "Whet up for a start!"

Mr. Barton drew a heavy silver watch from his fob, and carefully holding it so that the handful of glittering seals could be seen by everybody, appeared to meditate.

"Five minutes to one," he said at last. "No use in waiting much longer; 'tisn't good to keep the hounds fretting. Any signs of anybody else?"

The others, in response, turned towards the lane and highway. Some, with keen eyes, fancied they could detect a horseman through the wood. Presently Giles, from his perch at the door of the corncrib, cried out:

"There's somebody a-comin' up the meadow. I don't know the hoss; rides like Gilbert Potter. Gilbert it is, blast me! new-mounted."

"Another plow-horse!" suggested Mr. Joel Ferris, a young Pennsbury buck, who, having recently come into a legacy of four thousand pounds, wished it to be forgotten that he had never ridden any but plow-horses until within the year.

The others laughed, some contemptuously, glancing at their

own well-equipped animals the while, some constrainedly, for they knew the approaching guest, and felt a slight compunction in seeming to side with Mr. Ferris. Barton began to smile stiffly, but presently bit his lip and drew his brows together.

Pressing the handle of his riding-whip against his chin, he stared vacantly up the lane, muttering "We must wait, I suppose."

His lids were lifted in wonder the next moment; he seized Ferris by the arm, and exclaimed:

"Whom have we here?"

All eyes turned in the same direction, descried a dashing horseman in the lane.

"Upon my soul I don't know," said Ferris. "Anybody expected from the Fagg's Manor way?"

"Not of my inviting," Barton answered.

The other guests professed their entire ignorance of the stranger, who, having by this time passed the bars, rode directly up to the group. He was a short, broad-shouldered man of nearly forty, with a red, freckled face, keen, snapping gray eyes, and a close, wide mouth. Thick, jet-black whiskers, eyebrows and pigtail made the glance of those eyes, the gleam of his teeth, and the color of his skin where it was not reddened by the wind, quite dazzling. This violent and singular contrast gave his plain, common features an air of distinction. Although his mulberry coat was somewhat faded, it had a jaunty cut, and if his breeches were worn and stained, the short, muscular thighs and strong knees they covered, told of a practiced horseman.

He rode a large bay gelding, poorly groomed, and apparently not remarkable for blood, but with no marks of harness on his rough coat.

"Good-day to you, gentlemen!" said the stranger, familiarly knocking the handle of his whip against his cocked hat. "Squire Barton, how do you do?"

"How do you do, sir?" responded Mr. Barton, instantly flattered by the title, to which he had no legitimate right. "I believe," he added, "you have the advantage of me."

A broad smile, or rather grin, spread over the stranger's face. His teeth flashed, and his eyes shot forth a bright, malicious ray. He hesitated a moment, ran rapidly over the faces of the others without perceptibly moving his head, and noting the general curiosity, said at last:

"I hardly expected to find an acquaintance in this neighborhood, but a chase makes quick fellowship. I happened to hear of it at the Anvil Tavern—am on my way to Rising Sun; so, you see, if the hunt goes down Tuffkenamon, as is likely, it's so much of a lift on the way."

"All right,—glad to have you join us. What did you say your name was?" inquired Mr. Barton.

"I didn't say what; it's Fortune,—a fortune left to me by my father, ha! ha! Don't care if I do—"

With the latter words, Fortune (as we must now call him) leaned down from his saddle, took the black bottle from the unresisting hands of Mr. Ferris, inverted it against his lips, and drank so long and luxuriously as to bring water into the mouths of the spectators. Then, wiping his mouth with the back of his freckled hand, he winked and nodded his head approvingly to Mr. Barton.

Meanwhile the other horseman had arrived from the meadow, after dismounting and letting down the bars, over which his horse stepped slowly and cautiously—a circumstance which led some of the younger guests to exchange quiet, amused glances. Gilbert Potter, however, received a hearty greeting from all, including the host, though the latter, by an increased shyness in meeting his gaze, manifested some secret constraint.

"I was afraid I should have been too late," said Gilbert; "the old break in the hedge is stopped at last, so I came over the hill above, without thinking on the swampy bit, this side."

"Breaking your horse in to rough riding, eh?" said Mr. Ferris, touching a neighbor with his elbow.

Gilbert smiled good-humoredly, but said nothing, and a little laugh went around the circle.

Mr. Fortune seemed to understand the matter in a flash. He looked at the brown, shaggy-maned animal, standing behind its owner, with its head down, and said, in a low, sharp tone: "I see—where did you get him?"

Gilbert returned the speaker's gaze a moment before he answered. "From a drover," he then said.

"By the Lord!" ejaculated Mr. Barton, who had again conspicuously displayed his watch, "it's over half-past one. Look out for the hounds—we must start, if we mean to do any riding this day!"

The owners of the hounds picked out their several animals

and dragged them aside, in which operation they were uproariously assisted by the boys. The chase in Kennett, it must be confessed, was but a very faint shadow of the old English pastime. It had been kept up, in the neighborhood, from the force of habit in the Colonial times, and under the depression which the strong Quaker element among the people exercised upon all sports and recreations. The breed of hounds, not being restricted to close communion, had considerably degenerated, and few, even of the richer farmers, could afford to keep thoroughbred hunters for this exclusive object. Consequently all the features of the pastime had become rude and imperfect, and, although very respectable gentlemen still gave it their countenance, there was a growing suspicion that it was a questionable, if not demoralizing diversion. It would be more agreeable if we could invest the present occasion with a little more pomp and dignity; but we must describe the event precisely as it occurred.

The first to greet Gilbert were his old friends, Joe and Jake Fairthorn. These boys loudly lamented that their father had denied them the loan of his old gray mare, Bonnie; they could ride double on a gallop, they said; and wouldn't Gilbert take them along, one before and one behind him? But he laughed and shook his head.

"Well, we've got Watch, anyhow," said Joe, who thereupon began whispering very earnestly to Jake, as the latter seized the big family bulldog by the collar. Gilbert foreboded mischief, and kept his eye upon the pair.

A scuffle was heard in the corncrib, into which Giles had descended. The boys shuddered and chuckled in a state of delicious fear, which changed into a loud shout of triumph, as the soldier again made his appearance at the door, with the fox in his arms, and a fearless hand around its muzzle.

"By George! what a fine brush!" exclaimed Mr. Ferris.

A sneer, quickly disguised in a grin, ran over Fortune's face. The hounds howled and tugged; Giles stepped rapidly across the open space where the knoll sloped down to the meadow. It was a moment of intense expectation.

Just then, Joe and Jake Fairthorn let go their hold on the bulldog's collar; but Gilbert Potter caught the animal at the second bound. The boys darted behind the corncrib, scared less by Gilbert's brandished whip than by the wrath and astonishment in Mr. Barton's face.

"Cast him off, Giles!" the latter cried.

The fox, placed upon the ground, shot down the slope and through the fence into the meadow. Pausing then, as if first to assure himself of his liberty, he took a quick, keen survey of the ground before him, and then started off towards the left.

"He's making for the rocks!" cried Mr. Ferris; to which the stranger, who was now watching the animal with sharp interest, abruptly answered, "Hold your tongue!"

Within a hundred yards the fox turned to the right, and now, having apparently made up his mind to the course, struck away in a steady but not hurried trot. In a minute he had reached the outlying trees of the timber along the creek.

"He's a cool one, he is!" remarked Giles, admiringly.

By this time he was hidden by the barn from the sight of the hounds, and they were let loose. While they darted about in eager quest of the scent, the hunters mounted in haste. Presently an old dog gave tongue like a trumpet, the pack closed, and the horsemen followed. The boys kept pace with them over the meadow, Joe and Jake taking the lead, until the creek abruptly stopped their race, when they sat down upon the bank and cried bitterly, as the last of the hunters disappeared through the thickets on the further side.

It was not long before a high picket-fence confronted the riders. Mr. Ferris, with a look of dismay, dismounted. Fortune, Barton, and Gilbert Potter each threw off a heavy "rider," and leaped their horses over the rails. The others followed through the gaps thus made, and all swept across the field at full speed, guided by the ringing cry of the hounds.

When they reached the Wilmington road, the cry swerved again to the left, and most of the hunters, with Barton at their head, took the highway in order to reach the crossroad to New-Garden more conveniently. Gilbert and Fortune alone sprang into the opposite field, and kept a straight southwestern course for the other branch of Redley Creek. The field was divided by a stout thorn hedge from the one beyond it, and the two horse-men, careering neck and neck, glanced at each other curiously as they approached this barrier. Their respective animals were trans-formed; the unkempt manes were curried by the wind as they flew; their sleepy eyes were full of fire, and the splendid mus-cles, aroused to complete action, marked their hides with lines of beauty. There was no wavering in either; side by side they hung in flight above the hedge, and side by side struck the clean turf beyond.

Then Fortune turned his head, nodded approvingly to Gilbert, and muttered to himself: "He's a gallant fellow,—I'll not rob him of the brush." But he laughed a short, shrill, wicked laugh the next moment.

Before they reached the creek, the cry of the hounds ceased. They halted a moment on the bank, irresolute.

"He must have gone down towards the snuff-mill," said Gilbert, and was about to change his course.

"Stop," said the stranger; "if he has, we've lost him any way. Hark! hurrah!"

A deep bay rang from the westward, through the forest. Gilbert shouted: "The lime-quarry!" and dashed across the stream. A lane was soon reached, and as the valley opened, they saw the whole pack heading around the yellow mounds of earth which marked the locality of the quarry. At the same instant someone shouted in the rear, and they saw Mr. Alfred Barton, thundering after, and apparently bent on diminishing the distance between them.

A glance was sufficient to show that the fox had not taken refuge in the quarry, but was making a straight course up the center of the valley. Here it was not so easy to follow. The fertile floor of Tuffkenamon, stripped of woods, was crossed by lines of compact hedge, and, moreover, the huntsmen were not free to tear and trample the springing wheat of the thrifty Quaker farmers. Nevertheless, one familiar with the ground could take advantage of a gap here and there, choose the connecting pasture-fields, and favor his course with a bit of road, when the chase swerved towards either side of the valley. Gilbert Potter soon took the lead, closely followed by Fortune. Mr. Barton was perhaps better mounted than either, but both horse and rider were heavier, and lost in the moist fields, while they gained rapidly where the turf was firm.

After a mile and a half of rather toilsome riding, all three were nearly abreast. The old tavern of the Hammer and Trowel was visible, at the foot of the northern hill; the hounds, in front, bayed in a straight line towards Avondale Woods—but a long slip of undrained bog made its appearance. Neither gentleman spoke, for each was silently tasking his wits how to accomplish the passage most rapidly. The horses began to sink into the oozy soil; only a very practiced eye could tell where the surface was firmest, and even this knowledge was but slight advantage.

Nimbly as a cat Gilbert sprang from the saddle, still holding the pommel in his right hand, touched his horse's flank with the whip, and bounded from one tussock to another. The sagacious animal seemed to understand and assist his maneuver. Hardly had he gained firm ground than he was in his seat again, while Mr. Barton was still plunging in the middle of the bog.

By the time he had reached the road, Gilbert shrewdly guessed where the chase would terminate. The idlers on the tavern-porch cheered him as he swept around the corner; the level highway rang to the galloping hoofs of his steed, and in fifteen minutes he had passed the long and lofty oak woods of Avondale. At the same moment, fox and hounds broke into full view, sweeping up the meadow on his left. The animal made a last desperate effort to gain a lair among the bushes and loose stones on the northern hill; but the hunter was there before him, the hounds were within reach, and one faltering moment decided his fate.

Gilbert sprang down among the frantic dogs, and saved the brush from the rapid dismemberment which had already befallen its owner. Even then, he could only assure its possession by sticking it into his hat and remounting his horse. When he looked around, no one was in sight, but the noise of hoofs was heard crashing through the wood.

Mr. Ferris, with some dozen others, either anxious to spare their horses or too timid to take the hedges in the valley, had kept the crossroad to New-Garden, whence a lane along the top of the southern hill led them into the Avondale Woods. They soon emerged, shouting and yelling, upon the meadow.

The chase was up; and Gilbert Potter, on his "plow-horse," was the only huntsman in at the death.

CHAPTER 2

Who Shall Have the Brush?

Mr. Barton and Fortune, who seemed to have become wonderfully intimate during the half hour in which they had ridden together, arrived at the same time. The hunters, of whom a dozen were now assembled (some five or six inferior horses being still a mile in the rear), were all astounded, and some of them highly vexed, at the result of the chase. Gilbert's friends crowded about him, asking questions as to the course he had taken, and examining the horse, which had maliciously resumed its sleepy look, and stood with drooping head. The others had not sufficient tact to disguise their ill-humor, for they belonged to that class which, in all countries, possesses the least refinement—the uncultivated rich.

"The hunt started well, but it's a poor finish," said one of these.

"Never mind!" Mr. Ferris remarked; "such things come by chance."

These words struck the company to silence. A shock, felt rather than perceived, fell upon them, and they looked at each other with an expression of pain and embarrassment. Gilbert's face faded to a sallow paleness, and his eyes were fastened upon those of the speaker with a fierce and dangerous intensity. Mr. Ferris colored, turned away, and called to his hounds.

Fortune was too sharp an observer not to remark the disturbance. He cried out, and his words produced an instant, general sense of relief:

"It's been a fine run, friends, and we can't do better than ride back to the Hammer and Trowel, and take a 'smaller'*—or a 'bigger' for that matter—at my expense. You must let me pay

*Any drink of low alcoholic strength (ed.).

39

my footing* now, for I hope to ride with you many a time to come. Faith! If I don't happen to buy that place down by the Rising Sun, I'll try to find another, somewhere about New London or Westgrove, so that we can be nearer neighbors."

With that he grinned, rather than smiled; but although his manner would have struck a cool observer as being mocking instead of cordial, the invitation was accepted with great show of satisfaction, and the horsemen fell into pairs, forming a picturesque cavalcade as they passed under the tall, leafless oaks.

Gilbert Potter speedily recovered his self-possession, but his face was stern and his manner abstracted. Even the marked and careful kindness of his friends seemed secretly to annoy him, for it constantly suggested the something by which it had been prompted. Mr. Alfred Barton, however, whether under the influence of Fortune's friendship, or from a late suspicion of his duties as host of the day, not unkindly complimented the young man, and insisted on filling his glass. Gilbert could do no less than courteously accept the attention, but he shortly afterwards stole away from the noisy company, mounted his horse, and rode slowly towards Kennett Square.

As he thus rides, with his eyes abstractedly fixed before him, we will take the opportunity to observe him more closely. Slightly undersized, compactly built, and with strongly marked features, his twenty-four years have the effect of thirty. His short jacket and knee-breeches of gray velveteen cover a chest broad rather than deep, and reveal the fine, narrow loins and muscular thighs of a frame matured and hardened by labor. His hands, also, are hard and strong, but not ungraceful in form. His neck, not too short, is firmly planted, and the carriage of his head indicates patience and energy. Thick, dark hair enframes his square forehead, and straight, somewhat heavy brows. His eyes of soft dark gray are large, clear, and steady, and only change their expression under strong excitement. His nose is straight and short, his mouth a little too wide for beauty, and less firm now than it will be ten years hence, when the yearning tenderness shall have vanished from the corners of the lips; and the chin, in its broad curve, harmonizes with the square lines of the brow. Evidently a man whose youth has not been a holiday; who is reticent rather than demonstrative; who will be strong in

*A fee—usually either money or liquor—paid by a person admitted for the first time to a society (ed.).

his loves and long in his hates, and, without being of a despon-
dent nature, can never become heartily sanguine.

The spring day was raw and overcast, as it drew towards its
close, and the rider's musings seemed to accord with the change
in the sky. His face expressed a singular mixture of impatience,
determined will, and unsatisfied desire. But where most other
men would have sighed, or given way to some involuntary exclamation, he merely set his teeth, and tightened the grasp on
his whip-handle.

He was not destined, however, to a solitary journey. Scarcely
had he made three quarters of a mile, when, on approaching the
junction of a wood-road which descended to the highway from a
shallow little glen on the north, the sound of hoofs and voices
met his ears. Two female figures appeared, slowly guiding their
horses down the rough road. One, from her closely fitting riding-
habit of drab cloth, might have been a Quakeress, but for the
feather (of the same sober color) in her beaver hat, and rosette
of dark red ribbon at her throat. The other, in bluish gray, with
a black beaver and no feather, rode a heavy old horse with a
blind halter on his head, and held the stout leathern reins with a
hand covered with a blue woollen mitten. She rode in advance,
paying little heed to her seat, but rather twisting herself out of
shape in the saddle in order to chatter to her companion in the
rear.

"Do look where you are going, Sally!" cried the latter, as the
blinded horse turned aside from the road to drink at a little
brook that oozed forth from under the dead leaves.

Thus appealed to, the other lady whirled around with a half-
jump, and caught sight of Gilbert Potter and of her horse's head
at the same instant.

"Whoa there, Bonnie!" she cried. "Why, Gilbert, where did
you come from? Hold up your head, I say! Martha, here's Gilbert, with a brush in his hat! Don't be afraid, you beast; did
you never smell a fox? Here, ride in between, Gilbert, and tell
us all about it! No, not on that side, Martha; you can manage a
horse better than I can!"

In her efforts to arrange the order of march, she drove her
horse's head into Gilbert's back, and came near losing her balance. With amused screams, and bursts of laughter, and light,
rattling exclamations, she finally succeeded in placing herself at
his left hand, while her adroit and self-possessed companion

quietly rode up to his right. Then, dropping the reins on their horses' necks, the two ladies resigned themselves to conversation, as the three slowly jogged homewards abreast.

"Now, Gilbert!" exclaimed Miss Sally Fairthorn, after waiting a moment for him to speak; "did you really earn the brush, or beg it from one of them, on the way home?"

"Begging, you know, is my usual habit," he answered, mockingly.

"I know you're as proud as Lucifer, when you've a mind to be so. There!"

Gilbert was accustomed to the rattling tongue of his left-hand neighbor, and generally returned her as good as she gave. Today, however, he was in no mood for repartee. He drew down his brows and made no answer to her charge.

"Where was the fox earthed?" asked the other lady, after a rapid glance at his face.

Martha Deane's voice was of that quality which compels an answer, and a courteous answer, from the surliest of mankind. It was not loud, it could scarcely be called musical; but every tone seemed to exhale freshness as of dew, and brightness as of morning. It was pure, slightly resonant; and all the accumulated sorrows of life could not have veiled its inherent gladness. It could never grow harsh, never be worn thin, or sound husky from weariness; its first characteristic would always be youth, and the joy of youth, though it came from the lips of age.

Doubtless Gilbert Potter did not analyze the charm which it exercised upon him; it was enough that he felt and submitted to it. A few quiet remarks sufficed to draw from him the story of the chase, in all its particulars, and the lively interest in Martha Deane's face, the boisterous glee of Sally Fairthorn, with his own lurking sense of triumph, soon swept every gloomy line from his visage. His mouth relaxed from its set compression, and wore a winning sweetness; his eyes shone softly bright, and a nimble spirit of gayety gave grace to his movements.

"Fairly won, I must say!" exclaimed Miss Sally Fairthorn, when the narrative was finished. "And now, Gilbert, the brush?"

"The brush?"

"Who's to have it, I mean. Did you never get one before, as you don't seem to understand?"

"Yes, I understand," said he, in an indifferent tone; "it may be had for the asking."

"Then it's mine!" cried Sally, urging her heavy horse against him and making a clutch at his cap. But he leaned as suddenly away, and shot a length ahead, out of her reach. Miss Deane's horse, a light, spirited animal, kept pace with his.

"Martha!" cried the disappointed damsel, "Martha! one of us must have it; ask him, you!"

"No," answered Martha, with her clear blue eyes fixed on Gilbert's face, "I will not ask."

He returned her gaze, and his eyes seemed to say: "Will you take it, knowing what the acceptance implies?"

She read the question correctly; but of this he was not sure. Neither, if it were so, could he trust himself to interpret the answer. Sally had already resumed her place on his left, and he saw that the mock strife would be instantly renewed. With a movement so sudden as to appear almost ungracious, he snatched the brush from his cap and extended it to Martha Deane, without saying a word.

If she hesitated, it was at least no longer than would be required in order to understand the action. Gilbert might either so interpret it, or suspect that she had understood the condition in his mind, and meant to signify the rejection thereof. The language of gestures is wonderfully rapid, and all that could be said by either, in this way, was over, and the brush in Martha Deane's hand, before Sally Fairthorn became aware of the transfer.

"Well-done, Martha!" she exclaimed: "Don't let him have it again! Do you know to whom he would have given it: an A. and a W., with the look of an X,—so!"

Thereupon Sally pulled off her mittens and crossed her fore-fingers, an action which her companions understood—in combination with the mysterious initials—to be the rude, primitive symbol of a squint.

Gilbert looked annoyed, but before he could reply, Sally let go the rein in order to put on her mittens, and the blinded mare quickly dropping her head, the rein slipped instantly to the animal's ears. The latter perceived her advantage, and began snuffing along the edges of the road in a deliberate search for spring grass. In vain Sally called and kicked; the mare provokingly preserved her independence. Finally, a piteous appeal to Gilbert, who had pretended not to notice the dilemma, and was a hundred yards in advance, was Sally's only resource. The two halted and enjoyed her comical helplessness.

"That's enough, Gilbert," said Martha Deane, presently, "go now and pick up the rein."

He rode back, picked it up, and handed it to Sally without speaking.

"Gilbert," she said, with a sudden demure change of tone, as they rode on to where Miss Deane was waiting, "come and take supper with us at home. Martha has promised. You've hardly been to see us in a month."

"You know how much I have to do, Sally," he answered. "It isn't only that, today being a Saturday; but I've promised mother to be at home by dark, and fetch a quarter of tea from the store."

"When you've once promised, I know, oxen couldn't pull you the other way."

"I don't often see your mother, Gilbert," said Martha Deane; "she is well?"

"Thank you, Martha—too well, and yet not well enough."

"What do you mean?"

"I mean," he answered, "that she does more than she has strength to do. If she had less she would be forced to undertake less; if she had more, she would be equal to her undertaking."

"I understand you now. But you should not allow her to go on in that way; you should——"

What Miss Deane would have said must remain unwritten. Gilbert's eyes were upon her and held her own; perhaps a little more color came into her face, but she did not show the slightest embarrassment. A keen observer might have supposed that either a broken or an imperfect relation existed between the two, which the gentleman was trying to restore or complete without the aid of words; and that, furthermore, while the lady was the more skilful in the use of that silent language, neither rightly understood the other.

By this time they were ascending the hill from Redley Creek to Kennett Square. Martha Deane had thus far carried the brush carelessly in her right hand; she now rolled it into a coil and thrust it into a large velvet reticule which hung from the pommel of her saddle. A few dull orange streaks in the overcast sky, behind them, denoted sunset, and a raw, gloomy twilight crept up from the east.

"You'll not go with us?" Sally asked again, as they reached the corner, and the loungers on the porch of the Unicorn Tavern beyond, perceiving Gilbert, sprang from their seats to ask for news of the chase.

"Sally, I cannot!" he answered. "Good-night!"

Joe and Jake Fairthorn rushed up with a whoop, and before Gilbert could satisfy the curiosity of the tavern-idlers, the former sat behind Sally, on the old mare, with his face to her tail, while Jake, prevented by Miss Deane's riding-whip from attempting the same performance, capered behind the horses and kept up their spirits by flinging handfuls of sand.

Gilbert found another group in "the store"—farmers or their sons who had come in for a supply of groceries, or the weekly mail, and who sat in a sweltering atmosphere around the roaring stove. They, too, had heard of the chase, and he was obliged to give them as many details as possible while his quarter of tea was being weighed, after which he left them to supply the story from the narrative of Mr. Joel Ferris, who, a newcomer announced, had just alighted at the Unicorn, a little drunk, and in a very bad humor.

"Where's Barton?" Gilbert heard some one ask of Ferris, as he mounted.

"In his skin!" was the answer, "unless he's got into that fellow Fortune's. They're as thick as two pickpockets!"

Gilbert rode down the hill, and allowed his horse to plod leisurely across the muddy level, regardless of the deepening twilight.

He was powerfully moved by some suppressed emotion. The muscles of his lips twitched convulsively, and there was a hot surge and swell somewhere in his head, as of tears about to overrun their secret reservoir. But they failed to surprise him, this time. As the first drops fell from his dark eyelashes, he loosed the rein and gave the word to his horse. Over the ridge, along the crest, between dusky thorn hedges, he swept at full gallop, and so, slowly sinking towards the fair valley which began to twinkle with the lights of scattered farms to the eastward, he soon reached the last steep descent, and saw the gray gleam of his own barn below him.

By this time his face was sternly set. He clinched his hands, and muttered to himself—

"It will almost kill me to ask, but I must know, and—and she must tell."

It was dark now. As he climbed again from the bottom of the hill towards the house, a figure on the summit was drawn indistinctly against the sky, unconscious that it was thus betrayed. But it vanished instantly, and then he groaned—

"God help me! I cannot ask."

CHAPTER 3

Mary Potter and Her Son

While Gilbert was dismounting at the gate leading into his barnyard, he was suddenly accosted by a boyish voice:

"Got back, have you?"

This was Sam, the "bound-boy,"—the son of a tenant on the old Carson place, who, in consideration of three months' schooling every winter, and a "freedom suit" at the age of seventeen, if he desired then to learn a trade, was duly made over by his father to Gilbert Potter. His position was something between that of a poor relation and a servant. He was one of the family, eating at the same table, sleeping, indeed, (for economy of housework,) in the same bed with his master, and privileged to feel his full share of interest in domestic matters; but on the other hand bound to obedience and rigid service.

"Feed's in the trough," said he, taking hold of the bridle. "I'll fix him. Better go into th' house. Tea's wanted."

Feeling as sure that all the necessary evening's work was done as if he had performed it with his own hands, Gilbert silently followed the boy's familiar advice.

The house, built like most other old farmhouses in that part of the county, of hornblende stone, stood near the bottom of a rounded knoll, overhanging the deep, winding valley. It was two stories in neight, the gable looking towards the road, and showing, just under the broad double chimney, a limestone slab, upon which were rudely carved the initials of the builder and his wife, and the date "1727." A low portico, overgrown with woodbine and trumpet flower, ran along the front. In the narrow flower-bed under it, the crocuses and daffodils were beginning to thrust up their blunt, green points. A walk of flagstones separated them from the vegetable garden, which was bounded at the bottom by a millrace, carrying half the water of the creek to the saw and grist mill on the other side of the road.

Although this road was the principal thoroughfare between Kennett Square and Wilmington, the house was so screened from the observation of travellers, both by the barn, and by some huge, spreading apple trees which occupied the space between the garden and road, that its inmates seemed to live in absolute seclusion. Looking from the front door across a narrow green meadow, a wooded hill completely shut out all glimpse of the adjoining farms; while an angle of the valley, to the eastward, hid from sight the warm, fertile fields higher up the stream.

The place seemed lonelier than ever in the gloomy March twilight; or was it some other influence which caused Gilbert to pause on the flagged walk, and stand there, motionless, looking down into the meadow until a woman's shadow, crossing the panes, was thrown upon the square of lighted earth at his feet? Then he turned and entered the kitchen.

The cloth was spread and the table set. A kettle, humming on a heap of fresh coals, and a squat little teapot of blue china, were waiting anxiously for the brown paper parcel which he placed upon the cloth. His mother was waiting also, in a high straight-backed rocking chair, with her hands in her lap.

"You're tired waiting, Mother, I suppose?" he said, as he hung his hat upon a nail over the heavy oak mantelpiece.

"No, not tired, Gilbert, but it's hungry _you'll_ be. It won't take long for the tea to draw. Everything else has been ready this half hour."

Gilbert threw himself upon the settle under the front window, and mechanically followed her with his eyes, as she carefully measured the precious herb, even stooping to pick up a leaf or two that had fallen from the spoon to the floor.

The resemblance between mother and son was very striking. Mary Potter had the same square forehead and level eyebrows, but her hair was darker than Gilbert's, and her eyes more deeply set. The fire of a lifelong pain smouldered in them, and the throes of some never-ending struggle had sharpened every line of cheek and brow, and taught her lips to close, hard compression, which those of her son were also beginning to learn. She was about forty-five years of age, but there was even now a weariness in her motions, as if her prime of strength were already past. She wore a short gown of brown flannel, with a plain linen stomacher, and a coarse apron, which she removed when the supper had been placed upon the table. A simple cap, with a narrow frill, covered her head.

The entire work of the household devolved upon her hands alone. Gilbert would have cheerfully taken a servant to assist her, but this she positively refused, seeming to court constant labor, especially during his absence from the house. Only when he was there would she take occasion to knit or sew. The kitchen was a marvel of neatness and order. The bread-trough and dresser-shelves were scoured almost to the whiteness of a napkin, and the rows of pewter plates upon the latter flashed like silver scones. To Gilbert's eyes, indeed, the effect was sometimes painful. He would have been satisfied with less laborious order, a less eager and unwearied thrift. To be sure, all this was in furtherance of a mutual purpose; but he mentally determined that when the purpose had been fulfilled, he would insist upon an easier and more cheerful arrangement. The stern aspect of life from which his nature craved escape met him oftenest at home.

Sam entered the kitchen barefooted, having left his shoes at the back door. The tea was drawn, and the three sat down to their supper of bacon, bread and butter, and apple-sauce. Gilbert and his mother ate and drank in silence, but Sam's curiosity was too lively to be restrained.

"I say, how did Roger go?" he asked.

Mary Potter looked up, as if expecting the question to be answered, and Gilbert said:

"He took the lead, and kept it."

"O cracky!" exclaimed the delighted Sam.

"Then you think it's a good bargain, Gilbert. Was it a long chase? Was he well tried?"

"All right, Mother. I could sell him for twenty dollars advance—even to Joel Ferris," he answered.

He then gave a sketch of the afternoon's adventures, to which his mother listened with a keen, steady interest. She compelled him to describe the stranger, Fortune, as minutely as possible, as if desirous of finding some form or event in her own memory to which he could be attached; but without result.

After supper Sam squatted upon a stool in the corner of the fireplace, and resumed his reading of "The Old English Baron," by the light of the burning backlog, pronouncing every word to himself in something between a whisper and a whistle. Gilbert took an account-book, a leaden inkstand, and a stumpy pen from a drawer under the window, and calculated silently and somewhat laboriously. His mother produced a clocked stocking of blue wool, and proceeded to turn the heel.

In half an hour's time, however, Sam's whispering ceased; his head nodded violently, and the book fell upon the hearth.

"I guess I'll go to bed," he said; and having thus conscientiously announced his intention, he trotted up the steep backstairs on his hands and feet. In two minutes more, a creaking overhead announced that the act was accomplished.

Gilbert filliped the ink out of his pen into the fire, laid it in his book, and turned away from the table.

"Roger has bottom," he said at last, "and he's as strong as a lion. He and Fox will make a good team, and the roads will be solid in three days, if it don't rain."

"Why, you don't mean,"—she commenced.

"Yes, Mother. You were not for buying him, I know, and you were right, inasmuch as there is always *some* risk. But it will make a difference of two barrels of load, besides having a horse at home. If I plough both for corn and oats next week—and it will be all the better for corn, as the field next to Carson's is heavy—I can begin hauling the week after, and we'll have the interest by the first of April, without borrowing a penny."

"That would be good—very good, indeed," said she, dropping her knitting, and hesitating a moment before she continued; "only—only, Gilbert, I didn't expect you would be going so soon."

"The sooner I begin, Mother, the sooner I shall finish."

"I know that, Gilbert—I know that; but I'm always looking forward to the time when you won't be bound to go at all. Not that Sam and I can't manage awhile—but if the money was paid once."—

"There's less than six hundred now, altogether. It's a good deal to scrape together in a year's time, but if it can be done I will do it. Perhaps, then, you will let some help come into the house. I'm as anxious as you can be, Mother. I'm not of a roving disposition, that you know; yet it isn't pleasant to me to see you slave as you do, and for that very reason, it's a comfort when I'm away, that you've one less to work for."

He spoke earnestly, turning his face full upon her. "We've talked this over, often and often, but you never can make me see it in your way," he then added, in a gentler tone.

"Ay, Gilbert," she replied, somewhat bitterly, "I've had my thoughts. Maybe they were too fast; it seems so. I meant, and mean, to make a good home for you, and I'm happiest when I can do the most towards it. I want you to hold up your head and be beholden to no man. There are them in the neighborhood that were bound out as boys, and are now as good as the best."

"But they are not,"—burst from his lips, as the thought on which he so gloomily brooded sprang to the surface and took him by surprise. He checked his words by a powerful effort, and the blood forsook his face. Mary Potter placed her hand on her heart, and seemed to gasp for breath.

Gilbert could not bear to look upon her face. He turned away, placed his elbow on the table, and leaned his head upon his hand. It never occurred to him that the unfinished sentence might be otherwise completed. He knew that his *thought* was betrayed, and his heart was suddenly filled with a tumult of shame, pity, and fear.

For a minute there was silence. Only the long pendulum, swinging openly along the farther wall, ticked at each end of its vibration. Then Mary Potter drew a deep, weary breath, and spoke. Her voice was hollow and strange, and each word came as by a separate muscular effort.

"*What* are they not? What word was on your tongue, Gilbert?"

He could not answer. He could only shake his head, and bring forth a cowardly, evasive word—"Nothing."

"But there *is* something! Oh, I knew it must come some time!" she cried, rather to herself than to him. "Listen to me, Gilbert! Has anyone dared to say to your face that you are basely born?"

He felt, now, that no further evasion was possible; she had put into words the terrible question which he could not steel his own heart to ask. Perhaps it was better so—better a sharp, intense pain than a dull perpetual ache. So he answered honestly now, but still kept his head turned away, as if there might be a kindness in avoiding her gaze.

"Not in so many words, Mother," he said; "but there are ways, and ways of saying a thing; and the cruelest way is that which everybody understands, and I dare not. But I have long known what it meant. It is ten years, mother, since I have mentioned the word *'father'* in your hearing."

Mary Potter leaned forward, hid her face in her hands, and rocked to and fro, as if tortured with insupportable pain. She stifled her sobs, but the tears gushed forth between her fingers.

"O my boy—my boy!" she moaned. "Ten years!—and you believed it, all that time!"

He was silent. She leaned forward and grasped his arm.

"Did you—*do* you believe it? Speak, Gilbert!"

When he did speak, his voice was singularly low and gentle. "Never mind, Mother!" was all he could say. His head was still turned away from her, but she knew there were tears on his cheeks.

"Gilbert, it is a lie!" she exclaimed, with startling vehemence. "A lie—A LIE! You are my lawful son, born in wedlock! There is no stain upon your name, of my giving, and I know there will be none of your own."

He turned towards her, his eyes shining and his lips parted in breathless joy and astonishment.

"Is it—is it true?" he whispered.

"True as there is a God in Heaven."

"Then, Mother, give me my name! Now I ask you, for the first time, who was my father?"

She wrung her hands and moaned. The sight of her son's eager, expectant face, touched with a light which she had never before seen upon it, seemed to give her another and a different pang.

"That, too!" She murmured to herself.

"Gilbert," she then said, "Have I always been a faithful mother to you? Have I been true and honest in word and deed? Have I done my best to help you in all right ways—to make you comfortable, to spare you trouble? Have I ever—I'll not say acted, for nobody's judgment is perfect—but tried to act otherwise than as I thought it might be for your good?"

"You have done all that you could say, and more, Mother."

"Then, my boy, is it too much for me to ask that you should believe my word—that you should let it stand for the truth, without my giving proofs and testimonies? For, Gilbert, that I *must* ask of you, hard as it may seem. If you will only be content with the knowledge—but then, you have felt the shame all this while; it was my fault, mine, and I ought to ask your forgiveness—"

"Mother—Mother!" he interrupted, "don't talk that way! Yes —I believe you, without testimony. You never said, or thought, an untruth; and your explanation will be enough not only for me, but for the whole neighborhood, if all witnesses are dead or gone away. If you knew of the shameful report, why didn't you deny it at once? Why let it spread and be believed in?"

"Oh," she moaned again, "if my tongue was not tied—if my tongue was not tied! There was my fault, and what a punishment! Never—never was woman punished as I have been. Gilbert, whatever you do, bind yourself by no vow, except in the sight of men!"

"I do not understand you, Mother," said he.

"No, and I dare not make myself understood. Don't ask me anything more! It's hard to shut my mouth, and bear everything in silence, but it cuts my very heart in twain to speak and not tell!"

Her distress was so evident, that Gilbert, perplexed and bewildered as her words left him, felt that he dared not press her further. He could not doubt the truth of her first assertion; but, alas! it availed only for his own private consciousness—it took no stain from him, in the eyes of the world. Yet, now that the painful theme had been opened—not less painful, it seemed, since the suspected dishonor did not exist—he craved and decided to ask, enlightenment on one point.

"Mother," he said, after a pause, "I do not want to speak about this thing again. I believe you, and my greatest comfort in believing is for your sake, not for mine. I see, too, that you are bound in some way which I do not understand, so that we cannot be cleared from the blame that it put upon us. I don't mind that so much, either—for my own sake, and I will not ask for an explanation, since you say you dare not give it. But tell me one thing—will it always be so? Are you bound forever, and will I never learn anything more? I can wait; but, Mother, you know that these things work in a man's mind, and there will come a time when the knowledge of the worst thing that could be will seem better than no knowledge at all."

Her face brightened a little. "Thank you, Gilbert!" she said. "Yes; there will come a day when you shall know all—when you and me shall have justice. I do not know how soon; I cannot guess. In the Lord's good time. I have nigh out-suffered my fault, I think, and the reward cannot be far off. A few weeks, perhaps—yet, maybe, for oh, I am not allowed even to hope for it!—maybe a few years. It will all come to the light, after so long—so long—an eternity. If I had but known!"

"Come, we will say no more now. Surely I may wait a little while, when you have waited so long. I believe you, Mother. Yes, I believe you; I am your lawful son."

She rose, placed her hands on his shoulders, and kissed him. Nothing more was said.

Gilbert raked the ashes over the smouldering embers on the hearth, lighted his mother's night-lamp, and after closing the chamber-door softly behind her, stole upstairs to his own bed.

It was long past midnight before he slept.

CHAPTER 4

Fortune and Misfortune

On the same evening, a scene of a very different character occurred, in which certain personages of this history were actors. In order to describe it, we must return to the company of sportsmen whom Gilbert Potter left at the Hammer and Trowel Tavern, late in the afternoon.

No sooner had he departed than the sneers of the young bucks, who felt themselves humiliated by his unexpected success, became loud and frequent. Mr. Alfred Barton, who seemed to care little for the general dissatisfaction, was finally reproached with having introduced such an unfit personage at a gentleman's hunt; whereupon he turned impatiently, and retorted:

"There were no particular invitations sent out, as all of you know. Anybody that had a horse, and knew how to manage him, was welcome. Zounds! if you fellows are afraid to take hedges, am I to blame for that? A hunter's a hunter, though he's born on the wrong side of the marriage certificate."

"That's the talk, Squire!" cried Fortune, giving his friend a hearty slap between the shoulders. "I've seen riding in my day," he continued, "both down in Loudon and on the Eastern Shore —men born with spurs on their heels, and I tell you this Potter could hold his own, even with the Lees and the Tollivers. We took the hedge together, while you were making a round of I don't know how many miles on the road; and I never saw a thing neater done. If you thought there was anything unfair about him, why didn't you head him off?"

"Yes, damme," echoed Mr. Barton, bringing down his fist upon the bar, so that the glasses jumped, "why didn't you head him off?" Mr. Barton's face was suspiciously flushed, and he was more excited than the occasion justified.

There was no answer to the question, except that which none of the young bucks dared to make.

"Well, I've had about enough of this," said Mr. Joel Ferris, turning on his heel; "who's for home?"

"Me!" answered three or four, with more readiness than grammar. Some of the steadier young farmers, who had come for an afternoon's recreation, caring little who was first in at the death, sat awhile and exchanged opinions about crops and cattle; but Barton and Fortune kept together, whispering much, and occasionally bursting into fits of uproarious laughter. The former was so captivated by his new friend, that before he knew it every guest was gone. The landlord had lighted two or three tallow candles, and now approached with the question:

"Will you have supper, gentlemen?"

"That depends on what you've got," said Fortune.

This was not language to which the host was accustomed. His guests were also his fellow citizens: if they patronized him, he accommodated them, and the account was balanced. His meals were as good as anybody's, though he thought it that shouldn't, and people so very particular might stay away. But he was a mild, amiable man, and Fortune's keen eye and dazzling teeth had a powerful effect upon him. He answered civilly, in spite of an inward protest:

"There's ham and eggs, and frizzled beef."

"Nothing could be better!" Fortune exclaimed, jumping up. "Come 'Squire—if I stay over Sunday with you, you must at least take supper at my expense."

Mr. Barton tried to recollect whether he had invited his friend to spend Sunday with him. It must be so, of course; only, he could not remember when he had spoken, or what words he had used. It would be very pleasant, he confessed, but for one thing; and how was he to get over the difficulty?

However, here they were, at the table, Fortune heaping his plate like a bountiful host, and talking so delightfully about horses and hounds, and drinking-bouts, and all those wild experiences which have such a charm for bachelors of forty-five or fifty, that it was impossible to determine in his mind what he should do.

After the supper, they charged themselves with a few additional potations, to keep off the chill of the night air, mounted their horses, and took the New-Garden road. A good deal of confidential whispering had preceded their departure.

"They're off on a lark," the landlord remarked to himself, as they rode away, "and it's a shame, in men of their age."

After riding a mile, they reached the crossroad on the left, which the hunters had followed, and Fortune, who was a little in advance, turned into it.

"After what I told you, 'Squire," said he, "you won't wonder that I know the country so well. Let us push on; it's not more than two miles. I would be very clear of showing you one of my nests, if you were not such a good fellow. But mum's the word, you know."

"Never fear," Barton answered, somewhat thickly; "I'm an old bird, Fortune."

"That you are! Men like you and me are not made of the same stuff as those young nincompoops; we can follow a trail without giving tongue at every jump."

Highly flattered, Barton rode nearer, and gave his friend an affectionate punch in the side. Fortune answered with an arm around his waist and a tight hug, and so they rode onward through the darkness.

They had advanced for somewhat more than a mile on the crossroad, and found themselves in a hollow, with tall, dense woods on either side. Fortune drew rein and listened. There was no wind going, and the utmost stillness prevailed in every direction. There was something awful in the gloom and solitude of the forest, and Barton, in spite of his anticipations, began to feel uncomfortable.

"Good, so far!" said Fortune, at last. "Here we leave the road, and I must strike a light."

"Won't it be seen?" Barton anxiously inquired.

"No: it's a dark lantern—a most convenient thing. I would advise you to get one."

With that, he fumbled on his holsters and produced a small object, together with a tinderbox, and swiftly and skillfully struck a light. There was a little blue flash, as of sulphur, the snap of a spring, and the gleam disappeared.

"Stay!" he said, after satisfying himself that the lantern was in order. "I must know the time. Let me have your watch a minute."

Barton hauled up the heavy article from the depths of his fob, and handed it, with the bunch of jingling seals, to his friend. The latter thrust it into his waistcoat pocket, before opening the lantern, and then seemed to have forgotten his intention, for he turned the light suddenly on Barton's face.

"Now," said he, in a sharp tone, "I'll trouble you, 'Squire, for the fifty dollars young Ferris paid you before the start, and whatever other loose change you have about you."

Barton was so utterly astounded that the stranger's words conveyed no meaning to his ears. He sat with fixed eyes, open mouth, and hanging jaws, and was conscious only that the hair was slowly rising upon his head.

There was a rustling in one of Fortune's holsters, followed by a mysterious double click. The next moment, the lantern illumined a long, bright pistol-barrel, which pointed towards the victim's breast, and caused him to feel a sharp, wasp-like sting on that side of his body.

"Be quick, now! Hand over the money!" cried Fortune, thrusting the pistol an inch nearer.

With trembling hands, Barton took a pocketbook and purse of moleskin from his breast, and silently obeyed. The robber put up the pistol, took the ring of the lantern in his teeth, and rapidly examined the money.

"A hundred and twenty-five!" he said, with a grin—"not a bad haul."

"Fortune!" stammered Barton, in a piteous voice, "this is a joke, isn't it?"

"O yes, ha! ha!—a very good joke—a stroke of fortune for you! Look here!"

He turned full upon his face the lantern which he held in his left hand, while with the right he snatched off his hat, and—as it seemed to Barton's eyes—the greater part of his head. But it was only his black hair and whiskers, which vanished in the gloom, leaving a round, smooth face, and a head of close-cropped, red hair. With his wicked eyes and shining teeth, Barton imagined that he beheld a devil.

"Did you ever hear of Sandy Flash?" said the robber.

The victim uttered a cry and gave himself up for lost. This was the redoubtable highwayman—the terror of the county—who for two years had defied the law and all its ordinary and extraordinary agents, scouring the country at his will between the Schuylkill and the Susquehanna, and always striking his blows where no one expected them to fall. This was he in all his dreadful presence—a match for any twenty men, so the story went—and he, Alfred Barton, was in his clutches! A cold sweat broke out over his whole body; his face grew deadly pale, and his teeth chattered.

The highwayman looked at him and laughed. "Sorry I can't spend Sunday with you," said he; "I must go on towards the Rising Sun. When you get another fox, send me word." Then he leaned over, nearer the trembling victim, and added in a low, significant tone, "If you stir from this spot in less than one hour, you are a dead man."

Then he rode on, whistling "Money Musk" as he went. Once or twice he stopped, as if to listen, and Barton's heart ceased to beat; but by degrees the sound of his horse's hoofs died away. The silence that succeeded was full of terrors. Barton's horse became restive, and he would have dismounted and held him, but for the weakness in every joint which made him think that his body was falling asunder. Now and then a leaf rustled, or the scent of some animal, unperceived by his own nostrils, caused his horse to snort and stamp. The air was raw and sent a fearful chill through his blood. Moreover, how was he to measure the hour? His watch was gone; he might have guessed by the stars, but the sky was overcast. Fortune and Sandy Flash—for there were two individuals in his bewildered brain—would surely fulfil their threat if he stirred before the appointed time. What under heaven should he do?

Wait; that was all; and he waited until it seemed that morning must be near at hand. Then, turning his horse, he rode back very slowly towards the New-Garden road, and after many panics, to the Hammer and Trowel. There was still light in the barroom; should the door open, he would be seen. He put spurs to his horse and dashed past. Once in motion, it seemed that he was pursued, and along Tuffkenamon went the race, until his horse, panting and exhausted, paused to drink at Redley Creek. They had gone to bed at the Unicorn; he drew a long breath, and felt that the danger was over. In five minutes more he was at home.

Putting his horse in the stable, he stole quietly to the house, pulled off his boots in the woodshed, and entered by a back way through the kitchen. Here he warmed his chill frame before the hot ashes, and then very gently and cautiously felt his way to bed in the dark.

The next morning, being Sunday, the whole household, servants and all, slept an hour later than usual, as was then the country custom. Giles, the old soldier, was the first to appear. He made the fire in the kitchen, put on the water to boil, and then attended to the feeding of the cattle at the barn. When this was accomplished, he returned to the house and entered a bedroom adjoining the kitchen, on the ground floor. Here slept "Old Man Barton," as he was generally called—Alfred's father, by name Abiah, and now eighty-five years of age. For many years he had been a paralytic and unable to walk, but the disease had not affected his business capacity. He was the hardest, shrewdest, and cunningest miser in the county. There was not a penny of the income and expenditure of the farm, for any year, which he could not account for—not a date of a deed, bond, or note of hand, which he had ever given or received, that was not indelibly burnt upon his memory. No one, not even his sons, knew precisely how much he was worth. The old lawyer in Chester, who had charge of much of his investments, was as shrewd as himself, and when he made his annual visit, the first week in April, the doors were not only closed, but everybody was banished from hearing distance so long as he remained.

Giles assisted in washing and dressing the old man, then seated him in a rude armchair, resting on clumsy wooden castors, and poured out for him a small wineglass full of raw brandy. Once or twice a year, usually after the payment of delayed interest, Giles received a share of the brandy; but he never learned to expect it. Then a long hickory staff was placed in the old man's hand, and his armchair was rolled into the kitchen, to a certain station between the fire and the southern window, where he would be out of the way of his daughter Ann, yet could measure with his eye every bit of lard she put into the frying-pan, and every spoonful of molasses that entered into the composition of her pies.

She had already set the table for breakfast. The bacon and sliced potatoes were frying in separate pans, and Ann herself was lifting the lid of the tin coffeepot, to see whether the beverage had "come to a boil," when the old man entered, or, strictly speaking, *was* entered.

As his chair rolled into the light, the hideousness, not the grace and serenity of old age, was revealed. His white hair, thin and half-combed, straggled over the dark-red, purple-veined skin of his head; his cheeks were flabby bags of bristly, wrinkled leather; his mouth was a sunken, irregular slit, losing itself in the hanging folds at the corners, and even the life, gathered into his small, restless gray eyes, was half quenched under the red and heavy edges of the lids. The third and fourth fingers of his hands were crooked upon the skinny palms, beyond any power to open them.

When Ann—a gaunt spinster of fifty-five—had placed the coffee on the table, the old man looked around, and asked with a snarl: "Where's Alfred?"

"Not up yet, but you needn't wait, father."

"Wait?" was all he said, yet she understood the tone, and wheeled him to the table. As soon as his plate was filled, he bent forward over it, rested his elbows on the cloth, and commenced feeding himself with hands that trembled so violently that he could with great difficulty bring the food to his mouth. But he resented all offers of assistance, which implied any weakness beyond that of the infirmity which it was impossible for him to conceal. His meals were weary tasks, but he shook and jerked through them, and would have gone away hungry rather than acknowledge the infirmity of his great age.

Breakfast was nearly over before Alfred Barton made his appearance. No truant schoolboy ever dreaded the master's eye as he dreaded to appear before his father that Sunday morning. His sleep had been broken and restless; the teeth of Sandy Flash had again grinned at him in nightmare-dreams, and when he came to put on his clothes, the sense of emptiness in his breast-pocket and watch-fob impressed him like a violent physical pain. His loss was bad enough, but the inability to conceal it caused him even greater distress.

Buttoning his coat over the double void, and trying to assume his usual air, he went down to the kitchen and commenced his breakfast. Whenever he looked up, he found his father's eyes fixed upon him, and before a word had been spoken, he felt that he had already betrayed something, and that the truth would follow, sooner or later. A wicked wish crossed his mind, but was instantly suppressed, for fear lest that, also, should be discovered.

After Ann had cleared the table, and retired to her own room in order to array herself in the black cloth gown which she had worn every Sunday for the past fifteen years, the old man said, or rather wheezed out the words—

"Kennett meetin'?"

"Not today," said his son, "I've a sort of chill from yesterday." And he folded his arms and shivered very naturally.

"Did Ferris pay you?" the old man again asked.

"Y-yes."

"Where's the money?"

There was the question, and it must be faced. Alfred Barton worked the farm "on shares," and was held to a strict account by his father, not only for half of all the grain and produce sold, but of all the horses and cattle raised, as well as those which were bought on speculation. On his share he managed—thanks to the niggardly system enforced in the house—not only to gratify his vulgar taste for display, but even to lay aside small sums from time to time. It was a convenient arrangement, but might be annulled any time when the old man should choose, and Alfred knew that a prompt division of the profits would be his surest guarantee of permanence.

"I have not the money with me," he answered, desperately, after a pause, during which he felt his father's gaze travelling over him, from head to foot.

"Why not! You haven't spent it?" The latter question was a croaking shriek, which seemed to forebode, while it scarcely admitted, the possibility of such an enormity.

"I spent only four shillings, Father, but—but—but the money's all gone!"

The crooked fingers clutched the hickory staff, as if eager to wield it; the sunken gray eyes shot forth angry fire, and the broken figure uncurved and straightened itself with a wrathful curiosity.

"Sandy Flash robbed me on the way home," said the son, and now that the truth was out, he seemed to pluck up a little courage.

"What, what, what!" chattered the old man, incredulously; "no lies, boy, no lies!"

The son unbuttoned his coat, and showed his empty watch fob. Then he gave an account of the robbery, not strictly correct in all its details, but near enough for his father to know, without discovering inaccuracies at a later day. The hickory-stick was shaken once or twice during the recital, but it did not fall upon the culprit—though this correction (so the gossip of the neighborhood ran) had more than once been administered within the previous ten years. As Alfred Barton told his story, it was hardly a case for anger on the father's part, so he took his revenge in another way.

"This comes o' your races and your expensive company," he growled, after a few incoherent sniffs and snarls; "but I don't lose my half of the horse. No, no! I'm not paid till the money's been handed over. Twenty-five dollars, remember!—and soon, that I don't lose the use of it too long. As for *your* money and the watch, I've nothing to do with them. I've got along without a watch for eighty-five years, and I never wore as smart a coat as that in my born days. Young men understood how to save, in *my* time."

Secretly, however, the old man was flattered by his son's love of display, and enjoyed his swaggering air, although nothing would have induced him to confess the fact. His own father had come to Pennsylvania as a servant of one of the first settlers, and the reverence which he had felt, as a boy, for the members of the Quaker and farmer aristocracy of the neighborhood, had now developed into a late vanity to see his own family acknowledged as the equals of the descendants of the former. Alfred had long since discovered that when he happened to return home from the society of the Falconers, or the Caswells, or the Carsons, the old man was in an unusual good-humor. At such times, the son felt sure that he was put down for a large slice of the inheritance.

After turning the stick over and over in his skinny hands, and pressing the top of it against his toothless gums, the old man again spoke.

"See here, you're old enough now to lead a steady life. You might ha' had a farm o' your own, like Elisha, if you'd done as well. A very fair bit o' money he married—very fair—but I don't say you couldn't do as well, or, maybe, better."

"I've been thinking of that, myself," the son replied.

"Have you? Why don't you step up to her then? Ten thousand dollars aren't to be had every day, and you needn't expect to get it without the askin'! Where molasses is dropped, you'll always find more than one fly. Others than you have got their eyes on the girl."

The son's eyes opened tolerably wide when the old man began to speak, but a spark of intelligence presently flashed into them, and an expression of cunning ran over his face.

"Don't be anxious, Daddy!" said he, with assumed playfulness; "she's not a girl to take the first that offers. She has a mind of her own,—with her the more haste the less speed. I know what I'm about; I have my top eye open, and when there's a good chance, you won't find me sneaking behind the wood-house."

"Well, well!" muttered the old man, "we'll see—we'll see! A good family, too—not that I care for that. My family's as good as the next. But if you let her slip, boy"—and here he brought down the end of his stick with a significant whack, upon the floor. "This I'll tell you," he added, without finishing the broken sentence, "that whether you're a rich man or a beggar, depends on yourself. The more you have, the more you'll get; remember that! Bring me my brandy!"

Alfred Barton knew the exact value of his father's words. Having already neglected, or, at least, failed to succeed, in regard to two matches which his father had proposed, he understood the risk to his inheritance which was implied by a third failure. And yet, looking at the subject soberly, there was not the slightest prospect of success. Martha Deane was the girl in the old man's mind, and an instinct, stronger than his vanity, told him that she never would, or could, be his wife. But, in spite of that, it must be his business to create a contrary impression, and keep it alive as long as possible—perhaps until—until—

We all know what was in his mind. Until the old man should die.

CHAPTER *5*

Guests at Fairthorn's

The Fairthorn farm was immediately north of Kennett Square. For the first mile towards Unionville, the rich, rolling fields which any traveller may see to this day, on either side of the road, belonged to it. The house stood on the right, in the hollow into which the road dips, on leaving the village. Originally a large cabin of hewn logs, it now rejoiced in a stately stone addition, overgrown with ivy up to the eaves, and a long porch in front, below which two mounds of box guarded the flight of stone steps leading down to the garden. The hill in the rear kept off the north wind, and this garden caught the earliest warmth of spring. Nowhere else in the neighborhood did the crocuses bloom so early, or the peas so soon appear above ground. The lack of order, the air of old neglect about the place, in nowise detracted from its warm, cosy character; it was a pleasant nook, and the relatives and friends of the family (whose name was legion) always liked to visit there.

Several days had elapsed since the chase, and the eventful evening which followed it. It was baking day, and the plump arms of Sally Fairthorn were floury-white up to the elbows. She was leaning over the dough-trough, plunging her fists furiously into the spongy mass, when she heard a step on the porch. Although her gown was pinned up, leaving half of her short, striped petticoat visible, and a blue and white spotted handkerchief concealed her dark hair, Sally did not stop to think of that. She rushed into the front room, just as a gaunt female figure passed the window, at the sight of which she clapped her hands so that the flour flew in a little white cloud, and two or three strips of dough peeled off her arms and fell upon the floor.

The front door opened, and our old friend, Miss Betsy Lavender, walked into the room.

Any person, between Kildeer Hill and Hockessin, who did not know Miss Betsy, must have been an utter stranger to the country, or an idiot. She had a marvelous clairvoyant faculty for the approach of either joy or grief, and always turned up just at the moment when she was most wanted. Profession had she none; neither a permanent home, but for twenty years she had wandered hither and thither, in highly independent fashion, turning her hand to whatever seemed to require its cunning. A better housekeeper never might have lived, if she could have stuck to one spot; an admirable cook, nurse, seamstress, and spinner, she refused alike the high wages of wealthy farmers and the hands of poor widowers. She had a little money of her own, but never refused payment from those who were able to give it, in order that she might now and then make a present of her services to poorer friends. Her speech was blunt and rough, her ways odd and eccentric; her name was rarely mentioned without a laugh, but those who laughed at her esteemed her none the less. In those days of weekly posts and one newspaper, she was Politics, Art, Science, and Literature to many families.

In person, Miss Betsy Lavender was peculiar rather than attractive. She was nearly, if not quite, fifty years of age, rather tall, and a little stoop-shouldered. Her face, at first sight, suggested that of a horse, with its long, ridged nose, loose lips and short chin. Her eyes were dull gray, set near together, and much sharper in their operation than a stranger would suppose. Over a high, narrow forehead she wore thin bands of tan-colored hair, somewhat grizzled, and forming a coil at the back of her head, barely strong enough to hold the teeth of an enormous tortoise-shell comb. Yet her grotesqueness had nothing repellant; it was a genial caricature, at which no one could take offense.

"The very person I wanted to see!" cried Sally. "Father and Mother are going up to Uncle John's this afternoon; Aunt Eliza has an old woman's quilting-party, and they'll stay all night, and however am I to manage Joe and Jake by myself? Martha's half promised to come, but not till after supper. It will all go right, since you are here; come into Mother's room and take off your things!"

"Well," said Miss Betsy, with a snort, "*that's* to be my business, eh? I'll have my hands full; a pearter couple o' lads a'n't to be found this side o' Nottin'gam. They might ha' growed up wild on the Barrens, for all the manners they've got."

Sally knew that this criticism was true; also that Miss Betsy's task was no sinecure, and she therefore thought it best to change the subject.

"There!"said she, as Miss Betsy gave the thin rope of her back hair a fierce twist, and jammed her high comb inward and outward that the teeth might catch—"there! now you'll do! Come into the kitchen and tell me the news, while I set my loaves to rise."

"Loaves to rise," echoed Miss Betsy, seating herself on a tall, rush-bottomed chair near the window. She had an incorrigible habit of repeating the last three words of the person with whom she spoke—a habit which was sometimes mimicked good-humoredly, even by her best friends. Many persons, however, were flattered by it, as it seemed to denote an earnest attention to what they were saying. Between the two, there it was and there it would be, to the day of her death—Miss Lavender's "keel*-mark," as the farmers said of their sheep.

"Well," she resumed, after taking breath, "no news is good news, these days. Down Whitely Creek way, towards Strickersville, there's fever, they say; Richard Rudd talks o' buildin' higher up the hill—you know it's low and swampy about the old house—but Sarah, she says it'll be a mortal long ways to the springhouse, and so betwixt and between them I dunno how it'll turn out. Dear me! I was up at Aunt Buffin'ton's t' other day; she's lookin' poorly; her mother, I remember, went off in a decline, the same year the Tories burnt down their barn, and I'm afeard she's goin' the same way. But, yes! I guess there's one thing you'll like to hear. Old Man Barton is goin' to put up a new wagon-house, and Mark is to have the job."

"Law!" exclaimed Sally, "what's that to me?" But there was a decided smile on her face as she put another loaf into the pan, and, although her head was turned away, a pretty flush of color came up behind her ear, and betrayed itself to Miss Lavender's quick eye.

"Nothin' much, I reckon," the latter answered, in the most matter-of-fact way, "only I thought you might like to know it, Mark bein' a neighbor, like, and a right-down smart young fellow."

"Well, I *am* glad of it," said Sally, with sudden candor, "he's Martha's cousin."

*Keel, a local term for red chalk.

"Martha's cousin,—and I shouldn't wonder if he'd be something more to her, some day."

"No, indeed! What are you thinking of, Betsy?" Sally turned around and faced her visitor, regardless that her soft brunette face showed a decided tinge of scarlet. At this instant clattering feet were heard, and Joe and Jake rushed into the kitchen. They greeted their old friend with boisterous demonstrations of joy.

"Now we'll have doughnuts," cried Joe.

"No; 'lasses-wax!" said Jake. "Sally, where's mother? Dad's out at the wall, and Bonnie's jumpin' and prancin' like anything!"

"Go along!" exclaimed Sally, with a slap which lost its force in the air, as Jake jumped away. Then they all left the kitchen together, and escorted the mother to the garden-wall by the road, which served the purpose of a horse-block. Farmer Fairthorn—a hale, ruddy, honest figure, in broad-brimmed hat, brown coat and knee-breeches—already sat upon the old mare, and the pillion behind his saddle awaited the coming burden. Mother Fairthorn, a cheery little woman, with dark eyes and round brunette face, like her daughter, wore the scoop bonnet and drab shawl of a Quakeress, as did many in the neighborhood who did not belong to the sect. Never were people better suited to each other than these two: they took the world as they found it, and whether the crops were poor or abundant, whether money came in or had to be borrowed, whether the roof leaked, or a broken pale let the sheep into the garden, they were alike easy of heart, contented and cheerful.

The mare, after various obstinate whirls, was finally brought near the wall; the old woman took her seat on the pillion, and after a parting admonition to Sally: "Rake the coals and cover 'em up, before going to bed, whatever you do!"—they went off, deliberately, up the hill.

"Miss Betsy," said Joe, with a very grave air, as they returned to the kitchen, "I want you to tell me one thing,—whether it's true or not. Sally says I'm a monkey."

"I'm a monkey," repeated the unconscious Miss Lavender, whereupon both boys burst into shrieks of laughter, and made their escape.

"Much doughnuts they'll get from me," muttered the ruffled spinster, as she pinned up her sleeves and proceeded to help Sally. The work went on rapidly, and by the middle of the afternoon, the kitchen wore its normal aspect of homely neatness. Then came the hour or two of quiet and rest, nowhere in the world so grateful as in a country farmhouse, to its mistress and her daughters, when all the rough work of the day is over, and only the lighter task of preparing supper yet remains. Then, when the sewing or knitting has been produced, the little painted-pine work-stand placed near the window, and a pleasant neighbor drops in to enliven the softer occupation with gossip, the country wife or girl finds her life a very happy and cheerful possession. No dresses are worn with so much pleasure as those then made; no books so enjoyed as those then read, a chapter or two at a time.

Sally Fairthorn, we must confess, was not in the habit of reading much. Her education had been limited. She had ciphered as far as Compound Interest, read Murray's "Sequel," and Goldsmith's "Rome," and could write a fair letter, without misspelling many words; but very few other girls in the neighborhood possessed greater accomplishments than these, and none of them felt, or even thought of, their deficiencies. There were no "missions" in those days; it was fifty or sixty years before the formation of the "Kennett Psychological Society," and "Pamela," "Rasselas," and "Joseph Andrews," were lent and borrowed, as at present "Consuelo," Buckle, Ruskin, and "Enoch Arden."

One single work of art had Sally created, and it now hung, stately in a frame of curled maple, in the chilly parlor. It was a sampler, containing the alphabet, both large and small, the names and dates of birth of both her parents, a harp and willow-tree, the twigs whereof were represented by parallel rows of "herring-bone" stitch, a sharp zigzag spray of rosebuds, and the following stanza, placed directly underneath the harp and willow:

> "By Babel's streams we Sat and Wept
> When Zion we thought on:
> For Grief thereof, we Hang our Harp
> The Willow Tree upon."

Across the bottom of the sampler was embroidered the inscription: "Done by Sarah Ann Fairthorn, May, 1792, in the 16th year of her age."

While Sally went upstairs to her room, to put her hair into

order, and tie a finer apron over her cloth gown, Miss Betsy
Lavender was made the victim of a most painful experience.

Joe and Jake, who had been dodging around the house, half-
coaxing and half-teasing the ancient maiden whom they both
plagued and liked, had not been heard or seen for a while. Miss
Betsy was knitting by the front window, waiting for Sally, when
the door was hastily thrown open, and Joe appeared, panting,
scared, and with an expression of horror upon his face.

"Oh, Miss Betsy!" was his breathless exclamation, "Jake! the
cherry tree!"

Dropping her work upon the floor, Miss Lavender hurried out
of the house, with beating heart and trembling limbs, following
Joe, who ran towards the field above the barn, where near the
fence, there stood a large and lofty cherry tree. As she reached
the fence she beheld Jake, lying motionless on his back, on the
brown grass.

"The Lord have mercy!" she cried; her knees gave way, and
she sank upon the ground in an angular heap. When, with a
desperate groan, she lifted her head and looked through the
lower rails, Jake was not to be seen. With a swift, convulsive
effort she rose to her feet, just in time to catch a glimpse of the
two young scamps whirling over the farther fence into the wood
below.

She walked unsteadily back to the house. "It's given me such
a turn," she said to Sally, after describing the trick, "that I
dunno when I'll get over it."

Sally gave her some whiskey and sugar, which soon brought a
vivid red to the tip of her chin and the region of her cheek-
bones, after which she professed that she felt very comfortable.
But the boys, frightened at the effect of their thoughtless prank,
did not make their appearance. Joe, seeing Miss Betsy fall,
thought she was dead, and the two hid themselves in a bed of
dead leaves, beside a fallen log, not daring to venture home for
supper. Sally said they should have none, and would have
cleared the table; but Miss Betsy, whose kind heart had long
since relented, went forth and brought them to light, promising
that she would not tell their father, provided they "would never
do such a wicked thing again." Their behavior, for the rest of
the evening, was irreproachable.

Just as candles were being lighted, there was another step on
the porch, and the door opened on Martha Deane.

"I'm *so* glad!" cried Sally. "Never mind your pattens, Martha; Joe shall carry them into the kitchen. Come, let me take off your cloak and hat."

Martha's coming seemed to restore the fading daylight. Not boisterous or impulsive, like Sally, her nature burned with a bright and steady flame—white and cold to some, golden and radiant to others. Her form was slender, and every motion expressed a calm, serene grace, which could only spring from some conscious strength of character. Her face was remarkably symmetrical, its oval outline approaching the Greek ideal; but the brow was rather high than low, and the light brown hair covered the fair temples evenly, without a ripple. Her eyes were purely blue, and a quick, soft spark was easily kindled in their depths; the cheeks round and rosy, and the mouth clearly and delicately cut, with an unusual, yet wholly feminine firmness in the lines of the upper lip. This peculiarity, again, if slightly out of harmony with the pervading gentleness of her face, was balanced by the softness and sweetness of her dimpled chin, and gave to her face a rare union of strength and tenderness. It very rarely happens that decision and power of will in a young woman are not manifested by some characteristic rather masculine than feminine; but Martha Deane knew the art of unwearied, soft assertion and resistance, and her beautiful lips could pronounce, when necessary, a final word.

Joe and Jake came forward with a half-shy delight, to welcome "Cousin Martha," as she was called in the Fairthorn household, her mother and Sally's father having been "own" cousins.* There was a cheerful fire on the hearth, and the three ladies gathered in front of it, with the work-stand in the middle, while the boys took possession of the corner-nooks. The latter claimed their share of the gossip; they knew the family histories of the neighborhood much better than their school-books, and exhibited a precocious interest in this form of knowledge. The conversation, therefore, was somewhat guarded, and the knitting and sewing all the more assiduously performed, until, with great reluctance, and after repeated commands, Joe and Jake stole off to bed.

The atmosphere of the room then became infinitely more free and confidential. Sally dropped her hands in her lap, and settled

*First cousins (ed.).

herself more comfortably in her chair, while Miss Lavender, with an unobserved side-glance at her, said:

"Mark is to put up Barton's new wagon-house, I hear, Martha."

"Yes," Martha answered; "it is not much, but Mark, of course, is very proud of his first job. There is a better one in store, though he does not know of it."

Sally pricked up her ears. "What is it?" asked Miss Betsy.

"It is not to be mentioned, you will understand. I saw Alfred Barton today. He seems to take quite an interest in Mark, all at once, and he told me that the Hallowells are going to build a new barn this summer. He spoke to them of Mark, and thinks the work is almost sure."

"Well, now!" Miss Betsy exclaimed, "if he gets that, after a year's journeywork, Mark is a made man. And I'll speak to Richard Rudd the next time I see him. He thinks he's beholden to me, since Sarah had the fever so bad. I don't like folks to think that, but there's times when it appears to come handy."

Sally arose, flushed and silent, and brought a plate of cakes and a basket of apples from the pantry. The work was now wholly laid aside, and the stand cleared to receive the refreshments.

"Now pare your peels in one piece, girls," Miss Betsy advised, "and then whirl 'em to find the *itials* o' your sweethearts' names."

"You, too, Miss Betsy!" cried Sally, "we must find out the widower's name!"

"The widower's name," Miss Betsy gravely repeated, as she took a knife.

With much mirth the parings were cut, slowly whirled three times around the head, and then let fly over the left shoulder. Miss Betsy's was first examined and pronounced to be an A.

"Who's A?" she asked.

"Alfred!" said Sally. "Now, Martha, here's yours—an S, no it's a G!"

"The curl is the wrong way," said Martha, gravely, "it's a figure 3; so, I have three of them, have I?"

"And mine," Sally continued, "is a W!"

"Yes, if you look at it upside down. The inside of the peel is uppermost: you must turn it, and then it will be an M."

Sally snatched it up in affected vexation, and threw it into the fire. "Oh, I know a new way!" she cried; "did you ever try it, Martha—with the key and the Bible!"

"Old as the hills, but awful sure," remarked Miss Lavender. "When it's done serious, it's never been known to fail."

Sally took the house-key, and brought from the old walnut cabinet a plump octavo Bible, which she opened at the Song of Solomon, eighth chapter and sixth verse. The end of the key being carefully placed therein, the halves of the book were bound together with cords, so that it could be carried by the key-handle. Then Sally and Martha, sitting face to face, placed each the end of the forefinger of the right hand under the half the ring of the key nearest to her.

"Now, Martha," said Sally, "we'll try your fortune first. Say 'A,' and then repeat the verse: 'set me as a seal upon thy heart, as a seal upon thine arm; for love is strong as death, jealousy is cruel as the grave: the coals thereof are coals of fire, which hath a most vehement flame.' "

Martha did as she was bidden, but the book hung motionless. She was thereupon directed to say B, and repeat the verse; and so on, letter by letter. The slender fingers trembled a little with the growing weight of the book, and, although Sally protested that she was holding as still "as she knew how," the trembling increased, and before the verse which followed G had been finished, the ring of the key slowly turned, and the volume fell to the floor.

Martha picked it up with a quiet smile.

"It is easy to see who was in *your* mind, Sally," she said. "Now let me tell your fortune: we will begin at L—it will same time."

"Save time," said Miss Lavender, rising. "Have it out betwixt and between you, girls: I'm a-goin' to bed."

The two girls soon followed her example. Hastily undressing themselves in the chilly room, they lay down side by side, to enjoy the blended warmth and rest, and the tender, delicious interchanges of confidence which precede sleep. Though so different in every fibre of their natures, they loved each other with a very true and tender affection.

"Martha," said Sally, after an interval of silence, "did you think I *made* the Bible turn at G?"

"I think you thought it would turn, and therefore it did. Gilbert Potter was in your mind, of course."

"And not in yours, Martha?"

"If any man was seriously in my mind, Sally, do you think I would take the Bible and the door-key in order to find out his name?"

Sally was not adroit in speech: she felt that her question had not been answered, but was unable to see precisely how the answer had been evaded.

"I certainly was beginning to think that you liked Gilbert," she said.

"So I do. Anybody may know that who cares for the information." And Martha laughed cheerfully.

"Would you say so to Gilbert himself?" Sally timidly suggested.

"Certainly; but why should he ask? I like a great many young men."

"Oh, Martha!"

"Oh, Sally!—and so do you. But there's this I will say: if I were to love a man, neither he nor any other living soul should know it, until he had told me with his own lips that his heart had chosen me."

The strength of conviction in Martha's grave, gentle voice, struck Sally dumb. Her lips were sealed on the delicious secret she was longing, and yet afraid, to disclose. *He* had not spoken: she hoped he loved her, she was sure she loved him. Did she speak now, she thought, she would lower herself in Martha's eyes. With a helpless impulse, she threw one arm over the latter's neck, and kissed her cheek. She did not know that with the kiss she had left a tear.

"Sally," said Martha, in a tender whisper, "I only spoke for myself. Some hearts must be silent, while it is the nature of others to speak out. You are not afraid of me: it will be womanly in you to tell me everything. Your cheek is hot: you are blushing. Don't blush, Sally dear, for I know it already."

Sally answered with an impassioned demonstration of gratitude and affection. Then she spoke; but we will not reveal the secrets of her virgin heart. It is enough that, soothed and comforted by Martha's wise counsel and sympathy, she sank into happy slumber at her side.

CHAPTER 6

The New Gilbert

This time the weather, which so often thwarts the farmer's calculations, favored Gilbert Potter. In a week the two fields were ploughed, and what little farm-work remained to be done before the first of April, could be safely left to Sam. On the second Monday after the chase, therefore, he harnessed his four sturdy horses to the wagon, and set off before the first streak of dawn for Columbia, on the Susquehanna. Here he would take from twelve to sixteen barrels of flour (according to the state of the roads) and haul them, a two days' journey, to Newport, on the Christiana River. The freight of a dollar and a half a barrel, which he received, yielded him what in those days was considered a handsome profit for the service, and it was no unusual thing for farmers who were in possession of a suitable team, to engage in the business whenever they could spare the time from their own fields.

Since the evening when she had spoken to him, for the first time in her life, of the dismal shadow which rested upon their names, Mary Potter felt that there was an indefinable change in her relation to her son. He seemed suddenly drawn nearer to her, and yet, in some other sense which she could not clearly comprehend, thrust farther away. His manner, always kind and tender, assumed a shade of gentle respect, grateful in itself, yet disturbing, because new in her experience of him. His head was slightly lifted, and his lips, though firm as ever, less rigidly compressed. She could not tell how it was, but his voice had more authority in her ears. She had never before quite disentangled the man that he was from the child that he had been; but now the separation, sharp, sudden, and final, was impressed upon her mind. Under all the loneliness which came upon her, when the musical bells of his team tinkled into silence beyond the hill, there lurked a strange sense of relief, as if her nature would more readily adjust itself during his absence.

Instead of accepting the day with its duties as a sufficient burden, she now deliberately reviewed the past. It would give her pain, she knew; but what pain could she ever feel again, comparable to that which she had so recently suffered? Long she brooded over that bitter period before and immediately succeeding her son's birth, often declaring to herself how fatally she had erred, and as often shaking her head in hopeless renunciation of any present escape from the consequences of that error. She saw her position clearly, yet it seemed that she had so entangled herself in the meshes of a merciless fate, that the only reparation she could claim, either for herself or her son, would be thrown away by forestalling—after such endless, endless submission and suffering—the event which should set her free.

Then she recalled and understood, as never before, Gilbert's childhood and boyhood. For his sake she had accepted menial service in families where he was looked upon and treated as an incumbrance. The child, it had been her comfort to think, was too young to know or feel this—but now, alas! the remembrance of his shyness and sadness told her a different tale. So nine years had passed, and she was then forced to part with her boy. She had bound him to Farmer Fairthorn, whose good heart, and his wife's, she well knew, and now she worked for him alone, putting by her savings every year, and stinting herself to the utmost that she might be able to start him in life if he should live to be his own master. Little by little, the blot upon her seemed to fade out or be forgotten, and she hoped—oh, how she had hoped!—that he might be spared the knowledge of it.

She watched him grow up, a boy of firm will, strong temper, yet great self-control; and the easy Fairthorn rule, which would have spoiled a youth of livelier spirits, was, providentially, the atmosphere in which his nature grew more serene and patient. He was steady, industrious and faithful, and the Fairthorns loved him almost as their own son. When he reached the age of eighteen, he was allowed many important privileges: he hauled flour to Newport, having a share of the profits, and in other ways earned a sum which, with his mother's aid, enabled him to buy a team of his own, on coming of age.

Two years more of this weary, lonely labor, and the one absorbing aim of Mary Potter's life, which she had impressed upon him ever since he was old enough to understand it, drew near fulfillment. The farm upon which they now lived was sold, and Gilbert became the purchaser. There was still a debt of a thousand dollars upon the property, and she felt that until it was paid, they possessed no secure home. During the year which had elapsed since the purchase, Gilbert, by unwearied labor, had laid up about four hundred dollars, and another year, he had said, if he should prosper in his plans, would see them free at last! Then—let the world say what it chose! They had fought their way from shame and poverty to honest independence, and the respect which follows success would at least be theirs.

This was always the consoling thought to which Mary Potter returned, from the unallayed trouble of her mind. Day by day, Gilbert's new figure became more familiar, and she was conscious that her own manner towards him must change with it. The subject of his birth, however, and the new difficulties with which it beset her, would not be thrust aside. For years she had almost ceased to think of the possible release of which she had spoken; now it returned and filled her with a strange, restless impatience.

Gilbert, also, had ample time to review his own position during the fortnight's absence. After passing the hills and emerging upon the long, fertile swells of Lancaster, his experienced leaders but rarely needed the guidance of his hand or voice. Often, sunk in reverie, the familiar landmarks of the journey went by unheeded; often he lay awake in the crowded bedroom of a tavern, striving to clear a path for his feet a little way into the future. Only men of the profoundest culture make a deliberate study of their own natures, but those less gifted often act with an equal or even superior wisdom, because their qualities operate spontaneously, unwatched by an introverted eye. Such men may be dimly conscious of certain inconsistencies or unsolved puzzles in themselves, but instead of sitting down to unravel them, they seek the easiest way to pass by and leave them untouched. For them the material aspects of life are of the highest importance, and a true instinct shows them that beyond the merest superficial acquaintance with their own natures lie deep and distrubing questions, with which they are not fitted to grapple.

There comes a time, however, to every young man, even the most uncultivated, when he touches one of the primal, eternal forces of life, and is conscious of other needs and another destiny. This time had come to Gilbert Potter, forcing him to look upon the circumstances of his life from a loftier point of view. He had struggled, passionately but at random, for light— but, fortunately, every earnest struggle is towards the light, and it now began to dawn upon him.

He first became aware of one enigma, the consideration of which was not so easy to lay aside. His mother had not been deceived: there was a change in the man since that evening. Often and often, in gloomy broodings over his supposed disgrace, he had fiercely asserted to himself that *he* was free from stain, and the unrespect in which he stood was an injustice to be bravely defied. The brand which he wore, and which he fancied was seen by every eye he met, existed in his own fancy; his brow was as pure, his right to esteem and honor equal, to that of any other man. But it was impossible to act upon this reasoning; still when the test came he would shrink and feel the pain, instead of trampling it under his feet.

Now that the brand *was* removed, the strength which he had so desperately craved, was suddenly his. So far as the world was concerned, nothing was altered; no one knew of the revelation which his mother had made to him; he was still the child of her shame, but this knowledge was no longer a torture. Now he had a right to respect, not asserted only to his own heart, but which every man would acknowledge, were it made known. He was no longer a solitary individual, protesting against prejudice and custom. Though still feeling that the protest was just, and that his new courage implied some weakness, he could not conceal from himself the knowledge that this very weakness was the practical fountain of his strength. He was a secret and unknown unit of the great majority.

There was another, more intimate subject which the new knowledge touched very nearly; and here also, hope dawned upon a sense akin to despair. With all the force of his nature, Gilbert Potter loved Martha Deane. He had known her since he was a boy at Fairthorn's; her face had always been the brightest in his memory; but it was only since the purchase of the farm that his matured manhood had fully recongized its answering womanhood in her. He was slow to acknowledge the truth, even to his own heart, and when it could no longer be denied, he locked it up and sealed it with seven seals, determined never to betray it, to her or anyone. Then arose a wild hope, that respect might come with the independence for which he was laboring, and perhaps he might dare to draw nearer—near enough to guess if there were any answer in her heart. It was a frail support, but he clung to it as with his life, for there was none other.

Now—although his uncertainty was as great as ever—his approach could not humiliate her. His love brought no shadow of shame; it was proudly white and clean. Ah! he had forgotten that she did not know—that his lips were sealed until his mother's should be opened to the world. The curse was not to be shaken off so easily.

By the time he had twice traversed the long, weary road between Columbia and Newport, Gilbert reached a desperate solution of this difficulty. The end of his meditations was: "I will see if there be love in woman as in man!—love that takes no note of birth or station, but, once having found its mate, is faithful from first to last." In love, an honest and faithful heart touches the loftiest ideal. Gilbert knew that, were the case reversed, no possible test could shake his steadfast affection, and how else could he measure the quality of hers? He said to himself: "Perhaps it is cruel, but I cannot spare her the trial." He was prouder than he knew—but we must remember all that he endured.

It was a dry, windy March month that year, and he made four good trips before the first of April. Returning home from Newport by way of Wilmington, with seventy-five dollars clear profit in his pocket, his prospects seemed very cheerful. Could he accomplish two more months of hauling during the year, and the crops should be fair, the money from these sources, and the sale of his wagon and one span, would be something more than enough to discharge the remaining debt. He knew, moreover, how the farm could be more advantageously worked, having used his eyes to good purpose in passing through the rich, abundant fields of Lancaster. The land once his own—which, like his mother, he could not yet feel—his future, in a material sense, was assured.

Before reaching the Buck Tavern, he overtook a woman plodding slowly along the road. Her rusty beaver hat, tied down over her ears, and her faded gown, were in singular contrast to the shining new scarlet shawl upon her shoulders. As she stopped and turned, at the sound of his tinkling bells, she showed a hard red face, not devoid of a certain coarse beauty, and he recognized Deb. Smith, a lawless, irregular creature, well-known about Kennett.

"Good-day, Deborah!" said he; "if you are going my way, I can give you a lift."

"He calls me 'Deborah,'" she muttered to herself; then aloud —"Ay, and thank ye, Mr. Gilbert."

Seizing the tail of the near horse with one hand, she sprang upon the wagon-tongue, and the next moment sat upon the board at his side. Then, rummaging in a deep pocket, she produced, one after the other, a short black pipe, an eel-skin tabacco-pouch, flint, tinder, and a clumsy knife. With a dexterity which could only have come from long habit, she prepared and kindled the weed, and was presently puffing forth rank streams, with an air of the deepest satisfaction.

"Which way?" asked Gilbert.

"Your'n, as far as you go,—always providin' you takes me."

"Of course, Deborah, you're welcome. I have no load, you see."

"Mighty clever* in you, Mr. Gilbert; but you always was one o' the clever ones. Them as thinks themselves better born—"

"Come, Deborah, none of that!" he exclaimed.

"Ax your pardon," she said, and smoked her pipe in silence. When she had finished and knocked the ashes out against the front panel of the wagon, she spoke again, in a hard, bitter voice.—

"'Tisn't much difference what *I* am. I was raised on hard knocks, and now I must git my livin' by 'em. But I axes no 'un's help, I'm *that* proud, anyways. I go my own road, and a straighter one, too, damme, than I git credit for, but I let other people go their'n. You might have wuss company than me, though *I* say it."

These words hinted at an inward experience in some respects so surprisingly like his own, that Gilbert was startled. He knew the reputation of the woman, though he would have found it difficult to tell whereupon it was based. Everybody said she was bad, and nobody knew particularly why. She lived alone, in a log cabin in the woods; did washing and housecleaning; worked in the harvest-fields; smoked, and took her gill of whiskey with the best of them—but other vices, though inferred, were not

*Good-natured (ed.).

proven. Involuntarily, he contrasted her position, in this respect, with his own. The world, he had recently learned, was wrong in his case; might it not also be doing her injustice? Her pride, in its coarse way, was his also, and his life, perhaps, had only unfolded into honorable success through a mother's ever-watchful care and never-wearied toil.

"Deborah," he said, after a pause, "no man or woman who makes an honest living by hard work is bad company for me. I am trying to do the same thing that you are—to be independent of others. It's not an easy thing for anybody, starting from nothing, but I guess that it must be much harder for you than for me."

"Yes, you're a man!" she cried. "Would to God I'd been one, too! A man can do everything that I do, and it's all right and proper. Why did the Lord give me strength? Look at that!" She bared her right arm—hard, knitted muscle from wrist to shoulder—and clenched her fist. "What's that for?—not for a woman, I say; I could take two of 'em by the necks and pitch 'em over yon fence. I've felled an Irishman like an ox when he called me names. The anger's in me, and the boldness and the roughness, and the cursin'; I didn't put 'em there, and I can't git 'em out now, if I tried ever so much. Why did they snatch the sewin' from me when I wanted to learn women's work, and send me out to yoke th' oxen? I do believe I was a gal onc't, a six-month or so, but it's over long ago. I've been a man ever since!"

She took a bottle out of her pocket, and offered it to Gilbert. When he refused, she simply said: "You're right!" set it to her mouth, and drank long and deeply. There was a wild, painful gleam of truth in her words which touched his sympathy. How should he dare to judge this unfortunate creature, not knowing what perverse freak of nature and untoward circumstances of life had combined to make her what she was? His manner towards her was kind and serious, and by degrees this covert respect awoke in her a desire to deserve it. She spoke calmly and soberly, exhibiting a wonderful knowledge as they rode onwards, not only of farming, but of animals, trees, and plants.

The team, knowing that home and rest were near, marched cheerily up and down the hills along the border, and before sunset, emerging from the woods, they overlooked the little valley, the mill, and the nestling farmhouse. An Indian war whoop rang across the meadow, and Gilbert recognized Sam's welcome therein.

"Now, Deborah," said he, "you shall stop and have some supper, before you go any farther."

"I'm obliged, all the same," said she, "but I must push on. I've to go beyond the Square, and couldn't wait. But tell your mother if she wants a man's arm in housecleanin' time to let me know. And, Mr. Gilbert, let me say one thing: give me your hand."

The horses had stopped to drink at the creek. He gave her his right hand.

She held it in hers a moment, gazing intently on the palm. Then she bent her head and blew upon it gently, three times.

"Never mind: it's my fancy," she said. "You're born for trial and good luck, but the trials come first, all of a heap, and the good luck afterwards. You've got a friend in Deb. Smith, if you ever need one. Good-bye to ye!"

With these words she sprang from the wagon, and trudged off silently up the hill. The horses turned of themselves into the lane leading to the barn, and Gilbert assisted Sam in unharnessing and feeding them before entering the house. By the time he was ready to greet his mother, and enjoy, without further care, his first evening at home, he knew everthing that had occurred on the farm during his absence.

CHAPTER 7

Old Kennett Meeting

On the Sunday succeeding his return, Gilbert Potter proposed to his mother that they should attend the Friends' Meeting at Old Kennett.

The Quaker element, we have already stated, largely predominated in this part of the county; and even the many families who were not actually members of the sect were strongly colored with its peculiar characteristics. Though not generally using "the plain speech" among themselves, they invariably did so towards Quakers, varied but little from the latter in dress and habits, and, with very few exceptions, regularly attended their worship. In fact, no other religious attendance was possible, without a Sabbath journey too long for the well-used farmhorses. To this class belonged Gilbert and his mother, the Fairthorns, and even the Bartons. Farmer Fairthorn had a birthright, it is true, until his marriage, which having been a stolen match and not performed according to "Friends' ceremony," occasioned his excommunication. He might have been restored to the rights of membership by admitting his sorrow for the offense, but this he stoutly refused to do. The predicament was not an unusual one in the neighborhood; but a few, among whom was Dr. Deane, Martha's father, submitted to the required humiliation. As this did not take place, however, until after her birth, Martha was still without the pale, and preferred to remain so, for two reasons: first, that a scoop bonnet was monstrous on a young woman's head; and second, that she was passionately fond of music, and saw no harm in a dance. This determination of hers was, as her father expressed himself, a "great cross" to him; but she had a habit of paralyzing his argument by turning against him the testimony of the Friends in regard to forms and ceremonies, and their reliance on the guidance of the Spirit.

Herein Martha was strictly logical, and though she, and others who belonged to the same class, were sometimes characterized by a zealous Quaker in moments of bitterness as being "the world's people," they were generally regarded, not only with tolerance, but in a spirit of fraternity. The high seats in the gallery were not for them, but they were free to any other part of the meetinghouse during life, and to a grave in the grassy and briery enclosure adjoining, when dead. The necessity of belonging to some organized church was recognized but faintly, if at all; provided their lives were honorable, they were considered very fair Christians.

Mary Potter but rarely attended meeting, not from any lack of the need of worship, but because she shrank with painful timidity from appearing in the presence of the assembled neighborhood. She was, nevertheless, grateful for Gilbert's success, and her heart inclined to thanksgiving; besides, he desired that they should go, and she was not able to offer any valid objection. So, after breakfast, the two best horses of the team were very carefully groomed, saddled, and—Sam having been sent off on a visit to his father, with the house-key in his pocket—the mother and son took the road up the creek.

Both were plainly, yet very respectably, dressed, in garments of the same homemade cloth, of a deep, dark brown color, but Mary Potter wore under her cloak the new crape shawl which Gilbert had brought to her from Wilmington, and his shirt of fine linen displayed a modest ruffle in front. The resemblance in their faces was even more strongly marked, in the common expression of calm, grave repose, which sprang from the nature of their journey. A stranger meeting them that morning, would have seen that they were persons of unusual force of character, and bound to each other by an unusual tie.

Up the lovely valley, or rather glen, watered by the eastern branch of Redley Creek, they rode to the main highway. It was an early spring, and the low-lying fields were already green with the young grass; the weeping willows in front of the farmhouses seemed to spout up and fall like broad enormous geysers as the wind swayed them, and daffodils bloomed in all the warmer gardens. The dark foliage of the cedars skirting the road counteracted that indefinable gloom which the landscapes of early spring, in their grayness and incompleteness, so often inspire, and mocked the ripened summer in the close shadows which they threw. It was a pleasant ride, especially after mother and son had reached the main road, and other horsemen and horse-women issued from the gates of farms on either side, taking their way to the meetinghouse. Only two or three families could boast vehicles—heavy, cumbrous "chairs," as they were called, with a convex canopy resting on four stout pillars, and the bulging body swinging from side to side on huge springs of wood and leather. No healthy man or woman, however, unless he or she were very old, travelled otherwise than on horseback.

Now and then exchanging grave but kindly nods with their acquaintances, they rode slowly along the level upland, past the Anvil Tavern, through Logtown—a cluster of primitive cabins at the junction of the Wilmington Road—and reached the meeting-house in good season. Gilbert assisted his mother to alight at the stone platform built for that purpose near the women's end of the building, and then fastened the horses in the long, open shed in the rear. Then, as was the custom, he entered by the men's door, and quietly took a seat in the silent assembly.

The stiff, unpainted benches were filled with the congrega-tion, young and old, wearing their hats, and with a stolid, drowsy look upon their faces. Over a high wooden partition the old women in the gallery, but not the young women on the floor of the house, could be seen. Two stoves, with interminable lengths of pipe suspended by wires from the ceiling, created a stifling temperature. Every slight sound or motion—the moving of a foot, the drawing forth of a pocket-handkerchief, the lifting or lowering of a head—seemed to disturb the quiet as with a shock, and drew many of the younger eyes upon it; while in front, like the guardian statues of an Egyptian temple, sat the older members, with their hands upon their knees or clasped across their laps. Their faces were grave and severe.

After nearly an hour of this suspended animation, an old Friend rose, removed his broad-brimmed hat, and placing his hands upon the rail before him, began slowly swaying to and fro, while he spoke. As he rose into the chant peculiar to the sect, intoning alike his quotations from the Psalms and his utter-ances of plain, practical advice, an expression of quiet but al-most luxurious satisfaction stole over the faces of his aged brethren. With half-closed eyes and motionless bodies, they drank in the sound like a rich draught, with a sense of exquisite refreshment. A close connection of ideas, a logical derivation of

argument from text, would have aroused their suspicions that
the speaker depended rather upon his own active, conscious intellect, than upon the moving of the Spirit; but this aimless
wandering of a half-awake soul through the cadences of a language which was neither song nor speech, was, to their minds,
the evidence of genuine inspiration.

When the old man sat down, a woman arose and chanted
forth the suggestions which had come to her in the silence, in a
voice of wonderful sweetness and strength. Here music seemed
to revenge herself for the slight done to her by the sect. The
ears of the hearers were so charmed by the purity of tone, and
the delicate, rhythmical cadences of the sentences, that much of
the wise lessons repeated from week to week failed to reach
their consciousness.

After another interval of silence, the two oldest men reached
their hands to each other—a sign which the younger members
had anxiously awaited. The spell snapped in an instant; all arose
and moved into the open air, where all things at first appeared
to wear the same aspect of solemnity. The poplar trees, the
stone wall, the bushes in the corners of the fence, looked grave
and respectful for a few minutes. Neighbors said, "How does
thee do?" to each other, in subdued voices, and there was a
conscientious shaking of hands all around before they dared to
indulge in much conversation.

Gradually, however, all returned to the outdoor world and its
interests. The fences became so many posts and rails once more,
the bushes so many elders and blackberries to be cut away, and
the half-green fields so much sod for corn-ground. Opinions in
regard to the weather and the progress of spring labor were
freely interchanged, and the few unimportant items of social
news, which had collected in seven days, were gravely distrib-
uted. This was at the men's end of the meetinghouse; on their
side, the women were similarly occupied, but we can only conjecture the subjects of their conversation. The young men—as is
generally the case in religious sects of a rigid and clannish character—were by no means handsome. Their faces all bore the
stamp of *repression*, in some form or other, and as they talked
their eyes wandered with an expression of melancholy longing
and timidity towards the sweet, maidenly faces, whose bloom,
and pure, gentle beauty not even their hideous bonnets could
obscure.

One by one the elder men came up to the stone platform with the stable old horses which their wives were to ride home; the huge chair, in which sat a privileged couple, creaked and swayed from side to side, as it rolled with ponderous dignity from the yard; and now, while the girls were waiting their turn, the grave young men plucked up courage, wandered nearer, greeted, exchanged words, and so were helped into an atmosphere of youth.

Gilbert, approaching with them, was first recognized by his old friend, Sally Fairthorn, whose voice of salutation was so loud and cheery, as to cause two or three sedate old "women-friends" to turn their heads in grave astonishment. Mother Fairthorn, with her bright, round face, followed, and then—serene and strong in her gentle, symmetrical loveliness—Martha Deane. Gilbert's hand throbbed, as he held hers a moment, gazing into the sweet blue of her eyes; yet, passionately as he felt that he loved her in that moment, perfect as was the delight of her presence, a better joy came to his heart when she turned away to speak with his mother. Mark Deane—a young giant with curly yellow locks, and a broad, laughing mouth—had just placed a hand upon his shoulder, and he could not watch the bearing of the two women to each other; but all his soul listened to their voices, and he heard in Martha Deane's the kindly courtesy and respect which he did not see.

Mother Fairthorn and Sally so cordially insisted that Mary Potter and her son should ride home with them to dinner, that no denial was possible. When the horses were brought up to the block the yard was nearly empty, and the returning procession was already winding up the hill towards Logtown.

"Come, Mary," said Mother Fairthorn, "you and I will ride together, and you shall tell me all about your ducks and turkeys. The young folks can get along without us, I guess."

Martha Deane had ridden to meeting in company with her cousin Mark and Sally, but the order of the homeward ride was fated to be different. Joe and Jake, bestriding a single horse, like two of the Haymon's-children, were growing impatient, so they took the responsibility of dashing up to Mark and Sally, who were waiting in the road, and announcing,

"Cousin Martha says we're to go on; she'll ride with Gilbert."

Both well knew the pranks of the boys, but perhaps they found the message well-invented if not true; for they obeyed with secret alacrity, although Sally made a becoming show of reluctance. Before they reached the bottom of the hollow, Joe and Jake, seeing two schoolmates in advance, similarly mounted, dashed off in a canter to overtake them, and the two were left alone.

Gilbert and Martha naturally followed, since not more than two could conveniently ride abreast. But their movements were so quiet and deliberate, and the accident which threw them together was accepted so simply and calmly, that no one could guess what warmth of longing, of reverential tenderness, beat in every muffled throb of one of the two hearts.

Martha was an admirable horsewoman, and her slender, pliant figure never showed to greater advantage than in the saddle. Her broad beaver hat was tied down over the ears, throwing a cool gray shadow across her clear, joyous eyes and fresh cheeks. A pleasanter face never touched a young man's fancy, and every time it turned towards Gilbert it brightened away the distress of love. He caught, unconsciously, the serenity of her mood, and foretasted the peace which her being would bring to him if it were ever entrusted to his hands.

"Did you do well by your hauling, Gilbert," she asked, "and are you now home for the summer?"

"Until after corn-planting," he answered. "Then I must take two or three weeks, as the season turns out. I am not able to give up my team yet."

"But you soon will be, I hope. It must be very lonely for your mother to be on the farm without you."

These words touched him gratefully, and led him to a candid openness of speech which he would not otherwise have ventured—not from any inherent lack of candor, but from a reluctance to speak of himself.

"That's it, Martha," he said. "It is her work that I have the farm at all, and I only go away the oftener now, that I may the sooner stay with her altogether. The thought of her makes each trip lonelier than the last."

"I like to hear you say that, Gilbert. And it must be a comfort to you, withal, to know that you are working as much for your mother's sake as your own. I think I should feel so, at least, in your place. I feel my own mother's loss more now than when she died, for I was then so young that I can only just remember her face."

"But you have a father!" he exclaimed, and the words were scarcely out of his mouth before he became aware of their significance, uttered by his lips. He had not meant so much—only that she, like him, still enjoyed one parent's care. The blood came into his face; she saw and understood the sign, and broke a silence which would soon have become painful.

"Yes," she said, "and I am very grateful that he is spared; but we seem to belong most to our mothers."

"That is the truth," he said firmly, lifting his head with the impulse of his recovered pride, and meeting her eyes without flinching. "I belong altogether to mine. She has made me a man and set me upon my feet. From this time forward, my place is to stand between her and the world!"

Martha Deane's blood throbbed an answer to this assertion of himself. A sympathetic pride beamed in her eyes; she slightly bent her head, in answer, without speaking, and Gilbert felt that he was understood and valued. He had drawn a step nearer to the trial which he had resolved to make, and would now venture no further.

There was a glimmering spark of courage in his heart. He was surprised, in recalling the conversation afterwards, to find how much of his plans he had communicated to her during the ride, encouraged by the kindly interest she manifested, and the sensible comments she uttered. Joe and Jake, losing their mates at a crossroad, and finding Sally and Mark Deane not very lively company for them, rode back and disturbed these confidences, but not until they had drawn the two into a relation of acknowledged mutual interest.

Martha Deane had always, as she confessed to Sally, *liked* Gilbert Potter; she liked every young man of character and energy; but now she began to suspect that there was a rarer worth in his nature than she had guessed. From that day he was more frequently the guest of her thoughts than ever before. Instinct, in him, had performed the same service which men of greater experience of the world would have reached through keen perception and careful tact—in confiding to her his position, his labors and hopes, material as was the theme and seemingly unsuited to the occasion, he had in reality appreciated the serious, reflective nature underlying her girlish grace and gayety. What other young man of her acquaintance, she asked herself, would have done the same thing?

When they reached Kennett Square, Mother Fairthorn urged Martha to accompany them, and Sally impetuously seconded the invitation. Dr. Deane's horse was at his door, however, and his daughter, with her eyes on Gilbert, as if saying "for my father's sake," steadfastly declined. Mark, however, took her place, but there never had been, or could be, too many guests at the Fairthorn table.

When they reached the garden-wall, Sally sprang from her horse with such haste that her skirt caught on the pommel and left her hanging, being made of stuff too stout to tear. It was well that Gilbert was near, on the same side, and disengaged her in an instant; but her troubles did not end here. As she bustled in and out of the kitchen, preparing the dinner-table in the long sitting room, the hooks and door-handles seemed to have an unaccountable habit of thrusting themselves in her way, and she was ready to cry at each glance of Mark's laughing eyes. She had never heard the German proverb, "who loves, teases," and was too inexperienced, as yet, to have discovered the fact for herself.

Presently they all sat down to dinner, and after the first solemn quiet—no one venturing to eat or speak until the plates of all had been heaped with a little of everything upon the table—the meal became very genial and pleasant. A huge brown pitcher of stinging cider added its mild stimulus to the calm country blood, and under its mellowing influence Mark announced the most important fact of his life—he was to have the building of Hallowell's barn.

As Gilbert and his mother rode homewards that afternoon, neither spoke much, but both felt, in some indefinite way, better prepared for the life that lay before them.

CHAPTER 8

At Dr. Deane's

As she dismounted on the large flat stone outside the paling, Martha Deane saw her father's face at the window. It was sterner and graver than usual.

The Deane mansion stood opposite the Unicorn Tavern. When built, ninety years previous, it had been considered a triumph of architecture; the material was squared logs from the forest, dovetailed, and overlapping at the corners, which had the effect of rustic quoins, as contrasted with the front, which was plastered and yellow-washed. A small portico, covered with a tangled mass of eglantine and coral honeysuckle, with a bench at each end, led to the door; and the ten feet of space between it and the front paling were devoted to flowers and rose-bushes. At each corner of the front rose an old, picturesque, straggling cedar tree.

There were two front doors, side by side—one for the family sitting room, the other (rarely opened, except when guests arrived) for the parlor. Martha Deane entered the former, and we will enter with her.

The room was nearly square, and lighted by two windows. On those sides the logs were roughly plastered; on the others there were partitions of panelled oak, nearly black with age and smoke, as were the heavy beams of the same wood which formed the ceiling. In the corner of the room next the kitchen there was an open Franklin stove—an innovation at that time—upon which two or three hickory sticks were smouldering into snowy ashes. The floor was covered with a country-made rag carpet, in which an occasional strip of red or blue listing brightened the prevailing walnut color of the woof. The furniture was simple and massive, its only unusual feature being a tall cabinet with shelves filled with glass jars, and an infinity of small drawers. A few bulky volumes on the lower shelf constituted the medical library of Dr. Deane.

This gentleman was still standing at the window, with his hands clasped across his back. His quaker suit was of the finest drab broadcloth, and the plain cravat visible above his high, straight waistcoat, was of spotless cambric. His knee- and shoe-buckles were of the simplest pattern, but of good, solid silver, and there was not a wrinkle in the stockings of softest lamb's-wool, which covered his massive calves. There was always a faint odor of lavender, bergamot, or sweet marjoram about him, and it was a common remark in the neighborhood that the sight and smell of the Doctor helped a weak patient almost as much as his medicines.

In his face there was a curious general resemblance to his daughter, though the detached features were very differently formed. Large, unsymmetrical, and somewhat coarse—even for a man—they derived much of their effect from his scrupulous attire and studied air of wisdom. His long gray hair was combed back, that no portion of the moderate frontal brain might be covered; the eyes were gray rather than blue, and a habit of concealment had marked its lines in the corners, unlike the open, perfect frankness of his daughter's. The principal resemblance was in the firm, clear outline of the upper lip, which alone, in his face, had it been supported by the under one, would have made him almost handsome; but the latter was large and slightly hanging. There were marked inconsistencies in his face, but this was no disadvantage in a community unaccustomed to studying the external marks of character.

"Just home, Father? How did thee leave Dinah Passmore?" asked Martha, as she untied the strings of her beaver.

"Better," he answered, turning from the window; "but, Martha, who did I see thee riding with?"

"Does thee mean Gilbert Potter?"

"I do," he said, and paused. Martha, with her cloak over her arm and bonnet in her hand, in act to leave the room, waited, saying,

"Well, Father?"

So frank and serene was her bearing, that the old man felt both relieved and softened.

"I suppose it happened so," he said. "I saw his mother with Friend Fairthorn. I only meant thee shouldn't be seen in company with young Potter, when thee could help it; thee knows what I mean."

"I don't think, Father," she slowly answered, "there is anything against Gilbert Potter's life or character, except that which is no just reproach to *him*."

" 'The sins of the parents shall be visited upon the children, even to the third and fourth generation.' That is enough, Martha."

She went up to her room, meditating, with an earnestness almost equal to Gilbert's, upon this form of the world's injustice, which he was powerless to overcome. Her father shared it, and the fact did not surprise her; but her independent spirit had already ceased to be guided, in all things, by his views. She felt that the young man deserved the respect and admiration which he had inspired in her mind, and until a better reason could be discovered, she would continue so to regard him. The decision was reached rapidly, and then laid aside for any future necessity; she went downstairs again in her usual quiet, cheerful mood.

During her absence another conversation had taken place.

Miss Betsy Lavender (who was a fast friend of Martha, and generally spent her Sundays at the Doctor's) was sitting before the stove, drying her feet. She was silent until Martha left the room, when she suddenly exclaimed:

"Doctor! Judge not that ye be not judged."

"Thee may think as thee pleases, Betsy," said he, rather sharply: "it's thy nature, I believe, to take everybody's part."

"Put yourself in his place," she continued,—"remember them that's in bonds as bound with 'em—I disremember exackly how it goes, but no matter: I say your way a'n't right, and I'd say it seven times, if need be! There's no steadier or better-doin' young fellow in these parts than Gilbert Potter. Ferris, down in Pennsbury, or Alf Barton, here, for that matter, a'n't to be put within a mile of him. I could say something in Mary Potter's behalf, too, but I won't: for there's Scribes and Pharisees about."

Dr. Deane did not notice this thrust: it was not his habit to get angry. "Put *thyself* in *my* place, Betsy," he said. "He's a worthy young man, in some respects, I grant thee, but would thee like *thy* daughter to be seen riding home beside him from Meeting? It's one thing speaking for thyself, and another for thy daughter."

"Thy daughter!" she repeated. "Old or young can't make any difference, as I see."

There was something else on her tongue, but she forcibly withheld the words. She would not exhaust her ammunition until there was both a chance and a necessity to do some execution. The next moment Martha reëntered the room.

After dinner, they formed a quiet group in the front sitting room. Dr. Deane, having no more visits to make that day, took a pipe of choice tobacco—the present of a Virginia Friend, whose acquaintance he had made at Yearly Meeting—and seated himself in the armchair beside the stove. Martha, at the west window, enjoyed a volume of Hannah More, and Miss Betsy, at the front window, labored over the Psalms. The sun shone with dim, muffled orb, but the air without was mild, and there were already brown tufts, which would soon be blossoms, on the lilac twigs.

Suddenly Miss Betsy lifted up her head and exclaimed, "Well, I never!" As she did so, there was a knock at the door.

"Come in!" said Dr. Deane, and in came Mr. Alfred Barton, resplendent in blue coat, buff waistcoat, cambric ruffles, and silver-gilt buckles. But, alas! the bunch of seals—topaz, agate, and cornelian—no longer buoyed the deep-anchored watch. The money due his father had been promptly paid, through the agency of a three-months' promissory note, and thus the most momentous result of the robbery was overcome. This security for the future, however, scarcely consoled him for the painful privation of the present. Without the watch, Alfred Barton felt that much of his dignity and importance was lacking.

Dr. Deane greeted his visitor with respect, Martha with courtesy due to a guest, and Miss Betsy with the offhand, independent manner, under which she masked her private opinions of the persons whom she met.

"Mark isn't at home, I see," said Mr. Barton, after having taken his seat in the center of the room: "I thought I'd have a little talk with him about the wagon-house. I suppose he told you that I got Hallowell's new barn for him?"

"Yes, and we're all greatly obliged to thee, as well as Mark," said the Doctor. "The two jobs make a fine start for a young mechanic,* and I hope he'll do as well as he's been done by:

---

*Anyone having a manual occupation (ed.).

there's luck in a good beginning. By the bye, has thee heard anything more of Sandy Flash's doings?"

Mr. Barton fairly started at this question. His own misfortune had been carefully kept secret, and he could not suspect that the Doctor knew it; but he nervously dreaded the sound of that terrible name.

"What is it?" he asked, in a faint voice.

"He has turned up in Bradford, this time, and they say has robbed Jesse Frame, the Collector, of between four and five hundred dollars. The Sheriff and a posse of men from the valley hunted him for several days, but found no signs. Some think he has gone up into the Welch Mountain; but for my part, I should not be surprised if he were in this neighborhood."

"Good heavens!" exclaimed Mr. Barton, starting from his chair.

"Now's your chance," said Miss Betsy. "Git the young men together who won't feel afraid o' bein' twenty ag'in one: you know the holes and corners where he'll be likely to hide, and what's to hinder you from ketchin' him?"

"But he must have many secret friends," said Martha, "if what I have heard is true—that he has often helped a poor man with the money which he takes only from the rich. You know he still calls himself a Tory, and many of those whose estates have been confiscated would not scruple to harbor him, or even take his money."

"Take his money. That's a fact," remarked Miss Betsy, "and now I dunno whether I want him ketched. There's worse men goin' round, as respectable as you please, stealin' all their born days, only cunnin'ly jukin'* round the law instead o' battin' square through it. Why, old Liz Williams, o' Birmingham, herself told me with her own mouth, how she was ridin' home from Phildelphy market last winter, with six dollars, the price of her turkeys—and General Washin'ton's cook took one of 'em, but that's neither here nor there—in her pocket, and fearful as death when she come to Concord woods, and lo and behold! there she was overtook by a fresh-complected man, and she begged him to ride with her, for she had six dollars in her pocket and Sandy was known to be about. So he rode with her to her very lane-end, as kind and civil a person as she ever see, and then and

---

*Dialectal variant of "jouking," hence "dodging" (ed.).

there he said, 'Don't be afeard, Madam, for I, which have seen you home, is Sandy Flash himself, and here's somethin' more to remember me by—no sooner said than done, he put a goold guinea into her hand, and left her there as petrified as Lot's wife. Now *I* say, and it may be violation of the law, for all I know, but never mind, that Sandy Flash has got one corner of his heart in the right place, no matter where the other is. There's honor even among thieves, they say."

"Seriously, Alfred," said Dr. Deane, cutting Miss Betsy short before she had half expressed her sentiments, "it is time that something was done. If Flash is not caught soon, we shall be overrun with thieves, and there will be no security anywhere on the high roads, or in our houses. I wish that men of influence in the neighborhood, like thyself, would come together and plan, at least, to keep Kennett clear of him. Then other townships may do the same, and so the thing be stopped. If I were younger, and my practice were not so laborious, I would move in the matter, but thee is altogether a more suitable person."

"Do you think so?" Barton replied, with an irrepressible reluctance, around which he strove to throw an air of modesty. "That would be the proper way, certainly, but I—I don't know —that is, I can't flatter myself that I'm the best man to undertake it."

"It requires some courage, you know," Martha remarked, and her glance made him feel very uncomfortable, "and you are too dashing a fox-hunter not to have that. Perhaps the stranger who rode with you to Avondale—what was his name?—might be of service. If I were in your place, I should be glad of a chance to incur danger for the good of the neighborhood."

Mr. Alfred Barton was on nettles. If there were irony in her words his intellect was too muddy to detect it: her assumption of his courage could only be accepted as a compliment, but it was the last compliment he desired to have paid to himself, just at that time.

"Yes," he said, with a forced laugh, rushing desperately into the opposite extreme, "but the danger and the courage are not worth talking about. Any man ought to be able to face a robber, single-handed, and as for twenty men, why, when it's once known, Sandy Flash will only be too glad to keep away."

"Then, do thee do what I've recommended. It may be, as

thee says, that the being prepared is all that is necessary," remarked Dr. Deane.

Thus caught, Mr. Barton could do no less than acquiesce, and very much to his secret dissatisfaction, the Doctor proceeded to name the young men of the neighborhood, promising to summon such as lived on the lines of his professional journeys, that they might confer with the leader of the undertaking. Martha seconded the plan with an evident interest, yet it did not escape her that neither her father nor Mr. Barton had mentioned the name of Gilbert Potter.

"Is that all?" she asked, when a list of some eighteen persons had been suggested. Involuntarily, she looked at Miss Betsy Lavender.

"No, indeed!" cried the latter. "There's Jabez Travilla, up on the ridge, and Gilbert Potter, down at the mill."

"H'm, yes; what does thee say, Alfred?" asked the Doctor.

"They're both good riders, and I think they have courage enough, but we can never tell what a man is until he's been tried. They would increase the number, and that, it seems to me, is a consideration."

"Perhaps thee had better exercise thy own judgment there," the Doctor observed, and the subject, having been as fully discussed as was possible without consultation with other persons, it was dropped, greatly to Barton's relief.

But in endeavoring to converse with Martha he only exchanged one difficulty for another. His vanity, powerful as it was, gave way before that instinct which is the curse and torment of vulgar natures—which leaps into life at every contact of refinement, showing them the gulf between, which they know not how to cross. The impudence, the aggressive rudeness which such natures often exhibit, is either a mask to conceal their deficiency, or an angry protest against it. Where there is a drop of gentleness in the blood, it appreciates and imitates the higher nature.

This was the feeling which made Alfred Barton uncomfortable in the presence of Martha Deane—which told him, in advance, that natures so widely sundered, never could come into near relations with each other, and thus quite neutralized the attraction of her beauty and her ten thousand dollars. His game, however, was to pay court to her, and in so pointed a way that it should be remarked and talked about in the neighborhood. Let it once come through others to the old man's ears, he would have proved his obedience and could not be reproached if the result were fruitless.

"What are you reading, Miss Martha?" he asked, after a long and somewhat awkward pause.

She handed him the book in reply.

"Ah! Hannah More—a friend of yours? Is she one of the West-Whiteland Moores?"

Martha could not suppress a light, amused laugh, as she answered: "Oh, no, she is an Englishwoman."

"Then it's a Tory book," said he, handing it back; "I wouldn't read it, if I was you."

"It is a story, and I should think you might."

He heard other words than those she spoke. "As Tory as— what?" he asked himself. "As I am," of course; that is what she means. "Old Man Barton" had been one of the disloyal purveyors for the British army during its occupancy of Philadelphia in the winter of 1777-8, and though the main facts of the traffic, wherefrom he had drawn immense profits, never could be proved against him, the general belief hung over the family and made a very disagreeable cloud. Whenever Alfred Barton quarrelled with anyone, the taunt was sure to be flung into his teeth. That it came now, as he imagined, was as great a shock as if Martha had slapped him in the face with her own delicate hand, and his visage reddened from the blow.

Miss Betsy Lavender, bending laboriously over the Psalms, nevertheless kept her dull gray eyes in movement. She saw the misconception, and fearing that Martha did not, made haste to remark:

"Well, Mr. Alfred, and do *you* think it's a harm to read a story? Why, Miss Ann herself lent me 'Alonzo and Melissa,' and 'Midnight Horrors,' and I'l! be bound you've read 'em yourself on the sly. 'Ta'n't much other readin' men does, save and except the weekly paper, and law enough to git a tight hold on their debtors. Come, now, let's know what you *do* read?"

"Not much of anything, that's a fact," he answered, recovering himself, with a shudder at the fearful mistake he had been on the point of making, "but I've nothing against women reading stories. I was rather thinking of myself when I spoke to you, Miss Martha."

"So I suppose," she quietly answered. It was provoking. Everything she said made him think there was another meaning behind the words; her composed manner, though he knew it to be habitual, more and more disconcerted him. Never did an intentional wooer find his wooing so painful and laborious. After this attempt he addressed himself to Doctor Deane, for even the question of circumventing Sandy Flash now presented itself to his mind as a relief.

There he sat, and the conversation progressed in jerks and spirts, between pauses of embarrassing silence. The sun hung on the western hill in a web of clouds; Martha and Miss Betsy rose and prepared the tea table, and the guest, invited perforce, perforce accepted. Soon after the meal was over, however, he murmured something about cattle, took his hat and left.

Two or three horses were hitched before the Unicorn, and he saw some figures through the barroom window. A bright thought struck him; he crossed the road and entered.

"Hallo, Alf! Where from now? Why, you're as fine as a fiddler!" cried Mr. Joel Ferris, who was fast becoming familiar, on the strength of his inheritance.

"Over the way," answered the landlord, with a wink and a jerk of his thumb.

Mr. Ferris whistled, and one of the others suggested: "He must stand a treat, on that."

"But, I say!" said the former, "how is it you're coming away so soon in the evening?"

"I went very early in the afternoon," Barton answered, with a mysterious, meaning smile, as much as to say: "It's all right; I know what I'm about." Then he added aloud, "Step up, fellows; what'll you have?"

Many were the jests and questions to which he was forced to submit, but he knew the value of silence in creating an impression, and allowed them to enjoy their own inferences.

It is much easier to start a report, than to counteract it, when once started; but the first, only, was his business.

It was late in the evening when he returned home, and the household were in bed. Nevertheless, he did not enter by the back way, in his stockings, but called Giles down from the garret to unlock the front door, and made as much noise as he pleased on his way to bed.

The old man heard it, and chuckled under his coverlet.

CHAPTER 9

The Raising

Steadily and serenely the spring advanced. Old people shook their heads and said: "It will be April, this year, that comes in like a lamb and goes out like a lion,"—but it was not so. Soft, warm showers and frostless nights repaid the trustfulness of the early-expanding buds, and May came clothed completely in pale green, with a wreath of lilac and hawthorn bloom on her brow. For twenty years no such perfect spring had been known; and for twenty years afterwards the farmers looked back to it as a standard of excellence, whereby to measure the forwardness of their crops.

By the twentieth of April the young white-oak leaves were the size of a squirrel's ear—the old Indian sign of the proper time for corn-planting, which was still accepted by the new race, and the first of May saw many fields already specked with the green points of the springing blades. A warm, silvery vapor hung over the land, mellowing the brief vistas of the interlacing valleys, touching with a sweeter pastoral beauty the irregular alternation of field and forest, and lifting the wooded slopes, far and near, to a statelier and more imposing height. The park-like region of Kennett, settled originally by emigrants from Bucks and Warwickshire, reproduced to their eyes—as it does to this day—the characteristics of their original home, and they transplanted the local names to which they were accustomed, and preserved, even long after the War of Independence, the habits of their rural ancestry. The massive stone farmhouses, the walled gardens, the bountiful orchards, and, more than all, the well-trimmed hedges of hawthorn and blackthorn dividing their fields, or bordering their roads with the living wall, over which the clematis and wild-ivy love to clamber, made the region beautiful to their eyes. Although the large original grants, mostly given by the hand of William Penn, had been divided and sub-divided by three or four prolific generations, there was still enough and to spare—and even the golden promise held out by "the Backwoods," as the new States of Ohio and Kentucky were then called, tempted very few to leave their homes.

The people, therefore, loved the soil and clung to it with a fidelity very rare in any part of our restless nation. And truly, no one who had lived through the mild splendor of that spring, seeing day by day the visible deepening of the soft woodland tints, hearing the cheerful sounds of labor, far and wide, in the vapory air, and feeling at once the repose and the beauty of such a quiet, pastoral life, could have turned his back upon it, to battle with the inhospitable wilderness of the West. Gilbert Potter had had ideas of a new home, to be created by himself, and a life to which none should deny honor and respect: but now he gave them up forever. There was a battle to be fought—better here than elsewhere—here, where every scene was dear and familiar, and every object that met his eye gave a mute, gentle sense of consolation.

Restless, yet cheery labor was now the order of life on the farm. From dawn till dusk, Gilbert and Sam were stirring in field, meadow, and garden, keeping pace with the season and forecasting what was yet to come. Sam, although only fifteen, had a manly pride in being equal to the duty imposed upon him by his master's absence, and when the time came to harness the wagon-team once more, the mother and son walked over the fields together and rejoiced in the order and promise of the farm. The influences of the season had unconsciously touched them both: everything conspired to favor the fulfillment of their common plan, and, as one went forward to the repetition of his tedious journeys back and forth between Columbia and Newport, and the other to her lonely labor in the deserted farmhouse, the arches of bells over the collars of the leaders chimed at once to the ears of both, an anthem of thanksgiving and a melody of hope.

So May and the beginning of June passed away, and no important event came to any character of this history. When Gilbert had delivered the last barrels at Newport, and slowly cheered homewards his weary team, he was nearly two hundred dollars richer than when he started, and—if we must confess a universal if somewhat humiliating truth—so much the more a man in courage and determination.

The country was now covered with the first fresh magnificence of summer. The snowy pyramids of dogwood bloom had faded, but the tulip trees were tall cones of rustling green, lighted with millions of orange-colored stars, and all the underwood beneath the hemlock forests by the courses of streams, was rosy with laurels and azaleas. The vernal grass in the meadows was sweeter than any garden-rose, and its breath met that of the wild-grape in the thickets and struggled for preëminence of sweetness. A lush, tropical splendor of vegetation, such as England never knew, heaped the woods and hung the road-side with sprays which grew and bloomed and wantoned, as if growth were a conscious joy, rather than blind obedience to a law.

When Gilbert reached home, released from his labors abroad until October, he found his fields awaiting their owner's hand. His wheat hung already heavy-headed, though green, and the grass stood so thick and strong that it suggested the ripping music of the scythe blade which should lay it low. Sam had taken good care of the cornfield, garden, and the cattle, and Gilbert's few words of quiet commendation were a rich reward for all his anxiety. His ambition was, to be counted "a full hand,"—this was the *toga virilis*, which, once entitled to wear, would make him feel that he was any man's equal.

Without a day's rest, the labor commenced again, and the passion of Gilbert's heart, though it had only strengthened during his absence, must be thrust aside until the fortune of his harvest was secured.

In the midst of the haying, however, came a message which he could not disregard—a hasty summons from Mark Deane, who, seeing Gilbert in the upper hill-field, called from the road, bidding him to the raising of Hallowell's new barn, which was to take place on the following Saturday. "Be sure and come!" were Mark's closing words—"there's to be both dinner and supper, and the girls are to be on hand!"

It was the custom to prepare the complete frame of a barn—sills, plates, girders, posts, and stays—with all their mortises and pins, ready for erection, and then to summon all the able-bodied men of the neighborhood to assist in getting the timbers into place. This service, of course, was given gratuitously, and the farmer who received it could do no less than entertain, after the bountiful manner of the country, his helping neighbors, who therefore, although the occasion implied a certain amount of hard work, were accustomed to regard it as a sort of holiday, or merrymaking. Their opportunities for recreation, indeed, were so scanty, that a barn-raising, or a husking-party by moonlight, was a thing to be welcomed.

Hallowell's farm was just halfway between Gilbert's and Kennett Square, and the site of the barn had been well-chosen on a ridge, across the road, which ran between it and the farmhouse. The Hallowells were what was called "good providers," and as they belonged to the class of outside Quakers, which we have already described, the chances were that both music and dance would reward the labor of the day.

Gilbert, of course, could not refuse the invitation of so near a neighbor, and there was a hope in his heart which made it welcome. When the day came he was early on hand, heartily greeted by Mark, who exclaimed, "Give me a dozen more such shoulders and arms as yours, and I'll make the timbers spin!"

It was a bright, breezy day, making the wheat roll and the leaves twinkle. Ranges of cumuli moved, one after the other, like heaps of silvery wool, across the keen, dark blue of the sky. "A wonderful hay-day," the old farmers remarked, with a half-stifled sense of regret; but the younger men had already stripped themselves to their shirts and knee-breeches, and set to work with a hearty good-will. Mark, as friend, half-host and commander, bore his triple responsibility with a mixture of dash and decision, which became his large frame and ruddy, laughing face. It was—really, and not in an oratorical sense—the proudest day of his life.

There could be no finer sight than that of these lithe, vigorous specimens of a free, uncorrupted manhood, taking like sport the rude labor which was at once their destiny and their guard of safety against the assaults of the senses. As they bent to their work, prying, rolling, and lifting the huge sills to their places on the foundation-wall, they showed in every movement the firm yet elastic action of muscles equal to their task. Though Hallowell's barn did not rise, like the walls of Ilium, to music, a fine human harmony aided in its construction.

There was a plentiful supply of whiskey on hand, but Mark Deane assumed the charge of it, resolved that no accident or other disturbance should mar the success of this, his first raising. Everything went well, and by the time they were summoned to dinner, the sills and some of the uprights were in place, properly squared and tied.

It would require a Homeric catalogue to describe the dinner. To say that the table "groaned" is to give no idea of its condition. Mrs. Hallowell and six neighbors' wives moved from kitchen to dining-room, replenishing the dishes as fast as their contents diminished, and plying the double row of coatless guests with a most stern and exacting hospitality. The former would have been seriously mortified had not each man endeavored to eat twice his usual requirement.

After the slight rest which nature enforced—though far less than nature demanded, after such a meal—the work went on again with greater alacrity, since every timber showed. Rib by rib the great frame grew, and those perched aloft, pinning the posts and stays, rejoiced in the broad, bright landscape opened to their view. They watched the roads, in the intervals of their toil, and announced the approach of delayed guests, all alert for the sight of the first riding-habit.

Suddenly two ladies made their appearance, over the rise of the hill, one cantering lightly and securely, the other bouncing in her seat, from the rough trot of her horse.

"Look out! there they come!" cried a watcher.

"Who is it?" was asked from below.

"Where's Barton? He ought to be on hand—it's Martha Deane —and Sally with her; they always ride together."

Gilbert had one end of a handspike, helping lift a heavy piece of timber, and his face was dark with the strain; it was well that he dared not let go until the lively gossip which followed Barton's absence—the latter having immediately gone forward to take charge of the horses—had subsided. Leaning on the handspike, he panted—not entirely from fatigue. A terrible possibility of loss flashed suddenly across his mind, revealing to him in a new light the desperate force and desire of his love.

There was no time for meditation; his help was again wanted, and he expended therein the first hot tumult of his heart. By ones and twos the girls now gathered rapidly, and erelong they came out in a body to have a look at the raising. Their coming in no wise interrupted the labor; it was rather an additional stimulus, and the young men were right. Although they were not aware of the fact, they were never so handsome in their uneasy Sunday costume and awkward social ways, as thus in their free, joyous, and graceful element of labor. Greetings were interchanged, laughter and cheerful nothings animated the company, and when Martha Deane said,

"We may be in the way now—shall we go in?"

Mark responded,

"No, Martha! No, girls! I'll get twice as much work out o' my twenty-five 'jours,'* if you'll only stand where you are and look at 'em."

"Indeed!" Sally Fairthorn exclaimed. "But we have work to do as well as you. If you men can't get along without admiring spectators, we girls can."

The answer which Mark would have made to this pert speech was cut short by a loud cry of pain or terror from the old half-dismantled barn on the other side of the road. All eyes were at once turned in that direction, and beheld Joe Fairthorn rushing at full speed down the bank, making for the stables below. Mark, Gilbert Potter, and Sally, being nearest, hastened to the spot.

"You're in time!" cried Joe, clapping his hands in great glee. "I was awfully afeard he'd let go before I could git down to see him fall. Look quick—he can't hold on much longer!"

Looking into the dusky depths, they saw Jake, hanging by his hands to the edges of a hole in the floor above, yelling and kicking for dear life.

"You wicked, wicked boy!" exclaimed Sally, turning to Joe, "what have you been doing?"

"Oh," he answered, jerking and twisting with fearful delight, "there was such a nice hole in the floor! I covered it all over with straw, but I had to wait ever so long before Jake stepped onto it, and then he ketched hold goin' down, and nigh spoilt the fun."

Gilbert made for the barn-floor, to succor the helpless victim; but just as his step was heard on the boards, Jake's strength gave way. His fingers slipped, and with a last howl down he dropped, eight or ten feet, upon a bed of dry manure. Then his terror was instantly changed to wrath; he bounced upon his feet, seized a piece of rotten board, and made after Joe, who, anticipating the result, was already showing his heels down the road.

Meanwhile the other young ladies had followed, and so, after

*Journeymen (ed.).

discussing the incident with a mixture of amusement and horror, they betook themselves to the house, to assist in the preparations for supper. Martha Deane's eyes took in the situation, and immediately perceived that it was capable of a picturesque improvement. In front of the house stood a superb sycamore, beyond which a trellis of grapevines divided the yard from the kitchen-garden. Here, on the cool green turf, under shade, in the bright summer air, she proposed that the tables should be set, and found little difficulty in carrying her point. It was quite convenient to the outer kitchen door, and her ready invention found means of overcoming all other technical objections. Erelong the tables were transported to the spot, the cloth laid, and the aspect of the coming entertainment grew so pleasant to the eye that there was a special satisfaction in the labor.

An hour before sundown the frame was completed; the skeleton of the great barn rose sharp against the sky, its fresh white-oak timber gilded by the sunshine. Mark drove in the last pin, gave a joyous shout, which was answered by an irregular cheer from below, and lightly clambered down by one of the stays. Then the black jugs were produced, and passed from mouth to mouth, and the ruddy, glowing young fellows drew their shirtsleeves across their faces, and breathed the free, full breath of rest.

Gilbert Potter, sitting beside Mark—the two were mutually drawn towards each other, without knowing or considering why—had gradually worked himself into a resolution to be cool, and to watch the movements of his presumed rival. More than once, during the afternoon, he had detected Barton's eyes, fixed upon him with a more than accidental interest; looking up now, he met them again, but they were quickly withdrawn, with a shy, uneasy expression, which he could not comprehend. Was it possible that Barton conjectured the carefully hidden secret of his heart? Or had the gossip been free with his name, in some way, during his absence? Whatever it was, the dearer interests at stake prevented him from dismissing it from his mind. He was preternaturally alert, suspicious, and sensitive.

He was therefore a little startled when, as they were all rising in obedience to Farmer Hallowell's summons to supper, Barton suddenly took hold of his arm.

"Gilbert," said he, "we want your name in a list of young men we are getting together for the protection of our neighborhood. There are suspicions, you know, that Sandy Flash has some friends hereabouts, though nobody seems to know exactly who they are; and our only safety is in clubbing together, to smoke him out and hunt him down, if he ever comes near us. Now, you're a good hunter—"

"Put me down, of course!" Gilbert interrupted, immensely relieved to find how wide his suspicions had fallen from the mark. "That would be a more stirring chase than our last; it is a shame and a disgrace that he is still at large."

"How many have we now?" asked Mark, who was walking on the other side of Barton.

"Twenty-one, with Gilbert," the latter replied.

"Well, as Sandy is said to oount equal to twenty, we can meet him evenly, and have one to spare," laughed Mark.

"Has any one here ever seen the fellow?" asked Gilbert. "We ought to know his marks."

"He's short, thickset, with a red face, jet-black hair, and heavy whiskers," said Barton.

"Jet-black hair!" Mark exclaimed; "why, it's red as brick-dust! And I never heard that he wore whiskers."

"Pshaw! what was I thinking of? Red, of course—I meant red, all the time," Barton hastily assented, inwardly cursing himself for a fool. It was evident that the less he conversed about Sandy Flash, the better.

Loud exclamations of surprise and admiration interrupted them. In the shade of the sycamore, on the bright green floor of the silken turf, stood the long supper-table, snowily draped, and heaped with the richest products of cellar, kitchen, and dairy. Twelve chickens, stewed in cream, filled huge dishes at the head and foot, while hams and rounds of cold roast-beef accentuated the space between. The interstices were filled with pickles, pies, jars of marmalade, bowls of honey, and plates of cheese. Four coffeepots steamed in readiness on a separate table, and the young ladies, doubly charming in their fresh white aprons, stood waiting to serve the tired laborers. Clumps of crown-roses, in blossom, peered over the garden-paling, the woodbine filled the air with its nutmeg odors, and a broad sheet of sunshine struck the upper boughs of the arching sycamore, and turned them into a gilded canopy for the banquet. It might have been truly said of Martha Deane, that she touched nothing which she did not adorn.

In the midst of her duties as directress of the festival, she caught a glimpse of the three men, as they approached together, somewhat in the rear of the others. The embarrassed flush had not quite faded from Barton's face, and Gilbert's was touched by a lingering sign of his new trouble. Mark, light-hearted and laughing, precluded the least idea of mystery, but Gilbert's eye met hers with what she felt to be a painfully earnest, questioning expression. The next moment they were seated at the table, and her services were required on behalf of all.

Unfortunately for the social enjoyments of Kennett, eating had come to be regarded as part of labor; silence and rapidity were its principal features. Board and platter were cleared in a marvelously short time, the plates changed, the dishes replenished, and then the wives and maidens took the places of the young men, who lounged off to the road-side, some to smoke their pipes, and all to gossip.

Before dusk, Giles made his appearance with an old green bag under his arm. Barton, of course, had the credit of this arrangement, and it made him, for the time, very popular. After a pull at the bottle, Giles began to screw his fiddle, drawing now and then unearthly shrieks from its strings. The more eager of the young men thereupon stole to the house, assisted in carrying in the tables and benches, and in other ways busied themselves to bring about the moment when the aprons of the maidens could be laid aside, and their lively feet given to the dance. The moon already hung over the eastern wood, and a light breeze blew the dew-mist from the hill.

Finally, they were all gathered on the open bit of lawn between the house and the road. There was much hesitation at first, ardent coaxing and bashful withdrawal, until Martha broke the ice by boldly choosing Mark as her partner, apportioning Sally to Gilbert, and taking her place for a Scotch reel. She danced well and lightly, though in a more subdued manner than was then customary. In this respect, Gilbert resembled her; his steps, gravely measured, though sufficiently elastic, differed widely from Mark's springs, pigeonwings, and curvets. Giles played with a will, swaying head and fiddle up and down, and beating time with his foot; and the reel went off so successfully that there was no hesitation in getting up the next dance.

Mark was alert, and secured Sally this time. Perhaps Gilbert would have made the like exchange, but Mr. Alfred Barton

stepped before him, and bore off Martha. There was no appearance of design about the matter, but Gilbert felt a hot tingle in
his blood, and drew back a little to watch the pair. Martha
moved through the dance as if but half conscious of her partner's presence, and he seemed more intent on making the proper
steps and flourishes than on improving the few brief chances for
a confidential word. When he spoke, it was with the unnecessary
laugh, which is meant to show ease of manner, and betrays the
want of it. Gilbert was puzzled; either the two were unconscious
of the gossip which linked their names so intimately (which
seemed scarcely possible), or they were studiedly concealing an
actual tender relation. Among those simple-hearted people, the
shyness of love rivalled the secrecy of crime, and the ways by
which the lover sought to assure himself of his fortune were
made very difficult by the shrinking caution with which he concealed the evidence of his passion. Gilbert knew how well the
secret of his own heart was guarded, and the reflection that
others might be equally inscrutable smote him with sudden pain.

The figures moved before him in the splendid moonlight, and
with every motion of Martha's slender form the glow of his passion and the torment of his uncertainty increased. Then the
dance dissolved, and while he still stood with folded arms, Sally
Fairthorn's voice whispered eagerly in his ear,

"Gilbert—Gilbert! now is your chance to engage Martha for
the Virginia reel!"

"Let me choose my own partners, Sally!" he said, so sternly,
that she opened wide her black eyes.

Martha, fanning herself with her handkerchief spread over a
bent willow-twig, suddenly passed before him, like an angel in
the moonlight. A soft, tender star sparkled in each shaded eye, a
faint rose-tint flushed her cheeks, and her lips, slightly parted to
inhale the clover-scented air, were touched with a sweet, consenting smile.

"Martha!"

The word passed Gilbert's lips almost before he knew he had
uttered it. Almost a whisper, but she heard, and, pausing, turned
towards him.

"Will you dance with me now?"

"Am I your choice, or Sally's, Gilbert? I overheard your very
independent remark."

"Mine!" he said, with only half truth. A deep color shot into his face, and he knew the moonlight revealed it, but he forced his eyes to meet hers. Her face lost its playful expression, and she said, gently,

"Then I accept."

They took their places, and the interminable Virginia reel—under which name the old-fashioned Sir Roger de Coverley was known—commenced. It so happened that Gilbert and Mr. Alfred Barton had changed their recent places. The latter stood outside the space allotted to the dance, and appeared to watch Martha Deane and her new partner. The reviving warmth in Gilbert's bosom instantly died, and gave way to a crowd of torturing conjectures. He went through his part in the dance so abstractedly that when they reached the bottom of the line, Martha, out of friendly consideration for him, professed fatigue and asked his permission to withdraw from the company. He gave her his arm, and they moved to one of the benches.

"You, also, seem tired, Gilbert," she said.

"Yes—no!" he answered, confusedly, feeling that he was beginning to tremble. He stood before her as she sat, moved irresolutely as if to leave, and then, facing her with a powerful effort, he exclaimed,

"Martha, do you know what people say about Alfred Barton and yourself?"

"It would make no difference if I did," she answered; "people will say anything."

"But is it—is it true?"

"Is what true?" she quietly asked.

"That he is to marry you!" The words were said, and he would have given his life to recall them. He dropped his head, not daring to meet her eyes.

Martha Deane rose to her feet, and stood before him. Then he lifted his head; the moon shone full upon it, while her face was in shadow, but he saw the fuller light of her eye, the firmer curve of her lip.

"Gilbert Potter," she said, "what right have you to ask me such a question?"

"I have no right—none," he answered, in a voice whose suppressed, husky tones were not needed to interpret the pain and bitterness of his face. Then he quickly turned away and left her.

Martha Deane remained a minute, motionless, standing as he left her. Her heart was beating fast, and she could not immediately trust herself to rejoin the gay company. But now the dance was over, and the inseparable Sally hastened forward.

"Martha!" cried the latter, hot and indignant, "what is the matter with Gilbert? He is behaving shamefully; I saw him just now turn away from you as if you were a—a shock of corn. And the way he snapped me up—it is really outrageous!"

"It *seems* so, truly," said Martha. But she knew that Gilbert Potter loved her, and with what a love.

CHAPTER 10

The Rivals

With the abundant harvest of that year, and the sudden and universal need of extra labor for the fortnight, Gilbert Potter would have found his burden too heavy, but for welcome help from an unexpected quarter. On the very morning that he first thrust his sickle into the ripened wheat, Deb. Smith made her appearance, in a short-armed chemise and skirt of tow-cloth.

"I knowed ye'd want a hand," she said, "without sendin' to ask. I'll reap ag'inst the best man in Chester County, and you won't begrudge me my bushel o' wheat a day, when the harvest's in."

With this exordium, and a pull at the black jug under the elder bushes in the fence-corner, she took her sickle and bent to work. It was her boast that she could beat both men and women on their own ground. She had spun her twenty-four cuts of yarn, in a day, and husked her fifty shocks of heavy corn. For Gilbert she did her best, amazing him each day with a fresh performance, and was well worth the additional daily quart of whiskey which she consumed.

In this pressing, sweltering labor, Gilbert dulled, though he could not conquer, his unhappy mood. Mary Potter, with a true mother's instinct, surmised a trouble, but the indications were too indefinite for conjecture. She could only hope that her son had not been called upon to suffer a fresh reproach, from the unremoved stain hanging over his birth.

Miss Betsy Lavender's company at this time was her greatest relief, in a double sense. No ten persons in Kennett possessed half the amount of confidences which were entrusted to this single lady; there was that in her face which said: "I only blab what I choose, and what's locked up, *is* locked up." This was true; she was the greatest distributor of news, and the closest receptacle of secrets—anomalous as the two characters may seem—that ever blessed a country community.

Miss Betsy, like Deb. Smith, knew that she could be of service on the Potter farm, and, although her stay was perforce short on account of an approaching housewarming near Doe-Run, her willing arms helped to tide Mary Potter over the heaviest labor of harvest. There were thus hours of afternoon rest, even in the midst of the busy season, and during one of these the mother opened her heart in relation to her son's silent, gloomy moods.

"You'll perhaps say it's all my fancy, Betsy," she said, "and indeed I hope it is; but I know you see more than most people, and two heads are better than one. How does Gilbert seem to you?"

Miss Betsy mused awhile, with an unusual gravity on her long face. "I dunno," she remarked, at length; "I've noticed that some men have their vapors and tantrums, jist as some women have, and Gilbert's of an age to—well, Mary, has the thought of his marryin' ever come into your head?"

"No!" exclaimed Mary Potter, with almost a frightened air.

"I'll be bound! Some women are lookin' out for daughter-in-laws before their sons have a beard, and others think theirs is only fit to wear short jackets when they ought to be raisin' up families. I dunno but what it'll be a cross to you, Mary—you set so much store by Gilbert, and it's natural, like, that you should want to have him all to y'rself—but a man shall leave his father and mother and cleave unto his wife—or somethin' like it. Yes, I say it, although nobody clove unto me."

Mary Potter said nothing. Her face grew very pale, and such an expression of pain came into it that Miss Betsy, who saw everything without seeming to look at anything, made haste to add a consoling word.

"Indeed, Mary," she said, "now I come to consider upon it, you won't have so much of a cross. You a'n't the mother you've showed yourself to be, if you're not anxious to see Gilbert happy, and as for leavin' his mother, there'll be no leavin' needful, in his case, but on the contràry, quite the reverse, namely, a comin' to you. And it's no bad fortin', though I can't say it of my own experience; but never mind, all the same, I've seen the likes—to have a brisk, cheerful daughter-in-law keepin' house, and you a-settin' by the window, knittin' and restin' from mornin' till night, and maybe little caps and clothes to make, and lots o' things to teach, that young wives don't know o' theirselves. And then, after awhile you'll be called 'Granny,' but you won't mind it, for grandchildren's a mighty comfort, and no responsibility like your own. Why, I've knowed women that never seen what rest or comfort was, till they'd got to be grand-mothers!"

Something in this homely speech touched Mary Potter's heart, and gave her the relief of tears. "Betsy," she said at last, "I have had a heavy burden to bear, and it has made me weak."

"Made me weak," Miss Betsy repeated. "And no wonder. Don't think I can't guess that, Mary."

Here two tears trickled down the ridge of her nose, and she furtively wiped them off while adjusting her high comb. Mary Potter's face was turned towards her with a wistful, appealing expression, which she understood.

"Mary," she said, "I don't measure people with a two-foot rule. I take a ten-foot pole, and let it cover all that comes under it. Them that does their dooty to man, I guess won't have much trouble in squarin' accounts with the Lord. You know how I feel towards you without my tellin' of it, and them that's quick o' the tongue a'n't always full o' the heart. Now, Mary, I know as plain as if you'd said it, that there's somethin' on your mind, and you dunno whether to share it with me or not. What I say is, don't hurry yourself; I'd rather show fellow-feelin' than cur'osity; so, see your way clear first, and when the tellin' *me* anything can help, tell it—not before."

"It wouldn't help now," Mary Potter responded.

"Wouldn't help now. Then wait awhile. Nothin's so dangerous as speakin' before the time, whomsoever and wheresoever. Folks talk o' bridlin' the tongue; let 'em git a blind halter, say I, and a curb-bit, and a martingale! Not that I set an example, goodness knows, for mine runs like a mill-clapper, rickety-rick, rickety-rick; but never mind, it may be fast, but it isn't loose!"

In her own mysterious way, Miss Betsy succeeded in impart-ing a good deal of comfort to Mary Potter. She promised "to keep Gilbert under her eyes,"—which, indeed, she did, quite un-consciously to himself, during the last two days of her stay. At table she engaged him in conversation, bringing in references, in the most wonderfully innocent and random manner, to most of the families in the neighborhood. So skillfully did she operate that even Mary Potter failed to perceive her strategy. Deb.

Smith, sitting bare-armed on the other side of the table, and eating like six dragoons, was the ostensible target of her speech, and Gilbert was thus stealthily approached in flank. When she tied her bonnet-strings to leave, and the mother accompanied her to the gate, she left this indefinite consolation behind her:

"Keep up your sperrits, Mary. I think I'm on the right scent about Gilbert, but these young men are shy foxes. Let me alone awhile yet, and whatever you do, let *him* alone. There's no danger—not even a snarl, I guess. Nothin' to bother your head about, if you weren't his mother. Good lack! if I'm right, you'll see no more o' his tantrums in two months' time—and so, good-bye to you!"

The oats followed close upon the wheat harvest, and there was no respite from labor until the last load was hauled into the barn, filling its ample bays to the very rafters. Then Gilbert, mounted on his favorite Roger, rode up to Kennett Square one Saturday afternoon, in obedience to a message from Mr. Alfred Barton, informing him that the other gentlemen would there meet to consult measures for mutual protection against highwaymen in general and Sandy Flash in particular. As every young man in the neighborhood owned his horse and musket, nothing more was necessary than to adopt a system of action.

The meeting was held in the barroom of the Unicorn, and as every second man had his own particular scheme to advocate, it was both long and noisy. Many thought the action unnecessary, but were willing, for the sake of the community, to give their services. The simplest plan—to choose a competent leader, and submit to his management—never occurred to these free and independent volunteers, until all other means of unity had failed. Then Alfred Barton, as the originator of the measure, was chosen, and presented the rude but sufficient plan which had been suggested to him by Dr. Deane. The men were to meet every Saturday evening at the Unicorn, and exchange intelligence; but they could be called together at any time by a summons from Barton. The landlord of the Unicorn was highly satisfied with this arrangement, but no one noticed the interest with which the ostler, an Irishman named Dougherty, listened to the discussion.

Barton's horse was hitched beside Gilbert's, and as the two were mounting, the former said,

"If you're going home, Gilbert, why not come down our lane,

and go through by Carson's. We can talk the matter over a little; if there's any running to do, I depend a good deal on your horse."

Gilbert saw no reason for declining this invitation, and the two rode side by side down the lane to the Barton farmhouse. The sun was still an hour high, but a fragrant odor of broiled herring drifted out of the open kitchen-window. Barton thereupon urged him to stop and take supper, with a cordiality which we can only explain by hinting at his secret intention to become the purchaser of Gilbert's horse.

"Old Man Barton" was sitting in his arm-chair by the window, feebly brandishing his stick at the flies, and watching his daughter Ann as she transferred the herrings from the gridiron to a pewter platter.

"Father, this is Gilbert Potter," said Mr. Alfred, introducing his guest.

The bent head was lifted with an effort, and the keen eyes were fixed on the young man who came forward to take the crooked, half-extended hand.

"What Gilbert Potter?" he croaked.

Mr. Alfred bit his lips, and looked both embarrassed and annoyed. But he could do no less than say,

"Mary Potter's son."

Gilbert straightened himself proudly, as if to face a coming insult. After a long, steady gaze, the old man gave one of his hieroglyphic snorts, and then muttered to himself, "Looks like her."

During the meal, he was so occupied with the labor of feeding himself, that he seemed to forget Gilbert's presence. Bending his head sideways, from time to time, he jerked out a croaking question, which his son, whatever annoyance he might feel, was forced to answer according to the old man's humor.

"In at the Doctor's, boy?"

"A few minutes, Daddy, before we came together."

"See her? Was she at home?"

"Yes," came very shortly from Mr. Alfred's lips; he clenched his fists under the tablecloth.

"That's right, boy; stick up to her!" and he chuckled and munched together in a way which it made Gilbert sick to hear. The tail of the lean herring on his plate remained untasted; he swallowed the thin tea which Miss Ann poured out, and the heavy "half-Indian" bread* with a choking sensation. He had but one desire—to get away from the room, out of human sight and hearing.

Barton, ill at ease, and avoiding Gilbert's eye, accompanied him to the lane. He felt that the old man's garrulity ought to be explained, but knew not what to say. Gilbert spared him the trouble.

"When are we to wish you joy, Barton?" he asked, in a cold, hard voice.

Barton laughed in a forced way, clutched at his tawny whisker, and with something like a flush of his heavy face, answered in what was meant to be an indifferent tone:

"Oh, it's a joke of the old man's—don't mean anything."

"It seems to be a joke of the whole neighborhood, then; I have heard it from others."

"Have you?" Barton eagerly asked. "Do people talk about it much? What do they say?"

This exhibition of vulgar vanity, as he considered it, was so repulsive to Gilbert, in his desperate, excited condition, that for a moment he did not trust himself to speak. Holding the bridle of his horse, he walked mechanically down the slope, Barton following him.

Suddenly he stopped, faced the latter, and said, in a stern voice: "I must know, first, whether you are betrothed to Martha Deane."

His manner was so unexpectedly solemn and peremptory that Barton, startled from his self-possession, stammered,

"N—no: that is, not yet."

Another pause. Barton, curious to know how far gossip had already gone, repeated the question:

"Well, what do people say?"

"Some, that you and she will be married," Gilbert answered, speaking slowly and with difficulty, "and some that you won't. Which are right?"

"Damme, if *I* know!" Barton exclaimed, returning to his customary swagger. It was quite enough that the matter was generally talked about, and he had said nothing to settle it, in either way. But his manner, more than his words, convinced Gilbert that there was no betrothal as yet, and that the vanity

*Bread made partly of cornmeal (ed.).

of being regarded as the successful suitor of a lovely girl had a more prominent place than love, in his rival's heart. By so much was his torture lightened, and the passion of the moment subsided, after having so nearly betrayed itself.

"I say, Gilbert," Barton presently remarked, walking on towards the bars which led into the meadow-field; "it's time you were looking around in that way, hey?"

"It will be time enough when I am out of debt."

"But you ought, now, to have a wife in your house."

"I have a mother, Barton."

"That's true, Gilbert. Just as I have a father. The old man's queer, as you saw—kept me out of marrying when I was young, and now drives me to it. I might ha' had children grown——"

He paused, laying his hand on the young man's shoulder. Gilbert fancied that he saw on Barton's coarse, dull face, the fleeting stamp of some long-buried regret, and a little of the recent bitterness died out of his heart.

"Good-bye!" he said, offering his hand with greater ease than he would have thought possible, fifteen minutes sooner.

"Good-bye, Gilbert! Take care of Roger. Sandy Flash has a fine piece of horseflesh, but you beat him once—Damnation! You *could* beat him, I mean. If he comes within ten miles of us, I'll have the summonses out in no time."

Gilbert cantered lightly down the meadow. The soft breath of the summer evening fanned his face, and something of the peace expressed in the rich repose of the landscape fell upon his heart. But peace, he felt, could only come to him through love. The shame upon his name—the slow result of labor—even the painful store of memories which the years had crowded in his brain—might all be lightly borne, or forgotten, could his arms once clasp the now uncertain treasure. A tender mist came over his deep, dark eyes, a passionate longing breathed in his softened lips, and he said to himself,

"I would lie down and die at her feet, if that could make her happy; but how to live, and live without her?" This was a darkness which his mind refused to entertain. Love sees no justice on Earth or in Heaven, that includes not its own fulfilled desire.

Before reaching home, he tried to review the situation calmly. Barton's true relation to Martha Deane he partially suspected, so far as regarded the former's vanity and his slavish subservience to his father's will; but he was equally avaricious, and it was well known in Kennett that Martha possessed, or would possess, a handsome property in her own right. Gilbert, therefore, saw every reason to believe that Barton was an actual, if not a very passionate wooer.

That fact, however, was in itself of no great importance, unless Dr. Deane favored the suit. The result depended on Martha herself; she was called an "independent girl," which she certainly was, by contrast with other girls of the same age. It was this free, firm, independent, yet wholly womanly spirit which Gilbert honored in her, and which (unless her father's influence were too powerful) would yet save her to him, if she but loved him. Then he felt that his nervous, inflammable fear of Barton was incompatible with true honor for her, with trust in her pure and lofty nature. If she were so easily swayed, how could she stand the test which he was still resolved—nay, forced by circumstances—to apply?

With something like shame of his past excitement, yet with strength which had grown out of it, his reflections were terminated by Roger stopping at the barnyard gate.

CHAPTER 11

Guests at Potter's

A week or two later, there was trouble, but not of a very unusual kind, in the Fairthorn household. It was Sunday, the dinner was on the table, but Joe and Jake were not to be found. The garden, the corncrib, the barn, and the grove below the house were searched, without detecting the least sign of the truants. Finally Sally's eyes descried a remarkable object moving over the edge of the hill, from the direction of the Philadelphia road. It was a huge round creature, something like a cylindrical tortoise, slowly advancing upon four short, dark legs.

"What upon earth is that?" she cried.

All eyes were brought to bear upon this phenomenon, which gradually advanced until it reached the fence. Then it suddenly separated into three parts, the round back falling off, whereupon it was seized by two figures and lifted upon the fence.

"It's the best washtub, I do declare!" said Sally; "whatever have they been doing with it?"

Having crossed the fence, the boys lifted the inverted tub over their heads, and resumed their march. When they came near enough, it would be seen that their breeches and stockings were not only dripping wet, but streaked with black swamp-mud. This accounted for the unsteady, hesitating course of the tub, which at times seemed inclined to approach the house, and then tacked away towards the corner of the barnyard wall. A few vigorous calls, however, appeared to convince it that the direct course was the best, for it set out with a grotesque bobbing trot, which brought it speedily to the kitchen door.

Then Joe and Jake crept out, dripping to the very crowns of their heads, with their Sunday shirts and jackets in a horrible plight. The truth, slowly gathered from their mutual accusations, was this: they had resolved to have a boating excursion on

Redley Creek, and had abstracted the tub that morning when nobody was in the kitchen. Slipping down through the wood, they had launched it in a piece of still water. Joe got in first, and when Jake let go of the tub, it tilted over; then he held it for Jake, who squatted in the center, and floated successfully downstream until Joe pushed him with a pole, and made the tub lose its balance. Jake fell into the mud, and the tub drifted away; they had chased it nearly to the road before they recovered it.

"You bad boys, what shall I do with you?" cried Mother Fairthorn. "Put on your everyday clothes, and go to the garret. Sally, you can ride down to Potter's with the pears; they won't keep, and I expect Gilbert has no time to come for any, this summer."

"I'll go," said Sally, "but Gilbert don't deserve it. The way he snapped me up at Hallowell's—and he hasn't been here since!"

"Don't be hard on him, Sally!" said the kindly old woman; nor was Sally's more than a surface grudge. She had quite a sisterly affection for Gilbert, and was rather hurt than angered by what he had said in the fret of a mood which she could not comprehend.

The old mare rejoiced in a new bridle, with a headstall of scarlet morocco, and Sally would have made a stately appearance, but for the pears, which, stowed in the two ends of a grain-bag, and hung over the saddle, would not quite be covered by her riding-skirt. She trudged on slowly, down the lonely road, but had barely crossed the level below Kennett Square, when there came a quick sound of hoofs behind her.

It was Mark and Martha Deane, who presently drew rein, one on either side of her.

"Don't ride fast, please," Sally begged; "*I* can't, for fear of smashing the pears. Where are you going?"

"To Falconer's," Martha replied; "Fanny promised to lend me some new patterns; but I had great trouble in getting Mark to ride with me."

"Not if you will ride along, Sally," Mark rejoined. "We'll go with you first, and then you'll come with us. What do you say, Martha?"

"I'll answer for Martha!" cried Sally; "I am going to Potter's, and it's directly on your way."

"Just the thing," said. Mark; "I have a little business with Gilbert."

It was all settled before Martha's vote had been taken, and she accepted the decision without remark. She was glad, for Sally's sake, that they had fallen in with her, for she had shrewdly watched Mark, and found that, little by little, a serious liking for her friend was sending its roots down through the gay indifference of his surface mood. Perhaps she was not altogether calm in spirit at the prospect of meeting Gilbert Potter; but, if so, no sign of the agitation betrayed itself in her face.

Gilbert, sitting on the porch, half-hidden behind a mass of blossoming trumpet flower, was aroused from his Sabbath reverie by the sound of hoofs. Sally Fairthorn's voice followed, reaching even the ears of Mary Potter, who thereupon issued from the house to greet the unexpected guest. Mark had already dismounted, and although Sally protested that she would remain in the saddle, the strong arms held out to her proved too much of a temptation; it was so charming to put her hands on his shoulders, and to have [him] take her by the waist, and lift her to the ground so lightly!

While Mark was performing this service (and evidently with as much deliberation as possible), Gilbert could do no less than offer his aid to Martha Deane, whose sudden apparition he had almost incredulously realized. A bright, absorbing joy kindled his sad, strong features into beauty, and Martha felt her cheeks grow warm, in spite of herself, as their eyes met. The hands that touched her waist were firm, but no hands had ever before conveyed to her heart such a sense of gentleness and tenderness, and though her own gloved hand rested but a moment on his shoulder, the action seemed to her almost like a caress.

"How kind of you—all—to come!" said Gilbert, feeling that his voice expressed too much, and his words too little.

"The credit of coming is not mine, Gilbert," she answered. "We overtook Sally, and gave her our company for the sake of hers, afterwards. But I shall like to take a look at your place; how pleasant you are making it!"

"You are the first to say so; I shall always remember that!"

Mary Potter now advanced, with grave yet friendly welcome, and would have opened her best room to the guests, but the bowery porch, with its swinging scarlet bloom, haunted by hummingbirds and hawkmoths, wooed them to take their seats in its shade. The noise of a plunging cascade, which restored the idle mill-water to its parted stream, made a mellow, continuous music in the air. The highroad was visible at one point across the meadow, just where it entered the wood; otherwise, the seclusion of the place was complete.

"You could not have found a lovelier home, M—Mary," said Martha, terrified to think how near the words "*Mrs.* Potter" had been to her lips. But she had recovered herself so promptly that the hesitation was not noticed.

"Many people think the house ought to be upon the road," Mary Potter replied, "but Gilbert and I like it as it is. Yes, I hope it will be a good home, when we can call it our own."

"Mother is a little impatient," said Gilbert, "and perhaps I am also. But if we have health, it won't be very long to wait."

"That's a thing soon learned!" cried Mark. "I mean to be impatient. Why, when I was doing journeywork, I was as careless as the day's long, and so from hand to mouth didn't trouble me a bit; but now, I ha' n't been undertaking six months, and it seems that I feel worried if I don't get all the jobs going!"

Martha smiled, well pleased at this confession of the change, which she knew better how to interpret than Mark himself. But Sally, in her innocence, remarked:

"Oh Mark! that isn't right."

"I suppose it isn't. But maybe you've got to wish for more than you get, in order to get what you do. I guess I take things pretty easy, on the whole, for it's nobody's nature to be entirely satisfied. Gilbert, will you be satisfied when your farm's paid for?"

"No!" answered Gilbert with an emphasis, the sound of which, as soon as uttered, smote him to the heart. He had not thought of his mother. She clasped her hands convulsively, and looked at him, but his face was turned away.

"Why, Gilbert!" exclaimed Sally.

"I mean," he said, striving to collect his thoughts, "that there is something more than property"—but how should he go on? Could he speak of the family relation, then and there? Of honor in the community, the respect of his neighbors, without seeming to refer to the brand upon his and his mother's name? No; of none of these things. With sudden energy, he turned upon himself, and continued:

"I shall not feel satisfied until I am cured of my own impatience—until I can better control my temper, and get the weeds and rocks and stumps out of myself as well as out of my farm."

"Then you've got a job!" Mark laughed. "I think your fields are pretty tolerable clean, what I've seen of 'em. Nobody can say they're not well fenced in. Why, compared with you, I'm an open common, like the Wastelands, down on Whitely Creek, and everybody's cattle run over me!"

Mark's thoughtlessness was as good as tact. They all laughed heartily at his odd continuation of the simile, and Martha hastened to say:

"For my part, I don't think you are quite such an open common, Mark, or Gilbert so well fenced in. But even if you are, a great many things may be hidden in a clearing, and some people are tall enough to look over a high hedge. Betsy Lavender says some men tell all about themselves without saying a word, while others talk till Doomsday and tell nothing."

"And tell nothing," gravely repeated Mark, whereat no one could repress a smile, and Sally laughed outright.

Mary Potter had not mingled much in the society of Kennett, and did not know that this imitation of good Miss Betsy was a very common thing, and had long ceased to mean any harm. It annoyed her, and she felt it her duty to say a word for her friend.

"There is not a better or kinder-hearted woman in the county," she said, "than just Betsy Lavender. With all her odd ways of speech, she talks the best of sense and wisdom, and I don't know who I'd sooner take for a guide in times of trouble."

"You could not give Betsy a higher place than she deserves," Martha answered. "We all esteem her as a dear friend, and as the best helper where help is needed. She has been almost a mother to me."

Sally felt rebuked, and exclaimed tearfully, with her usual impetuous candor—"Now you know I meant no harm; it was all Mark's doing!"

"If you've anything against me, Sally, I forgive you for it. It isn't in my nature to bear malice," said Mark, with so serious an air, that poor Sally was more bewildered than ever. Gilbert and Martha, however, could not restrain their laughter at the fellow's odd, reckless humor, whereupon Sally, suddenly comprehending the joke, sprang from her seat. Mark leaped from the porch, and darted around the house, followed by Sally with mock-angry cries and brandishings of her riding-whip.

The scene was instantly changed to Gilbert's eyes. It was wonderful! There, on the porch of the home he so soon hoped to call his own, sat his mother, Martha Deane, and himself. The two former had turned towards each other, and were talking pleasantly; the hum of the hawkmoths, the mellow plunge of the water, and the stir of the soft summer breeze in the leaves, made a sweet accompaniment to their voices. His brain grew dizzy with yearning to fix that chance companionship, and make it the boundless fortune of his life. Under his habit of repression, his love for her had swelled and gathered to such an intensity that it seemed he must either speak or die.

Presently the rollicking couple made their appearance. Sally's foot had caught in her riding-skirt as she ran, throwing her at full length on the sward, and Mark, in picking her up, had possessed himself of the whip. She was not hurt in the least (her life having been a succession of tears and tumbles), but Mark's arm found it necessary to encircle her waist, and she did not withdraw from the support until they came within sight of the porch.

It was now time for the guests to leave, but Mary Potter must first produce her cakes and currant-wine—the latter an old and highly superior article, for there had been, alas! too few occasions which called for its use.

"Gilbert," said Mark, as they moved towards the gate, "why can't you catch and saddle Roger, and ride with us? You have nothing to do?"

"No; I would like—but where are you going?"

"To Falconer's; that is, the girls; but we won't stay for supper—I don't fancy quality company."

"Nor I," said Gilbert, with a gloomy face. "I have never visited Falconer's, and they might not thank you for introducing me."

He looked at Martha, as he spoke. She understood him, and gave him her entire sympathy and pity—yet it was impossible for her to propose giving up the visit, solely for his sake. It was not want of independence, but a maidenly shrinking from the inference of the act which kept her silent.

Mark, however, cut through the embarrassment. "I'll tell you what, Gilbert!" he exclaimed, "you go and get Roger from the field, while we ride on to Falconer's. If the girls will promise not to be too long about their patterns and their gossip, and what not, we can be back to the lane-end by the time you get there; then we'll ride up t' other branch o' Redley Creek, to the crossroad, and out by Hallowell's. I want to have a squint at the houses and barns down that way; nothing like business, you know!"

Mark thought he was very cunning in thus disposing of Martha during the ride, unconscious of the service he was offering to Gilbert. The latter's eagerness shone from his eyes, but still he looked at Martha, trembling for a sign that should decide his hesitation. Her lids fell before his gaze, and a faint color came into her face, yet she did not turn away. This time it was Sally Fairthorn who spoke.

"Five minutes will be enough for us, Mark," she said. "I'm not much acquainted with Fanny Falconer. So, Gilbert, hoist Martha into her saddle, and go for Roger."

He opened the gate for them, and then climbed over the fence into the hill-field above his house. Having reached the crest, he stopped to watch the three riding abreast, on a smart trot, down the glen. Sally looked back, saw him, and waved her hand; then Mark and Martha turned, giving no sign, yet to his eyes there seemed a certain expectancy in the movement.

Roger came from the farthest corner of the field at his call, and followed him down the hill to the bars, with the obedient attachment of a dog. When he had carefully brushed and then saddled the horse, he went to seek his mother, who was already making preparations for their early supper.

"Mother," he said, "I am going to ride a little way."

She looked at him wistfully and questioningly, as if she would fain have asked more; but only said,

"Won't you be home to supper, Gilbert?"

"I can't tell, but don't wait a minute, if I'm not here when it's ready."

He turned quickly, as if fearful of a further question, and the next moment was in the saddle.

The trouble in Mary Potter's face increased. Sighing sorely, she followed to the bridge of the barn, and presently descried him, beyond the mill, cantering lightly down the road. Then, lifting her arms, as in a blind appeal for help, she let them fall again, and walked slowly back to the house.

CHAPTER 12

The Events of an Evening

At the first winding of the creek, Gilbert drew rein, with a vague, half-conscious sense of escape. The eye which had followed him thus far was turned away at last.

For half a mile the road lay through a lovely solitude of shade and tangled bowery thickets, beside the stream. The air was soft and tempered, and filled the glen like the breath of some utterly peaceful and happy creature; yet over Gilbert's heart there brooded another atmosphere than this. The sultriness that precedes an emotional crisis weighed heavily upon him.

No man, to whom Nature has granted her highest gift—that of expression—can understand the pain endured by one of strong feelings, to whom not only this gift has been denied, but who must also wrestle with an inherited reticence. It is well that in such cases a kindly law exists, to aid the helpless heart. The least portion of the love which lights the world has been told in words; it works, attracts, and binds in silence. The eye never knows its own desire, the hand its warmth, the voice its tenderness, nor the heart its unconscious speech through these, and a thousand other vehicles. Every endeavor to hide the special fact betrays the feeling from which it sprang.

Like all men of limited culture, Gilbert felt his helplessness keenly. His mind, usually clear in its operations, if somewhat slow and cautious, refused to assist him here; it lay dead or apathetic in an air surcharged with passion. An anxious expectancy enclosed him with stifling pressure; he felt that it must be loosened, but knew not how. His craving for words—words swift, clear, and hot as lightning, through which his heart might discharge itself haunted him like a furious hunger.

The road, rising out of the glen, passed around the brow of a grassy hill, whence he could look across a lateral valley to the

Falconer farmhouse. Pausing here, he plainly descried a stately "chair" leaning on its thills, in the shade of the weeping willow, three horses hitched side by side to the lane-fence, and a faint glimmer of color between the mounds of box which almost hid the porch. It was very evident to his mind that the Falconers had other visitors, and that neither Mark nor Sally (whatever might be Martha Deane's inclination) would be likely to prolong their stay; so he slowly rode on, past the lane-end, and awaited them at the ford beyond.

It was not long—though the wood on the western hill already threw its shadow into the glen—before the sound of voices and hoofs emerged from the lane. Sally's remark reached him first:

"They may be nice people enough, for ought I know, but their ways are not my ways, and there's no use in trying to mix them."

"That's a fact!" said Mark. "Hallo, here's Gilbert, ahead of us!"

They rode into the stream together, and let their horses drink from the clear, swift-flowing water. In Mark's and Sally's eyes, Gilbert was as grave and impassive as usual, but Martha Deane was conscious of a strange, warm, subtle power, which seemed to envelop her as she drew near him. Her face glowed with a sweet, unaccustomed flush; his was pale, and the shadow of his brows lay heavier upon his eyes. Fate was already taking up the invisible, floating filaments of these two existences, and weaving them together.

Of course it happened, and of course by the purest accident, that Mark and Sally first reached the opposite bank, and took the narrow wood-road, where the loose, briery sprays of the thickets brushed them on either side. Sally's hat, and probably her head, would have been carried off by a projecting branch, had not Mark thrown his arm around her neck and forcibly bent her forwards. Then she shrieked and struck at him with her riding-whip, while Mark's laugh woke all the echoes of the woods.

"I say, Gilbert!" he cried, turning back in his saddle, "I'll hold *you* responsible for Martha's head; it's as much as *I* can do to keep Sally's on her shoulders."

Gilbert looked at his companion as she rode slowly by his side through the cool, mottled dusk of the woods. She had drawn the strings of the beaver through a button-hole of her riding-habit, and allowed it to hang upon her back. The motion of the horse gave a gentle, undulating grace to her erect, self-reliant figure, and her lips, slightly parted, breathed maidenly trust and consent. She turned her face towards him and smiled, at Mark's words.

"The warning is unnecessary," he said. "You will give me no chance to take care of you, Martha."

"Is it not better so?" she asked.

He hesitated; he would have said "No," but finally evaded a direct answer.

"I would be glad enough to do you a service—even so little as that," were his words, and the tender tone in which they were spoken made itself evident to his own ears.

"I don't doubt it, Gilbert," she answered, so kindly and cordially that he was smitten to the heart. Had she faltered in her reply—had she blushed and kept silence—his hope would have seized the evidence and rushed to the trial; but this was the frankness of friendship, not the timidity of love. She could not, then, suspect his passion, and ah, how the risks of its utterance were multiplied!

Meanwhile, the wonderful glamour of her presence—that irresistible influence which at once takes hold of body and spirit—had entered into every cell of his blood. Thought and memory were blurred into nothingness by this one overmastering sensation. Riding through the lonely woods, out of shade into yellow, level sunshine, in the odors of minty meadows and moist spices of the creekside, they twain seemed to him to be alone in the world. If they loved not each other, why should not the leaves shrivel and fall, the hills split asunder, and the sky rain death upon them? Here she moved at his side—he could stretch out his hand and touch her; his heart sprang towards her, his arms ached for very yearning to clasp her—his double nature demanded her with the will and entreated for her with the affection! Under all, felt though not suspected, glowed the vast primal instinct upon which the strength of manhood and of womanshood is based.

Sally and Mark, a hundred yards in advance, now thrown into sight and now hidden by the windings of the road, were so pleasantly occupied with each other that they took no heed of the pair behind them. Gilbert was silent; speech was mockery, unless it gave the words which he did not dare to pronounce.

His manner was sullen and churlish in Martha's eyes, he suspected; but so it must be, unless a miracle were sent to aid him. She, riding as quietly, seemed to meditate, apparently unconscious of his presence; how could he know that she had never before been so vitally conscious of it?

The long rays of sunset withdrew to the tree-tops, and a deeper hush fell upon the land. The road which had mounted along the slope of a stubble-field, now dropped again into a wooded hollow, where a tree, awkwardly felled, lay across it. Roger pricked up his ears and leaped lightly over. Martha's horse followed, taking the log easily, but she reined him up the next moment, uttering a slight exclamation, and stretched out her hand wistfully towards Gilbert.

To seize it and bring Roger to a stand was the work of an instant. "What is the matter, Martha?" he cried.

"I think the girth is broken," said she. "The saddle is loose, and I was nigh losing my balance. Thank you, I can sit steadily now."

Gilbert sprang to the ground and hastened to her assistance.

"Yes, it is broken," he said, "but I can give you mine. You had better dismount, though; see, I will hold the pommel firm with one hand, while I lift you down with the other. Not too fast, I am strong; place your hands on my shoulders—so!"

She bent forward and laid her hands upon his shoulders. Then as she slid gently down, his right arm crept around her waist, holding her so firmly and securely that she had left the saddle and hung in its support while her feet had not yet touched the earth. Her warm breath was on Gilbert's forehead; her bosom swept his breast, and the arm that until then had supported, now swiftly, tenderly, irresistibly embraced her. Trembling, thrilling from head to foot, utterly unable to control the mad impulse of the moment, he drew her to his heart and laid his lips to hers. All that he would have said—all, and more than all, that words could have expressed—was now said, without words. His kiss clung as if it were the last this side of death—clung until he felt that Martha feebly strove to be released.

The next minute they stood side by side, and Gilbert, by a revulsion equally swift and overpowering, burst into a passion of tears.

He turned and leaned his head against Roger's neck. Presently a light touch came upon his shoulder.

"Gilbert!"

He faced her then, and saw that her own cheeks were wet. "Martha!" he cried, "unless you love me with a love like mine for you, you can never forgive me!"

She came nearer; she laid her arms around him, and lifted her face to his. Then she said, in a tender, tremulous whisper,

"Gilbert—Gilbert! I forgive you."

A pang of wonderful, incredulous joy shot through his heart. Exalted by his emotion above the constraints of his past and present life, he arose and stood free and strong in his full stature as a man. He held her softly and tenderly embraced, and a purer bliss than the physical delight of her warm, caressing presence shone upon his face as he asked,

"Forever, Martha?"

"Forever."

"Knowing what I am?"

"Because I know what you are, Gilbert!"

He bowed his head upon her shoulder, and she felt softer tears—tears which came this time without sound or pang—upon her neck. It was infinitely touching to see this strong nature so moved, and the best bliss that a true woman's heart can feel—the knowledge of the boundless bounty which her love brings with it—opened upon her consciousness. A swift instinct revealed to her the painful struggles of Gilbert's life—the stern, reticent strength they had developed—the anxiety and the torture of his long-suppressed passion, and the powerful and purity of that devotion with which his heart had sought and claimed her. She now saw him in his true character—firm as steel, yet gentle as dew, patient and passionate, and purposely cold only to guard the sanctity of his emotions.

The twilight deepened in the wood, and Roger, stretching and shaking himself, called the lovers to themselves. Gilbert lifted his head and looked into Martha's sweet, unshrinking eyes.

"May the Lord bless you, as you have blessed me!" he said, solemnly. "Martha, did you guess this before?"

"Yes," she answered, "I felt that it must be so."

"And you did not draw back from me—you did not shun the thought of me! You were—"

He paused; was there not blessing enough, or must he curiously question its growth?

Martha, however, understood the thought in his mind. "No,

Gilbert!" she said, "I cannot truly say that I loved you at the time when I first discovered your feeling towards me. I had always esteemed and trusted you, and you were much in my mind; but when I asked myself if I could look upon you as my husband, my heart hesitated with the answer. I did not deserve your affection then, because I could not repay it in the same measure. But, although the knowledge seemed to disturb me, sometimes, yet it was very grateful, and therefore I could not quite make up my mind to discourage you. Indeed, I knew not what was right to do, but I found myself more and more strongly drawn towards you; a power came from you when we met, that touched and yet strengthened me, and then I thought, 'Perhaps I *do* love him.' Today, when I first saw your face, I knew that I did. I felt your heart calling to me like one that cries for help, and mine answered. It has been slow to speak, Gilbert, but I know it has spoken truly at last!"

He replaced the broken girth, lifted her into the saddle, mounted his own horse, and they resumed their ride along the dusky valley. But how otherwise their companionship now!

"Martha," said Gilbert, leaning towards her and touching her softly as he spoke, as if fearful that some power in his words might drive them apart—"Martha, have you considered what I am called? That the family name I bear is in itself a disgrace? Have you imagined what it is to love one so dishonored as I am?"

The delicate line of her upper lip grew clear and firm again, temporarily losing its relaxed gentleness. "I have thought of it," she answered, "but not in that way. Gilbert, I honored you before I loved you. I will not say that this thing makes no difference, for it does—a difference in the name men give you, a difference in your work through life (for you must deserve more esteem to gain as much as other men)—and a difference in my duty towards you. They call me 'independent,' Gilbert, because, though a woman, I dare to think for myself; I know not whether they mean praise by the word, or no; but I think it would frighten away the thought of love from many men. It has not frightened you; and you, however you were born, are the faithfulest and best man I know. I love you with my whole heart, and I will be true to you!"

With these words, Martha stretched out her hand. Gilbert took and held it, bowing his head fondly over it, and inwardly thanking God that the test which his pride had exacted was over at last. He could reward her truth, spare her the willing sacrifice —and he would.

"Martha," he said, "if I sometimes doubted whether you could share my disgrace, it was because I had bitter cause to feel how heavy it is to bear. God knows I would have come to you with a clean and honorable name, if I could have been patient to wait longer in uncertainty. But I could not tell how long the time might be—I could not urge my mother, nor even ask her to explain—"

"No, no, Gilbert! Spare *her!*" Martha interrupted.

"I *have*, Martha—God bless you for the words!—and I *will*; it would be the worst wickedness not to be patient, now! But I have not yet told you—"

A loud halloo rang through the dusk.

"It is Mark's voice," said Martha; "answer him!"

Gilbert shouted, and a double cry instantly replied. They had reached the crossroad from New-Garden, and Mark and Sally, who had been waiting impatiently for a quarter of an hour, rode to meet them. "Did you lose the road?" "Whatever kept you so long?" were the simultaneous questions.

"My girth broke in jumping over the tree," Martha answered, in her clear, untroubled voice. "I should have been thrown off, but for Gilbert's help. He had to give me his own girth, and so we have ridden slowly, since he has none."

"Take my breast-strap," said Mark.

"No," said Gilbert, "I can ride Roger bareback, if need be, with the saddle on my shoulder."

Something in his voice struck Mark and Sally singularly. It was grave and subdued, yet sweet in its tones as never before; he had not yet descended from the solemn exaltation of his recent mood. But the dusk sheltered his face, and its new brightness was visible only to Martha's eyes.

Mark and Sally again led the way, and the lovers followed in silence up the hill, until they struck the Wilmington road, below Hallowell's. Here Gilbert felt that it was best to leave them.

"Well, you two are cheerful company!" exclaimed Sally, as they checked their horses. "Martha, how many words has Gilbert spoken to you this evening?"

"As many as I have spoken to him," Martha answered; "but I will say three more—Good-night, Gilbert!"

"Good-night!" was all he dared say, in return, but the pressure of his hand burned long upon her fingers.

He rode homewards in the starlight, transformed by love and gratitude, proud, tender, strong to encounter any fate. His mother sat in the lonely kitchen, with the New Testament in her lap; she had tried to read, but her thoughts wandered from the consoling text. The table was but half-cleared, and the little old teapot still squatted beside the coals.

Gilbert strove hard to assume his ordinary manner, but he could not hide the radiant happiness that shone from his eyes and sat upon his lips.

"You've not had supper?" Mary Potter asked.

"No, Mother! but I'm sorry to keep things waiting; I can do well enough without."

"It's not right to go without your regular meals, Gilbert. Sit up to the table!"

She poured out the tea, and Gilbert ate and drank in silence. His mother said nothing, but he knew that her eye was upon him, and that he was the subject of her thoughts. Once or twice he detected a wistful, questioning expression, which, in his softened mood, touched him almost like a reproach.

When the table had been cleared and everything put away, she resumed her seat, breathing an unconscious sigh as she dropped her hands into her lap. Gilbert felt that he must now speak, and only hesitated while the considered how he could best do so, without touching her secret and mysterious trouble.

"Mother!" he said at last, "I have something to tell you."

"Ay, Gilbert?"

"Maybe it'll seem good news to you; but maybe not. I have asked Martha Deane to be my wife!"

He paused, and looked at her. She clasped her hands, leaned forward, and fixed her dark, mournful eyes intently upon his face.

"I have been drawn towards her for a long time," Gilbert continued. "It has been a great trouble to me, because she is so pretty, and withal so proud in the way a girl should be—I liked her pride, even while it made me afraid—and they say she is rich also. It might seem like looking too high, Mother, but I couldn't help it."

"There's no woman too high for you, Gilbert!" Mary Potter exclaimed. Then she went on, in a hurried, unsteady voice: "It isn't that—I mistrusted it would come so, some day, but I hoped—only for your good, my boy, only for that—I hoped not so soon. You're still young—not twenty-five, and there's debt on the farm;—couldn't you ha' waited a little, Gilbert?"

"I have waited, Mother," he said, slightly turning away his head, that he might not see the tender reproach in her face, which her question seemed to imply. "I *did* wait—and for that reason. I wanted first to be independent, at least; and I doubt that I would have spoken so soon, but there were others after Martha, and that put the thought of losing her into my head. It seemed like a matter of life or death. Alfred Barton tried to keep company with her—he didn't deny it to my face; the people talked of it. Folks always say more than they know, to be sure, but then, the chances were so much against *me*, mother! I was nigh crazy, sometimes. I tried my best and bravest to be patient, but today we were riding alone—Mark and Sally gone ahead—and—and then it came from my mouth, I don't know how; I didn't expect it. But I shouldn't have doubted Martha; she let me speak; she answered me—I can't tell you her words, Mother, though I'll never forget one single one of 'em to my dying day. She gave me her hand and said she would be true to me forever."

Gilbert waited, as if his mother might here speak, but she remained silent.

"Do you understand, Mother?" he continued. "She pledged herself to me—she will be my wife. And I asked her—you won't be hurt, for I felt it to be my duty—whether she knew how disgraced I was in the eyes of the people—whether my name would not be a shame for her to bear? She couldn't know what we know: she took me even with the shame—and she looked prouder than ever when she stood by me in the thought of it! She would despise me, now, if I should offer to give her up on account of it, but she may know as much as I do, Mother? She deserves it."

There was no answer. Gilbert looked up.

Mary Potter sat perfectly still in her high rocking chair. Her arms hung passively at her sides, and her head leaned back and was turned to one side, as if she were utterly exhausted. But in the pale face, the closed eyes, and the blue shade about the parted lips, he saw that she was unconscious of his words. She had fainted.

CHAPTER 13

Two Old Men

Shortly after Martha Deane left home for her eventful ride to Falconer's, the Doctor also mounted his horse and rode out of the village in the opposite direction. Two days before, he had been summoned to bleed "Old Man Barton," on account of a troublesome buzzing in the head, and, although not bidden to make a second professional visit, there was sufficient occasion for him to call upon his patient in the capacity of a neighbor.

Dr. Deane never made a step outside the usual routine of his business without a special and carefully considered reason. Various causes combined to inspire his movement in the present instance. The neighborhood was healthy; the village was so nearly deserted that no curious observers lounged upon the tavern-porch, or sat upon the horse-block at the corner store; and Mr. Alfred Barton had been seen riding towards Avondale. There would have been safety in a much more unusual proceeding; this, therefore, might be undertaken in that secure, easy frame of mind which the Doctor both cultivated and recommended to the little world around him.

The Barton farmhouse was not often molested by the presence of guests, and he found it as quiet and lifeless as an uninhabited island of the sea. Leaving his horse hitched in the shade of the corncrib, he first came upon Giles, stretched out under the holly bush, and fast asleep, with his head upon his jacket. The door and window of the family-room were open, and Dr. Deane, walking softly upon the thick grass, saw that Old Man Barton was in his accustomed seat. His daughter Ann was not visible; she was at that moment occupied in taking out the drawers of her queer old bureau, in her narrow bedroom upstairs, various bits of lace and ribbon, done up in lavender, and perchance (for we must not be too curious) a broken sixpence or a lock of dead hair.

136

The old man's back was towards the window, but the Doctor could hear that papers were rustling and crackling in his trembling hands, and could see that an old casket of very solid oak, bound with iron, stood on the table at his elbow. Thereupon he stealthily retraced his steps to the gate, shut it with a sharp snap, cleared his throat, and mounted the porch with slow, loud, deliberate steps. When he reached the open door, he knocked upon the jamb without looking into the room. There was a jerking, dragging sound for a moment, and then the old man's snarl was heard:

"Who's there?"

Dr. Deane entered, smiling, and redolent of sweet marjoram. "Well, Friend Barton," he said, "let's have a look at thee now!"

Thereupon he took a chair, placed in in front of the old man, and sat down upon it, with his legs spread wide apart, and his ivory-headed cane (which he also used as a riding-whip) bolt upright between them. He was very careful not to seem to see that a short quilt, which the old man usually wore over his knees, now lay in a somewhat angular heap upon the table.

"Better, I should say—yes, decidedly better," he remarked, nodding his head gravely. "I had nothing to do this afternoon— the neighborhood is very healthy—and thought I would ride down and see how thee's getting on. Only a friendly visit, thee knows."

The old man had laid one shaking arm and crooked hand upon the edge of the quilt, while with the other he grasped his hickory staff. His face had a strange, ashy color, through which the dark, corded veins on his temples showed with singular distinctness. But his eye was unusually bright and keen, and its cunning, suspicious expression did not escape the Doctor's notice.

"A friendly visit—ay!" he growled—"not like doctors' visits generally, eh? Better?—of course I'm better. It's no harm to tap one of a full-blooded breed. At our age, Doctor, a little blood goes a great way."

"No doubt, no doubt!" the Doctor assented. "Especially in thy case. I often speak of thy wonderful constitution."

"Neighborly, you say, Doctor—only neighborly?" asked the old man. The Doctor smiled, nodded, and seemed to exhale a more powerful herbaceous odor.

"Maybe, then, you'll take a bit of a dram?—a thimble-full

won't come amiss. You know the shelf where it's kep'—reach to, and help yourself, and then help me to a drop."

Dr. Deane rose and took down the square black bottle and the diminutive wineglass beside it. Half-filling the latter—a thimble-full in verity—he drank it in two or three delicate little sips, puckering his large underlip to receive them.

"It's right to have the best, Friend Barton," he said, "there's more life in it!" as he filled the glass to the brim and held it to the slit in the old man's face.

The latter eagerly drew off the top fullness, and then seized the glass in his shaky hand. "Can help myself," he croaked— "don't need waitin' on; not so bad as that!"

His color presently grew, and his neck assumed a partial steadiness. "What news, what news?" he asked. "You gather up a plenty in your goin's-around. It's a little I get, except the bones, after they've been gnawed over by the whole neighborhood."

"There is not much now, I believe," Dr. Deane observed. "Jacob and Leah Gilpin have another boy, but thee hardly knows them, I think. William Byerly died last week in Birmingham; thee's heard of him—he had a wonderful gift of preaching. They say Maryland cattle will be cheap, this fall: does Alfred intend to fatten many? I saw him riding towards New-Garden."

"I guess he will," the old man answered,—"must make somethin' out o' the farm. That pastur'-bottom ought to bring more than it does."

"Alfred doesn't look to want for much," the Doctor continued. "It's a fine farm he has."

"*Me*, I say!" old Barton exclaimed, bringing down the end of his stick upon the floor. "The farm's mine!"

"But it's the same thing, isn't it?" asked Dr. Deane, in his cheeriest voice and with his pleasantest smile.

The old man looked at him for a moment, gave an incoherent grunt, the meaning of which the Doctor found it impossible to decipher, and presently, with a cunning leer, said,

"Is all your property the same thing as your daughter's?"

"Well—well," replied the Doctor, softly rubbing his hands, "I should hope so—yes, I should hope so."

"Besides what she has in her own right?"

"Oh, thee knows that will be hers without my disposal. What I should do for her would be apart from that. I am not likely, at my time of life, to marry again—but we are led by the Spirit, thee knows; we cannot say, I will do thus and so, and these and such things shall happen, and those and such other shall not."

"Ay, that's my rule, too, Doctor," said the old man, after a pause, during which he had intently watched his visitor, from under his wrinkled eyelids.

"I thought," the Doctor resumed, "thee was pretty safe against another marriage, at any rate, and thee had perhaps made up thy mind about providing for thy children. It's better for us old men to have our houses set in order, that we may spare ourselves worry and anxiety of mind. Elisha is already established in his own independence, and I suppose Ann will give thee no particular trouble; but if Alfred, now, should take a notion to marry, he couldn't, thee sees, be expected to commit himself without having some idea of what thee intends to do for him."

Dr. Deane, having at last taken up his position and uncovered his front of attack, waited for the next movement of his adversary. He was even aware of a slight professional curiosity to know how far the old man's keen, shrewd, wary faculties had survived the wreck of his body.

The latter nodded his head, and pressed the top of his hickory stick against his gums several times, before he answered. He enjoyed the encounter, though not so sure of its issue as he would have been ten years earlier.

"I'd do the fair thing, Doctor!" he finally exclaimed; "whatever it might be, it'd be fair. Come, isn't that enough?"

"In a general sense, it is. But we are talking now as neighbors. We are both old men, Friend Barton, and I think we know how to keep our own counsel. Let us suppose a case—just to illustrate the matter, thee understands. Let us say that Friend Paxson—a widower, thee knows—had a daughter Mary, who had—well, a nice little penny in her own right—and that thy son Alfred desired her in marriage. Friend Paxson, as a prudent father, knowing his daughter's portion, both what it is and what it will be—he would naturally wish, in Mary's interest, to know that Alfred would not be dependent on her means, but that the children they might have would inherit equally from both. Now, it strikes me that Friend Paxson would only be right in asking thee what thee would do for thy son—nay, that, to be safe, he would want to see some evidence that would hold in law. Things are so uncertain, and a wise man guardeth his own household."

The old man laughed until his watery eyes twinkled. "Friend Paxson is a mighty close and cautious one to deal with," he said. "Mayhap he'd like to manage to have me bound, and himself go free?"

"Thee's mistaken, indeed!" Dr. Deane protested. "He's not that kind of a man. He only means to do what's right, and to ask for the same security from thee, which thee—I'm sure of it, Friend Barton!—would expect *him* to furnish."

The old man began to find this illustration uncomfortable; it was altogether one-sided. Dr. Deane could shelter himself behind Friend Paxson and the imaginary daughter, but the applications came personally home to him. His old patience had been weakened by his isolation from the world, and his habits of arbitrary rule. He knew, moreover, the probable amount of Martha's fortune, and could make a shrewd guess at the Doctor's circumstances; but if the settlements were to be equal, each must give his share its highest valuation in order to secure more from the other. It was a difficult game, because these men viewed it in the light of a business transaction, and each considered that any advantage over the other would be equivalent to a pecuniary gain on his own part.

"No use beatin' about the bush, Doctor," the old man suddenly said. "You don't care for Paxson's daughter, that never was; why not put your Martha in her place. She has a good penny, I hear—five thousand, some say."

"Ten, every cent of it!" exclaimed Dr. Deane, very nearly thrown off his guard. "That is, she will have it, at twenty-five; and sooner, if she marries with my consent. But why does thee wish particularly to speak of her?"

"For the same reason you talk about Alfred. He hasn't been about your house lately, I s'pose, hey?"

The Doctor smiled, dropping his eyelids in a very sagacious way. "He *does* seem drawn a little our way, I must confess to thee," he said, "but we can't always tell how much is meant. Perhaps thee knows his mind better than I do?"

"Mayhap I do—know what it will be, if *I* choose! But I don't begrudge sayin' that he likes your girl, and I shouldn't wonder if he'd showed it."

"Then thee sees, Friend Barton," Dr. Deane continued, "that the case is precisely like the one I supposed; and what I would consider right for Friend Paxson, would even be right for myself. I've no doubt thee could do more for Alfred than I can do for Martha, and without wrong to thy other children—Elisha, as I said, being independent, and Ann not requiring a great deal—and the two properties joined together would be a credit to us, and to the neighborhood. Only, thee knows, there must be some legal assurance beforehand. There is nothing certain—even thy mind is liable to change—ah, the mind of man is an unstable thing!"

The Doctor delivered these words in his most impressive manner, uplifting both eyes and hands.

The old man, however, seemed to pay but little attention to it. Turning his head on one side, he said, in a quick, sharp voice: "Time enough for that when we come to it. How's the girl inclined? Is the money hers, anyhow, at twenty-five—how old now? Sure to be a couple, hey?—settle that first!"

Dr. Deane crossed his legs carefully, so as not to crease the cloth too much, laid his cane upon them, and leaned back a little in his chair. "Of course I've not spoken to Martha," he presently said; "I can only say that she hasn't set her mind upon anybody else, and that is the main thing. She has followed my will in all, except as to joining the Friends, and there I felt that I couldn't rightly command, where the Spirit had not spoken. Yes, the money will be hers at twenty-five—she is twenty-one now—but I hardly think it necessary to take that into consideration. If thee can answer for Alfred, I think I can answer for her."

"The boy's close about *his* money," broke in the old man, with a sly, husky chuckle. "What he has, Doctor, you understand, goes toward balancin' what she has, afore you come onto me, at all. Yes, yes, I know what I'm about. A good deal, off and on, has been got out o' this farm, and it hasn't all gone into *my* pockets. I've a trifle put out, but you can't expect me to strip myself naked, in my old days. But I'll do what's fair—I'll do what's fair!"

"There's only this," the Doctor added, meditatively, "and I want thee to understand, since we've, somehow or other, come to mention the matter, that we'd better have another talk, after we've had more time to think of it. Thee can make up thy mind, and let me know *about* what thee'll do; and I the same. Thee *has* a starting-point on my side, knowing the amount of Martha's fortune—*that*, of course, thee must come up to first, and then we'll see about the rest!"

Old Man Barton felt that he was here brought up to the rack. He recognized Dr. Deane's advantage, and could only evade it by accepting his proposition for delay. True, he had already gone over the subject, in his lonely, restless broodings beside the window, but this encounter had freshened and resuscitated many points. He knew that the business would be finally arranged, but nothing would have induced him to hasten it. There was a great luxury in this preliminary skirmishing.

"Well, well!" said he, "we needn't hurry. You're right there, Doctor. I s'pose you won't do anything to keep the young ones apart?"

"I think I've shown my own wishes very plainly, Friend Barton. It is necessary that Alfred should speak for himself, though, and after all we've said, perhaps it might be well if thee should give him a hint. Thee must remember that he has never yet mentioned the subject to me."

Dr. Deane thereupon arose, smoothed his garments, and shook out, not only sweet marjoram, but lavender, cloves, and calamus. His broad-brimmed drab hat had never left his head during the interview. There were steps on the creaking floor overhead, and the Doctor perceived that the private conference must now close. It was nearly a drawn game, so far; but the chance of advantage was on his side.

"Suppose I look at thy arm—in a neighborly way, of course," he said, approaching the old man's chair.

"Never mind—took the bean off this mornin'—old blood, you know, but lively yet. Gad, Doctor! I've not felt so brisk for a year." His eyes twinkled so, under their puffy lids, the flabby folds in which his mouth terminated worked so curiously—like those of a bellows, where they run together towards the nozzle— and the two movable fingers on each hand opened and shut with such a menacing, clutching motion, that for one moment the Doctor felt a chill, uncanny creep run over his nerves.

"Brandy!" the old man commanded. "I've not talked so much at once't for months. You might take a little more, maybe. No? well, you hardly need it. Good brandy's powerful dear, these times."

Dr. Deane had too much tact to accept the grudging invitation. After the old man had drunk, he carefully replaced the bottle and glass on their accustomed shelf, and disposed himself to leave. On the whole, he was well satisfied with the afternoon's work, not doubting but that he had acted the part of a tender and most considerate parent towards his daughter.

Before they met, she also had disposed of her future, but in a very different way.

Miss Ann descended the stairs in time to greet the Doctor before his departure. She would have gladly retained him to tea, as a little relief to the loneliness and weariness of the day; but she never dared to give an invitation except when it seconded her father's, which, in the present case, was wanting.

CHAPTER 14

Doubts and Surmises

Gilbert's voice, sharpened by his sudden and mortal fear, recalled Mary Potter to consciousness. After she had drunk of the cup of water which he brought, she looked slowly and wearily around the kitchen, as if some instinct taught her to fix her thoughts on the signs and appliances of her everyday life, rather than allow them to return to the pang which had overpowered her. Little by little she recovered her calmness and a portion of her strength, and at last, noticing her son's anxious face, she spoke.

"I have frightened you, Gilbert; but there is no occasion for it. I wasn't rightly prepared for what you had to say—and—and—but, please, don't let us talk any more about it tonight. Give me a little time to think—if I *can* think. I'm afraid it's but a sad home I'm making for you, and sure it's a sad load I've put upon you, my poor boy! But oh, try, Gilbert, *try* to be patient a little while longer—it can't be for long—for I begin to see now that I've worked out my fault, and that the Lord in Heaven owes me justice!"

She clenched her hands wildly, and rose to her feet. Her steps tottered, and he sprang to her support.

"Mother," he said, "let me help you to your room. I'll not speak of this again; I wouldn't have spoken tonight, if I had mistrusted that it could give you trouble. Have no fear that I can ever be impatient again; patience is easy to me now!"

He spoke kindly and cheerfully, registering a vow in his heart that his lips should henceforth be closed upon the painful theme, until his mother's release (whatever it was and whenever it might come) should open them.

But competent as he felt in that moment to bear the delay cheerfully, and determined as he was to cast no additional weight on his mother's heart, it was not so easy to compose his thoughts, as he lay in the dusky, starlit bedroom upstairs. The events of the day, and their recent consequences, had moved his strong nature to its very foundations. A chaos of joy, wonder, doubt, and dread surged through him. Over and over he recalled the sweet pressure of Martha Deane's lip, the warm curve of her bosom, the dainty, delicate firmness of her hand. Was this—could this possession really be his? In his mother's mysterious secret there lay an element of terror. He could not guess why the revelation of his fortunate love should agitate her so fearfully, unless—and the suspicion gave him a shock—her history were in some way involved with that of Martha Deane.

This thought haunted and perplexed him, continually returning to disturb the memory of those holy moments in the twilight dell, and to ruffle the bright current of joy which seemed to gather up and sweep away with it all the forces of his life. Any fate but to lose her, he said to himself; let the shadow fall anywhere, except between them! There would be other troubles, he foresaw—the opposition of her father; the rage and hostility of Alfred Barton; possibly, when the story became known (as it must be in the end), the ill will or aversion of the neighborhood. Against all these definite and positive evils, he felt strong and tolerably courageous, but the something which evidently menaced him through his mother made him shrink with a sense of cowardice.

Hand in hand with this dread he went into the world of sleep. He stood upon the summit of the hill behind Falconer's farmhouse, and saw Martha beckoning to him from the hill on the other side of the valley. They stretched and clasped hands through the intervening space; the hills sank away, and they found themselves suddenly below, on the banks of the creek. He threw his arms around her, but she drew back, and then he saw that it was Betsy Lavender, who said: "I am your father—did you never guess it before?" Down the road came Dr. Deane and his mother, walking arm in arm; their eyes were fixed on him, but they did not speak. Then he heard Martha's voice, saying: "Gilbert, why did you tell Alfred Barton? Nobody must know that I am engaged to both of you." Betsy Lavender said: "He can only marry with my consent—Mary Potter has nothing to do with it." Martha then came towards him smiling, and said: "I will not send back your saddle-girth—see, I am wearing it as a belt!" He took hold of the buckle and drew her nearer; she began to weep, and they were suddenly standing side by side, in a dark room, before his dead mother, in her coffin.

This dream, absurd and incoherent as it was, made a strange impression upon Gilbert's mind. He was not superstitious, but in spite of himself the idea became rooted in his thoughts that the truth of his own parentage affected, in some way, some member of the Deane family. He taxed his memory in vain for words or incidents which might help him to solve his doubt. Something told him that his obligation to his mother involved the understanding that he would not even attempt to discover her secret; but he could not prevent his thoughts from wandering around it, and making blind guesses as to the vulnerable point.

Among these guesses came one which caused him to shudder; he called it impossible, incredible, and resolutely barred it from his mind. But with all his resolution, it only seemed to wait at a little distance, as if constantly seeking an opportunity to return. What if Dr. Deane were his own father? In that case Martha would be his half sister, and the stain of illegitimacy would rest on her, not on him! There was ruin and despair in the supposition; but, on the other hand, he asked himself why should the fact of his love throw his mother into a swoon? Among the healthy, strong-nerved people of Kennett, such a thing as a swoon was of the rarest occurrence, and it suggested some terrible cause to Gilbert's mind. It was sometimes hard for him to preserve his predetermined patient, cheerful demeanor in his mother's presence, but he tried bravely, and succeeded.

Although the harvest was well over, there was still much work to do on the farm, in order that the month of October might be appropriate to hauling—the last time, Gilbert hoped, that he should be obliged to resort to this source of profit. Though the price of grain was sure to decline on account of the extraordinary harvest, the quantity would make up for this deficiency. So far, his estimates had been verified. A good portion of the money was already on hand, and his coveted freedom from debt in the following spring became now tolerably secure. His course, in this respect, was in strict accordance with the cautious, plodding, conscientious habits of the community in which he lived. They were satisfied to advance steadily and slowly, never establishing a new mark until the old one had been reached.

Gilbert was impatient to see Martha again, not so much for

the delight of love, as from the sense of the duty which he owed to her. His mother had not answered his question—possibly not even heard it—and he did not dare to approach her with it again. But so much as he knew might be revealed to the wife of his heart; of that he was sure. If she could but share his confidence in his mother's words, and be equally patient to await the solution, it would give their relation a new sweetness, an added sanctity and trust.

He made an errand to Fairthorn's at the close of the week, hoping that chance might befriend him, but almost determined, in any case, to force an interview. The dread he had trampled down still hung around him, and it seemed that Martha's presence might dissipate it. Something, at least, he might learn concerning Dr. Deane's family, and here his thoughts at once reverted to Miss Betsy Lavender. In her he had the true friend, the close mouth, the brain crammed with family intelligence!

The Fairthorns were glad to see their "boy," as the old woman still called him. Joe and Jake threw their brown legs over the barnyard fence and clamored for a ride upon Roger. "Only along the level, t'other side o' the big hill, Gilbert!" said Joe, whereupon the two boys punched each other in the sides and nearly smothered with wicked laughter. Gilbert understood them; he shook his head, and said: "You rascals, I think I see you doing that again!" But he turned away his face, to conceal a smile at the recollection.

It was, truly, a wicked trick. The boys had been in the habit of taking the farm-horses out of the field and riding them up and down the Unionville road. It was their habit, as soon as they had climbed "the big hill," to use stick and voice with great energy, force the animals into a gallop, and so dash along the level. Very soon, the horses knew what was expected of them, and whenever they came abreast of the great chestnut tree on the top of the hill, they would start off as if possessed. If any business called Farmer Fairthorn to the Street Road, or up Marlborough way, Joe and Jake, dancing with delight, would dart around the barn, gain the wooded hollow, climb the big hill behind the limekiln, and hide themselves under the hedge, at the commencement of the level road. Here they could watch their father, as his benign, unsuspecting face came in sight, mounting the hill, either upon the gray mare, Bonnie, or the brown gelding, Peter. As the horse neared the chestnut tree, they fairly

shook with eager expectancy—then came the start, the astonishment of the old man, his frantic "Whoa, there, whoa!" his hat
soaring off on the wind, his short, stout body bouncing in the
saddle, as, half-unseated, he clung with one hand to the mane
and the other to the bridle!—while the wicked boys, after
breathlessly watching him out of sight, rolled over and over on
the grass, shrieking and yelling in a perfect luxury of fun.

Then they knew that a test would come, and prepared themselves to meet it. When, at dinner, Farmer Fairthorn turned to
his wife and said: "Mammy," (so he always addressed her) "I
don't know what's the matter with Bonnie; why, she came nigh
runnin' off with me!"—Joe, being the oldest and boldest, would
look up in well-affected surprise, and ask, "Why, how, Daddy?"
while Jake would bend down his head and whimper,—"Somethin' 's got into my eye." Yet the boys were very good-hearted
fellows at bottom, and we are sorry that we must chronicle so
many things to their discredit.

Sally Fairthorn met Gilbert in her usual impetuous way. She
was glad to see him, but she could not help saying: "Well, have
you got your tongue yet, Gilbert? Why, you're growing to be as
queer as Dick's hat-band! I don't know any more where to find
you, or how to place you; whatever is the matter?"

"Nothing, Sally," he answered, with something of his old
playfulness, "nothing except that the pears were very good.
How's Mark?"

"Mark!" she exclaimed with a very well assumed sneer. "As if
I kept an account of Mark's comings and goings!" But she could
not prevent an extra color from rising into her face.

"I wish you did, Sally," Gilbert gravely remarked. "Mark is a
fine fellow, and one of my best friends, and he'd be all the
better, if a smart, sensible girl like yourself would care a little
for him."

There was no answer to this, and Sally, with a hasty "I'll tell
Mother you're here!" darted into the house.

Gilbert was careful not to ask many questions during his visit;
but Sally's rattling tongue supplied him with all he would have
been likely to learn, in any case. She had found Martha at home
the day before, and had talked about him, Gilbert. Martha
hadn't noticed anything "queer" in his manner, whereupon she,
Sally, had said that Martha was growing "queer" too; then
Martha remarked that—but here Sally found that she had been

talking altogether too fast, so she bit her tongue and blushed a little. The most important piece of news, however, was that Miss Lavender was then staying at Dr. Deane's.

On his way to the village, Gilbert chose the readiest and simplest way of accomplishing his purpose. He would call on Betsy Lavender, and ask her to arrange her time so that she could visit his mother during his approaching absence from home. Leaving his horse at the hitching-post in front of the store, he walked boldly across the road and knocked at Dr. Deane's door.

The Doctor was absent. Martha and Miss Lavender were in the sitting room, and a keen, sweet throb in his blood responded to the voice that bade him enter.

"Gilbert Potter, I'll be snaked!" exclaimed Miss Lavender, jumping up with a start that overturned her footstool.

"Well, Gilbert!" and "Well, Martha!" were the only words the lovers exchanged, on meeting, but their hands were quick to clasp and loath to loose. Martha Deane was too clearheaded to be often surprised by an impulse of the heart, but when the latter experience came to her, she never thought of doubting its justness. She had not been fully, vitally aware of her love for Gilbert until the day when he declared it, and now, in memory, the two circumstances seemed to make but one fact. The warmth, the beauty, the spiritual expansion which accompany love had since then dawned upon her nature in their true significance. Proudly and cautiously as she would have guarded her secret from an intrusive eye, just as frank, tender, and brave was she to reveal every emotion of her heart to her lover. She was thoroughly penetrated with the conviction of his truth, of the integral nobility of his manhood; and these, she felt, were the qualities her heart had unconsciously craved. Her mind was made up inflexibly; it rejoiced in his companionship, it trusted in his fidelity, and if she considered conventional difficulties, it was only to estimate how they could most speedily be overthrown. Martha Deane was in advance of her age—or, at least, of the community in which she lived.

They could only exchange commonplaces, of course, in Miss Lavender's presence; and perhaps they were not aware of the gentle, affectionate way in which they spoke of the weather and similar topics. Miss Lavender was; her eyes opened widely, then nearly closed with an expression of superhuman wisdom; she looked out of the window and nodded to the lilac bush, then exclaiming in desperate awkwardness: "Goodness me, I must have a bit o' sage!" made for the garden, with long strides.

Gilbert was too innocent to suspect the artifice—not so Martha. But while she would have foiled the inference of any other woman, she accepted Betsy's without the least embarrassment, and took Gilbert's hand again in her own before the door had fairly closed.

"O Martha!" he cried, "if I could but see you oftener—but for a minute, every day! But there—I won't be impatient. I've thought of you ever since, and I ask myself, the first thing when I wake, morning after morning, is it really true?"

"And I say to myself, every morning, it *is* true," she answered. Her lovely blue eyes smiled upon him with a blissful consent, so gentle and so perfect, that he would fain have stood thus and spoken no word more.

"Martha," he said, returning to the thought of his duty, "I have something to say. You can hear it now. My mother declares that I am her lawful son, born in wedlock—she gave me her solemn word—but more than that she will not allow me to ask, saying she's bound for a time, and something, I don't know what, must happen before she can set herself right in the eyes of the world. I believe her, Martha, and I want that you should believe her, for her sake and for mine. I can't make things clear to you, now, because they're not clear to myself; only, what she has declared is and must be true! I am not baseborn, and it'll be made manifest, I'm sure; the Lord will open her mouth in his own good time—and until then, we must wait! Will you wait with me?"

He spoke earnestly and hurriedly, and his communication was so unexpected that she scarcely comprehended its full import. But for his sake, she dared not hesitate to answer.

"Can you ask it, Gilbert? Whatever your mother declares to you must be true; yet I scarcely understand it."

"Nor can I! I've wearied my brains, trying to guess why she can't speak, and what it is that'll give her the liberty at last. I daren't ask her more—she fainted dead away, the last time."

"Strange things sometimes happen in this world," said Martha, with a grave tenderness, laying her hand upon his arm, "and this seems to be one of the strangest. I am glad you have told me, Gilbert—it will make so much difference to you!"

"So it don't take you from me, Martha," he groaned, in a return of his terrible dread.

"Only Death can do that—and then but for a little while."

Here Miss Betsy Lavender made her appearance, but without the sage.

"How far a body can see, Martha," she exclaimed, "since the big gum-tree's been cut down. It lays open the sight o' the road across the creek, and I seen your father ridin' down the hill, as plain as could be!"

"Betsy," said Gilbert, "I wanted to ask you about coming down our way."

"Our way. Did you? I see your horse hitched over at the store. I've an arrand—sewin'-thread and pearl buttons—and so I'll git my bonnet and you can tell me on the way."

The lovers said farewell, and Betsy Lavender accompanied Gilbert, proposing to walk a little way with him and get the articles on her return.

"Gilbert Potter," she said, when they were out of sight and earshot of the village, "I want you to know that I've got eyes in my head. *I'm* a safe body, as you can see, though it mayn't seem the proper thing in me to say it, but all other folks isn't, so look out!"

"Betsy!" he exclaimed, "you seem to know everything about everybody—at least, you know what I am, perhaps better than I do myself; now suppose I grant you're right, what do you think of it?"

"Think of it? Go 'long!—you know what you want me to say, that there never was such a pair o' lovyers under the firmament! Let my deeds prove what I think, say I—for here's a case where deeds is wanted!"

"You can help me, Betsy—you can help me now! Do you know—can you guess—who was my father?"

"Good Lord!" was her surprised exclamation—"No, I don't, and that's the fact."

"Who was Martha Deane's mother?"

"A Blake—Naomi, one o' the Birmingham Blakes, and a nice woman she was, too. I was at her weddin', and I helped nuss her when Martha was born."

"Had Dr. Deane been married before?"

"Married before? Well—no!" Here Miss Betsy seemed to be suddenly put upon her guard. "Not to that extent, I should say. However, it's neither here nor there. Good lack, boy!" she cried, noticing a deadly paleness on Gilbert's face—"a-h-h-h, I begin to

understand now. Look here, Gilbert! Git that nonsense out o'
y'r head, jist as soon as *you* can. There's enough o' trouble
ahead, without borrowin' any more out o' y'r wanderin' wits. I
don't deny but what I was holdin' back somethin', but it's another thing as ever was. I'll speak *you* clear o' your misdoubtin's, if that's y'r present bother. You don't feel quite as much
like a live corpse, now, I reckon, hey?"

"O, Betsy!" he said, "if you knew how I have been perplexed, you wouldn't wonder at my fancies!"

"I can fancy all that, my boy," she gently answered, "and I'll
tell you another thing, Gilbert—your mother has a heavy secret
on her mind, and I rather guess it concerns your father. No—
don't look so eager-like—I don't know it. All I do know is that
you were born in Phildelphy."

"In Philadelphia! I never heard that."

"Well—it's neither here nor there. I've had my hands too full
to spy out other people's affairs, but many a thing has come to
me in a nateral way, or half-unbeknown. You can't do better
than leave all sich wild guesses and misdoubtin's to me, that's
better able to handle 'em. Not that I'm a-goin' to preach and
declare anything until I know the rights of it, whatever and
wherever. Well, as I was sayin'—for there's Beulah Green comin'
up the road, and you must git your usual face onto you, though
Goodness knows, mine's so crooked, I've often said nothin'
short o' Death'll ever make much change in it—but never mind,
I'll go down a few days to your mother, when you're off,
though I don't promise to do much, except, maybe, cheer her
up a bit; but we'll see, and so remember me to her, and good-
bye!"

With these words and a sharp, bony wring of his hand, Miss
Betsy strode rapidly back to the village. It did not escape Gilbert's eye that, strongly as she had pronounced against his secret
fear, the detection of it had agitated her. She had spoken hurriedly, and hastened away as if desiring to avoid further questions. He could not banish the suspicion that she knew something which might affect his fortune; but she had not forbidden
his love for Martha—she had promised to help him, and that was
a great consolation. His cheerfulness, thenceforth, was not assumed, and he rejoiced to see a very faint, shadowy reflection of
it, at times, in his mother's face.

CHAPTER 15

Alfred Barton Between Two Fires

For some days after Dr. Deane's visit, Old Man Barton was a continual source of astonishment to his son Alfred and his daughter Ann. The signs of gradual decay which one of them, at least, had watched with the keenest interest, had suddenly disappeared; he was brighter, sharper, more talkative than at any time within the previous five years. The almost worn-out machinery of his life seemed to have been mysteriously repaired, whether by Dr. Deane's tinkering, or by one of those freaks of Nature which sometimes bring new teeth and hair to an aged head, neither the son nor the daughter could guess. To the former this awakened activity of the old man's brain was not a little annoying. He had been obliged to renew his note for the money borrowed to replace that which had been transferred to Sandy Flash, and in the meantime was concocting an ingenious device by which the loss should not entirely fall on his own half-share of the farm-profits. He could not have endured his father's tyranny without the delight of the cautious and wary revenges of this kind which he sometimes allowed himself to take.

Another circumstance, which gave him great uneasiness, was this: the old man endeavored in various ways, both direct and indirect, to obtain knowledge of the small investments which he had made from time to time. The most of these had been through the agency of the old lawyer at Chester, consolidated into a first-class mortgage; but it was Alfred's interest to keep his father in ignorance of the other sums, not because of their importance, but because of their insignificance. He knew that the old man's declaration was true—"The more you have, the more you'll get!"

The following Sunday, as he was shaving himself at the back kitchen-window—Ann being upstairs, at her threadbare toilet—

Old Barton, who had been silent during breakfast, suddenly addressed him:

"Well, boy, how stands the matter now?"

The son knew very well what was meant, but he thought it best to ask, with an air of indifference,

"What matter, Daddy?"

"What matter, eh? The colt's lame leg, or the farrow o' the big sow? Gad, boy! don't you ever think about the gal, except when I put it into your head?"

"Oh, that!" exclaimed Alfred, with a smirk of well-assumed satisfaction—"that, indeed! Well, I think I may say, Daddy, that all's right in that quarter."

"Spoken to her yet?"

"N—no, not right out, that is; but since other folks have found out what I'm after, I guess it's plain enough to her. And a good sign is, that she plays a little shy."

"Shouldn't wonder," growled the old man. "Seems to me *you* play a little shy, too. Have to take it in my own hands, if it ever comes to anything."

"Oh, it isn't at all necessary; I can do my own courting," Alfred replied, as he wiped his razor and laid it away.

"Do it, then, boy, in short order! You're too old to stand in need o' much billin' and cooin'—but the gal's rayther young, and may expect it—and I s'pose it's the way. But I'd sooner you'd step up to the Doctor, bein' as I can only take him when he comes here to me loaded and primed. He's mighty cute and sharp, but if you've got any gumption, we'll be even with him."

Alfred turned around quickly and looked at his father.

"Ay, boy, I've had one bout with him, last Sunday, and there's more to come."

"What was it?"

"Set yourself down on that cheer, and keep your head straight a bit, so that what goes into one ear don't fly out at the t'other."

While Alfred, with a singular expression of curiosity and distrust, obeyed this command, the old man deliberated, for the last time, on the peculiar tactics to be adopted, so that his son should be made an ally, as against Dr. Deane, and yet be prevented from becoming a second foe, as against his own property. For it was very evident that while it was the father's interest to exaggerate the son's presumed wealth, it was the latter's interest to underrate it. Thus a third element came into play, making this a triangular game of avarice. If Alfred could have understood his true position, he would have been more courageous; but his father had him at a decided advantage.

"Hark ye, boy!" said he, "I've waited e'en about long enough, and it's time this thing was either a hit or a flash in the pan. The Doctor's ready for 't; for all his cunnin' he couldn't help lettin' me see that; but he tries to cover both pockets with one hand while he stretches out the t'other. The gal's money's safe, ten thousand of it, and we've agreed that it'll be share and share; only, your'n bein' more than her'n, why, of course he must make up the difference."

The son was far from being as shrewd as the father, or he would have instantly chosen the proper tack; but he was like a vessel caught in stays, and experienced considerable internal pitching and jostling. In one sense it was a relief that the old man supposed him to be worth much more than was actually the case, but long experience hinted that a favorable assumption of this kind often led to a damaging result. So with a wink and grin, the miserable hypocrisy of which was evident to his own mind, he said:

"Of course he must make up the difference, and more too! I know what's fair and square."

"Shut your mouth, boy, till I give you leave to open it. Do you hear?—the gal's ten thousand dollars must be put ag'inst the ten thousand you've saved off the profits o' the farm; then, the rest you've made bein' properly accounted for, he must come down with the same amount. Then, you must find out to a hair what he's worth of his own—not that it concerns you, but *I* must know. What you've got to do is about as much as you've wits for. Now, open your mouth!"

"Ten thousand!" exclaimed Alfred, beginning to comprehend the matter more clearly; "why, it's hardly quite ten thousand altogether, let alone anything over!"

"No lies, no lies! I've got it all in my head, if you haven't. Twenty years on shares—first year, one hundred and thirty-seven dollars—that was the year the big flood swep' off half the corn on the bottom; second year, two hundred and fifteen, with interest on the first, say six on a hundred, allowin' the thirty-seven for your squanderin's, two hundred and twenty-one; third year, three hundred and five, with interest, seventeen, makes three hundred and twenty-two, and twenty, your half of the bay horse sold to Sam Falconer, forty-two; fourth year—"

"Never mind, Daddy!" Alfred interrupted; "I've got it all down in my books; you needn't go over it."

The old man struck his hickory staff violently upon the floor. "I *will* go over it!" he croaked, hoarsely. "I mean to show you, boy, to your own eyes and your own ears, that you're now worth thirteen thousand, two hundred and forty-nine dollars and fifteen cents! And ten thousand of it balances the gal's ten thousand, leavin' three thousand two hundred and forty-nine and fifteen cents, for the Doctor to make up to *you*! And you'll show him your papers, for you're no son of mine if you've put out your money without securin' it. I don't mind your goin' your own road with what you've arned, though, for your proper good, you needn't ha' been so close; but now you've got to show what's in your hand, if you mean to git it double!"

Alfred Barton was overwhelmed by the terrors of this unexpected dilemma. His superficial powers of dissimulation forsook him; he could only suggest, in a weak voice:

"Suppose my papers don't show that much?"

"You've made that, or nigh onto it, and your papers *must* show it! If money can't stick to your fingers, do you s'pose I'm goin' to put more into 'em? Fix it any way you like with the Doctor, so you square accounts. Then, afterwards, let him come to me—ay, let him come!"

Here the old man chuckled until he brought on a fit of coughing, which drove the dark purple blood into his head. His son hastened to restore him with a glass of brandy.

"There, that'll do," he said, presently; "now you know what's what. Go up to the Doctor's this afternoon, and have it out before you come home. I can't dance at your weddin', but I wouldn't mind help nuss another grandchild or two—eh, boy?"

"Damme, and so you shall, Dad!" the son exclaimed, relapsing into his customary swagger, as the readiest means of flattering the old man's more amiable mood. It was an easier matter to encounter Dr. Deane—to procrastinate and prolong the settlement of terms, or shift the responsibility of the final result from his own shoulders. Of course, the present command must be obeyed, and it was by no means an agreeable one; but Alfred Barton had courage enough for any emergency not yet arrived. So he began to talk and joke very comfortably about his possible marriage, until Ann, descending to the kitchen in her solemn black gown, interrupted the conference.

That afternoon, as Alfred took his way by the footpath to the village, he seated himself in the shade, on one end of the log which spanned the creek, in order to examine his position, before venturing on a further step. We will not probe the depths of his meditations; probably they were not very deep, even when most serious; but we may readily conjecture those considerations which were chiefly obvious to his mind. The affair, which he had so long delayed, through a powerful and perhaps a natural dread, was now brought to a crisis. He could not retreat without extreme risk to his prospects of inheritance; since his father and Dr. Deane had come to an actual conference, he was forced to assume the part which was appropriate to him. Sentiment, he was aware, would not be exacted, but a certain amount of masculine anticipation belonged to his character of lover; should he assume this, also, or meet Dr. Deane on a hard business ground?

It is a matter of doubt whether any vulgar man suspects the full extent of his vulgarity; but there are few who are not conscious, now and then, of a very uncomfortable difference between themselves and the refined natures with whom they come in contact. Alfred Barton had never been so troubled by this consciousness as when in the presence of Martha Deane. He was afraid of her; he foresaw that she, as his wife, would place him in a more painful subjection than that which his father now enforced. He was weary of bondage, and longed to draw a free, unworried breath. With all his swagger, his life had not always been easy or agreeable. A year or two more might see him, in fact and in truth, his own master. He was fifty years old; his habits of life were fixed; he would have shrunk from the semi-servitude of marriage, though with a woman after his own heart, and there was nothing in this (except the money) to attract him.

"I see no way!" he suddenly exclaimed, after a fit of long and unsatisfactory musing.

"Nor I neither, unless you make room for me!" answered a shrill voice at his side.

He started as if shot, becoming aware of Miss Betsy Lavender, who had just emerged from the thicket.

"Skeered ye, have I?" said she. "Why, how you do color up, to be sure! I never was that red, even in my blushin' days; but never mind, what's said to nobody is nobody's business."

He laughed a forced laugh. "I was thinking, Miss Betsy," he said, "how to get the grain threshed and sent to the mills before prices come down. Which way are you going?"

She had been observing him through half-closed eyes, with her head a little thrown back. First slightly nodding to herself, as if assenting to some mental remark, she asked,

"Which way are *you* going'? For my part I rather think we're changin' places—me to see Miss Ann, and you to see Miss Martha."

"You're wrong!" he exclaimed. "I was only going to make a little neighborly call on the Doctor."

"On the Doctor! Ah-ha! it's come to that, has it? Well, I won't be in the way."

"Confound the witch!" he muttered to himself, as she sprang upon the log and hurried over.

Mr. Alfred Barton was not acquainted with the Greek drama, or he would have had a very real sense of what is meant by fate. As it was, he submitted to circumstances, climbed the hill, and never halted until he found himself in Dr. Deane's sitting room.

Of course, the Doctor was alone and unoccupied; it always happens so. Moreover he knew, and Alfred Barton knew that he knew, the subject to be discussed; but it was not the custom of the neighborhood to approach an important interest except in a very gradual and roundabout manner. Therefore the Doctor said, after the first greeting,

"Thee'll be getting thy crops to market soon, I imagine?"

"I'd like to," Barton replied, "but there's not force enough on our place, and the threshers are wanted everywhere at once. What would you do—hurry off the grain now, or wait to see how it may stand in the spring?"

Dr. Deane meditated a moment, and then answered with great deliberation: "I never like to advise, where the chances are about even. It depends, thee knows, on the prospect of next year's crops. But, whichever way thee decides, it will make less difference to thee than to them that depend altogether upon their yearly earnings."

Barton understood this· stealthy approach to the important subject, and met it in the same way. "I don't know," he said; "it's slow saving on half-profits. I have to look mighty close, to make anything decent."

"Well," said the Doctor, "what isn't laid up *by* thee, is laid up *for* thee, I should judge."

"I should hope so, Doctor; but I guess you know the old man as well as I do. If anybody could tell what's in his mind, it's Lawyer Stacy, and he's as close as a steel-trap. I've hardly had a fair chance, and it ought to be made up to me."

"It will be, no doubt." And then the Doctor, resting his chin upon his cane, relapsed into a grave, silent, expectant mood, which his guest well understood.

"Doctor," he said at last, with an awkward attempt at a gay, confidential manner, "you know what I come for today. Perhaps I'm rather an old boy to be here on such an errand; I've been a bit afraid lest you might think me so; and for that reason I haven't spoken to Martha at all (though I think she's smart enough to guess how my mind turns), and won't speak, till I have first have your leave. I'm not so young as to be light-headed in such matters; and, most likely, I'm not everything that Martha would like; but—but—there's other things to be con-sidered—not that I mind 'em much, only the old man, you know, is very particular about 'em, and so I've come up to see if we can't agree without much trouble."

Dr. Deane took a small pinch of Rappee, and then touched his nose lightly with his lavendered handkerchief. He drew up his hanging underlip until it nearly covered the upper, and lifted his nostrils with an air at once of reticence and wisdom. "I don't deny," he said slowly, "that I've suspected something of what is in thy mind, and I will further say that thee's done right in coming first to me. Martha being an only child, I have her welfare much at heart, and if I had known anything seriously to thy discredit, I would not have permitted thy attentions. So far as that goes, thee may feel easy. I *did* hope, however, that thee would have some assurance of what thy father intends to do for thee—and perhaps thee has—Elisha being established in his own independence, and Ann not requiring a great deal, thee would inherit considerable, besides the farm. And it seems to me that I might justly, in Martha's interest, ask for some such assurance."

If Alfred Barton's secret thought had been expressed in words, it would have been: "Curse the old fool—he knows what the old man is, as well as I do!" But he twisted a respectful hypocrisy out of his whisker, and said,

"Ye-e-es, that seems only fair. How am *I* to get at it, though?

I daren't touch the subject with a ten-foot pole, and yet it stands both to law and reason that I should come in for a handsome slice o' the property. You might take it for granted, Doctor?"

"So I might, if *thy* father would take for granted what *I* might be able to do. I can see, however, that it's hardly thy place to ask him; that might be left to me."

This was an idea which had not occurred to Alfred Barton. A thrill of greedy curiosity shot through his heart; he saw that, with Dr. Deane's help, he might be able to ascertain the amount of the inheritance which must so soon fall to him. This feeling, fed by the impatience of his long subjection, took complete possession of him, and he resolved to further his father's desires, without regard to present results.

"Yes, that might be left to me," the Doctor repeated, "after the other matter is settled. Thee knows what I mean. Martha will have ten thousand dollars in her own right, at twenty-five— and sooner, if she marries with my approbation. Now, thee or thy father must bring an equal sum; that is understood between us—and I think thy father mentioned that thee could do it without calling upon him. Is that the case?"

"Not quite—but, yes, very nearly. That is, the old man's been so close with me, that I'm a little close with him, Doctor, you see! He doesn't know exactly how much I have got, and as he threatens to leave me according to what I've saved, why, I rather let him have his own way about the matter."

A keen, shrewd smile flitted over the Doctor's face.

"But if it isn't quite altogether ten thousand, Doctor," Barton continued, "I don't say but what it could be easily made up to that figure. You and I could arrange all that between our two selves, without consulting the old man—and, indeed, it's not *his* business, in any way—and so, you might go straight to the other matter at once."

"H'm," mused the Doctor, with his chin again upon his stick, "I should perhaps be working in thy interest, as much as in mine. Then thee can afford to come up fair and square to the mark. Of course, thee has all the papers to show for thy own property?"

"I guess there'll be no trouble about that," Barton answered, carelessly. "I lend on none but the best security. 'Twill take a little time—must go to Chester—so we needn't wait for that; 'twill be all right!"

"Oh, no doubt; but hasn't thee overlooked one thing?"

"What?"

"That Martha should first know thy mind towards her."

It was true; he had overlooked that important fact, and the suggestion came to him very like an attack of cramp. He laughed, however, took out a red silk handkerchief, and tried to wipe a little eagerness into his face.

"No, Doctor!" he exclaimed, "not forgot, only keeping the best for the last. I wasn't sure but you might want to speak to her yourself, first; but she knows, doesn't she?"

"Not to my direct knowledge; and I wouldn't like to venture to speak in her name."

"Then, I'll—that is, you think I'd better have a talk with her. A little tough, at my time of life, ha! ha!—but faint heart never won fair lady; and I hadn't thought of going that far today, though of course, I'm anxious—been in my thoughts so long—and perhaps—perhaps—"

"I'll tell thee," said the Doctor, seeming not to notice Barton's visible embarrassment, which he found very natural; "do thee come up again next First-day afternoon, prepared to speak thy mind. I will give Martha a hint of thy purpose beforehand, but only a hint, mind thee; the girl has a smart head of her own, and thee'll come on faster with her if thee pleads thy own cause with thy own mouth."

"Yes, I'll come then!" cried Barton, so relieved at his present escape that his relief took the expression of joy. Dr. Deane was a fair judge of character; he knew all of Alfred Barton's prominent traits, and imagined that he was now reading him like an open book; but it was like reading one of those Latin sentences which, to the ear, are made up of English words. The signs were all correct, only they belonged to another language.

The heavy wooer shortly took his departure. While on the return path, he caught sight of Miss Betsy Lavender's beaver, bobbing along behind the pickets of the hill-fence, and rather than encounter its wearer in his present mood, he stole into the shelter of one of the cross-hedges, and made his way into the timber bottom below.

CHAPTER 16

Martha Deane

Little did Dr. Deane suspect the nature of the conversation which had that morning been held in his daughter's room, between herself and Betsy Lavender.

When the latter returned from her interview with Gilbert Potter the previous evening, she found the Doctor already arrived. Mark came home at supper-time, and the evening was so prolonged by his rattling tongue that no room was left for any confidential talk with Martha, although Miss Betsy felt that something ought to be said, and it properly fell to her lot to broach the delicate subject.

After breakfast on Sunday morning, therefore, she slipped up to Martha's room, on the transparent pretense of looking again at a new dress which had been bought some days before. She held the stuff to the light, turned it this way and that, and regarded it with an importance altogether out of proportion to its value.

"It seems as if I couldn't git the color rightly set in my head," she remarked; " 'ta'n't quiet laylock, nor yit vi'let, and there ought, by rights, to be quilled ribbon round the neck, though the Doctor might consider it too gay; but never mind, he'd dress you in drab or slate if he could, and I dunno, after all—"

"Betsy!" exclaimed Martha, with an impetuousness quite unusual to her calm nature, "throw down the dress! Why won't you speak of what is in your mind; don't you see I'm waiting for it?"

"You're right, child!" Miss Betsy cried, flinging the stuff to the farthest corner of the room; "I'm an awkward old fool, with all my exper'ence. Of course I seen it with half a wink; there! don't be so trembly now. I know how you feel, Martha; you wouldn't think it, but I do. I can tell the real signs from the passin' fancies, and if ever I see true-love in my born days, I see it in you, child, and in *him*."

Martha's face glowed in spite of herself. The recollection of Gilbert's embrace in the dusky glen came to her, already for the thousandth time, but warmer, sweeter at each recurrence. She felt that her hand trembled in that of the spinster, as they sat knee to knee, and that a tender dew was creeping into her eyes; leaning, forward, she laid her face a moment on her friend's shoulder, and whispered,

"It is all very new and strange, Betsy; but I am happy."

Miss Lavender did not answer immediately. With her hand on Martha's soft, smooth hair, she was occupied in twisting her arm so that the sleeve might catch and conceal two troublesome tears which were at that moment trickling down her nose. Besides, she was not at all sure of her voice, until something like a dry crust of bread in her throat had been forcibly swallowed down.

Martha, however, presently lifted her head with a firm, courageous expression, though the rosy flush still suffused her cheeks. "I'm not as independent as people think," she said, "for I couldn't help myself when the time came, and I seem to belong to him, ever since."

"Ever since. Of course you do!" remarked Miss Betsy, with her head down and her hands busy at her high comb and thin twist of hair; "every woman, savin' and exceptin' myself, and no fault o' mine, must play Jill to somebody's Jack; it's man's way and the Lord's way, but worked out with a mighty variety, though I say it, but why not, my eyes bein' as good as anybody else's! Come now, you're lookin' again after your own brave fashion; and so, you're sure o' your heart, Martha?"

"Betsy, my heart speaks once and for all," said Martha, with kindling eyes.

"Once and for all. I knowed it—and so the Lord help us! For here I smell wagon-loads o' trouble; and if you weren't a girl to know her own mind and stick to it, come weal, come woe, and he with a bulldog's jaw that'll never let go, and I mean no runnin' of him down, but on the contràry, quite the reverse, I'd say to both, git over it somehow for it won't be, and no matter if no use, it's my dooty—well, it's t'other way, and I've got to give a lift where I can, and pull this way, and shove that way, and hold back everybody, maybe, and fit things to things, and unfit other things—Good Lord, child, you've made an awful job for *me*!"

Therewith Miss Betsy laughed, with a dry, crisp, cheerfulness which quite covered up and concealed her forebodings. Nothing pleased her better than to see realized in life her own views of what ought to be, and the possibility of becoming one of the shaping and regulating powers to that end stirred her nature to its highest and most joyous activity.

Martha Deane, equally brave, was more sanguine. The joy of her expanding love foretold its fulfillment to her heart. "I know, Betsy," she said, "that Father would not hear of it now; but we are both young and can wait, at least until I come into my property—*ours*, I ought to say, for I think of it already as being as much Gilbert's as mine. What other trouble can there be?"

"Is there none on his side, Martha?"

"His birth? Yes, there is—or was, though not to me—never to me! I am so glad, for his sake—but, Betsy, perhaps you do not know—"

"If there's anything I need to know, I'll find it out, soon or late. He's worried, that I see, and no wonder, poor boy! But as you say, there's time enough, and my single and solitary advice to both o' you is, don't look at one another before folks, if you can't keep your eyes from blabbin'. Not a soul suspicions anything now, and if you two'll only fix it betwixt and between you to keep quiet and patient, and as forbearin' in showin' feelin' as people that hate each other like snakes, why, who knows but somethin' may turn up, all unexpected, to make the way as smooth for ye as a pitch-pine plank!"

"Patient!" Martha murmured to herself. A bright smile broke over her face, as she thought how sweet it would be to match, as best a woman might, Gilbert's incomparable patience and energy of purpose. The tender humility of her love, so beautifully interwoven with the texture of its pride and courage, filled her heart with a balmy softness and peace. She was already prepared to lay her firm, independent spirit at his feet, or exercise it only as her new, eternal duty to him might require. Betsy Lavender's warning could not ripple the bright surface of her happiness; she knew that no one (hardly even Gilbert, as yet) suspected that in her heart the love of a strong and faithful and noble man outweighed all other gifts or consequences of life—

that, to keep it, she would give up home, friends, father, the conventional respect of everyone she knew!

"Well, child!" exclaimed Miss Lavender, after a long lapse of silence; "the words is said that can't be taken back, accordin' to *my* views o' things, though, Goodness knows, there's enough and enough thinks different, and you must abide by 'em; and what I think of it all I'll tell you when the end comes, not before, so don't ask me now; but one thing more, there's another sort of a gust brewin', and goin' to break soon, if ever, and that is, Alf. Barton—though you won't believe it—he's after you in his stupid way, and your father favors him. And my advice is, hold him off as much as you please, but say nothin' o' Gilbert!"

This warning made no particular impression upon Martha. She playfully tapped Miss Betsy's high comb, and said: "Now, if you are going to be so much worried about me, I shall be sorry that you found it out."

"Well I won't!—and now let me hook your gownd."

Often, after that, however, did Martha detect Miss Betsy's eyes fixed upon her with a look of wistful, tender interest, and she knew, though the spinster would not say it, that the latter was alive with sympathy, and happy in the new confidence between them. With each day, her own passion grew and deepened, until it seemed that the true knowledge of love came after its confession. A sweet, warm yearning for Gilbert's presence took its permanent seat in her heart; not only his sterling manly qualities, but his form, his face—the broad, square brow; the large, sad, deep-set gray eyes; the firm, yet impassioned lips—haunted her fancy. Slowly and almost unconsciously as her affection had been developed, it now took the full stature and wore the radiant form of her maiden dream of love.

If Dr. Deane noticed the physical bloom and grace which those days brought to his daughter, he was utterly innocent of the true cause. Perhaps he imagined that his own eyes were first fairly opened to her beauty by the prospect of soon losing her. Certainly she had never seemed more obedient and attractive. He had not forgotten his promise to Alfred Barton; but no very convenient opportunity for speaking to her on the subject occurred until the following Sunday morning. Mark was not at home, and he rode with her to Old Kennett Meeting.

As they reached the top of the long hill beyond the creek, Martha reined in her horse to enjoy the pleasant westward view over the fair September landscape. The few houses of the village crowned the opposite hill; but on this side the winding, wooded vale meandered away, to lose itself among the swelling slopes of clover and stubble-field; and beyond, over the blue level of Tuffkenamon, the oak-woods of Avondale slept on the horizon. It was a landscape such as one may see, in a more cultured form, on the road from Warwick to Stratford. Every one in Kennett enjoyed the view, but none so much as Martha Deane, upon whom its harmonious, pastoral aspect exercised an indescribable charm.

To the left, on the knoll below, rose the chimneys of the Barton farmhouse, over the round tops of the apple trees, and in the nearest field Mr. Alfred's Maryland cattle were fatterning on the second growth of clover.

"A nice place, Martha!" said Dr. Deane, with a wave of his arm, and a whiff of sweet herbs.

"Here, in this first field, is the true place for the house," she answered, thinking only of the landscape beauty of the farm.

"Does thee mean so?" the Doctor eagerly asked, deliberating with himself how much of his plan it was safe to reveal. "Thee may be right, and perhaps thee might bring Alfred to thy way of thinking."

She laughed. "It's hardly worth the trouble."

"I've noticed, of late," her father continued, "that Alfred seems to set a good deal of store by thee. He visits us pretty often."

"Why, Father!" she exclaimed, as they rode onward, "it's rather *thee* that attracts him, and cattle, and crops, and the plans for catching Sandy Flash! He looks frightened whenever I speak to him."

"A little nervous, perhaps. Young men are often so, in the company of young women, I've observed."

Martha laughed so cheerily that her father said to himself: "Well, it doesn't displease her, at any rate." On the other hand, it was possible that she might have failed to see Barton in the light of a wooer, and therefore a further hint would be required.

"Now that we happen to speak of him, Martha," he said, "I might as well tell thee that, in my judgment, he seems to be drawn towards thee in the way of marriage. He may be a little awkward in showing it, but that's a common case. When he was at our house, last First-day, he spoke of thee frequently, and said that he would like to—well, to see thee soon. I believe he intends coming up this afternoon."

Martha became grave, as Betsy Lavender's warning took so suddenly a positive form. However, she had thought of this contingency as a possible thing, and must prepare herself to meet it with firmness.

"What does thee say?" the Doctor asked, after waiting a few minutes for an answer.

"Father, I hope thee's mistaken. Alfred Barton is not overstocked with wit, I know, but he can hardly be that foolish. He is almost as old as thee."

She spoke quietly, but with that tone of decision which Dr. Deane so well knew. He set his teeth and drew up his underlip to a grim pout. If there was to be resistance, he thought, she would not find him so yielding as on other points; but he would first try a middle course.

"Understand me, Martha," he said; "I do not mean to declare what Alfred Barton's sentiments really are, but what, in my judgment, they *might* be. And thee had better wait and learn, before setting thy mind either for or against him. It's hardly putting much value upon thyself, to call him foolish."

"It is a humiliation to me, if thee is right, Father," she said.

"I don't see that. Many young women would be proud of it. I'll only say one thing, Martha; if he seeks thee, and *does* speak his mind, do thee treat him kindly and respectfully."

"Have I ever treated thy friends otherwise?" she asked.

"My friends! thee's right—he *is* my friend."

She made no reply, but her soul was already courageously arming itself for battle. Her father's face was stern and cold, and she saw, at once, that he was on the side of the enemy. This struggle safely over, there would come another and a severer one. It was well that she had given herself time, setting the fulfilment of her love so far in advance.

Nothing more was said on this theme, either during the ride to Old Kennett, or on the return. Martha's plan was very simple: she would quietly wait until Alfred Barton should declare his sentiments, and then reject him once and forever. She would speak clearly, and finally; there should be no possibility of misconception. It was not a pleasant task; none but a vain and heartless woman would be eager to assume it; and Martha Deane hoped that it might be spared her.

But she, no less than her irresolute lover (if we can apply that word to Alfred Barton), was an instrument in the hands of an uncomfortable fate. Soon after dinner a hesitating knock was heard at the door, and Barton entered with a more uneasy air than ever before. Erelong, Dr. Deane affected to have an engagement with an invalid on the New-Garden road; Betsy Lavender had gone to Fairthorn's for the afternoon, and the two were alone.

For a few moments, Martha was tempted to follow her father's example, and leave Alfred Barton to his own devices. Then she reflected that this was a cowardly feeling; it would only postpone her task. He had taken his seat, as usual, in the very centre of the room; so she came forward and seated herself at the front window, with her back to the light, thus, woman-like, giving herself all the advantages of position.

Having his large, heavy face before her, in full light, she was at first a little surprised on finding that it expressed not even the fond anxiety, much less the eagerness, of an aspiring wooer. The hair and whiskers, it is true, were so smoothly combed back that they made long lappets on either side of his face; unusual care had been taken with his cambric cravat and shirt-ruffles, and he wore his best blue coat, which was entirely too warm for the season. In strong contrast to this external preparation, were his restless eyes which darted hither and thither in avoidance of her gaze, the fidgety movements of his thick fingers, creeping around buttons and in and out of buttonholes, and finally the silly, embarrassed half-smile which now and then came to his mouth and made the platitudes of his speech almost idiotic.

Martha Deane felt her courage rise as she contemplated this picture. In spite of the disgust which his gross physical appearance, and the contempt which his awkward helplessness inspired, she was conscious of a lurking sense of amusement. Even a curiosity, which we cannot reprehend, to know by what steps and in what manner he would come to the declaration, began to steal into her mind, now that it was evident her answer could not possibly wound any other feeling than vanity.

In this mood, she left the burden of the conversation to him. He might flounder, or be completely stalled, as often as he pleased; it was no part of her business to help him.

In about three minutes after she had taken her seat by the window, he remarked, with a convulsive smile,

"Apples are going to be good, this year."

"Are they?" she said.

"Yes; do you like 'em? Most girls do."

"I believe I do—except russets," Martha replied, with her hands clasped in her lap, and her eyes full upon his face.

He twisted the smoothness out of one whisker, very much disconcerted at her remark, because he could not tell—he never could, when speaking with her—whether or not she was making fun of him. But he could think of nothing to say, except his own preferences in the matter of apples—a theme which he pursued until Martha was very tired of it.

He next asked after Mark Deane, expressing at great length his favorable opinion of the young carpenter, and relating what pains he had taken to procure for him the building of Hallowell's barn. But to each observation Martha made the briefest possible replies, so that in a short time he was forced to start another topic.

Nearly an hour had passed, and Martha's sense of the humorous had long since vanished under the dreary monotony of the conversation, when Alfred Barton seemed to have come to a desperate resolution to end his embarrassment. Grasping his knees with both hands, and dropping his head forward so that the arrows of her eyes might glance from his fat forehead, he said,

"I suppose you know why I come here today, Miss Martha?"

All her powers were awake and alert in a moment. She scrutinized his face keenly, and, although his eyes were hidden, there were lines enough visible, especially about the mouth, to show that the bitter predominated over the sweet in his emotions.

"To see my father, wasn't it? I'm sorry he was obliged to leave home," she answered.

"No, Miss Martha, I come to see you. I have something to say to you, and I'm sure you know what I mean by this time, don't you?"

"No. How should I?" She coolly replied. It was not true; but the truest-hearted woman that ever lived could have given no other answer.

Alfred Barton felt the sensation of a groan pass through him, and it very nearly came out of his mouth. Then he pushed on, in a last wild effort to perform the remainder of his exacted task in one piece:

"I want you to be—to be—my—wife! That is, my father and yours are agreed about it, and they think I ought to speak to you. I'm a good deal older, and—and perhaps you mightn't fancy me in all things, but they say it'll make little difference; and if you haven't thought about it much, why, there's no hurry as to making up your mind. I've told you now, and to be sure you ought to know, while the old folks are trying to arrange property matters, and it's my place, like, to speak to you first."

Here he paused; his face was very red, and the perspiration was oozing in great drops from every pore. He drew forth the huge red silk handkerchief, and mopped his cheeks, his nose, and his forehead; then lifted his head and stole a quick glance at Martha. Something in his face puzzled her, and yet a sudden presentiment of his true state of feeling flashed across her mind. She still sat, looking steadily at him, and for a few moments did not speak.

"Well?" he stammered.

"Alfred Barton," she said, "I must ask you one question; do you love me?"

He seemed to feel a sharp sting; The muscles of his mouth twitched; he bit his lip, sank his head again, and murmured,

"Y—yes."

"He does not," she said to herself. "I am spared this humiliation. It is a mean, low nature, and fears mine—fears, and would soon hate. He shall not see even so much of me as would be revealed by a frank, respectful rejection. I must punish him a little for the deceit, and I now see how to do it."

While these thoughts passed rapidly through her brain, she waited until he should again venture to meet her eye. When he lifted his head, she exclaimed,

"You have told an untruth! Don't turn your head away; look me in the face, and hear me tell you that you do not love me—that you have not come to me of your own desire, and that you would rather ten thousand times I should say No, if it were not for a little property of mine! But suppose I, too, were of a similar nature; suppose I cared not for what is called love, but only for money and lands such as you will inherit; suppose I found the plans of my father and your father very shrewd and reasonable, and were disposed to enter into them—what then?"

Alfred Barton was surprised out of the last remnant of his hypocrisy. His face, so red up to this moment, suddenly became sallow; his chin dropped, and an expression of amazement and fright came into the eyes fixed on Martha's.

The game she was playing assumed a deeper interest; here was something which she could not yet fathom. She saw what influence had driven him to her, against his inclination, but his motive for seeming to obey, while dreading success, was a puzzle. Singularly enough, a slight feeling of commiseration began to soften her previous contempt, and hastened her final answer.

"I see that these suppositions would not please you," she said, "and thank you for the fact. Your face is more candid than your speech. I am now ready to say, Alfred Barton— because I am sure the knowledge will be agreeable to you—that no lands, no money, no command of my father, no degree of want, or misery, or disgrace, could ever make me your wife!"

She had risen from her chair while speaking, and he also started to his feet. Her words, though such an astounding relief in one sense, had nevertheless given him pain; there was a sting in them which cruelly galled his self-conceit. It was enough to be rejected; she need not have put an eternal gulf between their natures.

"Well," said he, sliding the rim of his beaver backwards and forwards between his fingers, "I suppose I'll have to be going. You're very plain-spoken, as I might ha' known. I doubt whether we two would make a good team, and no offense to you, Miss Martha. Only, it'll be a mortal disappointment to the old man, and—look here, it a'n't worth while to say anything about it, is it?"

Alfred Barton was strongly tempted to betray the secret reason which Martha had not yet discovered. After the strong words he had taken from her, she owed him a kindness, he thought; if she would only allow the impression that the matter was still undecided—that more time (which a coy young maiden might reasonably demand) had been granted! On the other hand, he feared that her clear, firm integrity of character would be repelled by the nature of his motive. He was beginning to feel, greatly to his own surprise, a profound respect for her.

"If my father questions me about your visit," she said, "I shall tell him simply that I have declined your offer. No one else is likely to ask me."

"I don't deny," he continued, still lingering near the door, "that I've been urged by my father—yours, too, for that matter

—to make the offer. But I don't want you to think hard of me. I've not had an easy time of it, and if you knew everything, you'd see that a good deal isn't rightly to be laid to my account."

He spoke sadly, and so genuine a stamp of unhappiness was impressed upon his face, that Martha's feeling of commiseration rose to the surface.

"You'll speak to me, when we happen to meet?" he said.

"If I did not," she answered, "everyone would suspect that something had occurred. That would be unpleasant for both of us. Do not think that I shall bear malice against you; on the contrary, I wish you well."

He stooped, kissed her hand, and then swiftly, silently, and with averted head, left the room.

CHAPTER 17

·   Consultations

When Dr. Deane returned home, in season for supper, he found Martha and Betsy Lavender employed about their little household matters. The former showed no lack of cheerfulness or composure, nor, on the other hand, any such nervous unrest as would be natural to a maiden whose hand had just been asked in marriage. The Doctor could not at all guess, from her demeanor, whether anything had happened during his absence. That Alfred Barton had not remained was rather an unfavorable circumstance; but then, possibly, he had not found courage to speak. All things being considered, it seemed best that he should say nothing to Martha, until he had had another interview with his prospective son-in-law.

At this time Gilbert Potter, in ignorance of the cunning plans which were laid by the old men, was working early and late to accomplish all necessary farm labor by the first of October. That month he had resolved to devote to the road between Columbia and Newport, and if but average success attended his hauling, the earnings of six round trips, with the result of his bountiful harvest, would at last place in his hands the sum necessary to defray the remaining debt upon the farm. His next year's wheat-crop was already sowed, the seed-clover cut, and the fortnight which still intervened was to be devoted to threshing. In this emergency, as at reaping-time, when it was difficult to obtain extra hands, he depended on Deb. Smith, and she did not fail him.

Her principal home, when she was not employed on farm-work, was a log hut on the edge of a wood belonging to the next farm north of Fairthorn's. This farm—the "Woodrow property," as it was called—had been stripped of its stock and otherwise pillaged by the British troops (Howe and Cornwallis having had their headquarters at Kennett Square), the day previous to the Battle of Brandywine, and the proprietor had never since recovered from his losses. The place presented a ruined and desolated appearance, and Deb. Smith, for that reason perhaps, had settled herself in the original log cabin of the first settler, beside a swampy bit of ground near the road. The Woodrow farmhouse was on a ridge beyond the wood, and no other dwelling was in sight.

The mysterious manner of life of this woman had no doubt given rise to the bad name which she bore in the neighborhood. She would often disappear for a week or two at a time, and her return seemed to take place invariably in the night. Sometimes a belated farmer would see the single front window of her cabin lighted at midnight, and hear the dulled sound of voices in the stillness. But no one cared to play the spy upon her movements very closely; her great strength and fierce, reckless temper made her dangerous, and her hostility would have been worse than the itching of ungratified curiosity. So they let her alone, taking the revenge in the character they ascribed to her, and the epithets they attached to her name.

When Gilbert, after hitching his horse in a corner of the zig-zag picket-fence, climbed over and approached the cabin, Deb. Smith issued from it to meet him, closing the heavy plank door carefully behind her.

"So, Mr. Gilbert!" she cried, stretching out her hard, red hand, "I reckon you want me ag'in. I've been holdin' off from many jobs o' thrashin', this week, because I suspicioned ye'd be comin' for me."

"Thank you, Deborah!" said he, "you're a friend in need."

"Am I? There you speak the truth. Wait till you see me thump the Devil's tattoo with my old flail on your thrashin'-floor! But you look as cheery as an Easter-mornin' sun; you've not much for to complain of, these days, I guess?"

Gilbert smiled.

"Take care!" she cried, a kindly softness spreading over her rough face, "good luck's deceitful! If I had the strands o' your fortin' in *my* hands, maybe I wouldn't twist 'em even; but I ha'n't, and my fingers is too thick to manage anything smaller'n a rope-knot. You're goin'? Well, look out for me bright and early o' Monday, and my sarvice to your mother!"

As he rode over the second hill, on his way to the village,

Gilbert's heart leaped, as he beheld Betsy Lavender just turning into Fairthorn's gate. Except his mother, she was the only person who knew of his love, and he had great need of her kind and cautious assistance.

He had not allowed his heart simply to revel in the ecstasy of its wonderful fortune, or to yearn with inexpressible warmth for Martha's dearest presence, though these emotions haunted him constantly; he had also endeavored to survey the position in which he stood, and to choose the course which would fulfill both his duty towards her and towards his mother. His coming independence would have made the prospect hopefully bright, but for the secret which lay across it like a threatening shadow. Betsy Lavender's assurances had only partially allayed his dread; something hasty and uncertain in her manner still lingered uneasily in his memory, and he felt sure that she knew more than she was willing to tell. Moreover, he craved with all the strength of his heart for another interview with Martha, and he knew of no way to obtain it without Betsy's help.

Her hand was on the gate-latch when his call reached her ears. Looking up the road, she saw that he had stopped his horse between the high, bushy banks, and was beckoning earnestly. Darting a hasty glance at the ivy-draped windows nearest the road, and finding that she was not observed, she hurried to meet him.

"Betsy," he whispered, "I *must* see Martha again before I leave, and you must tell me how."

"Tell me how. Folks say that lovyers' wits are sharp," said she, "but I wouldn't give much for either o' your'n. I don't like underhanded goin's-on, for my part, for things done in darkness'll come to light, or somethin' like it; but never mind, if they're crooked everyway they won't run in straight tracks, all 't once't. This I see, and you see, and she sees, that we must all keep as dark as sin."

"But there must be some way," Gilbert insisted. "Do you never walk out together? And couldn't we arrange a time—you, too, Betsy, I want you as well!"

"I'm afeard I'd be like the fifth wheel to a wagon."

"No, no! You must be there—you must hear a good part of what I have to say."

"A good part—that'll do; thought you didn't mean the whole. Don't fret so, lad; you'll have Roger trampin' me down, next thing. Martha and me talk o' walkin' over to Polly Withers's. She promised Martha a pa'tridge-breasted aloe, and they say you've got to plant it in pewter sand, and only water it once't a month, and how it can grow I can't see; but never mind, all the same—s'pose we say Friday afternoon about three o'clock, goin' through the big woods between the Square and Witherses, and you might have a gun, for the squirls is plenty, and so acciden-tal-like, if anybody should come along—"

"That's it, Betsy!" Gilbert cried, his face flashing, "thank you, a thousand times!"

"A thousand times," she repeated. "Once't is enough."

Gilbert rode homewards, after a pleasant call at Fairthorn's, in a very joyous mood. Not daring to converse with his mother on the one subject which filled his heart, he showed her the calcula-tions which positively assured his independence in a short time. She was never weary of going over the figures, and although her sad, cautious nature always led her to anticipate disappoint-ments, there was now so much already in hand that she was forced to share her son's sanguine views. Gilbert could not help noticing that this idea of independence, for which she had la-bored so strenuously, seemed to be regarded, in her mind, as the first step towards her mysterious and long-delayed justification; she was so impatient for its accomplishment, her sad brow light-ened so, her breath came so much freer as she admitted that his calculations were correct!

Nevertheless, as he frequently referred to the matter, on the following days, she at last said,

"Please, Gilbert, don't always talk so certainly of what isn't over and settled! It makes me fearsome, so to take Providence for granted beforehand. I don't think the Lord likes it, for I've often noticed that it brings disappointment; and I'd rather be humble and submissive in heart, and better to deserve our good fortune when it comes."

"You may be right, mother," he answered; "but it's pleasant to me to see you looking a little more hopeful."

"Ay, lad, I'd never look otherwise, for your sake, if I could." And nothing more was said.

Before sunrise on Monday morning, the rapid, alternate beats of three flails on Gilbert's threshing-floor made the autumnal music which the farmer loves to hear. Two of these—Gilbert's and Sam's—kept time with each other, one falling as the other rose; but the third—quick, loud, and filling all the pauses with thundering taps—was wielded by the arm of Deb. Smith. Day by day, the pile of wheat-sheaves lessened in the great bay, and the cone of golden straw rose higher in the barnyard. If a certain black jug behind the barn door needed frequent replenishing, Gilbert knew that the strength of its contents passed into the red, bare, muscular arms which shamed his own, and that Deb., while she was under his roof, would allow herself no coarse excess, either of manner or speech. The fierce, defiant look left her face, and when she sat, of an evening, with her pipe in the chimney-corner, both mother and son found her very entertaining company. In Sam she inspired at once admiration and despair. She could take him by the slack of the waistband and lift him at arm's-length, and he felt that he should never be "a full hand," if he were obliged to equal her performances with the flail.

Thus, his arm keeping time to the rhythm of joy in his heart, and tasting the satisfaction of labor as never before in his life, the days passed to Gilbert Potter. Then came the important Friday, hazy with "the smoke of burning summer," and softly colored with the drifts of goldenrods and crimson sumac leaves along the edges of the yet green forests. Easily feigning an errand to the village, he walked rapidly up the road in the warm afternoon, taking the crossroad to New-Garden just before reaching Hallowell's, and then struck to the right across the fields.

After passing the crest of the hill, the land sloped gradually down to the eastern end of Tuffkenamon valley, which terminates at the ridge upon which Kennett Square stands. Below him, on the right, lay the field and hedge, across which he and Fortune (he wondered what had become of the man) had followed the chase; and before him, on the level, rose the stately trees of the wood which was to be his trysting-place. It was a sweet, peaceful scene, and but for the undercurrent of trouble upon which all his sensations floated, he could have recognized the beauty and the bliss of human life which such golden days suggest.

It was scarcely yet two o'clock, and he watched the smooth field nearest the village for full three-quarters of an hour before his sharp eyes could detect any moving form upon its surface. To impatience succeeded doubt, to doubt, at its most cruel height, a shock of certainty. Betsy Lavender and Martha Deane had entered the field at the bottom, and, concealed behind the hedge of blackthorn, had walked halfway to the wood before he discovered them, by means of a lucky break in the hedge. With breathless haste he descended the slope, entered the wood at its lower edge, and traversed the tangled thickets of dogwood and haw, until he gained the footpath winding through the very heart of the shade.

It was not many minutes before the two advancing forms glimmered among the leaves. As he sprang forward to meet them, Miss Betsy Lavender suddenly exclaimed, "Well, I never, Martha! here's wintergreen!" and was down on her knees, on the dead leaves, with her long nose nearly touching the plants.

When the lovers saw each other's eyes, one impulse drew them heart to heart. Each felt the clasp of the other's arms, and the sweetness of that perfect kiss, which is mutually given, as mutually taken—the ripe fruit of love, which having once tasted, all its first timid tokens seem ever afterwards immature and unsatisfactory. The hearts of both had unconsciously grown in warmth, in grace and tenderness; and they now felt, for the first time, the utter, reciprocal surrender of their natures which truly gave them to each other.

As they slowly unwound the blissful embrace, and, holding each other's hands, drew their faces apart until either's eyes could receive the other's beloved countenance, no words were spoken—and none were needed. Thenceforward, neither would ever say to the other, "Do you love me as well as ever?" or "Are you sure you can never change?"—for theirs were natures to which such tender doubt and curiosity were foreign. It was not the age of introversion or analytical love; they were sound, simple, fervent natures, and believed forever in the great truth which had come to them.

"Gilbert," said Martha, presently, "it was right that we should meet before you leave home. I have much to tell you—for now you must know everything that concerns me; it is your right."

Her words were very grateful. To hear her say "It is your right," sent a thrill of purely unselfish pride through his breast. He admitted an equal right, on her part; the moments were precious, and he hastened to answer her declaration by one as frank and confiding.

"And I," he said, "could not take another step until I had seen you. Do not fear, Martha, to test my patience or my faith in you, for anything you may put upon me will be easy to bear. I have turned our love over and over in my mind; tried to look at it—as we both must, sooner or later—as something which, though it don't in any wise belong to others, yet with which others have the power to interfere. The world isn't made quite right, Martha, and we're living in it."

Martha's lip took a firmer curve. "Our love is right, Gilbert," she exclaimed, "and the world must give way!"

"It must—I've sworn it! Now let us try to see what are the mountains in our path, and how we can best get around or over them. First, this is my position."

Thereupon Gilbert clearly and rapidly explained to her his precise situation. He set forth his favorable prospects of speedy independence, the obstacle which his mother's secret threw in their way, and his inability to guess any means which might unravel the mystery, and hasten his and her deliverance. The disgrace once removed, he thought, all other impediments to their union would be of trifling importance.

"I see all that clearly," said Martha, when he had finished; "now, this is *my* position."

She told him frankly her father's plans concerning her, and gave him, with conscientious minuteness, all the details of Alfred Barton's interview. At first his face grew dark, but at the close he was able to view the subject in its true character, and to contemplate it with as careless a merriment as her own.

"You see, Gilbert," were Martha's final words, "how we are situated. If I marry, against my father's consent, before I am twenty-five—"

"Don't speak of your property, Martha!" he cried; "I never took that into mind!"

"I know you didn't, Gilbert, but *I* do! It is mine, and must be mine, to be yours; here you must let me have my own way—I will obey you in everything else. Four years is not long for us to wait, having faith in each other; and in that time, I doubt not, your mother's secret will be revealed. You cannot, must not, press her further; in the meantime we will see each other as often as possible—"

"Four years!" Gilbert interrupted, in a tone almost of despair.

"Well—not quite," said Martha, smiling archly; "since you must know my exact age, Gilbert, I was twenty-one on the second of last February; so that the time is really three years, four months, and eleven days."

"I'd serve seven years, as Jacob served, if need be," he said. "It's not alone the waiting; it's the anxiety, the uncertainty, the terrible fear of that which I don't know. I'm sure that Betsy Lavender guesses something about it; have you told her what my mother says?"

"It was *your* secret, Gilbert."

"I didn't think," he answered, softly. "But it's well she should know. She is the best friend we have. Betsy!"

"A mortal long time afore *I'm* wanted!" exclaimed Miss Lavender, with assumed grimness, as she obeyed the call. "I s'pose you thought there was no watch needed, and both ends o' the path open to all the world. Well—what am *I* to do?—move mountains like a grain o' mustard-seed (or however it runs), dip out th' ocean with a pint-pot, or ketch old birds with chaff, eh?"

Gilbert, aware that she was familiar with the particular difficulties on Martha's side, now made her acquainted with his own. At the mention of his mother's declaration in regard to his birth, she lifted her hands and nodded her head, listening, thenceforth to the end, with half-closed eyes and her loose lips drawn up in a curious pucker.

"What do you think of it?" he asked as she remained silent.

"Think of it? About as pretty a snarl as ever I see. I can't say as I'm so over and above taken aback by what your mother says. I've all along had a hankerin' suspicion of it in my bones. Some things seems to me like the smell o' watermelons, that I've knowed to come with fresh snow; you know there *is* no watermelons, but then, there's the smell of 'em! But it won't do to hurry a matter o' this kind—long-sufferin' and slow to anger, though that don't quite suit, but never mind, all the same my opinion is, ye've both o' ye got to wait!"

"Betsy, do you know nothing about it? Can you guess nothing?" Gilbert persisted.

She stole a quick glance at Martha, which he detected, and a chill ran through his blood. His face grew pale.

"Nothin' that fits your case," said Miss Lavender, presently. She saw the renewal of Gilbert's suspicion, and was casting about in her mind how to allay it without indicating something else which she wished to conceal. "This I'll say," she exclaimed at last, with desperate frankness, "that I *do* know somethin' that may be o' use, when things comes to the wust, as I hope they won't, but it's neither here nor there so far as *you two* are concerned; so don't ask me, for I won't tell, and if it's to be done, *I'm* the only one to do it! If I've got my little secrets, I'm keepin' 'em in your interest, remember that!"

There was the glimmer of a tear in each of Miss Lavender's eyes before she knew it.

"Betsy, my dear friend!" cried Gilbert, "we know you and trust you. Only say this, for my sake—that you think my mother's secret is nothing which will part Martha and me!"

"Martha and me. I *do* think so—am I a dragon, or a—what's that Job talks about?—a behemoth? It's no use; we must all wait and see what'll turn up. But, Martha, I've rather a bright thought, for a wonder; what if we could bring Alf. Barton into the plot, and git him to help us for the sake o' *his* bein' helped?"

Martha looked surprised, but Gilbert flushed up to the roots of his hair, and set his lips firmly together.

"I dunno as it'll do," continued Miss Betsy, with perfect indifference to these signs, "but then it *might*. First and foremost, we must try to find out what he wants, for it isn't you, Martha; so you, Gilbert, might as well be a little more of a cowcumber than you are at this present moment. But if it's nothin' ag'inst the law, and not likely, for he's too cute, we might even use a vessel—well, not exackly o' wrath, but somethin' like it. There's more'n one concern at work in all this, it strikes *me*, and it's wuth while to know 'em all."

Gilbert was ashamed of his sensitiveness in regard to Barton, especially after Martha's frank and merry confession; so he declared himself entirely willing to abide by her judgment.

"It would not be pleasant to have Alfred Barton associated with us, even in the way of help," she said. "I have a woman's curiosity to know what he means, I confess; but, unless Betsy could make the discovery without me, I would not take any steps towards it."

"Much would be fittin' to me, child," said Miss Lavender, "that wouldn't pass for you, at all. We've got six weeks till Gilbert comes back, and no need o' hurry, except our arrand to

Polly Withers's, which'll come to nothin', unless you each take leave of other mighty quick, while I'm lookin' for some more wintergreen."

With these words she turned short around and strode away.

"It had best be our own secret yet, Martha?" he asked.

"Yes, Gilbert, and all the more precious."

They clasped hands and kissed, once, twice, thrice, and then the underwood slowly deepened between them and the shadows of the forest separated them from each other.

CHAPTER 18

Sandy Flash Reappears

During the month of October, while Gilbert Potter was occupied with his lonely and monotonous task, he had ample
leisure to evolve a clear, calm, happy purpose from the tumult
of his excited feelings. This was, first, to accomplish his own
independence, which now seemed inevitably necessary, for his
mother's sake, and its possible consequences to her; then, strong
in the knowledge of Martha Deane's fidelity, to wait with her.

With the exception of a few days of rainy weather, his hauling prospered, and he returned home after five weeks' absence,
to count up the gains of the year and find that very little was
lacking of the entire amount to be paid.

Mary Potter, as the prospect of release drew so near, became
suddenly anxious and restless. The knowledge that a very large
sum of money (as she considered it) was in the house, filled her
with a thousand new fears. There were again rumors of Sandy
Flash lurking around Marlborough, and she shuddered and trembled whenever his name was mentioned. Her uneasiness became
at last so great that Gilbert finally proposed writing to the conveyancer in Chester who held the mortgage, and asking whether
the money might not as well be paid at once, since he had it in
hand, as wait until the following spring.

"It's not the regular way," said she, "but then, I suppose it'll
hold in law. You can ask Mr. Trainer about that. O Gilbert, if it
can be done, it'll take a great load off my mind!"

"Whatever puts the mortgage into my hands, Mother," said
he, "is legal enough for us. I needn't even wait to sell the grain;
Mark Deane will lend me the seventy-five dollars still to be made
up, if he has them—or, if he can't, somebody clsc will. I was
going to the Square this evening; so I'll write the letter at once,
and put it in the office."

The first thing Gilbert did, on reaching the village, was to post the letter in season for the mail-rider, who went once a week to and fro between Chester and Peach-bottom Ferry, on the Susquehanna. Then he crossed the street to Dr. Deane's, in order to inquire for Mark, but with the chief hope of seeing Martha for one sweet moment, at least. In this, however, he was disappointed; as he reached the gate, Mark issued from the door.

"Why, Gilbert, old boy!" he shouted; "the sight o' you's good for sore eyes! What have you been about since that Sunday evening we rode up the west branch? I was jist steppin' over to the tavern to see the fellows—come along, and have a glass o' rye!"

He threw his heavy arm over Gilbert's shoulder, and drew him along.

"In a minute, Mark; wait a bit—I've a little matter of business with you. I need to borrow seventy-five dollars for a month or six weeks, until my wheat is sold. Have you that much that you're not using?"

"That and more comin' to me soon," said Mark, "and of course you can have it. Want it right away?"

"Very likely in ten or twelve days."

"Oh, well, never fear—I'll have some accounts squared by that time! Come along!" And therewith the good-natured fellow hurried his friend into the barroom of the Unicorn.

"Done pretty well, haulin', this time?" asked Mark, as they touched glasses.

"Very well," answered Gilbert, "seeing it's the last time. I'm at an end with hauling now."

"You don't say so? Here's to your good luck!" exclaimed Mark, emptying his glass.

A man, who had been tilting his chair against the wall, in the farther corner of the room, now arose and came forward. It was Alfred Barton.

During Gilbert's absence, neither this gentleman's plan nor that of his father, had made much progress. It was tolerably easy, to be sure, to give the old man the impression that the preliminary arrangements with regard to money were going on harmoniously; but it was not so easy to procure Dr. Deane's acceptance of the part marked out for him. Alfred had sought an interview with the latter soon after that which he had had with Martha, and the result was not at all satisfactory. The wooer had been obliged to declare that his suit was unsuccessful; but, he believed, only temporarily so. Martha had been taken by surprise; the question had come upon her so suddenly that she could scarcely be said to know her own mind, and time must be allowed her. Although this statement seemed probable to Dr. Deane, as it coincided with his own experience in previously sounding his daughter's mind, yet Alfred's evident anxiety that nothing should be said to Martha upon the subject, and that the Doctor should assume to his father that the question of balancing her legacy was a good as settled (then proceed at once to the discussion of the second and more important question), excited the Doctor's suspicions. He could not well avoid giving the required promise in relation to Martha, but he insisted on seeing the legal evidences of Alfred Barton's property before going a step further.

The latter was therefore in a state of great perplexity. The game he was playing seemed safe enough, so far, but nothing had come of it, and beyond this point it could not be carried, without great increase of risk. He was more than once tempted to drop it entirely, confessing his complete and final rejection, and allowing his father to take what course he pleased; but presently the itching of his avaricious curiosity returned in full force, and suggested new expedients.

No suspicion of Gilbert Potter's relation to Martha Deane had ever entered his mind. He had always had a liking for the young man, and would, no doubt, have done him any good service which did not require the use of money. He now came forward very cordially and shook hands with the two.

Gilbert had self-possession enough to control his first impulse, and to meet his rival with his former manner. Secure in his own fortune, he even felt that he could afford to be magnanimous, and thus, by degrees, the dislike wore off which Martha's confession had excited.

"What is all this talk about Sandy Flash?" he asked.

"He's been seen up above," said Barton; "some say, about Marlborough, and some, along the Strasburg road. He'll hardly come this way; he's too cunning to go where the people are prepared to receive him."

If either of the three had happened to look steadily at the back window of the barroom, they might have detected, in the dusk, the face of Dougherty, the Irish ostler of the Unicorn

Tavern. It disappeared instantly, but there was a crack nearly half an inch wide between the bottom of the back door and the sill under it, and to that crack a large, flat ear was laid.

"If he comes any nearer, you must send word around at once," said Gilbert—"not wait until he's already among us."

"Let me alone for that!" Barton exclaimed; "Damn him, I only wish he had pluck enough to come!"

Mark was indignant. "What's the sheriff and constables good for?" he cried. "It's a burnin' shame that the whole country has been plundered so long, and the fellow still runnin' at large. Much he cares for the five hundred dollars on his head."

"It's a thousand, now," said Barton. "They've doubled it."

"Come, that'd be a good haul for us. We're not bound to keep inside of our township; I'm for an up-and-down chase all over the country, as soon as the fall work's over!"

"And I, too," said Gilbert.

"You're fellows after my own heart, both o' you!" Barton asserted, slapping them upon the back. "What'll you take to drink?"

By this time several others had assembled, and the conversation became general. While the flying rumors about Sandy Flash were being produced and discussed, Barton drew Gilbert aside.

"Suppose we step out on the back porch," he said, "I want to have a word with you."

The door closed between them and the noisy barroom. There was a rustling noise under the porch, as of a fowl disturbed on its roost, and then everything was still.

"Your speaking of your having done well by hauling put it into my head, Gilbert," Barton continued. "I wanted to borrow a little money for a while, and there's reasons why I shouldn't call upon anybody who'd tell of it. Now, as you've got it, lying idle—"

"It happens to be just the other way, Barton," said Gilbert, interrupting him. "I came here tonight to borrow."

"How's that?" Barton could not help asking, with a momentary sense of chagrin. But the next moment he added, in a milder tone, "I don't mean to pry into your business."

"I shall very likely have to use my money soon," Gilbert explained, "and must at least wait until I hear from Chester. That will be another week, and then, if the money should not be wanted, I can accommodate you. But, to tell you the truth, I don't think there's much chance of that."

"Shall you have to go down to Chester?"

"I hope so."

"When?"

"In ten or twelve days from now."

"Then," said Barton, "I'll fix it this way. 'Tisn't only the money I want, but to have it paid in Chester, without the old man or Stacy knowing anything of the matter. If I was to go myself, Stacy'd never rest till he found out my business—Faith! I believe if I was hid in the hayloft o' the William Penn Tavern, he'd scent me out. Now, I can get the money of another fellow I know, if you'll take it down and hand it over for me. Would you be that obliging?"

"Of course," Gilbert answered. "If I go it will be no additional trouble."

"All right," said Barton, "between ourselves, you understand."

A week later, a letter, with the following address was brought to the post office by the mail-rider—

> *"To Mr. Gilbert Potter, Esqre*
> *Kennett Square P. O.*
> *These, with Care and Speed."*

Gilbert, having carefully cut around the wafer and unfolded the sheet of strong eyllowish paper, read this missive—

"Sir: Y^r resp^d favour of y^e * 11th came duly to hand, and ye proposition w^h it contains has been submitted to Mr Jones, ye present houlder of ye mortgage. He wishes me to inform you that he did not anticipate ye payment before ye first day of April, 1797, w^h was ye term agreed upon at ye payment of ye first note; nevertheless, being required to accept full and lawful payment, whensoever tendered, he hath impowered me to receive ye moneys at y^r convenience, providing ye settlement be full and compleat, as aforesaid, and not merely ye payment of a part of portion thereof.

"Y^r ob't serv't,

"Isaac Trainer."

---

*This form of the article, though in general disuse at the time, was still frequently employed in epistolary writing, in that part of Pennsylvania.

Gilbert, with his limited experience of business matters, had entirely overlooked the fact that the permission of the creditor is not necessary to the payment of a debt. He had a profound respect for all legal forms, and his indebtedness carried with it a sense of stern and perpetual responsibility, which, alas! has not always been inherited by the descendants of that simple and primitive period.

Mary Potter received the news with a sigh of relief. The money was again counted, the interest which would be due somewhat laboriously computed, and finally nothing remaining but the sum which Mark Deane had promised to furnish. This Mark expected to receive on the following Wednesday, and Gilbert and his mother agreed that the journey to Chester should be made at the close of the same week.

They went over these calculations in the quiet of the Sabbath afternoon, sitting alone in the neat, old-fashioned kitchen, with the dim light of an Indian-summer sun striking through the leafless trumpet vines, and making a quaint network of light and shade on the whitewashed windowframe. The pendulum ticked drowsily along the opposite wall, and the hickory backlog on the hearth hummed a lamentable song through all its simmering pores of sap. Peaceful as the happy landscape without, dozing in dreams of the departed summer, cheery as the tidy household signs within, seemed at last the lives of the two inmates. Mary Potter had not asked how her son's wooing had further sped, but she felt that he was contented of heart; she, too, indulging finally in the near consummation of her hopes—which touched her like the pitying sympathy of the power that had dealt so singularly with her life—was nearer the feeling of happiness than she had been for long and weary years.

Gilbert was moved by the serenity of her face, and the trouble which he knew it concealed seemed to his mind to be wearing away. Carefully securing the doors, they walked over the fields together, pausing on the hilltop to listen to the caw of the gathering crows, or to watch the ruby disc of the beamless sun stooping to touch the western rim of the valley. Many a time had they thus gone over the farm together, but never before with such a sense of peace and security. The day was removed, mysteriously, from the circle of its fellows, and set apart by a peculiar influence which prevented either from ever forgetting it, during all the years that come after.

They were not aware that at the very moment this influence was profoundest in their hearts, new rumors of Sandy Flash's movements had reached Kennett Square, and were being excitedly discussed at the Unicorn Tavern. He had been met on the Street Road, riding towards the Red Lion, that very afternoon, by a man who knew his face; and later in the evening came a second report, that an individual of his build had crossed the Philadelphia Road, this side of the Anvil, and gone southward into the woods. Many were the surmises, and even detailed accounts, of robberies that either had been or might be committed, but no one could say precisely how much was true.

Mark Deane was not at home, and the blacksmith was commissioned to summon Alfred Barton, who had ridden over to Pennsbury on a friendly visit to Mr. Joel Ferris. When he finally made his appearance towards ten o'clock, he was secretly horror-stricken at the great danger he had escaped; but it gave him an admirable opportunity to swagger. He could do no less than promise to summon the volunteers in the morning, and provision was made accordingly for desptaching as many messengers as the village could afford.

Since the British occupation nearly twenty years before, Kennett Square had not known as lively a day as that which followed. The men and boys were in the street grouped in front of the tavern, the women at the windows, watching, some with alarmed, but many with amused faces. Sally Fairthorn, although it was washing-day, stole up through Dr. Deane's garden and into Martha's room, for at least half an hour, but Joe and Jake left their overturned shocks of corn unhusked for the whole day.

Some of the young farmers to whom the message had been sent, returned answer that they were very busy and could not leave their work; the horses of others were lame; the guns of others broken. By ten o'clock, however, there were nine volunteers, very irregularly armed and mounted, in attendance; by eleven o'clock, thirteen, and Alfred Barton, whose place as leader was anything but comfortable, began to swell with an air of importance, and set about examining the guns of his command. Neither he nor any one else noticed particularly that the Irish ostler appeared to be a great connoisseur in muskets, and was especially interested in the structure of the flints and pans.

"Let's look over the roll, and see how many are true blue,"

said Barton, drawing a paper from his pocket. "There's failing nine or ten, among 'em some I fully counted on—Withers, he *may* come yet; Ferris, hardly time to get word; but Carson, Potter, and Travilla ought to turn up curst soon, or we'll have the sport without 'em!"

"Give me a horse, Mr. Barton, and I'll ride down for Gilbert!" cried Joe Fairthorn.

"No use—Giles went this morning," growled Barton.

"It's time we were starting; which road would be best to take?" asked one of the volunteers.

"All roads lead to Rome, but all don't lead to Sandy Flash, ha! ha!" said another, laughing at his own smartness.

"Who knows where he was seen last?" Barton asked, but it was not easy to get a coherent answer. One had heard one report, and another another; he had been seen from the Street Road on the north all the way around eastward by the Red Lion and the Anvil, and in the rocky glen below the Barton farm, to the lime-quarries of Tuffkenamon on the west.

"Unless we scatter, it'll be like looking for a needle in a haystack," remarked one of the more courageous volunteers.

"If they'd all had spunk enough to come," said Barton, "we might ha' made four parties, and gone out on each road. As it is, we're only strong enough for two."

"Seven to one?—that's too much odds in Sandy's favor!" cried a light-headed youth, whereat the others all laughed, and some of them blushed a little.

Barton bit his lip, and with a withering glance at the young man, replied, "Then we'll make three parties, and you shall be the third."

Another quarter of an hour having elapsed, without any accession to the troop, Barton reluctantly advised the men to get their arms, which had been carelessly placed along the tavern porch, and to mount for the chase.

Just then Joe and Jake Fairthorn, who had been dodging back and forth through the village, watching the roads, made their appearance with the announcement,

"Hurray—there's another—comin' up from below, but it a'n't Gilbert. He's stuck full o' pistols, but he's a-foot, and you must git him a horse. I tell you, he looks like a real buster!"

"Who can it be?" asked Barton.

"We'll see, in a minute," said the nearest volunteers, taking up their muskets.

"There he is—there he is!" cried Joe.

All eyes, turned towards the crossing of the roads, beheld just rounding the corner house, fifty paces distant, a short, broad-shouldered, determined figure, making directly for the tavern. His face was red and freckled, his thin lips half-parted with a grin which showed the flash of white teeth between them, and his eyes sparkled with the light of a cold, fierce courage. He had a double-barreled musket on his shoulder, and there were four pistols in the tight leathern belt about his waits.

Barton turned deadly pale as he beheld this man. An astonished silence fell upon the group, but, the next moment some voice exclaimed, in an undertone, which, nevertheless, everyone heard,

"By the living Lord! Sandy Flash himself!"

There was a general confused movement, of which Alfred Barton took advantage to partly cover his heavy body by one of the porch pillars. Some of the volunteers started back, others pressed closer together. The pert youth alone, who was to form the third party, brought his musket to his shoulder.

Quick as lightning Sandy Flash drew a pistol from his belt and leveled it at the young man's breast.

"Ground arms!" he cried, "or you are a dead man."

He was obeyed, although slowly and with grinding teeth.

"Stand aside!" he then commanded. "*You* have pluck, and I should hate to shoot you. Make way, the rest o' ye! I've saved ye the trouble o' ridin' far to find me. Whoever puts finger to trigger, falls. Back, back, I say, and open the door for me!"

Still advancing as he spoke, and shifting his pistol so as to cover now one, now another of the group, he reached the tavern porch. Someone opened the door of the barroom, which swung inwards. The highwayman strode directly to the bar, and there stood, facing the open door, while he cried to the trembling barkeeper,

"A glass o' rye, good and strong!"

It was set before him. Holding the musket in his arm, he took the glass, drank, wiped his mouth with the back of his hand, and then, spinning a silver dollar into the air, said, as it rang upon the floor,

"*I* stand treat today; let the rest o' the gentlemen drink at my expense!"

He then walked out, and slowly retreated backwards towards the corner house, covering his retreat with the leveled pistol, and the flash of his dauntless eye.

He had nearly reached the corner, when Gilbert Potter dashed up behind him, with Roger all in a foam. Joe Fairthorn, seized with deadly terror when he heard the terrible name, had set off at full speed for home; but descrying Gilbert approaching on a gallop, changed his course, met the latter, and gasped out the astounding intelligence. All this was the work of a minute, and when Gilbert reached the corner, a single glance showed him the true state of affairs. The confused group in front of the tavern, some faces sallow with cowardice, some red with indignation and shame; the solitary, retreating figure, alive in every nerve with splendid courage, told him the whole story, which Joe's broken words had only half hinted.

Flinging himself from his horse, he leveled his musket, and cried out,

"Surrender!"

Sandy Flash, with a sudden spring, placed his back against the house, pointed his pistol at Gilbert, and said: "Drop your gun, or I fire!"

For answer, Gilbert drew the trigger; the crack of the explosion rang sharp and clear, and a little shower of mortar covered Sandy Flash's cocked hat. The ball had struck the wall about four inches above his head.

He leaped forward; Gilbert clubbed his musket and awaited him. They were scarcely two yards apart; the highwayman's pistol-barrel was opposite Gilbert's heart, and the two men were looking into each other's eyes. The group in front of the tavern stood as if paralyzed, every man holding his breath.

"Halt!" said Sandy Flash. "Halt! I hate bloodshed, and besides that, young Potter, you're not the man that'll take me prisoner. I could blow your brains out by movin' this finger, but *you're* safe from any bullet o' mine, whoever a'n't!"

At the last words a bright, mocking, malicious grin stole over his face. Gilbert, amazed to find himself known to the highwayman, and puzzled with certain familiar marks in the latter's countenance, was swiftly enlightened by this grin. It was Fortune's face before him, without the black hair and whiskers—and Fortune's voice that spoke!

Sandy Flash saw the recognition. He grinned again. "You'll know your friend, another time," he said, sprang five feet backward, whirled, gained the cover of the house, and was mounting his horse among the bushes at the bottom of the garden before any of the others reached Gilbert, who was still standing as if thunderstruck.

By this time Sandy Flash had leaped the hedge and was careering like lightning towards the shelter of the woods. The interest now turned upon Gilbert Potter, who was very taciturn and thoughtful and had little to relate. They noticed, however, that his eyes were turned often and inquiringly upon Alfred Barton, and that the latter as steadily avoided meeting them.

When Gilbert went to bring Roger, who had quietly waited at the crossing of the roads, Deb. Smith suddenly made her appearance.

"I seen it all," she said. "I was a bit up the road, but I seen it. You shouldn't ha' shot, Mr. Gilbert, though it isn't him that's born to be hit with a bullet; but *you're* safe enough from *his* bullets, anyhow—whatever happens, *you're* safe!"

"What do you mean, Deborah?" he exclaimed, as she almost repeated to him Sandy Flash's very words.

"I mean what I say," she answered. "*You* wouldn't be afeard, but it'll be a comfort to your mother. I must have a drink o' whiskey after that sight."

With these words she elbowed her way into the barroom. Most of the Kennett Volunteers were there engaged in carrying out a similar resolution. They would gladly have kept the whole occurrence secret, but that was impossible. It was known all over the country in three days, and the story of it has not yet died out of the local annals.

CHAPTER 19

The Husking Frolic

Jake Fairthorn rushed into Dr. Deane's door with a howl of terror.

"Cousin Martha! Betsy!" he cried; "he's goin' to shoot Gilbert!"

"None o' your tricks, boy!" Betsy Lavender exclaimed, in her most savage tone, as she saw the paleness of Martha's face. "I'm up to 'em. Who'd shoot Gilbert Potter? Not Alf. Barton, I'll be bound; he'd be afeard to shoot even Sandy Flash!"

"It's Sandy Flash—he's there! Gilbert shot his hat off!" cried Jake.

"The Lord have mercy!" And the next minute Miss Betsy found herself, she scarcely knew how, in the road.

Both had heard the shot, but supposed that it was some volunteer discharging an old load from his musket; they knew nothing of Sandy's visit to the Unicorn, and Jake's announcement seemed simply incredible.

"O you wicked boy! What'll become o' you?" cried Miss Lavender, as she beheld Gilbert Potter approaching, leading Roger by the bridle. But at the same instant she saw, from the faces of the crowd, that something unusual had happened. While the others instantly surrounded Gilbert, the young volunteer who alone had made any show of fight, told the story to the two ladies. Martha Deane's momentary shock of terror disappeared under the rush of mingled pride and scorn which the narrative called up in her heart.

"What a pack of cowards!" she exclaimed, her cheeks flushing—"to stand still and see the life of the only man that dares to face a robber at the mercy of the robber's pistol!"

Gilbert approached. His face was grave and thoughtful, but his eye brightened as it met hers. No two hands ever conveyed so many and such swift messages as theirs, in the single moment when they touched each other. The other women of the village crowded around, and he was obliged, though with evident reluctance, to relate his share in the event.

In the meantime the volunteers had issued from the tavern, and were loudly discussing what course to pursue. The most of them were in favor of instant pursuit. To their credit it must be said that very few of them were actual cowards; they had been both surprised by the incredible daring of the highwayman, and betrayed by the cowardly inefficiency of their own leader. Barton, restored to his usual complexion by two glasses of whiskey, was nearly ready to head a chase which he suspected would come to nothing; but the pert young volunteer, who had been whispering with some of the younger men, suddenly cried out,

"I say, fellows, we've had about enough o' Barton's command; and I, for one, am a-goin' to enlist under Captain Potter."

"Good!" "Agreed!" responded a number of others, and some eight or ten stepped to one side. The few remaining around Alfred Barton began to look doubtful, and all eyes were turned curiously upon him.

Gilbert, however, stepped forward and said: "It's bad policy to divide our forces just now, when we ought to be off on the hunt. Mr. Barton, we all know, got up the company, and I am willing to serve under him, if he'll order us to mount at once! If not, rather than lose more time, I'll head as many as are ready to go."

Barton saw how the tide was turning, and suddenly determined to cover up his shame, if possible, with a mantle of magnanimity.

"The fellows are right, Gilbert!" he said. "You deserve to take the lead today, so go ahead; I'll follow you! '

"Mount, then, all of you!" Gilbert cried, without further hesitation. In a second he was on Roger's back. "You, Barton," he ordered, "take three with you and make for the New-Garden crossroad as fast as you can. Pratt, you and three more towards the Hammer and Trowel; while I, with the rest, follow the direct trail."

No more time was wasted in talking. The men took their guns and mounted, the two detached commands were told off, and in five minutes the village was left to its own inhabitants.

Gilbert had a long and perplexing chase, but very little came of it. The trail of Sandy Flash's horse was followed without much difficulty until it struck the west branch of Redley Creek. There it suddenly ceased, and more than an hour elapsed before someone discovered it, near the road, a quarter of a mile further up the stream. Thence it turned towards the Hammer and Trowel, but no one at the farmhouses on the road had seen anyone pass except a Quaker, wearing the usual broad-brimmed hat and drab coat, and mounted on a large, sleepy-looking horse.

About the middle of the afternoon, Gilbert detected, in one of the lanes leading across to the Street Road, the marks of a galloping steed, and those who had a little lingering knowledge of woodcraft noticed that the gallop often ceased suddenly, changed to a walk, and was then as suddenly resumed. Along the Street Road no one had been seen except a Quaker, apparently the same person. Gilbert and his hunters now suspected the disguise, but the difficulty of following the trail had increased with every hour of lost time; and after scouring along the Brandywine and then crossing into the Pocopsin valley, they finally gave up the chase, late in the day. It was the general opinion that Sandy had struck northward, and was probably safe in one of his lairs among the Welch Mountains.

When they reached the Unicorn tavern at dusk, Gilbert found Joe Fairthorn impatiently waiting for him. Sally had been "tearin' around like mad," (so Joe described his sister's excitement), having twice visited the village during the afternoon in the hope of seeing the hero of the day—after Sandy Flash, of course, who had, and deserved, the first place.

"And, Gilbert," said Joe, "I wasn't to forgit to tell you that we're a-goin' to have a huskin' frolic o' Wednesday night—day after tomorrow, you know. Dad's behind-hand with huskin', and the moon's goin' to be full, and Mark he said Let's have a frolic, and I'm comin' home to meet Gilbert anyhow, and so I'll be there. And Sally she said I'll have Martha and lots o' girls, only we shan't come out into the field till you're nigh about done. Then Mark he said That won't take long, and if you don't help me with my shocks I won't come, and Sally she hit him, and so it's all agreed. And you'll come, Gilbert, won't you?"

"Yes, yes, Joe," Gilbert answered, a little impatiently; "tell Sally I'll come." Then he turned Roger's head towards home.

He was glad of the solitary ride which allowed him to collect his thoughts. Fearless as was his nature, the danger he had escaped might well have been cause for grave self-congratulation; but the thought of it scarcely lingered beyond the moment of the encounter. The astonishing discovery that the stranger, Fortune, and the redoubtable Sandy Flash were one and the same person; the mysterious words which this person had addressed to him; the repetition of the same words by Deb. Smith—all these facts, suggesting, as their common solution, some secret which concerned himself, perplexed his mind, already more than sufficiently occupied with mystery.

It suddenly flashed across his memory, as he rode homeward, that on the evening when he returned from the fox-chase, his mother had manifested an unusual interest in the strange huntsman, questioning him minutely as to the latter's appearance. Was she—or, rather, had she been, at one time of her life—acquainted with Sandy Flash? And if so—

"No!" he cried aloud, "it is impossible! It could not—cannot be!" The new possibility which assailed him was even more terrible than his previous belief in the dishonor of his birth. Better, a thousand times, he thought, be basely born than the son of an outlaw! It seemed that every attempt he made to probe his mother's secret threatened to overwhelm him with a knowledge far worse than the fret of his ignorance. Why not be patient, therefore, leaving the solution to her and to time?

Nevertheless, a burning curiosity led him to relate to his mother, that evening, the events of the day. He watched her closely as he described his encounter with the highwayman, and repeated the latter's words. It was quite natural that Mary Potter should shudder and turn pale during the recital—quite natural that a quick expression of relief should shine from her face at the close; but Gilbert could not be sure that her interest extended to any one except himself. She suggested no explanation of Sandy Flash's words, and he asked none.

"I shall know no peace, child," she said, "until the money has been paid, and the mortgage is in your hands."

"You won't have long to wait, now, mother," he answered cheerily. "I shall see Mark on Wednesday evening, and therefore can start for Chester on Friday, come rain or shine. As for Sandy Flash, he's no doubt up on the Welch Mountain by this time. It isn't his way to turn up twice in succession in the same place."

"You don't know him, Gilbert. He won't soon forget that you shot at him."

"I seem to be safe enough, if he tells the truth," Gilbert could not help remarking.

Mary Potter shook her head, and said nothing.

Two more lovely Indian-summer days went by, and as the wine-red sun slowly quenched his lower limb in the denser smoke along the horizon, the great bronzed moon struggled out of it, on the opposite rim of the sky. It was a weird light and a weird atmosphere, such as we might imagine overspreading Babylonian ruins, on the lone plains of the Euphrates; but no such fancies either charmed or tormented the lusty, wide-awake, practical lads and lasses, whom the brightening moon beheld on their way to the Fairthorn farm. "The best night for huskin' that ever was," comprised the sum of their appreciation.

At the old farmhouse there was great stir of preparation. Sally, with her gown pinned up, dodged in and out of kitchen and sitting room, catching herself on every door-handle, while Mother Fairthorn, beaming with quiet content, stood by the fire, and inspected the great kettles which were to contain the materials for the midnight supper. Both were relieved when Betsy Lavender made her appearance, saying,

"Let down your gownd, Sally, and give *me* that ladle. What'd be a mighty heap o' work for you in that flustered condition is child's-play to the likes o' me, that's as steady as a cart-horse—not that self-praise, as the sayin' is, is any recommendation—but my kickin' and prancin' days is over, and high time, too."

"No, Betsy, I'll not allow it!" cried Sally. "You must enjoy yourself, too." But she had parted with the ladle while speaking, and Miss Lavender, repeating the words "Enjoy yourself, too!" quietly took her place in the kitchen.

The young men, as they arrived, took their way to the cornfield, piloted by Joe and Jake Fairthorn. These boys each carried a wallet over his shoulders, the jug in the front end balancing that behind, and the only casualty that occurred was when Jake, jumping down from a fence, allowed his jugs to smite together, breaking one of them to shivers.

"There, that'll come out o' your pig-money," said Joe.

"I don't care," Jake retorted, "if Daddy only pays me the rest."

The boys, it must be known, received every year the two smallest pigs of the old sow's litter, with the understanding that these were to be their separate property, on condition of their properly feeding and fostering the whole herd. This duty they performed with great zeal and enthusiasm, and numberless and splendid were the castles which they built with the coming money; yet, alas! when the pigs were sold, it always happened that Farmer Fairthorn found some inconvenient debt pressing him, and the boys' pig-money was therefore taken as a loan—only as a loan—and permanently invested.

There were between three and four hundred shocks to husk, and the young men, armed with husking-pegs of hickory, fastened by a leathern strap over the two middle fingers, went bravely to work. Mark Deane, who had reached home that afternoon, wore the seventy-five dollars in a buckskin belt around his waist, and anxiously awaited the arrival of Gilbert Potter, of whose adventure he had already heard. Mark's presumed obligations to Alfred Barton prevented him from expressing his overpowering contempt for that gentleman's conduct, but he was not obliged to hold his tongue about Gilbert's pluck and decision, and he did not.

The latter, detained at the house by Mother Fairthorn and Sally—both of whom looked upon him as one arisen from the dead—did not reach the field until the others had selected their rows, overturned the shocks, and were seated in a rustling line, in the moonlight.

"Gilbert!" shouted Mark, "come here! I've kep' the row next to mine for you! And I want to get a grip o' your hand, my bold boy!"

He sprang up, flinging an armful of stalks behind him, and with difficulty restrained an impulse to clasp Gilbert to his broad breast. It was not the custom of the neighborhood; the noblest masculine friendship would have been described by the people in no other terms than "They are very thick," and men who loved each other were accustomed to be satisfied with the knowledge. The strong moonlight revealed to Gilbert Potter the honest heart which looked out of Mark's blue eyes, as the latter held his hand like a vise, and said,

"I've heard all about it."

"More than there was occasion for, very likely," Gilbert replied. "I'll tell you my story some day, Mark; but tonight we must work and not talk."

"All right, Gilbert. I say, though, I've got the money you wanted; we'll fix the matter after supper."

The rustling of the cornstalks recommenced, and the tented lines of shocks slowly fell as the huskers worked their way over the brow of the hill, whence the ground sloped down into a broad belt of shade, cast by the woods in the bottom. Two or three dogs which had accompanied their masters coursed about the field, or darted into the woods in search of an opossum-trail. Joe and Jake Fairthorn would gladly have followed them, but were afraid of venturing into the mysterious gloom; so they amused themselves with putting on the coats which the men had thrown aside, and gravely marched up and down the line, commending the rapid and threatening the tardy workers.

Erelong, the silence was broken by many a shout of exultation or banter, many a merry sound of jest or fun, as the back of the night's task was fairly broken. One husker mimicked the hoot of an owl in the thickets below; another sang a melody popular at the time, the refrain of which was,

> "Be it late or early, be it late or soon,
> It's I will enjoy the sweet rose in June!"

"Sing out, boys!" shouted Mark, "so the girls can hear you! It's time they were comin' to look after us."

"Sing, yourself!" someone replied. "You can out-bellow the whole raft."

Wihout more ado, Mark opened his mouth and began chanting, in a ponderous voice,

> "On yonder mountain summit
> My castle you will find,
> Renown'd in ann-cient historee,—
> My name it's Rinardine!"

Presently, from the upper edge of the wood, several feminine voices were heard, singing another part of the same song:

> "Beware of meeting Rinar,
> All on the mountains high!"

Such a shout of fun ran over the field that the frighted owl ceased his hooting in the thicket. The moon stood high, and turned the night-haze into diffused silver. Though the hollows were chill with gathering frost, the air was still mild and dry on the hills, and the young ladies, in their warm gowns of home-made flannel, enjoyed both the splendor of the night and the lively emulation of the scattered laborers.

"Turn to, and give us a lift, girls," said Mark.

"Beware of meeting Rinar!" Sally laughed.

"Because you know what you promised him, Sally," he retorted. "Come, a bargain's a bargain; there's the outside row standin'—not enough of us to stretch all the way acrost the field—so let's you and me take that and bring it down square with th' others. The rest may keep my row a-goin', if they can."

Two or three of the other maidens had cut the supporting stalks of the next shock, and overturned it with much laughing. "I can't husk, Mark," said Martha Deane, "but I'll promise to superintend these, if you will keep Sally to her word."

There was a little running hither and thither, a show of fight, a mock scramble, and it ended by Sally tumbling over a pumpkin, and then being carried off by Mark to the end of the outside row of shocks, some distance in the rear of the line of work. Here he laid the stalks straight for her, doubled his coat and placed it on the ground for a seat, and then took his place on the other side of the shock.

Sally husked a few ears in silence, but presently found it more agreeable to watch her partner, as he bent to the labor, ripping the covering from each ear with one or two rapid motions, snapping the cob, and flinging the ear over his shoulder into the very center of the heap, without turning his head. When the shock was finished, there were five stalks on her side, and fifty on Mark's.

He laughed at the extent of her help, but, seeing how bright and beautiful her face looked in the moonlight, how round and supple her form, contrasted with his own rough proportions, he added, in a lower tone,

"Never mind the work, Sally—I only wanted to have you with me."

Sally was silent but happy, and Mark proceeded to overthrow the next shock.

When they were again seated face to face, he no longer bent so steadily over the stalks, but lifted his head now and then to watch the gloss of the moon on her black hair, and the mellow gleam that seemed to slide along her cheek and chin, playing with the shadows, as she moved.

"Sally!" he said at last, "you must ha' seen, over and over ag'in, that I like to be with you. Do you care for me at all?"

She flushed and trembled a little as she answered, "Yes, Mark, I do."

He husked half a dozen ears rapidly, then looked up again and asked,

"Do you care enough for me, Sally, to take me for good and all? I can't put it into fine speech, but I love you dearly and honestly; will you marry me?"

Sally bent down her head, so choked with the long-delayed joy that she found it impossible to speak. Mark finished the few remaining stalks and put them behind him; he sat upon the ground at her feet.

"There's my hand, Sally; will you take it, and me with it?"

Her hand slowly made its way into his broad, hard palm. Once the surrender expressed, her confusion vanished; she lifted her head for his kiss, then leaned it on his shoulder and whispered,

"Oh, Mark, I've loved you for ever and ever so long a time!"

"Why, Sally, deary," said he, "that's my case, too; and I seemed to feel it in my bones that we was to be a pair; only, you know, I had to get a foothold first. I couldn't come to you with empty hands—though, faith! there's not much to speak of in 'em!"

"Never mind that, Mark—I'm *so* glad you want me!"

And indeed she was; why should she not, therefore, say so?

"There's no need o' broken sixpences, or true lovers' knots, I guess," said Mark, giving her another kiss. "I'm a plainspoken fellow, and when I say I want you for my wife, Sally, I mean it. But we mustn't be settin' here, with the row unhusked; that'll never do. See if I don't make the ears spin! And I guess you can help me a little now, can't you?"

With a jolly laugh, Mark picked up the corn-cutter and swung it above the next shock. In another instant it would have fallen, but a loud shriek burst out from the bundled stalks, and Joe Fairthorn crept forth on his hands and knees.

The lovers stood petrified. "Why, you young devil!" exclaimed Mark, while the single word "JOE!" which came from Sally's lips, contained the concentrated essence of a thousand slaps.

"Don't—don't!" whimpered Joe. "I'll not tell anybody, indeed I won't!"

"If you do," threatened Mark, brandishing the corn-cutter, "it isn't your legs I shall cut off, but your head, even with the shoulders. What were you doin' in that shock?"

"I wanted to hear what you and Sally were sayin' to each other. Folks said you two was a-courtin'," Joe answered.

The comical aspect of the matter suddenly struck Mark, and he burst into a roar of laughter.

"Mark, how can you?" said Sally, bridling a little.

"Well—it's all in the fam'ly, after all. Joe, tarnation scamp as he is, is long-headed enough to keep his mouth shut, rather than have people laugh at his relations—eh, Joe?"

"I said I'd never say a word," Joe affirmed, "and I won't. You see if I even tell Jake. But I say, Mark, when you and Sally get married, will you be my uncle?"

"It depends on your behavior," Mark gravely answered, seating himself to husk. Joe magnanimously left the lovers, and pitched over the third shock ahead, upon which he began to husk with might and main, in order to help them out with their task.

By the time the outside row was squared, the line had reached the bottom of the slope, where the air was chill, although the shadows of the forest had shifted from the field. Then there was a race among the huskers for the fence, the girls promising that he whose row was first husked out should sit at the head of the table, and be called King of the Corn-field. The stalks rustled, the cobs snapped, the ears fell like a shower of golden cones, and amid much noise and merriment, not only the victor's row but all the others were finished, and Farmer Fairthorn's field stood husked from end to end.

Gilbert Potter had done his share of the work steadily, and as silently as the curiosity of the girls, still excited by his recent adventure, would allow. It was enough for him that he caught a chance word, now and then, from Martha. The emulation of the race with which the husking closed favored them, and he gladly lost a very fair chance of becoming King of the Corn-field for the opportunity of asking her to assist him in contriving a brief interview on the way to the house.

Where two work together to the same end, there is no doubt about the result, especially as, in this case, the company preferred returning through the wood instead of crossing the open, high-fenced fields. When they found themselves together, out of earshot of the others, Gilbert lost no time in relating the partic-

ulars of his encounter with Sandy Flash, the discovery he had
made, and the mysterious assurance of Deb. Smith.

Martha listened with the keenest interest. "It is very, very
strange," she said, "and the strangest of all is that he should be
that man, Fortune. As for his words, I do not find them so
singular. He has certainly the grandest courage, robber as he is,
and he admires the same quality in you; no doubt you made a
favorable impression upon him on the day of the fox-chase; and
so, although you are hunting him down, he will not injure you,
if he can help it. I find all that very natural, in a man of his
nature."

"But Deb. Smith?" Gilbert asked.

"That," said Martha, "is rather a curious coincidence, but
nothing more, I think. She is said to be a superstitious creature,
and if you have ever befriended her—and you may have done so,
Gilbert, without your good heart being aware of it—she thinks
that her spells, or charms, or what not, will save you from harm.
No, I was wrong; it is not so very strange, except Fortune's
intimacy with Alfred Barton, which everybody was talking about
at the time."

Gilbert drew a deep breath of relief. How the darkness of his
new fear vanished in the light of Martha's calm, sensible words!
"How wonderfully you have guessed the truth!" he cried. "So it
is; Deb. Smith thinks she is beholden to me for kind treatment;
she blew upon my palm, in a mysterious way, and said she
would stand by me in time of need! But that about Fortune
puzzles me. I can see that Barton is very shy of me since he
thinks I've made the discovery."

"We must ask Betsy Lavender's counsel, there," said Martha.
"It is beyond my depth."

The supper smoked upon the table when they reached the
farmhouse, It had been well earned, and it was enjoyed, both in
a physical and social sense, to the very extent of the guests'
capacities. The King sat at the head of the table, and Gilbert
Potter—forced into that position by Mark—at the foot. Sally
Fairthorn insisted on performing her duty as handmaiden, although, as Betsy Lavender again and again declared, her room
was better than her help.*

Sally's dark eyes fairly danced and sparkled; her full, soft lips

---

*Her absence was more helpful than her presence (ed.).

shone with a scarlet bloom. she laughed with a wild, nervous
joyousness, and yet rushed about haunted with a fearful dread
of suddenly busting into tears. Her ways were so well known,
however, that a little extra impulsiveness excited no surprise.
Martha Deane was the only person who discovered what had
taken place. As the girls were putting on their hats and cloaks in
the bedroom, Sally drew her into the passage, kissed her a number of times with passionate vehemence, and then darted off
without saying a word.

Gilbert rode home through the splendid moonlight, in the
small hours of the morning, with a light heart, and Mark's
money-belt buckled around his waist.

CHAPTER *20*

Gilbert on the Road to Chester

Being now fully prepared to undertake his journey to Chester, Gilbert remembered his promise to Alfred Barton. As the subject had not again been mentioned between them—probably owing to the excitement produced by Sandy Flash's visit to Kennett Square, and its consequences—he felt bound to inform Barton of his speedy departure, and to renew his offer of service.

He found the latter in the field, assisting Giles, who was hauling home the sheaves of corn-fodder in a harvest-wagon. The first meeting of the two men did not seem to be quite agreeable to either. Gilbert's suspicions had been aroused, although he could give them no definite form, and Barton shrank from any reference to what had now become a very sore topic.

"Giles," said the latter, after a moment of evident embarrassment, "I guess you may drive home with that load, and pitch it off; I'll wait for you here."

When the rustling wain had reached a convenient distance, Gilbert began,

"I only wanted to say that I'm going to Chester tomorrow."

"Oh, yes!" Barton exclaimed, "about that money? I suppose you want all o' yours?"

"It's as I expected. But you said you could borrow elsewhere, and send it by me."

"The fact is," said Barton, "that I've both borrowed and sent. I'm obliged to you, all the same, Gilbert; the will's as good as the deed, you know; but I got the money from—well, from a friend, who was about going down on his own business, and so that stone killed both my birds. I ought to ha' sent you word, by rights."

"Is your *friend*," Gilbert asked, "a safe and trusty man?"

"Safe enough, I guess—a little wild, at times, maybe; but he's not such a fool as to lose what he'd never have a chance of getting again."

"Then," said Gilbert, "it's hardly likely that he's the same friend you took such a fancy to, at the Hammer and Trowel, last spring?"

Alfred Barton started as if he had been shot, and a deep color spread over his face. His lower jaw slackened and his eyes moved uneasily from side to side.

"Who—who do you mean?" he stammered.

The more evident his embarrassment became, the more Gilbert was confirmed in his suspicion that there was some secret understanding between the two men. The thing seemed incredible, but the same point, he remembered, had occurred to Martha Deane's mind, when she so readily explained the other circumstances.

"Barton," he said, sternly, "you know very well whom I mean. What became of your friend Fortune? Didn't you see him at the tavern, last Monday morning?"

"Y-yes—oh, yes! I know who he is *now*, the damned scoundrel! I'd give a hundred dollars to see him dance upon nothing!"

He clenched his fists, and uttered a number of other oaths, which need not be repeated. His rage seemed so real that Gilbert was again staggered. Looking at the heavy, vulgar face before him—the small, restless eyes, the large sensuous mouth, the forehead whose very extent, in contradiction to ordinary laws, expressed imbecility rather than intellect—it was impossible to associate great cunning and shrewdness with such a physiognomy. Every line, at that moment, expressed pain and exasperation. But Gilbert felt bound to go a step further.

"Barton," he said, "didn't you know who Fortune was, on that day?"

"N-no—no! On that *day*—NO! Blast me if I did!"

"Not before you left him?"

"Well, I'll admit that a suspicion of it came to me at the very last moment—too late to be of any use. But come, damme! that's all over, and what's the good o' talking? *You* tried your best to catch the fellow, too, but he was too much for you! 'tisn't such an easy job, eh?"

This sort of swagger was Alfred Barton's only refuge when he was driven into a corner. Though some color still lingered in his face, he spread his shoulders with a bold, almost defiant air, and

met Gilbert's eye with a steady gaze. The latter was not prepared to carry his examination further, although he was still far
from being satisfied.

"Come, come, Gilbert!" Barton presently resumed, "I mean
no offense. You showed yourself to be true blue, and you led
the hunt as well as any man could ha' done; but the very
thought o' the fellow makes me mad, and I'll know no peace till
he's strung up. If I was your age, now! A man seems to lose his
spirit as he gets on in years, and I'm only sorry you weren't
made captain at the start, instead o' me. You *shall* be, from this
time on; I won't take it again!"

"One thing I'll promise you," said Gilbert, with a meaning
look, "that I won't let him walk into the barroom of the Unicorn without hindrance."

"I'll bet you won't!" Barton exclaimed. "All *I'm* afraid of is,
that he won't try it again."

"We'll see; this highway-robbery must have an end. I must
now be going. Good-bye!"

"Good-bye, Gilbert; take care o' yourself!" said Barton, in a
very good humor, now that the uncomfortable interview was
over. "And, I say," he added, "remember that I stand ready to
do you a good turn, whenever I can!"

"Thank you!" responded Gilbert, as he turned Roger's head;
but he said to himself, "when all other friends fail, I may come
to *you*, not sooner."

The next morning showed signs that the Indian summer had
reached its close. All night long the wind had moaned and lamented in the chimneys, and the sense of dread in the outer
atmosphere crept into the house and weighed upon the slumber-
ing inmates. There was a sound in the forest as of sobbing
Dryads, waiting for the swift death and the frosty tomb. The
blue haze of dreams which had overspread the land changed into
an ashy, livid mist, dragging low, and clinging to the features of
the landscape like a shroud to the limbs of a corpse.

The time, indeed, had come for a change. It was the end of
November; and after a summer and autumn beautiful almost
beyond parallel, a sudden and severe winter was generally anticipated. In this way, even the most ignorant field-hand recognized the eternal balance of nature.

Mary Potter, although the day had arrived for which she had
so long and fervently prayed, could not shake off the depressing

influence of the weather. After breakfast, when Gilbert began to make preparations for the journey, she found herself so agitated that it was with difficulty she could give him the usual assistance. The money, which was mostly in silver coin, had been sewed into tight rolls, was was now to be carefully packed in the saddlebags; the priming of the pistols was to be renewed, and the old, shrivelled covers of the holsters so greased, hammered out, and padded that they would keep the weapons dry in case of rain. Although Gilbert would reach Chester that evening—the distance being not more than twenty-four miles—the preparations, principally on account of his errand, were conducted with a grave and solemn sense of their importance.

When, finally, everything was in readiness—the saddlebags so packed that the precious rolls could not rub or jimgle; the dinner of sliced bread and pork placed over them, in a folded napkin; the pistols, intended more for show than use, thrust into the antiquated holsters; and all these deposited and secured on Roger's back—Gilbert took his mother's hand, and said,

"Good-bye, Mother! Don't worry, now, if I shouldn't get back until late tomorrow evening; I can't tell exactly how long the business will take."

He had never looked more strong and cheerful. The tears came to Mary Potter's eyes, but she held them back by a powerful effort. All she could say—and her voice trembled in spite of herself—was,

"Good-bye, my boy! Remember that I've worked, and thought, and prayed, for you alone—and that I'd do more—I'd do *all*, if I only could!"

His look said "I do not forget!" He sat already in the saddle, and was straightening the folds of his heavy cloak, so that it might protect his knees. The wind had arisen, and the damp mist was driving down the glen, mixed with scattered drops of a coming rainstorm. As he rode slowly away, Mary Potter lifted her eyes to the dense gray of the sky, darkening from moment to moment, listened to the murmur of the wind over the wooded hills opposite, and clasped her hands with the appealing gesture which had now become habitual to her.

"Two days more!" she sighed, as she entered the house—"two days more of fear and prayer! Lord forgive me that I am so weak of faith—that I make myself trouble where I ought to be humble and thankful!"

Gilbert rode slowly, because he feared the contents of his saddlebags would be disturbed by much jolting. Proof against wind and weather, he was not troubled by the atmospheric signs, but rather experienced a healthy glow and exhilaration of the blood as the mist grew thicker and beat upon his face like the blown spray of a waterfall. By the time he had reached the Carson farm, the sky contracted to a low, dark arch of solid wet, in which there was no positive outline of cloud, and a dull, universal roar, shorn of all windy sharpness, hummed over the land.

From the hill behind the farmhouse, whence he could overlook the bottom-lands of Redley Creek, and easily descry, on a clear day, the yellow front of Dr. Deane's house in Kennett Square, he now beheld a dim twilight chaos, wherein more and more of the distance was blotted out. Yet still some spell held up the suspended rain, and the drops that fell seemed to be only the leakage of the airy cisterns before they burst. The fields on either hand were deserted. The cattle huddled behind the stacks or crouched disconsolately in fence-corners. Here and there a farmer made haste to cut and split a supply of wood for his kitchen fire, or mended the rude roof on which his pigs depended for shelter; but all these signs showed how soon he intended to be snugly housed, to bide out the storm.

It was a day of no uncertain promise. Gilbert confessed to himself, before he reached the Philadelphia road, that he would rather have chosen another day for the journey; yet the thought of returning was farthest from his mind. Even when the rain, having created its little pools and sluices in every hollow of the ground, took courage, and multiplied its careering drops, and when the wet gusts tore open his cloak and tugged at his dripping hat, he cheerily shook the moisture from his cheeks and eyelashes, patted Roger's streaming neck, and whistled a bar or two of an old carol.

There were pleasant hopes enough to occupy his mind, without dwelling on these slight external annoyances. He still tried to believe that his mother's release would be hastened by the independence which lay folded in his saddlebags, and the thud of the wet leather against Roger's hide was a sound to cheer away any momentary foreboding. Then, Martha—dear, noble girl! She was his; it was but to wait, and waiting must be easy when the end was certain. He felt, moreover, that in spite of his unexplained disgrace, he had grown in the respect of his neighbors; that his persevering integrity was beginning to bring its reward, and he thanked God very gratefully that he had been saved from adding to his name any stain of his own making.

In an hour or more the force of the wind somewhat abated, but the sky seemed to dissolve into a massy flood. The rain rushed down, not in drops, but in sheets, and in spite of his cloak, he was wet to the skin. For half an hour he was obliged to halt in the wood between Old Kennett and Chadd's Ford, and here he made the discovery that with all his care the holsters were nearly full of water. Brown streams careered down the long, meadowy hollow on his left, wherein many Hessian soldiers lay buried. There was money buried with them, the people believed, but no one cared to dig among the dead at midnight, and many a wild tale of frighted treasure-seekers recurred to his mind.

At the bottom of the long hill flowed the Brandywine, now rolling swift and turbid, level with its banks. Roger bravely breasted the flood, and after a little struggle, reached the opposite side. Then across the battle-meadow, in the teeth of the storm, along the foot of the low hill, around the brow of which the entrenchments of the American army made a clayey streak, until the ill-fated field, sown with grapeshot and bullets which the farmers turned up every spring with their furrows, lay behind him. The story of the day was familiar to him, from the narratives of scores of eyewitnesses, and he thought to himself, as he rode onward, wet, lashed by the furious rain, yet still of good cheer, "Though the fight was lost, the cause was won."

After leaving the lovely lateral valley which stretches eastward for two miles at right angles to the course of the Brandywine, he entered a rougher and wilder region, more thickly wooded and deeply indented with abrupt glens. Thus far he had not met with a living soul. Chester was now not more than eight or ten miles distant, and, as nearly as he could guess, it was about two o'clock in the afternoon. With the best luck, he could barely reach his destination by nightfall, for the rain showed no signs of abating, and there were still several streams to be crossed.

His blood leaped no more so nimbly along his veins; the continued exposure had at last chilled and benumbed him. Letting the reins fall upon Roger's neck, he folded himself closely in his wet cloak, and bore the weather with a grim, patient endurance.

The road dropped into a rough glen, crossed a stony brook, and then wound along the side of a thickly wooded hill. On his right the bank had been cut away like a wall; on the left a steep slope of tangled thicket descended to the stream.

One moment, Gilbert knew that he was riding along this road, Roger pressing close to the bank for shelter from the wind and rain; the next, there was a swift and tremendous grip on his collar, Roger slid from under him, and he was hurled backwards, with great force, upon the ground. Yet even in the act of falling, he seemed to be conscious that a figure sprang down upon the road from the bank above.

It was some seconds before the shock, which sent a crash through his brain and a thousand fiery sparkles into his eyes, passed away. Then a voice, keen, sharp, and determined, which it seemed that he knew, exclaimed,

"Damn the beast! I'll have to shoot him."

Lifting his head with some difficulty, for he felt weak and giddy, and propping himself on his arm, he saw Sandy Flash in the road, three or four paces off, fronting Roger, who had whirled around, and with levelled ears and fiery eyes, seemed to be meditating an attack.

The robber wore a short overcoat, made entirely of muskrat skins, which completely protected the arms in his belt. He had a large hunting knife in his left hand, and appeared to be feeling with his right for the stock of a pistol. It seemed to Gilbert that nothing but the singular force of his eye held back the horse from rushing upon him.

"Keep as you are, young man!" he cried, without turning his head, "or a bullet goes into your horse's brain. I know the beast, and don't want to see him slaughtered. If *you* don't, order him to be quiet!"

Gilbert, although he knew every trait of the noble animal's nature better than those of many a human acquaintance, was both surprised and touched at the instinct with which he had recognized an enemy, and the fierce courage with which he stood on the defensive. In that moment of bewilderment, he thought only of Roger, whose life hung by a thread, which his silence would instantly snap. He might have seen—had there been time for reflection—that nothing would have been gained, in any case, by the animal's death; for, stunned and unarmed as he was, he was no match for the powerful, wary highwayman.

Obeying the feeling which entirely possessed him, he cried, "Roger! Roger, old boy!"

The horse neighed a shrill, glad neigh of recognition, and pricked up his ears. Sandy Flash stood motionless; he had let go of the pistol, and concealed the knife in a fold of his coat.

"Quiet, Roger, quiet!" Gilbert again commanded.

The animal understood the tone, if not the words. He seemed completely reassured, and advanced a step or two nearer. With the utmost swiftness and dexterity, combined with an astonishing gentleness—making no gesture which might excite Roger's suspicion—Sandy Flash thrust his hand into the holsters, smiled mockingly, cut the straps of the saddlebags with a single movement of his keen-edged knife, tested the weight of the bags, nodded, grinned, and then, stepping aside, he allowed the horse to pass him. But he watched every motion of the head and ears, as he did so.

Roger, however, seemed to think only of his master. Bending down his head, he snorted warmly into Gilbert's pale face, and then swelled his sides with a deep breath of satisfaction. Tears of shame, grief, and rage swam in Gilbert's eyes. "Roger," he said, "I've lost everything but you!"

He staggered to his feet and leaned against the bank. The extend of his loss—the hopelessness of its recovery—the impotence of his burning desire to avenge the outrage—overwhelmed him. The highwayman still stood, a few paces off, watching him with a grim curiosity.

With a desperate effort, Gilbert turned towards him. "Sandy Flash," he cried, "do you know what you are doing?"

"I rather guess so,"—and the highwayman grinned. "I've done it before, but never quite so neatly as this time."

"I've heard it said, to your credit," Gilbert continued, "that, though you rob the rich, you sometimes give to the poor. This time you've robbed a poor man."

"I've only borrowed a little from one able to spare a good deal more than I've got—and the grudge I owe him isn't paid off yet."

"It is not so!" Gilbert cried. "Every cent has been earned by my own and my mother's hard work. I was taking it to Chester, to pay off a debt upon the farm; and the loss and the disappointment will well-nigh break my mother's heart. According to your views of things, you owe me a grudge, but you are outside of the law, and I did my duty as a lawful man by trying to shoot you!"

"And I *bein'* outside o' the law, as you say, have let you off mighty easy, young man!" exclaimed Sandy Flash, his eyes shining angrily and his teeth glittering. "I took you for a fellow o' pluck, not for one that'd lie, even to the robber they call me! What's all this pitiful story about Barton's money?"

"Barton's money!"

"Oh—ay! You didn't agree to take some o' his money to Chester?" The mocking expression on the highwayman's face was ·perfectly diabolical. He slung the saddlebags over his shoulders, and turned to leave.

Gilbert was so amazed that for a moment he knew not what to say. Sandy Flash took three strides up the road, and then sprang down into the thicket.

"It's not Barton's money!" Gilbert cried, with a last desperate appeal—"it is mine, mine and my mother's!"

A short, insulting laugh was the only answer.

"Sandy Flash!" he cried again, raising his voice almost to a shout, as the crashing of the robber's steps through the brushwood sounded father and farther down the glen, "Sandy Flash! You have plundered a widow's honest earnings today, and a curse goes with such plunder! Hark you! if never before, you are cursed from this hour forth! I call upon God, in my mother's name, to mark you!"

There was no sound in reply, except the dull, dreary hum of the wind and the steady lashing of the rain. The growing darkness of the sky told of approaching night, and the wild glen, bleak enough before, was now a scene of utter and hopeless desolation to Gilbert's eyes. He was almost unmanned, not only by the cruel loss, but also by the stinging sense of outrage which it had left behind. A mixed feeling of wretched despondency and shame filled his heart, as he leaned, chill, weary, and still weak from the shock of his fall, upon Roger's neck.

The faithful animal turned his head from time to time, as if to question his master's unusual demeanor. There was a look of almost human sympathy in his large eyes; he was hungry and restless, yet would not move until the word of command had been given.

"Poor fellow!" said Gilbert, patting his cheek, "we've both fared ill today. But you mustn't suffer any longer for my sake."

He then mounted and rode onward through the storm.

CHAPTER 21

Roger Repays His Master

A mile or more beyond the spot where Gilbert Potter had been waylaid, there was a lonely tavern, called the "Drovers' Inn." Here he dismounted, more for his horse's sake than his own, although he was sore, weary, and sick of heart. After having carefully groomed Roger with his own hands, and commended him to the special attentions of the ostler, he entered the warm public room, wherein three or four stormbound drovers were gathered around the roaring fire of hickory logs.

The men kindly made way for the pale, dripping, wretched-looking stranger; and the landlord, with a shrewd glance and a suggestion of "Something hot, I reckon?" began mixing a compound proper for the occasion. Laying aside his wet cloak, which was sent to the kitchen to be more speedily dried, Gilbert presently sat in a cloud of his own steaming garments, and felt the warmth of the potent liquor in his chilly blood.

All at once, it occurred to him that the highwayman had not touched his person. There was not only some loose silver in his pockets, but Mark Deane's money-belt was still around his waist. So much, at least, was rescued, and he began to pluck up a little courage. Should he continue his journey to Chester, explain the misfortune to the holder of his mortgage, and give notice to the County Sheriff of this new act of robbery? Then the thought came into his mind that in that case he might be detained a day or two, in order to make depositions, or comply with some unknown legal form. In the meantime the news would spread over the country, no doubt with many exaggerations, and might possibly reach Kennett—even the ears of his mother. That reflection decided his course. She must first hear the truth from his mouth; he would try to give her cheer and encouragement, though he felt none himself; then, calling his friends together, he would hunt Sandy Flash like a wild beast until they had tracked him to his lair.

"Unlucky weather for ye, it seems?" remarked the curious landlord, who, seated in a corner of the fireplace, had for full ten minutes been watching Gilbert's knitted brows, gloomy, brooding eyes, and compressed lips.

"Weather?" he exclaimed, bitterly. "It's not the weather. Landlord, will you have a chance of sending to Chester to-morrow?"

"I'm going, if it clears up," said one of the drovers.

"Then, my friend," Gilbert continued, "will you take a letter from me to the Sheriff?"

"If it's nothing out of the way," the man replied.

"It's in the proper course of law—if there is any law to protect us. Not a mile and a half from here, landlord, I have been waylaid and robbed on the public road!"

There was a general exclamation of surprise, and Gilbert's story, which he had suddenly decided to relate in order that the people of the neighborhood might be put upon their guard, was listened to with an interest only less than the terror which it inspired. The landlady rushed into the barroom, followed by the red-faced kitchen wench, and both interrupted the recital with cries of "Dear, dear!" and "Lord save us!" The landlord, meanwhile, had prepared another tumbler of hot and hot, and brought it forward, saying,

"You need it, the Lord knows, and it shall cost you nothing."

"What I most need now," Gilbert said, "is pen, ink, and paper, to write out my account. Then I suppose you can get me up a cold check,* for I must start homewards soon."

"Not 'a cold check' after all that drenching and mishandling!" the landlord exclaimed. "We'll have a hot supper in half an hour, and you shall stay, and welcome. Wife, bring down one of Liddy's pens the schoolmaster made for her, and put a little vinegar into th' ink-bottle; it's most dried up!"

In a few minutes the necessary materials for a letter, all of the rudest kind, were supplied, and the landlord and drovers hovered around as Gilbert began to write, assisting him with the most extraordinary suggestions.

"I'd threaten," said a drover, "to write straight to General

---

*A local term, in use at the time, signifying a "lunch."

Washington, unless they promise to catch the scoundrel in no time!"

"And don't forget the knife and pistol!" cried the landlord.

"And say the Tory farmers' houses ought to be searched!"

"And give his marks, to a hair!"

Amid all this confusion, Gilbert managed to write a brief, but sufficiently circumstantial account of the robbery, calling upon the County authorities to do their part in effecting the capture of Sandy Flash. He offered his services and those of the Kennett troop, announcing that he should immediately start upon the hunt, and expected to be seconded by the law.

When the letter had been sealed and addressed, the drovers—some of whom carried money with them, and had agreed to travel in company, for better protection—eagerly took charge of it, promising to back the delivery with very energetic demands for assistance.

Night had fallen, and the rain fell with it, in renewed torrents. The dreary, universal hum of the storm rose again, making all accidental sounds of life impertinent, in contrast with its deep, tremendous monotone. The windows shivered, the walls sweat and streamed, and the wild wet blew in under the doors, as if beseiging that refuge of warm, red firelight.

"This beats the Lammas flood o' '68," said the landlord, as he led the way to supper. "I was a young man at that time, and remember it well. Half the dams on Brandywine went that night."

After a bountiful meal, Gilbert completely dried his garments and prepared to set out on his return, resisting the kindly persuasion of the host and hostess that he should stay all night. A restless, feverish energy filled his frame. He felt that he could not sleep, that to wait idly would be simple misery, and that only in motion towards the set aim of his fierce, excited desires, could he bear his disappointment and shame. But the rain still came down with a volume which threatened soon to exhaust the cisterns of the air, and in that hope he compelled himself to wait a little.

Towards nine o'clock the great deluge seemed to slacken. The wind arose, and there were signs of its shifting, erelong, to the northwest, which would bring clear weather in a few hours. The night was dark, but not pitchy; a dull phosphoric gleam overspread the under surface of the sky. The woods were full of noises, and every gully at the roadside gave token, by its stony rattle, of the rain-born streams.

With his face towards home and his back to the storm, Gilbert rode into the night. The highway was but a streak of less palpable darkness; the hills on either hand scarcely detached themselves from the low, black ceiling of sky behind them. Sometimes the light of a farmhouse window sparkled faintly, like a glowworm, but whether far or near, he could not tell; he only knew how blest must be the owner, sitting with wife and children around his secure hearthstone—how wretched his own life, cast adrift in the darkness—wife, home, and future, things of doubt!

He had lost more than money, and his wretchedness will not seem unmanly when we remember the steady strain and struggle of his previous life. As there is nothing more stimulating to human patience, and courage, and energy, than the certain prospect of relief at the end, so there is nothing more depressing than to see that relief suddenly snatched away, and the same round of toil thrust again under one's feet! This is the fate of Tantalus and Sisyphus in one.

Not alone the money; a year, or two years, of labor would no doubt replace what he had lost. But he had seen, in imagination, his mother's feverish anxiety at an end; household help procured, to lighten her over-heavy toil; the possibility of her release from some terrible obligation brought nearer, as he hoped and trusted, and with it the strongest barrier broken down which rose between him and Martha Deane. All these things which he had, as it were, held in his hand, had been stolen from him, and the loss was bitter because it struck down to the roots of the sweetest and strongest fibres of his heart. The night veiled his face, but if some hotter drops than those of the storm were shaken from his cheek, they left no stain upon his manhood.

The sense of outrage, of personal indignity, which no man can appreciate who has not himself been violently plundered, added its sting to his miserable mood. He thirsted to avenge the wrong; Barton's words involuntarily came back to him—"I'll know no peace till the villain has been strung up!" Barton! How came Sandy Flash to know that Barton intended to send money by him? Had not Barton himself declared that the matter should be kept secret? Was there some complicity between the latter and Sandy Flash? Yet, on the other hand, it seemed that the highwayman believed that he was robbing Gilbert of Barton's money. Here was an enigma which he could not solve.

All at once, a hideous solution presented itself. Was it possible that Barton's money was to be only *apparently* stolen—in reality returned to him privately, afterwards? Possibly the rest of the plunder divided between the two confederates? Gilbert was not in a charitable mood; the human race was much more depraved, in his view, than twelve hours before; and the inference which he would have rejected as monstrous, that very morning, now assumed a possible existence. One thing, at least, was certain; he would exact an explanation, and if none should be furnished, he would make public the evidence in his hands.

The black, dreary night seemed interminable. He could only guess, here and there, at a landmark, and was forced to rely more upon Roger's instinct of the road than upon the guidance of his senses. Towards midnight, as he judged by the solitary crow of a cock, the rain almost entirely ceased. The wind began to blow, sharp and keen, and the hard vault of the sky to lift a little. He fancied that the hills on his right had fallen away, and that the horizon was suddenly depressed towards the north. Roger's feet began to splash in constantly deepening water, and presently a roar, distinct from that of the wind, filled the air.

It was the Brandywine. The stream had overflowed its broad meadow-bottoms, and was running high and fierce beyond its main channel. The turbid waters made a dim, dusky gleam around him; soon the fences disappeared, and the flood reached to his horse's belly. But he knew that the ford could be distinguished by the break in the fringe of timber; moreover, that the creek-bank was a little higher than the meadows behind it, and so far, at least, he might venture. The ford was not more than twenty yards across, and he could trust Roger to swim that distance.

The faithful animal pressed bravely on, but Gilbert soon noticed that he seemed at fault. The swift water had forced him out of the road, and he stopped, from time to time, as if anxious and uneasy. The timber could now be discerned, only a short distance in advance, and in a few minutes they would gain the bank.

What was that? A strange rustling, hissing sound, as of cattle trampling through dry reeds—a sound which quivered and shook, even in the breath of the hurrying wind! Roger snorted, stood still, and trembled in every limb; and a sensation of awe and terror struck a chill through Gilbert's heart. The sound drew swiftly nearer, and became a wild, seething roar, filling the whole breadth of the valley.

"Great God!" cried Gilbert, "the dam!—the dam has given way!" He turned Roger's head, gave him the rein, struck, spurred, cheered, and shouted. The brave beast struggled through the impeding flood, but the advance wave of the coming inundation already touched his side. He staggered; a line of churning foam bore down upon them, the terrible roar was all around and over them, and horse and rider were whirled away.

What happened during the first few seconds, Gilbert could never distinctly recall. Now they were whelmed in the water, now riding its careering tide, torn through the tops of brushwood, jostled by floating logs and timbers of the dam-breast, but always, as it seemed, remorselessly held in the heart of the tumult and the ruin.

He saw, at last, that they had fallen behind the furious onset of the flood, but Roger was still swimming with it, desperately throwing up his head from time to time, and snorting the water from his nostrils. All his efforts to gain a foothold failed; his strength was nearly spent, and unless some help should come in a few minutes, it would come in vain. And in the darkness, and the rapidity with which they were borne along, how should help come?

All at once, Roger's course stopped. He became an obstacle to the flood, which pressed him against some other obstacle below, and rushed over horse and rider. Thrusting out his hand, Gilbert felt the rough bark of a tree. Leaning towards it and clasping the log in his arms, he drew himself from the saddle, while Roger, freed from his burden, struggled into the current and instantly disappeared.

As nearly as Gilbert could ascertain, several timbers, thrown over each other, had lodged, probably upon a rocky islet in the stream, the uppermost one projecting slantingly out of the flood. It required all his strength to resist the current which sucked, and whirled, and tugged at his body, and to climb high enough to escape its force without over-balancing his support. At last, though still half immersed, he found himself comparatively safe for a time, yet as far as ever from a final rescue.

He must await the dawn, and an eternity of endurance lay in

those few hours. Meantime, perhaps, the creek would fall, for the rain had ceased and there were outlines of moving cloud in the sky. It was the night which made his situation so terrible, by concealing the chances of escape. At first, he thought most of Roger. Was his brave horse drowned, or had he safely gained the bank below? Then, as the desperate moments went by, and the chill of exposure and the fatigue of exertion began to creep over him, his mind reverted, with a bitter sweetness, a mixture of bliss and agony, to the two beloved women to whom his life belonged—the life which, alas! he could not now call his own, to give.

He tried to fix his thoughts on death, to commend his soul to Divine Mercy; but every prayer shaped itself into an appeal that he might once more see the dear faces and hear the dear voices. In the great shadow of the fate which hung over him, the loss of his property became as dust in the balance, and his recent despair smote him with shame. He no longer fiercely protested against the injuries of fortune, but entreated pardon and pity for the sake of his love.

The clouds rolled into distincter masses, and the northwest wind still hunted them across the sky, until there came, first a tiny rift for a star, then a gap for a whole constellation, and finally a broad burst of moonlight. Gilbert now saw that the timber to which he clung was lodged nearly in the center of the channel, as the water swept with equal force on either side of him. Beyond the banks there was a wooded hill on the left; on the right an overflowed meadow. He was too weak and benumbed to trust himself to the flood, but he imagined that it was beginning to subside, and therein lay his only hope.

Yet a new danger now assailed him, from the increasing cold. There was already a sting of frost, a breath of ice, in the wind. In another hour the sky was nearly swept bare of clouds, and he could note the lapse of the night by the sinking of the moon. But he was by this time hardly in a condition to note anything more. He had thrown himself, face downwards, on the top of the log, his arms mechanically clasping it, while his mind sank into a state of torpid, passive suffering, growing nearer to the dreamy indifference which precedes death. His cloak had been torn away in the first rush of the inundation, and the wet coat began to stiffen in the wind from the ice gathering over it.

The moon was low in the west, and there was a pale glimmer

of the coming dawn in the sky when Gilbert Potter suddenly raised his head. Above the noise of the water and the whistle of the wind, he heard a familiar sound—the shrill, sharp neigh of a horse. Lifting himself, with great exertion, to a sitting posture, he saw two men, on horseback, in the flooded meadow, a little below him. They stopped, seemed to consult, and presently drew nearer.

Gilbert tried to shout, but the muscles of his throat were stiff, and his lungs refused to act. The horse neighed again. This time there was no mistake; it was Roger that he heard! Voice came to him, and he cried aloud—a hoarse, strange, unnatural cry.

The horsemen heard it, and rapidly pushed up the bank until they reached a point directly opposite to him. The prospect of escape brought a thrill of life to his frame; he looked around and saw that the flood had indeed fallen.

"We have no rope," he heard one of the men say. "How shall we reach him?"

"There is no time to get one, now," the other answered. "My horse is stronger than yours. I'll go into the creek just below, where it's broader and not so deep, and work my way up to him."

"But one horse can't carry both."

"His will follow, be sure, when it sees me."

As the last speaker moved away, Gilbert saw a led horse plunging through the water, beside the other. It was a difficult and dangerous undertaking. The horseman and the loose horse entered the main stream below, where its divided channel met and broadened, but it was still above the saddle-girths, and very swift. Sometimes the animals plunged, losing their foothold; nevertheless, they gallantly breasted the current, and inch by inch worked their way to a point about six feet below Gilbert. It seemed impossible to approach nearer.

"Can you swim?" asked the man.

Gilbert shook his head. "Throw me the end of Roger's bridle!" he then cried.

The man unbuckled the bridle and threw it, keeping the end of the rein in his hand. Gilbert tried to grasp it, but his hands were too numb. He managed, however, to get one arm and his head through the opening, and relaxed his hold on the log.

A plunge, and the man had him by the collar. He felt himself lifted by a strong arm and laid across Roger's saddle. With his failing strength and stiff limbs, it was no slight task to get into place, and the return, though less laborious to the horses, was equally dangerous, because Gilbert was scarcely able to support himself without help.

"You're safe now," said the man, when they reached the bank, "but it's a downright mercy of God that you're alive!"

The other horseman joined them, and they rode slowly across the flooded meadow. They had both thrown their cloaks around Gilbert, and carefully steadied him in the saddle, one on each side. He was too much exhausted to ask how they had found him, or whither they were taking him—too numb for curiosity, almost for gratitude.

"Here's your saviour!" said one of the men, patting Roger's shoulder. "It was all along of him that we found you. Want to know how? Well—about three o'clock it was, maybe a little earlier, maybe a little later, my wife woke me up. 'Do you hear that?' she says. I listened and heard a horse in the lane before the door, neighing—I can't tell you exactly how it was—like as if he'd call up the house. 'Twas rather queer, I thought, so I got up and looked out of window, and it seemed to me he had a saddle on. He stamped, and pawed, and then he gave another yell, and stamped again. Says I to my wife, 'There's something wrong here,' and I dressed and went out. When he saw me, he acted the strangest you ever saw; thinks I, if ever an animal wanted to speak, that animal does. When I tried to catch him, he shot off, run down the lane a bit, and then came back as strangely acting as ever. I went into the house and woke up my brother, here, and we saddled our horses and started. Away went yours ahead, stopping every minute to look around and see if we followed. When we came to the water, I kind o' hesitated, but 'twas no use; the horse would have us go on, and on, till we found you. I never heard tell of the like of it, in my born days!"

Gilbert did not speak, but two large tears slowly gathered in his eyes, and rolled down his cheeks. The men saw his emotion, and respected it.

In the light of the cold, keen dawn, they reached a snug farmhouse a mile from the Brandywine. The men lifted Gilbert from the saddle, and would have carried him immediately into the house, but he first leaned upon Roger's neck, took the faithful creature's head in his arms, and kissed it.

The good housewife was already up, and anxiously awaiting the return of her husband and his brother. A cheery fire crackled on the hearth, and the coffeepot was simmering beside it. When Gilbert had been partially revived by the warmth, the men conducted him into an adjoining bedroom, undressed him, and rubbed his limbs with whiskey. Then, a large bowl of coffee having been administered, he was placed in bed, covered with half a dozen blankets, and the curtains were drawn over the windows. In a few minutes he was plunged in a slumber almost as profound as that of the death from which he had been so miraculously delivered.

It was two hours past noon when he awoke, and he no sooner fully comprehended the situation and learned how the time had sped, than he insisted on rising, although still sore, weak, and feverish. The good farmer's wife had kept a huge portion of dinner hot before the fire, and he knew that without compelling a show of appetite, he would not be considered sufficiently recovered to leave. He had but one desire—to return home. So recently plucked from the jaws of death, his life still seemed to be an uncertain possession.

Finally Roger was led forth, quiet and submissive as of old— having forgotten his good deed as soon as it had been accomplished—and Gilbert, wrapped in the farmer's cloak, retraced his way to the main road. As he looked across the meadow, which told of the inundation in its sweep of bent, muddy grass, and saw, between the creek-bank trees, the lodged timber to which he had clung, the recollection of the night impressed him like a frightful dream. It was a bright, sharp, wintry day—the most violent contrast to that which had preceded it. The hills on either side, whose outlines he could barely guess in the darkness, now stood out from the air with a hard, painful distinctness; the sky was an arch of cold, steel-tinted crystal; and the north wind blew with a shrill, endless whistle through the naked woods.

As he climbed the long hill west of Chadd's Ford, Gilbert noticed how the meadow on his right had been torn by the flood gathered from the fields above. In one place a Hessian skull had been snapped from the buried skeleton, and was rolled to light, among the mud and pebbles. Not far off, something was moving among the bushes, and he involuntarily drew rein.

The form stopped, appeared to crouch down for a moment,

then suddenly rose and strode forth upon the grass. It was a woman, wearing a man's flannel jacket, and carrying a long, pointed staff in her hand. As she approached with rapid strides, he recognized Deb. Smith.

"Deborah!" he cried, "what are doing here?"

She set her pole to the ground and vaulted over the high picket-fence, like an athlete.

"Well," she said, "if I'd ha' been shy o' you, Mr. Gilbert, you wouldn't ha' seen me. I'm not one of them as goes prowlin' around among dead bodies' bones at midnight; what I want, I looks for in the daytime."

"Bones?" he asked. "You're surely not digging up the Hessians?"

"Not exackly; but, you see, the rain's turned out a few, and some on 'em, folks says, was buried with lots o' goold platted up in their pigtails. I know o' one man that dug up two or three to git their teeth (to sell to the tooth-doctors, you know), and when he took hold o' the pigtail to lift the head by, the hair come off in his hand, and out rattled ten good goolden guineas. Now, if any money's washed out, there's no harm in a body's pickin' of it up, as I see."

"What luck have you had?" asked Gilbert.

"Nothin' to speak of; a few buttons, and a thing or two. But I say, Mr. Gilbert, what luck ha' *you* had?" She had been keenly and curiously inspecting his face.

"Deborah!" he exclaimed, "you're a false prophet! You told me that, whatever happened, I was safe from Sandy Flash."

"Eh?"

There was a shrill tone of surprise and curiosity in this exclamation.

"You ought to know Sandy Flash better, before you prophesy in his name," Gilbert repeated, in a stern voice.

"Oh, Mr. Gilbert, tell me what you mean?" She grasped his leg with one hand, while she twisted the other in Roger's mane, as if to hold both horse and rider until the words were explained.

Thereupon he related to her in a brief, fierce way, all that had befallen him. Her face frew red and her eyes flashed; she shook her fist and swore under her breath, from time to time, while he spoke.

"You'll be righted, Mr. Gilbert!" she then cried, "you'll be righted, never fear! Leave it to me! Haven't I always kep' my word to you? You're believin' I lied the last time, and no wonder; but I'll prove the truth o' my words yet—may be the Devil git my soul, if I don't!"

"Don't think that I blame you, Deborah," he said. "You were too sure of my good luck, because you wished me to have it—that's all."

"Thank ye for that! But it isn't enough for me. When I promise a thing, I have power to keep my promise. Ax me no more questions; bide quiet awhile, and if the money isn't back in your pocket by New Year, I give ye leave to curse me, and kick me, and spit upon me!"

Gilbert smiled sadly and incredulously, and rode onward. He made haste to reach home, for a dull pain began to throb in his head, and chill shudders ran over his body. He longed to have the worst over which yet awaited him, and gain a little rest for body, brain, and heart.

CHAPTER 22

Martha Deane Takes a Resolution

Mary Potter had scarcely slept during the night of her son's absence. A painful unrest, such as she never remembered to have felt before, took complete possession of her. Whenever the monotony of the drenching rain outside lulled her into slumber for a few minutes, she was sure to start up in bed with a vague, singular impression that someone had called her name. After midnight, when the storm fell, the shrill wailing of the rising wind seemed to forebode disaster. Although she believed Gilbert to be safely housed in Chester, the fact constantly slipped from her memory, and she shuddered at every change in the wild weather as if he were really exposed to it.

The next day, she counted the hours with a feverish impatience. It seemed like tempting Providence, but she determined to surprise her son with a supper of unusual luxury for their simple habits, after so important and so toilsome a journey. Sam had killed a fowl; it was picked and dressed, but she had not courage to put it into the pot, until the fortune of the day had been assured.

Towards sunset she saw, through the back kitchen-window, a horseman approaching from the direction of Carson's. It seemed to be Roger, but could that rider, in the faded brown cloak, be Gilbert? His cloak was blue; he always rode with his head erect, not hanging like this man's, whose features she could not see. Opposite the house, he lifted his head—it *was* Gilbert, but how old and haggard was his face!

She met him at the gate. His cheeks were suddenly flushed, his eyes bright, and the smile with which he looked at her seemed to be joyous; yet it gave her a sense of pain and terror.

"Oh, Gilbert!" she cried; "what has happened?"

He slid slowly and wearily off the horse, whose neck he fondled a moment before answering her.

227

"Mother," he said at last, "you have to thank Roger that I am here tonight. I have come back to you from the gates of death; will you be satisfied with that for a while?"

"I don't understand you, my boy! You frighten me; haven't you been at Chester?"

"No," he answered, "there was no use of going."

A presentiment of the truth came to her, but before she could question him further, he spoke again.

"Mother, let us go into the house. I am cold and tired; I want to sit in your old rocking chair, where I can rest my head. Then I'll tell you everything; I wish I had an easier task!"

She noticed that his steps were weak and slow, felt that his hands were like ice, and saw his blue lips and chattering teeth. She removed the strange cloak, placed her chair in front of the fire, seated him in it, and then knelt upon the floor to draw off his stiff, sodden top boots. He was passive as a child in her hands. Her care for him overcame all other dread, and not until she had placed his feet upon a stool, in the full warmth of the blaze, given him a glass of hot wine and lavender, and placed a pillow under his head, did she sit down at his side to hear the story.

"I thought of this, last night," he said, with a faint smile; "not that I ever expected to see it. The man was right; it's a mercy of God that I ever got out alive!"

"Then be grateful to God, my boy!" she replied, "and let me be grateful, too. It will balance misfortune—for that there *is* misfortune in store for us, I see plainly."

Gilbert then spoke. The narrative was long and painful, and he told it wearily and brokenly, yet with entire truth, disguising nothing of the evil that had come upon them. His mother sat beside him, pale, stony, stifling the sobs that rose in her throat, until he reached the period of his marvelous rescue, when she bent her head upon his arm and wept aloud.

"That's all, Mother!" he said at the close; "it's hard to bear, but I'm more troubled on your account than on my own."

"Oh, I feared we were over-sure!" she cried. "I claimed payment before it was ready. The Lord chooses His own time, and punishes them that can't wait for His ways to be manifest! It's terribly hard; and yet, while His left hand smites, His right hand gives mercy! He might ha' taken you, my boy, but He makes a miracle to save you for me!"

When she had outwept her passionate tumult of feeling, she grew composed and serene. "Haven't I yet learned to be patient, in all these years?" she said. "Haven't I sworn to work out with open eyes the work I took in blindness? And after waiting twenty-five years, am I to murmur at another year or two? No, Gilbert! It's to be done; I *will* deserve my justice! Keep your courage, my boy; be brave and patient, and the sight of you will hold me from breaking down!"

She arose, felt his hands and feet, set his pillow aright, and then stooped and kissed him. His chills had ceased; a feeling of heavy, helpless languor crept over him.

"Let Sam see to Roger, Mother!" he murmured. "Tell him not to spare the oats."

"I'd feed him with my own hands, Gilbert, if I could leave you. I'd put fine wheat bread into his manger, and wrap him in blankets off my own bed! To think that Roger—that I didn't want you to buy—Lord forgive me, I was advising your own death!"

It was fortunate for Mary Potter that she saw a mysterious Providence, which, to her mind, warned and yet promised while it chastised, in all that had occurred. This feeling helped her to bear a disappointment which would otherwise have been very grievous. The idea of an atoning ordeal which she must endure in order to be crowned with the final justice, and so behold her life redeemed, had become rooted in her nature. To Gilbert much of this feeling was inexplicable, because he was ignorant of the circumstances which had called it into existence. But he saw that his mother was not yet hopeless, that she did not seem to consider her deliverance as materially postponed, and a glimmer of hope was added to the relief of having told his tale.

He was still feverish, dozing and muttering in uneasy dreams, as he lay back in the old rocking chair, and Mary Potter, with Sam's help, got him to bed, after administering a potion which she was accustomed to use in all complaints, from mumps to typhus fever.

As for Roger, he stood knee-deep in clean litter, with half a bushel of oats before him.

The next morning Gilbert did not arise, and as he complained of great soreness in every part of his body, Sam was dispatched for Dr. Deane.

It was the first time this gentleman had ever been summoned

to the Potter farmhouse. Mary Potter felt considerable trepidation at his arrival, both on account of the awe which his imposing presence inspired, and the knowledge of her son's love for his daughter—a fact which, she rightly conjectured, he did not suspect. As he brought his ivory-headed cane, his sleek drab broadcloth, and his herbaceous fragrance into the kitchen, she was almost overpowered.

"How is thy son ailing?" he asked. "He always seemed to me to be a very healthy young man."

She described the symptoms with a conscientious minuteness.

"How was it brought on?" he asked again.

She had not intended to relate the whole story, but only so much of it as was necessary for the Doctor's purposes; but the commencement excited his curiosity, and he knew so skillfully how to draw one word after another, suggesting further explanations without directly asking them, that Mary Potter was led on and on, until she had communicated all the particulars of her son's misfortune.

"This is a wonderful tale thee tells me," said the Doctor—"wonderful! Sandy Flash, no doubt, has reason to remember thy son, who, I'm told, faced him very boldly on Second-day morning. It is really time the country was aroused; we shall hardly be safe in our own houses. And all night in the Brandywine flood—I don't wonder thy son is unwell. Let me go up to him."

Dr. Deane's prescriptions usually conformed to the practice of his day—bleeding and big doses—and he would undoubtedly have applied both of these in Gilbert's case, but for the latter's great anxiety to be in the saddle and on the hunt of his enemy. He stoutly refused to be bled, and the Doctor had learned, from long observation, that patients of a certain class must be humored rather than coerced. So he administered a double dose of Dover's Powders, and prohibited the drinking of cold water. His report was, on the whole, reassuring to Mary Potter. Provided his directions were strictly followed, he said, her son would be up in two or three days; but there *might* be a turn for the worse, as the shock to the system had been very great, and she ought to have assistance.

"There's no one I can call upon," said she, "without it's Betsy Lavender, and I must ask you to tell her for me, if you think she can come."

"I'll oblige thee, certainly," the Doctor answered. "Betsy *is* with us, just now, and I don't doubt but she can spare a day or two. She may be a little headstrong in her ways, but thee'll find her a safe nurse."

It was really not necessary, as the event proved. Rest and warmth were what Gilbert most needed. But Dr. Deane always exaggerated his patient's condition a little, in order that the credit of the latter's recovery might be greater. The present case was a very welcome one, not only because it enabled him to recite a most astonishing narrative at secondhand, but also because it suggested a condition far more dangerous than that which the patient actually suffered. He was the first person to bear the news to Kennett Square, where it threw the village into a state of great excitement, which rapidly spread over the neighborhood.

He related it at his own tea table that evening to Martha and Miss Betsy Lavender. The former could with difficulty conceal her agitation; she turned red and pale, until the Doctor finally remarked,

"Why, child, thee needn't be so frightened."

"Never mind!" exclaimed Miss Betsy, promptly coming to the rescue, "it's enough to frighten anybody. It fairly makes me shiver in my shoes. If Alf. Barton had ha' done his dooty like a man, this wouldn't ha' happened!"

"I've no doubt Alfred did the best he could, under the circumstances," the Doctor sternly remarked.

"Fiddle-de-dee!" was Miss Betsy's contemptuous answer. "He's no more gizzard than a rabbit. But that's neither here nor there; Mary Potter wants me to go down and help, and go I will!"

"Yes, I think thee might as well go down tomorrow morning, though I'm in hopes the young man may be better, if he minds my directions," said the Doctor.

"Tomorrow mornin'? Why not next week? When help's wanted, give it *right away*; don't let the grass grow under your feet, say I! Good luck that I gev up Mendenhall's homecomin' over t' the Lion, or I wouldn't ha' been here; so another cup o' tea, Martha, and I'm off!"

Martha left the table at the same time, and followed Miss Betsy upstairs. Her eyes were full of tears, but she did not tremble, and her voice came firm and clear.

"I am going with you," she said.

Miss Lavender whirled around and looked at her a minute, without saying a word.

"I see you mean it, child. Don't think me hard or cruel, for I know your feelin's as well as if they was mine; but all the same, I've got to look ahead, and back'ards, and on this side and that, and so lookin', and so judgin', accordin' to my light, which a'n't all tied up in a napkin, what I've got to say is, and ag'in don't think me hard, it won't do!"

"Betsy," Martha Deane persisted, "a misfortune like this brings my duty with it. Besides, he may be in great danger; he may have got his death—"

"Don't begin talkin' that way," Miss Lavender interrupted, "or you'll put me out o' patience. I'll say that for your father, he's always mortal concerned for a bad case, Gilbert Potter or not; and I can mostly tell the heft of a sickness by the way he talks about it—so that's settled; and as to dooties, it's very well and right, I don't deny it, but never mind, all the same, I said before, the whole thing's a snarl, and I say it ag'in, and unless you've got the end o' the ravellin's in your hand, the harder you pull, the wuss you'll make it!"

There was good sense in these words, and Martha Deane felt it. Her resolution began to waver, in spite of the tender instinct which told her that Gilbert Potter now needed precisely the help and encouragement which she alone could give.

"Oh, Betsy," she murmured, her tears falling without restraint, "it's hard for me to seem so strange to him, at such a time!"

"Yes," answered the spinster, setting her comb tight with a fierce thrust, "it's hard every one of us can't have our own ways in this world! But don't take on now, Martha dear; we only have your father's word, and not to be called a friend's, but *I'll* see how the land lays, and tomorrow evenin', or next day at th' outside, you'll know everything fair and square. Neither you nor Gilbert is inclined to do things rash, and what you *both* agree on, after a proper understandin', I guess'll be pretty nigh right. There! where's my knittin'-basket?"

Miss Lavender trudged off, utterly fearless of the night walk of two miles, down the lonely road. In less than an hour she knocked at the door of the farmhouse, and was received with open arms by Mary Potter. Gilbert had slept the greater part of the day but was now awake, and so restless from the desire to leave his bed, that his mother could with difficulty restrain him.

"Set down and rest yourself, Mary!" Miss Betsy exclaimed. "I'll go up and put him to rights."

She took a lamp and mounted to the bedroom. Gilbert, drenched in perspiration, and tossing uneasily under a huge pile of blankets, sprang up as her gaunt figure entered the door. She placed the lamp on a table, pressed him down on the pillow by main force, and covered him up to the chin.

"Martha?" he whispered, his face full of intense, piteous eagerness.

"Will you promise to lay still and sweat, as you're told to do?"

"Yes, yes!"

"Now let me feel your pulse. That'll do; now for your tongue! Tut, tut! the boy's not so bad. I give you my word you may get up and dress yourself tomorrow mornin', if you'll only hold out tonight. And as for thorough-stem tea.* and what not, I guess you've had enough of 'em; but you can't jump out of a sick-spell into downright peartness, at one jump!"

"Martha, Martha!" Gilbert urged.

"You're both of a piece, I declare! There was she, this very night, dead set on comin' down with me, and mortal hard it was to persuade her to be reasonable!"

Miss Lavender had not a deal to relate, but Gilbert compelled her to make up by repetition what she lacked in quantity. And at every repetition the soreness seemed to decrease in his body, and the weakness in his muscles, and hope and courage to increase in his heart.

"Tell her," he exclaimed, "it was enough that she wanted to come. That alone has put new life into me!"

"I see it has," said Miss Lavender, "and now, maybe, you've got life enough to tell me all the ups and downs o' this affair, for I can't say as I rightly understand it."

The conference was long and important. Gilbert related every circumstance of his adventure, including the mysterious allusion to Alfred Barton, which he had concealed from his mother. He was determined, as his first course, to call the volunteers to-

---

*Possibly a reference to tea made with thoroughwort, an English medicinal herb (ed.).

gether and organize a thorough hunt for the highwayman. Until that had been tried, he would postpone all further plans of action. Miss Lavender did not say much, except to encourage him in this determination. She felt that there was grave matter for reflection in what had happened. The threads of mystery seemed to increase, and she imagined it possible that they might all converge to one unknown point.

"Mary," she said, when she descended to the kitchen, "I don't see but what the boy's goin' on finely. Go to bed, you, and sleep quietly; I'll take the settle, here, and I promise you I'll go up every hour through the night to see whether he's kicked his coverin's off."

Which promise she faithfully kept, and in the morning Gilbert came down to breakfast, a little haggard, but apparently as sound as ever. Even the Doctor, when he arrived, was slightly surprised at the rapid improvement.

"A fine constitution for medicines to work on," he remarked. "I wouldn't wish thee to be sick, but when thee *is*, it's a pleasure to see how thy system obeys the treatment."

Martha Deane, during Miss Lavender's absence, had again discussed in her heart her duty to Gilbert. Her conscience was hardly satisfied with the relinquishment of her first impulse. She felt that there was, there must be, something for her to do in this emergency. She knew that he had toiled, and dared, and suffered for her sake, while she had done nothing. It was not pride—at least not the haughty quality which bears an obligation uneasily—but rather the impulse, at once brave and tender, to stand side by side with him in the struggle, and win an equal right to the final blessing.

In the afternoon Miss Lavender returned, and her first business was to give a faithful report of Gilbert's condition and the true story of his misfortune, which she repeated, almost word for word, as it came from his lips. It did not differ materially from that which Martha had already heard, and the direction which her thoughts had taken in the meantime seemed to be confirmed. The gentle, steady strength of purpose that looked from her clear blue eyes, and expressed itself in the firm, sharp curve of her lip, was never more distinct than when she said,

"Now, Betsy, all is clear to me. You were right before, and I am right now. I must see Gilbert when he calls the men together, and after that I shall know how to act."

Three days afterwards, there was another assemblage of the Kennett Volunteers at the Unicorn Tavern. This time, however, Mark Deane was on hand, and Alfred Barton did not make his appearance. That Gilbert Potter should take the command was an understood matter. The preliminary consultation was secretly held, and when Dougherty, the Irish ostler, mixed himself, as by accident, among the troop, Gilbert sharply ordered him away. Whatever the plan of the chase was, it was not communicated to the crowd of country idlers; and there was, in consequence, some grumbling at, and a great deal of respect for, the new arrangement.

Miss Betsy Lavender had managed to speak to Gilbert before the others arrived; therefore, after they had left, to meet the next day, equipped for a possible absence of a week, he crossed the road and entered Dr. Deane's house.

This time the two met, not so much as lovers, but rather as husband and wife might meet after long absence and escape from imminent danger. Martha Deane knew how cruel and bitter Gilbert's fate must seem to his own heart, and she resolved that all the cheer which lay in her buoyant, courageous nature should be given to him. Never did a woman more sweetly bend the tones of regret and faith, sympathy and encouragement.

"The time has come, Gilbert," she said at last, "when our love for each other must no longer be kept a secret—at least from the few who, under other circumstances, would have a right to know it. We must still wait, though no longer (remember that!) than we were already agreed to wait; but we should betray ourselves, sooner or later, and then the secret, discovered by others, would seem to hint at a sense of shame. We shall gain respect and sympathy, and perhaps help, if we reveal it ourselves. Even if you do not take the same view, Gilbert, think of this, that it is my place to stand beside you in your hour of difficulty and trial; that other losses, other dangers, may come, and you could not, you must not, hold me apart when my heart tells me we should be together!"

She laid her arms caressingly over his shoulders, and looked into his face. A wonderful softness and tenderness touched his pale, worn countenance. "Martha," he said, "remember that my disgrace will cover you, yet awhile."

"Gilbert!"

That one word, proud, passionate, reproachful, yet forgiving, sealed his lips.

"So be it!" he cried. "God knows, I think but of you. If I selfishly considered myself, do you think I would hold back my own honor?"

"A poor honor," she said, "that I sit comfortably at home and love you, while you are face to face with death!"

Martha Deane's resolution was inflexibly taken. That same evening she went into the sitting room, where her father was smoking a pipe before the open stove, and placed her chair opposite to his.

"Father," she said, "thee has never asked any questions concerning Alfred Barton's visit."

The Doctor started, and looked at her keenly, before replying. Her voice had its simple, natural tone, her manner was calm and self-possessed; yet something in her firm, erect posture and steady eye impressed him with the idea that she had determined on a full and final discussion of the question.

"No, child," he answered, after a pause. "I saw Alfred, and he said thee was rather taken by surprise. He thought, perhaps, thee didn't rightly know thy own mind, and it would be better to wait a little. That is the chief reason why I haven't spoken to thee."

"If Alfred Barton said that, he told thee false," said she. "I knew my own mind, as well then as now. I said to him that nothing could ever make me his wife."

"Martha!" the Doctor exclaimed, "don't be hasty! If Alfred is a little older—"

"Father!" she interrupted, "never mention this thing again! Thee can neither give me away, nor sell me; though I am a woman, I belong to myself. Thee knows I'm not hasty in anything. It was a long time before I rightly knew my own heart; but when I did know it and found that it had chosen truly, I gave it freely, and it is gone from me forever!"

"Martha, Martha!" cried Dr. Deane, starting from his seat, "what does all this mean?"

"It means something which it is thy right to know, and therefore I have made up my mind to tell thee, even at the risk of incurring thy lasting displeasure. I means that I have followed the guidance of my own heart and bestowed it on a man a thousand times better and nobler than Alfred Barton ever was, and if the Lord spares us to each other, I shall one day be his wife!"

The Doctor glared at his daughter in speechless amazement. But she met his gaze steadily, although her face grew a shade paler, and the expression of the pain she could not entirely suppress, with the knowledge of the struggle before her, trembled ·a little about the corners of her lips.

"Who is this man?" he asked.

"Gilbert Potter."

Dr. Deane's pipe dropped from his hand and smashed upon the iron hearth.

"Martha Deane!" he cried. "Does the d— *what* possesses thee? Wasn't it enough that thee should drive away the man I had picked out for thee, with a single view to thy own interest and happiness; but must thee take up, as a wicked spite to thy father, with almost the only man in the neighborhood who brings thee nothing but poverty and disgrace? It shall not be—it shall never be!"

"It *must* be, Father," she said gently. "God hath joined our hearts and our lives, and no man—not even thee—shall put them asunder. If there were disgrace, in the eyes of the world—which I now know there is not—Gilbert has wiped it out by his courage, his integrity, and his sufferings. If he is poor, I am well-to-do."

"Thee forgets," the Doctor interrupted, in a stern voice, "the time isn't up!"

"I know that unless thee gives thy consent, we must wait three years; but I hope, Father, when thee comes to know Gilbert better, thee will not be so hard. I am thy only child, and my happiness cannot be indifferent to thee. I have tried to obey thee in all things—"

He interrupted her again. "Thee's adding another cross to them I bear for thee already! Am I not, in a manner, thy keeper, and responsible for thee before the world and in the sight of the Lord? But thee hardened thy heart against the direction of the Spirit, and what wonder, then, that it's hardened against me?"

"No, Father," said Martha, rising and laying her hand softly upon his arm, "I *obeyed* the Spirit in that other matter, as I obey my conscience in this. I took my duty into my own hands, and considered it in a humble, and, I hope, a pious spirit. I saw that there were innocent needs of nature, pleasant enjoyments of life, which did not conflict with sincere devotion, and that I was not called upon to renounce them because others happened to see the world in a different light. In this sense, thee is not my keeper; I must render an account, not to thee, but to Him who gave me my soul. Neither is thee the keeper of my heart and its affections. In the one case and the other my right is equal—nay, it stands as far above thine as Heaven is above the earth!"

In the midst of his wrath, Dr. Deane could not help admiring his daughter. Foiled and exasperated as he was by the sweet, serene, lofty power of her words, they excited a wondering respect which he found it difficult to hide.

"Ah, Martha!" he said, "thee has a wonderful power, if it were only directed by the true Light! But now, it only makes the cross heavier. Don't think that I'll ever consent to see thee carry out thy strange and wicked fancies! Thee must learn to forget this man Potter, and the sooner thee begins, the easier it will be!"

"Father," she answered, with a sad smile, "I'm sorry thee knows so little of my nature. The wickedness would be in forgetting. It is very painful to me that we must differ. Where my duty was wholly owed to thee, I have never delayed to give it; but here it is owed to Gilbert Potter—owed, and will be given."

"Enough, Martha!" cried the Doctor, trembling with anger; "don't mention his name again!"

"I will not, except when the same duty requires it to be mentioned. But, Father, try to think less harshly of the name; it will one day be mine!"

She spoke gently and imploringly, with tears in her eyes. The conflict had been, as she said, very painful; but her course was plain, and she dared not flinch a step at the outset. The difficulties must be met face to face, and resolutely assailed, if they were ever to be overcome.

Dr. Deane strode up and down the room in silence, with his hands behind his back. Martha stood by the fire, waiting his further speech, but he did not look at her, and at the end of half an hour, commanded shortly and sharply, without turning his head,

"Go to bed!"

"Good-night, Father," she said, in her usual clear sweet voice, and quietly left the room.

CHAPTER 23

A Cross-Examination

The story of Gilbert Potter's robbery and marvellous escape from death ran rapidly through the neighborhood, and coming, as if did, upon the heels of his former adventure, created a great excitement. He became almost a hero in the minds of the people. It was not their habit to allow any man to *quite* assume so lofty a character as that, but they granted to Gilbert fully as much interest as, in their estimation, any human being ought properly to receive. Dr. Deane was eagerly questioned, wherever he went; and if his garments could have exhaled the odors of his feelings, his questioners would have smelled aloes and asafoetida instead of sweet marjoram and bergamot. But—in justice to him be it said—he told and retold the story very correctly; the tide of sympathy ran so high and strong that he did not venture to stem it on grounds which could not be publicly explained.

The supposed disgrace of Gilbert's birth seemed to be quite forgotten for the time; and there was no young man of spirit in the four townships who was not willing to serve under his command. More volunteers offered, in fact, than could be profitably employed. Sandy Flash was not the game to be unearthed by a loud, numerous, sweeping hunt; traps, pitfalls, secret and unwearied following of his many trails were what was needed. So much time had elapsed that the beginning must be a conjectural beating of the bushes, and to this end several small companies were organized, and the country between the Octorara and the Delaware very effectually scoured.

When the various parties reunited after several days, neither of them brought any positive intelligence, but all the greater store of guesses and rumors. Three or four suspicious individuals had been followed and made to give an account of themselves; certain hiding-places, especially the rocky lairs along the Brandywine and the North Valley-Hill, were carefully examined, and some traces of occupation, though none very recent, were discovered. Such evidence as there was seemed to indicate that part of the eastern branch of the Brandywine, between the forks of the stream and the great Chester Valley, as being the probable retreat of the highwayman, and a second expedition was at once organized. The Sheriff, with a posse of men from the lower part of the county, undertook to watch the avenues of escape towards the river.

This new attempt was not more successful, so far as its main object was concerned, but it actually stumbled upon Sandy Flash's trail, and only failed by giving tongue too soon and following too impetuously. Gilbert and his men had a tantalizing impression (which later intelligence proved to have been correct) that the robber was somewhere near them—buried in the depths of the very wood they were approaching, dodging behind the next barn as it came into view, or hidden under dead leaves in some rain-washed gulley. Had they but known, one gloomy afternoon in late December, that they were riding under the cedar tree in whose close, cloudy foliage he was coiled, just above their heads! Had they but guessed who the deaf old woman was, with her face muffled from the cold, and six cuts of blue yarn in her basket! But detection had not then become a science, and they were far from suspecting the extent of Sandy Flash's devices and disguises.

Many of the volunteers finally grew tired of the fruitless chase and returned home; others could only spare a few days from their winter labors; but Gilbert Potter, with three or four faithful and courageous young fellows—one of whom was Mark Deane—returned again and again to the search, and not until the end of December did he confess himself baffled. By this time all traces of the highwayman were again lost; he seemed to have disappeared from the country.

"I believe Pratt's right," said Mark, as the two issued from the Marlborough woods, on their return to Kennett Square. "Chester County is too hot to hold him."

"Perhaps so," Gilbert answered, with a gloomy face. He was more keenly disappointed at the failure than he would then confess, even to Mark. The outrage committed upon him was still unavenged, and thus his loss, to his proud, sensitive nature, carried a certain shame with it. Moreover, the loss itself must speedily be replaced. He had half flattered himself with the hope of capturing not only Sandy Flash, but his plunder; it was hard to forget that, for a day or two, he had been independent—hard to stoop again to be a borrower and a debtor!

"What are the county authorities good for?" Mark exclaimed. "Between you and me, the Sheriff's a reg'lar puddin'-head. I wish you was in his place.

"If Sandy is safe in Jersey, or down on the Eastern Shore, that would do no good. It isn't enough that he leaves us alone, from this time on; he has a heavy back-score to settle."

"Come to think on it, Gilbert," Mark continued, "isn't it rather queer that you and him should be thrown together in such ways? There was Barton's fox-chase last spring; then your shootin' at each other, at the Square; and then the robbery on the road. It seems to me as if he picked you out to follow you, and yet I don't know why."

Gilbert started. Mark's words reawakened the dark, incredible suspicion which Martha Deane had removed. Again he declared to himself that he would not entertain the thought, but he could not reject the evidence that there was something more than accident in all these encounters. If anyone besides Sandy Flash were responsible for the last meeting, it must be Alfred Barton. The latter, therefore, owed him an explanation, and he would demand it.

When they reached the top of the "big hill" north of the Fairthorn farmhouse, whence they looked eastward down the sloping corn-field which had been the scene of the husking frolic, Mark turned to Gilbert with an honest blush all over his face, and said,

"I don't see why you shouldn't know it, Gilbert. I'm sure Sally wouldn't care; you're almost like a brother to her."

"What?" Gilbert asked, yet with a quick suspicion of the coming intelligence.

"Oh, I guess you know well enough, old fellow. I asked her that night, and it's all right between us. What do you say to it, now?"

"Mark, I'm glad of it; I wish you joy, with all my heart!" Gilbert stretched out his hand, and as he turned and looked squarely into Mark's half-bashful yet wholly happy face, he re-membered Martha's words, at their last interview.

"You are like a brother to me, Mark," he said, "and you shall have *my* secret. What would you say if I had done the same thing?"

"No!" Mark exclaimed; "who?"

"Guess!"

"Not—not Martha?"

Gilbert smiled.

"By the Lord! It's the best day's work *you've* ever done! Gi' me y'r hand ag'in; we'll stand by each other faster than ever, now!"

When they stopped at Fairthorn's, the significant pressure of Gilbert's hand brought a blush into Sally's cheek; but when Mark met Martha with his telltale face, she answered with a proud and tender smile.

Gilbert's first business after his return was to have a consultation with Miss Betsy Lavender, who alone know of the suspicions attaching to Alfred Barton. The spinster had, in the meantime, made the matter the subject of profound and somewhat painful cogitation. She had ransacked her richly stored memory of persons and events, until her brain was like a drawer of tumbled clothes; had spent hours in laborious mental research, becoming so absorbed that she sometimes gave crooked answers when spoken to, and was haunted with a terrible dread of having thought aloud; and had questioned the oldest gossips right and left, coming as near the hidden subject as she dared. When they met, she communicated the result to Gilbert in this wise:

" 'T a'n't agreeable for a body to allow they're flummuxed, but if *I* a'n't, this time, I'm mighty near onto it. It's like lookin' for a set o' buttons that'll match, in a box full o' tail ends o' things. This'n 'd do, and that'n 'd do; but you can't put this'n and that'n together; and here's got to be square work, everything fitting' tight and hangin' plumb, or it'll be throwed back onto your hands, and all to be done over ag'in. I dunno when I've done so much headwork and to no purpose, follerin' here and guessin' there, and nosin' into everything that's past and gone; and so my opinion is, whether you like it or not, but never mind, all the same, I can't do no more than give it, that we'd better drop what's past and gone, and look a little more into these present times!"

"Well, Betsy," said Gilbert, with a stern, determined face, "this is what I shall do. I am satisfied that Barton is connected, in some way, with Sandy Flash. What it is, or whether the knowledge will help us, I can't guess; but I shall force Barton to tell me!"

"To tell me. That might do, as far as it goes," she remarked, after a moment's reflection. "It won't be easy; you'll have to threaten as well as coax, but I guess you can git it out of him in the long run, and maybe I can help you here, two bein' better than one, if one is but a sheep's-head."

"I don't see, Betsy, that I need to call on you."

"This way, Gilbert. It's a strong p'int o' law, I've heerd tell, not that I know much o' law, Goodness knows, nor ever want to, but never mind, it's a strong p'int when there's two witnesses to a thing—one to clinch what the t'other drives in; and you must have a show o' law to work on Alf. Barton, or I'm much mistaken!"

Gilbert reflected a moment. "It can do no harm," he then said; "can you go with me, now?"

"Now's the time! If we only git the light of a farden-candle* out o' him, it'll do me a mortal heap o' good; for with all this rakin' and scrapin' for nothin', I'm like a heart pantin' after the water-brooks, though a mouth would be more like it, to my thinkin', when a body's so awful dry as that comes to!"

The two thereupon took the footpath down through the frozen fields and the dreary timber of the creek-side, to the Barton farmhouse. As they approached the barn, they saw Alfred Barton sitting on a pile of straw and watching Giles, who was threshing wheat. He seemed a little surprised at their appearance; but as Gilbert and he had not met since their interview in the corn-field before the former's departure for Chester, he had no special cause for embarrassment.

"Come into the house," he said, leading the way.

"No," Gilbert answered, "I came here to speak with you privately. Will you walk down the lane?"

"No objection, of course," said Barton, looking from Gilbert to Miss Lavender, with a mixture of curiosity and uneasiness. "Good news, I hope; got hold of Sandy's tracks, at last?"

"One of them."

"Ah, you don't say so! Where?"

"Here!"

Gilbert stopped and faced Barton. They were below the barn, and out of Giles's hearing.

*Dialectal variant of "farthing candle"—hence, something of small size or value (ed.).

"Barton," he resumed, "you know what interest I have in the arrest of that man, and you won't deny my right to demand of you an account of your dealings with him. When did you first make his acquaintance?"

"I've told you that, already; the matter has been fully talked over between us," Barton answered, in a petulant tone.

"It has not been fully talked over. I require to know, first of all, precisely when, and under what circumstances, you and Sandy Flash came together. There is more to come, so let us begin at the beginning."

"Damme, Gilbert, *you* were there, and saw as much as I did. How could I know who the cursed black-whiskered fellow was?"

"But you found it out," Gilbert persisted, "and the manner of your finding it out must be explained."

Barton assumed a bold, insolent manner. "I don't see as that follows," he said. "It has nothing in the world to do with his robbery of you; and as for Sandy Flash, I wish to the Lord you'd get hold of him yourself, instead of trying to make me accountable for his comings and goings!"

"He's tryin' to fly off the handle," Miss Lavender remarked. "I'd drop that part o' the business a bit, if I was you, and come to the t'other proof."

"What the devil have *you* to do here?" asked Barton.

"Miss Betsy is here because I asked her," Gilbert said. "Because all that passes between us may have to be repeated in a court of justice, and two witnesses are better than one!"

He took advantage of the shock which these words produced upon Barton, and repeated to him the highwayman's declarations, with the inference they might bear if not satisfactorily explained. "I kept my promise," he added, "and said nothing to any living soul of your request that I should carry money for you to Chester. Sandy Flash's information, therefore, must have come, either directly or indirectly, from you."

Barton had listened with open mouth and amazed eyes.

"Why, the man is a devil!" he cried. "I, neither, never said a word of the matter to any living soul!"

"Did you really send any money?" Gilbert asked.

"That I did! I got it of Joel Ferris, and it happened he was bound for Chester the very next day, on his own business; and so, instead of turning it over to me, he just paid it there, according to my directions. You'll understand, this is between ourselves?"

He darted a sharp, suspicious glance at Miss Betsy Lavender, who gravely nodded her head.

"The difficulty is not yet explained," said Gilbert, "and perhaps you'll *now* not deny my right to know something more of your first acquaintance with Sandy Flash?"

"Have it then!" Barton exclaimed, desperately—"and much good may it do you! I thought his name was Fortune, as much as you did, till nine o'clock that night, when he put a pistol to my breast in the woods! If you think I'm colloguing* with him, why did he rob me under threat of murder—money, watch, and everything?"

"Ah-ha!" said Miss Lavender, "and so that's the way your watch has been gittin' mended all this while? Mainspring broke, as I've heerd say; well, I don't wonder! Gilbert, I guess this much is true. Alf. Barton'd never live so long without that watch, and that half-peck o' seals, if he could help it!"

"This, too, may as well be kept to ourselves," Barton suggested. "It isn't agreeable to a man to have it known that he's been so taken in as I was, and that's just the reason why I kept it to myself; and, of course, I shouldn't like it to get around."

Gilbert could do no less than accept this part of the story, and it rendered his later surmises untenable. But the solution which he sought was as far off as ever.

"Barton," he said, after a long pause, "will you do your best to help me in finding out how Sandy Flash got the knowledge?"

"Only show me a way! The best would be to catch him and get it from his own mouth."

He looked so earnest, so eager, and—as far as the traces of cunning in his face would permit—so honest, that Gilbert yielded to a sudden impulse, and said,

"I believe you, Barton. I've done you wrong in my thoughts— not willingly, for I don't want to think badly of you or anyone else—but because circumstances seemed to drive me to it. It would have been better if you had told me of your robbery at the start."

"You're right there, Gilbert! I believe I was an outspoken, fellow enough, when I was young, and all the better for it, but the old man's driven me into a curst way of keeping dark about everything, and so I go on heaping up trouble for myself."

---

*Privately in confederacy (ed.).

"Trouble for myself. Alf. Barton," said Miss Lavender, "that's the truest word you've said this many a day. Murder will out, you know, and so will robbery, and so will—other things. More o' your doin's is known, not that they're agreeabler, but on the contràry, quite the reverse, and as full need to be explained, though it don't seem to matter much, yet it may, who can tell? And now look here, Gilbert; my crow is to be picked, and you've seen the color of it, but never mind, all the same since Martha's told the Doctor, it can't make much difference to you. And this is all between ourselves, you understand?"

The last words were addressed to Barton, with a comical, unconscious imitation of his own manner. He guessed something of what was coming, though not the whole of it, and again became visibly uneasy; but he stammered out,

"Yes; oh, yes! of course."

Gilbert could form a tolerably correct idea of the shape and size of Miss Lavender's crow. He did not feel sure that this was the proper time to have it picked, or even that it should be picked at all; but he imagined that Miss Lavender had either consulted Martha Deane, or that she had wise reasons of her own for speaking. He therefore remained silent.

"First and foremost," she resumed, "I'll tell you, Alf. Barton, what we know o' your doin's, and then it's for you to judge whether we'll know any more. Well, you've been tryin' to git Martha Deane for a wife, without wantin' her in your heart, but rather the contràry, though it seems queer enough when a body comes to think of it, but never mind; and your father's druv you to it; and you were of a cold shiver for fear she'd take you, and yet you want to let on it a'n't settled betwixt and between you—oh, you needn't chaw your lips and look yaller about the jaws, it's the Lord's truth; and now answer me this, *what do you mean?* and maybe you'll say what right have I got to ask, but never mind, all the same, if I haven't, Gilbert Potter has, for it's him that Martha Deane has promised to take for a husband!"

It was a day of surprises for Barton. In his astonishment at the last announcement, he took refuge from the horror of Miss Lavender's first revelations. One thing was settled—all the fruits of his painful and laborious plotting were scattered to the winds. Denial was of no use, but neither could an honest explanation, even if he should force himself to give it, be of any possible service.

"Gilbert," he asked, "is this true?—about *you*, I mean."

"Martha Deane and I are engaged, and were already at the time when you addressed her," Gilbert answered.

"Good heavens! I hadn't the slightest suspicion of it. Well—I don't begrudge you your luck, and of course I'll draw back, and never say another word, now or ever."

"*You* wouldn't ha' been comfortable with Martha Deane, anyhow," Miss Lavender grimly remarked. " 'Tisn't good to hitch a colt-horse and an old spavined critter in one team. But that's neither here nor there; you ha'n't told us why you made up to her for a purpose, and kep' on pretendin' she didn't know her own mind."

"I've promised Gilbert that I won't interfere, and that's enough," said Barton, doggedly.

Miss Lavender was foiled for a moment, but she presently returned to the attack. "I dunno as it's enough, after what's gone before," she said. "Couldn't you go a step furder, and lend Gilbert a helpin' hand, whenever and whatever?"

"Betsy!" Gilbert exclaimed.

"Let me alone, lad! I don't speak in Gilbert's name, nor yet in Martha's; only out o' my own mind. I don't ask you to do anything, but I want to know how it stands with your willin'ness."

"I've offered, more than once, to do him a good turn, if I could; but I guess my help wouldn't be welcome," Barton answered. The sting of the suspicion rankled in his mind, and Gilbert's evident aversion sorely wounded his vanity.

"Wouldn't be welcome. Then I'll only say this; maybe I've got it in my power, and 'tisn't sayin' much, for the mouse gnawed the mashes o' the lion's net, to help you to what you're after, bein' as it isn't Martha, and can't be her money. S'pose I did it o' my own accord, leavin' you to feel beholden to me, or not, after all's said and done?"

But Alfred Barton was proof against even this assault. He was too dejected to enter at once into a new plot, the issue of which would probably be as fruitless as the others. He had already accepted a sufficiency of shame, for one day. This last confession, if made, would place his character in a still grosser and meaner light; while, if withheld, the unexplained motive might be presented as a partial justification of his course. He had been surprised into damaging admissions; but here he would take a firm stand.

"You're right so far, Betsy," he said, "that I had a reason—a good reason, it seemed to me, but I may be mistaken—for what I did. It concerns no one under Heaven but my own self; and though I don't doubt your willingness to do me a good turn, it would make no difference—you couldn't help one bit. I've given the thing up, and so let it be!"

There was nothing more to be said, and the two cross-examiners took their departure. As they descended to the creek, Miss Lavender remarked, as if to herself,

"No use—it can't be screwed out of him! So there's one cur'osity the less; not that I'm glad of it, for not knowin' worries more than knowin', whatsoever and whosoever. And I dunno as I think any the wuss of him for shuttin' his teeth so tight onto it."

Alfred Barton waited until the two had disappeared behind the timber in the bottom. Then he slowly followed, stealing across the fields and around the stables, to the back door of the Unicorn barroom. It was noticed that, although he drank a good deal that afternoon, his ill-humor was not, as usual, diminished thereby.

CHAPTER 24

Deb. Smith Takes a Resolution

It was a raw, overcast evening in the early part of January. Away to the west there was a brownish glimmer in the dark-gray sky, denoting sunset, and from that point there came barely sufficient light to disclose the prominent features of a wild, dreary, uneven landscape.

The foreground was a rugged clearing in the forest, just where the crest of a high hill began to slope rapidly down to the Brandywine. The dark meadows, dotted with irregular lakes of ice, and long dirty drifts of unmelted snow, but not the stream itself, could be seen. Across the narrow valley rose a cape, or foreland, of the hills beyond, timbered nearly to the top, and falling, on either side, into deep lateral glens—those warm nooks which the first settlers loved to choose, both from their snug aspect of shelter, and from the cold, sparkling springs of water which every one of them held in its lap. Back of the summits of all the hills stretched a rich, rolling upland, cleared and mapped into spacious fields, but showing everywhere an edge of dark, wintry woods against the darkening sky.

In the midst of this clearing stood a rough cabin, or rather half-cabin, of logs; for the back of it was formed by a ledge of slaty rocks, some ten or twelve feet in height, which here cropped out of the hillside. The raw clay with which the crevices between the logs had been stopped, had fallen out in many places; the roof of long strips of peeled bark was shrivelled by wind and sun, and held in its place by stones and heavy branches of trees, and a square tower of plastered sticks in one corner very imperfectly suggested a chimney. There was no inclosed patch of vegetable-ground near, no stable, improvised of corn-shocks, for the shelter of cow or pig, and the habitation seemed not only to be untenanted, but to have been forsaken years before.

Yet a thin, cautious thread of smoke stole above the rocks, and just as the starless dusk began to deepen into night, a step was heard, slowly climbing upward through the rustling leaves and snapping sticks of the forest. A woman's figure, wearily scaling the hill under a load which almost concealed the upper part of her body, for it consisted of a huge wallet, a rattling collection of articles tied in a blanket, and two or three bundles slung over her shoulders with a rope. When at last, panting from the strain, she stood beside the cabin, she shook herself, and the articles, with the exception of the wallet, tumbled to the ground. The latter she set down carefully, thrust her arm into one of the ends and drew forth a heavy jug, which she raised to her mouth. The wind was rising, but its voice among the trees was dull and muffled; now and then a flake of snow dropped out of the gloom, as if some cowardly, insulting creature of the air were spitting at the world under cover of the night.

"It's likely to be a good night," the woman muttered, "and he'll be on the way by this time. I must put things to rights."

She entered the cabin by a narrow door in the southern end. Her first care was to rekindle the smouldering fire from a store of boughs and dry brushwood piled in one corner. When a little flame leaped up from the ashes, it revealed an interior bare and dismal enough, yet very cheery in contrast with the threatening weather outside. The walls were naked logs and rock, the floor of irregular flat stones, and no furniture remained except some part of a cupboard or dresser, near the chimney. Two or three short saw-cuts of logs formed as many seats, and the only sign of a bed was a mass of dry leaves, upon which a blanket had been thrown, in a hollow under the overhanging base of the rock.

Untying the blanket, the woman drew forth three or four rude cooking utensils, some dried beef and smoked sausages, and two huge round loaves of bread, and arranged them upon the one or two remaining shelves of the dresser. Then she seated herself in front of the fire, staring into the crackling blaze, which she mechanically fed from time to time, muttering brokenly to herself in the manner of one accustomed to be much alone.

"It was a mean thing, after what I'd said—my word used to be wuth somethin', but times seems to ha' changed. If they have, why shouldn't I change with 'em, as well's anybody else?

Well, why need it matter? I've got a bad name. ... No, that'll do! Stick to what you're about, or you'll be wuthlesser, even, than they says you are!"

She shook her hard fist, and took another pull at the jug.

"It's well I laid in a good lot o' *that*," she said. "No better company for a lonesome night, and it'll stop his cussin', I reckon, anyhow. Eh? What's that?"

From the wood came a short, quick yelp, as from some stray dog. She rose, slipped out the door, and peered into the darkness, which was full of gathering snow. After listening a moment, she gave a low whistle. It was not answered, but a stealthy step presently approached, and a form, dividing itself from the gloom, stood at her side.

"All right, Deb.?"

"Right as I can make it. I've got meat and drink, and I come straight from the Turk's Head, and Jim says the Sheriff's gone back to Chester, and there's been nobody out these three days. Come in and take bite and sup, and then tell me everything."

They entered the cabin. The door was carefully barred, and then Sandy Flash, throwing off a heavy overcoat, such as the drovers were accustomed to wear, sat down by the fire. His face was redder than its wont from cold and exposure, and all its keen, fierce lines were sharp and hard. As he warmed his feet and hands at the blaze and watched Deb. Smith while she set the meat upon the coals, and cut the bread with a heavy hunting-knife, the wary, defiant look of a hunted animal gradually relaxed, and he said,

"Faith, Deb., this is better than hidin' in the frost. I believe I'd ha' froze last night, if I hadn't got down beside an ox for a couple o' hours. It's a dog's life they've led me, and I've had just about enough of it."

"Then why not give it up, Sandy, for good and all? I'll go out with you to the Backwoods, after—after things is settled."

"And let 'em brag they frightened me away!" he exclaimed, with an oath. "Not by a long shot, Deb. I owe 'em a score for this last chase—I'll make the rich men o' Chester County shake in their shoes, and the officers o' the law, and the Volunteers, damme! before I've done with 'em. When I go away for good, I'll leave somethin' behind me for them to remember me by!"

"Well, never mind; eat a bit—the meat's ready, and see here, Sandy! I carried this all the way."

He seized the jug and took a long draught. "You're a good 'un, Deb.," he said. "A man isn't half a man when his belly's cold and empty."

He fell to, and ate long and ravenously. Warmed at last, both by fire and fare, and still more by his frequent potations, he commenced the story of his disguises and escapes, laughing at times with boisterous self-admiration, swearing brutally and bitterly at others, over the relentless energy with which he had been pursued. Deb. Smith listened with eager interest, slapping him upon the back with a force of approval which would have felled an ordinary man, but which Sandy Flash cheerfully accepted as a caress.

"You see," he said at the close, "after I sneaked between Potter's troop and the Sheriff's, and got down into the lower corner o' the county, I managed to jump aboard a grain-sloop bound for Newport, but they were froze in at the mouth o' Christeen; so I went ashore, dodged around Wilmington (where I'm rather too well known), and come up Whitely Creek as a drover from Mar'land. But from Grove up to here, I've had to look out mighty sharp, takin' nigh onto two days for what I could go straight through in half a day."

"Well, I guess you're safe here, Sandy," she said; "they'll never think o' lookin' for you twice't in the same place. Why didn't you send word for me before? You've kep' me a mortal long time a-waitin', and down on the Woodrow farm would ha' done as well as here."

"It's a little too near that Potter. He'd smell me out as quick as if I was a skunk to windward of him. Besides, it's time I was pitchin' on a few new holes; we must talk it over together, Deb."

He lifted the jug again to his mouth. Deb. Smith, although she had kept nearly even pace with him, was not so sensible to the potency of the liquor, and was watching for the proper degree of mellowness, in order to broach the subject over which she had been secretly brooding since his arrival.

"First of all, Sandy," she now said, "I want to talk to you about Gilbert Potter. The man's my friend, and I thought you cared enough about me to let my friends alone."

"So I do, Deb., when they let me alone. I had a right to shoot the fellow, but I let him off easy, as much for your sake as because he was carryin' another man's money."

"That's not true!" she cried. "It was his own money, every cent of it—hard-earned money, meant to pay off his debts; and I can say it because I helped him earn it, mowin' and reapin' beside him in the harvest-field, thrashin' beside him in the barn, eatin' at his table, and sleepin' under his roof. I gev him my word he was safe from you, but you've made me out a liar, with no more thought o' me than if I'd been a stranger or an enemy!"

"Come, Deb., don't get into your tantrums. Potter may be a decent fellow, as men go, for anything I know, but you're not beholden to him because he treated you like a Christian as you are. You seem to forgit that he tried to take my life—that he's hardly yet giv' up huntin' me like a wild beast! Damn him, if the money *was* his, which I don't believe, it wouldn't square accounts between us. You think more o' his money than o' my life, you huzzy!"

"No I don't, Sandy!" she protested, "no I don't. You know me better 'n that. What am I here for, tonight? Have I never helped you, and hid you, and tramped the country for you back and forth, by day and by night—and for what? Not for money, but because I'm your wife, whether or not priest or 'squire has said it. I thought you cared for me, I did, indeed; I thought you might do one thing to please me!"

There was a quivering motion in the muscles of her hard face; her lips were drawn convulsively, with an expression which denoted weeping, although no tears came to her eyes.

"Don't be a fool!" Sandy exclaimed. "S'pose you have served me, isn't it somethin' to have a man to serve? What other husband is there for you in the world, than me—the only man that isn't afeard o' your fist? You've done your duty by me, I'll allow, and so have I done mine by you!"

"Then," she begged, "do this one thing over and above your duty. Do it, Sandy, as a bit o' kindness to me, and put upon me what work you please, till I've made it up to you! You dunno what it is, maybe, to have one person in the world as shows a sort o' respect for you—that gives you his hand honestly, like a gentleman, and your full Chris'en name. It does good when a body's been banged about as I've been, and more used to curses than kind words, and not a friend to look after me if I was layin' at death's door—and I don't say *you* wouldn't come, Sandy, but you can't. And there's no denyin' that he had the law on his side, and isn't more an enemy than any other man. Maybe he'd even be a friend in need, as far as he dared, if you'd only do it—"

"Do what? What in the Devil's name is the woman drivin' at?" yelled Sandy Flash.

"Give back the money; it's his'n, not Barton's—I know it. Tell me where it is, and I'll manage the whole thing for you. It's got to be paid in a month or two, folks says, and they'll come on him for it, maybe take and sell his farm—sell th' only house, Sandy, where I git my rights, th' only house where I git a bit o' peace an' comfort! You wouldn't be that hard on me?"

The highwayman took another deep drink and rose to his feet. His face was stern and threatening. "I've had enough o' this foolery," he said. "Once and for all, Deb., don't you poke your nose into my affairs! Give back the money? Tell you where it is? Pay him for huntin' me down? I could take you by the hair and knock your head ag'in the wall, for them words!"

She arose also and confronted him. The convulsive twitching of her mouth ceased, and her face became as hard and defiant as his. "Sandy Flash, mark my words!" she exclaimed. "You're a-goin' the wrong way, when you stop takin' only from the Collectors and the proud rich men, and sparin' the poor. Instead o' doin' good to balance the bad, it'll soon be all bad, and you no better 'n a common thief! You needn't show your teeth; it's true, and I say it square to y'r face!"

She saw the cruel intensity of his anger, but did not flinch. They had had many previous quarrels, in which neither could claim any very great advantage over the other; but the highwayman was now in an impatient and exasperated mood, and she dared more than she suspected in defying him.

"You ———!" (the epithet he used cannot be written) "will you stop your jaw, or shall I stop it for you? I'm your master, and I give you your orders, and the first order is, Not another word, now and never, about Potter or his money!"

He had never before outraged her by such a word, never before so brutally asserted his claim to her obedience. All the hot, indignant force of her fierce, coarse nature rose in resistance. She was thoroughly aroused and fearless. The moment had come, she felt, when the independence which had been her compensation amid all the hardships and wrongs of her life, was threatened—when she must either preserve it by a desperate effort, or be trampled underfoot by this man whom she both loved and feared, and in that moment, hated.

"I'll not hold my jaw!" she cried, with flashing eyes. "Not even at your biddin', Sandy Flash! I'll not rest till I have the money out o' you; there's no law ag'inst stealin' from a thief!"

The answer was a swift, tremendous blow of the highwayman's fist, delivered between her eyes. She fell, and lay for a moment stunned, the blood streaming from her face. Then with a rapid movement, she seized the hunting-knife which lay beside the fire, and sprang to her feet.

The knife was raised in her right hand, and her impulse was to plunge it into his heart. But she could not avoid his eyes; they caught and held her own, as if by some diabolical fascination. He stood motionless, apparently awaiting the blow. Nothing in his face or attitude expressed fear; only all the power of the man seemed to be concentrated in his gaze, and to hold her back. The impulse once arrested, he knew, it would not return. The eyes of each were fixed on the other's, and several minutes of awful silence thus passed.

Finally, Deb. Smith slightly shuddered, as if with cold, her hand slowly fell, and without a word she turned away to wash her bloody face.

Sandy Flash grinned, took another drink of whiskey, resumed his seat before the fire, and then proceeded to fill his pipe. He lit and smoked it to the end, without turning his head or seeming to pay the least attention to her movements. She, meanwhile, had stopped the flow of blood from her face, bound a rag around her forehead, and lighted her own pipe, without speaking. The highwayman first broke the silence.

"As I was a-sayin'," he remarked, in his ordinary tone, "we've got to look out for new holes, where the scent isn't so strong as about these. What do you think o' th' Octorara?"

"Where?" she asked. Her voice was hoarse and strange, but he took no notice of it, gazing steadily into the fire as he puffed out a huge cloud of smoke.

"Well, pretty well down," he said. "There's a big bit o' woodland, nigh onto two thousand acres, belongin' to somebody in Baltimore that doesn't look at once't in ten years, and my thinkin' is, it'd be as safe as the Backwoods. I must go to—it's no difference where—tomorrow mornin', but I'll be back day after tomorrow night, and you needn't stir from here till I come. You've grub enough for that long, eh?"

"It'll do," she muttered.

"Then, that's enough. I must be off an hour before day, and I'm devilish fagged and sleepy, so here goes!"

With these words he rose, knocked the ashes out of his pipe, and stretched himself on the bed of leaves. She continued to smoke her pipe.

"Deb.," he said, five minutes afterwards, "I'm not sure o' wakin'. You look out for me—do you hear?"

"I hear," she answered, in the same low, hoarse voice, without turning her head. In a short time Sandy Flash's deep breathing announced that he slept. Then she turned and looked at him with a grim, singular smile, as the wavering firelight drew clear pictures of his face which the darkness as constantly wiped out again. By and by she noiselessly moved her seat nearer to the wall, leaned her head against the rough logs, and seemed to sleep. But, even if it were sleep, she was conscious of his least movement, and started into alert wakefulness, if he turned, muttered in dreams, or crooked a finger among the dead leaves. From time to time she rose, stole out of the cabin and looked at the sky. Thus the night passed away.

There was no sign of approaching dawn in the dull, overcast, snowy air; but a blind, animal instinct of time belonged to her nature, and about two hours before sunrise, she set about preparing a meal. When all was ready, she bent over Sandy Flash, seized him by the shoulder, and shook his eyes open.

"Time!" was all she said.

He sprang up, hastily devoured the bread and meat, and emptied the jug of its last remaining contents.

"Hark ye, Deb.," he exclaimed, when he had finished, "you may as well trudge over to the Turk's Head and fill this while I'm gone. We'll need all of it, and more, tomorrow night. Here's a dollar, to pay for 't. Now I must be on the tramp, but you may look for me tomorrow, an hour after sun."

He examined his pistols, stuck them in his belt, threw his drover's cloak over his shoulders, and strode out of the cabin. She waited until the sound of his footsteps had died away in the cold, dreary gloom, and then threw herself upon the pallet which he had vacated. This time she slept soundly, until hours after the gray winter day had come up the sky.

Her eyes were nearly closed by the swollen flesh, and she laid handfuls of snow upon her face, to cool the inflammation. At first, her movements were uncertain, expressing a fierce conflict, a painful irresolution of feeling; she picked up the hunting-knife, looked at it with a ghastly smile, and then threw it from her. Suddenly, however, her features changed, and every trace of her former hesitation vanished. After hurriedly eating the fragments left from Sandy's breakfast, she issued from the cabin and took a straight and rapid course eastward, up and over the hill.

During the rest of that day and the greater part of the next, the cabin was deserted.

It was almost sunset, and not more than an hour before Sandy Flash's promised return, when Deb. Smith again made her appearance. Her face was pale (except for the dark blotches around the eyes), worn, and haggard; she seemed to have grown ten years older in the interval.

Her first care was to rekindle the fire and place the replenished jug in its accustomed place. Then she arranged and rearranged the rude blocks which served for seats, the few dishes and the articles of food on the shelf, and, when all had been done, paced back and forth along the narrow floor, as if pushed by some invisible, tormenting power.

Finally a whistle was heard, and in a minute afterwards Sandy Flash entered the door. The bright blaze of the hearth shone upon his bold, daring, triumphant face.

"That's right, Deb.," he said. "I'm dry and hungry, and here's a rabbit you can skin and set to broil in no time. Let's look at you, old gal! The devil!—I didn't mean to mark you like that. Well, bygones is bygones, and better times is a-comin'."

"Sandy!" she cried, with a sudden, appealing energy, "Sandy —once't more! Won't you do for me what I want o' you?"

His face darkened in an instant. "Deb.!" was all the word he uttered, but she understood the tone.

He took off his pistol-belt and laid it on the shelf. "Lay there, pets!" he said; "I won't want you tonight. A long tramp it was, and I'm glad it's over. Deb., I guess I've nigh tore off one o' my knee-buckles, comin' through the woods."

Placing his foot upon one of the logs, he bent down to examine the buckle. Quick as lightning, Deb., who was standing behind him, seized each of his arms, just above the elbows, with her powerful hands, and drew them towards each other upon his back. At the same time she uttered a shrill, wild cry—a scream so strange and unearthly in its character that Sandy Flash's blood chilled to hear it.

"Curse you, Deb., what are you doin? Are you clean mad?" he ejaculated, struggling violently to free his arms.

"Which is strongest now?" she asked; "my arms, or your'n? I've got you, I'll hold you, and I'll only let go when I please!"

He swore and struggled, but he was powerless in her iron grip. In another minute the door of the cabin was suddenly burst open, and two armed men sprang upon him. More rapidly than the fact can be related, they snapped a pair of heavy steel handcuffs upon his wrists, pinioned his arms at his sides, and bound his knees together. Then, and not till then, Deb. Smith relaxed her hold.

Sandy Flash made one tremendous muscular effort, to test the strength of his bonds, and then stood motionless. His white teeth flashed between his parted lips, and there was a dull, hard glare in his eyes which told that though struck dumb with astonishment and impotent rage, he was still fearless, still unsubdued. Deb. Smith, behind him, leaned against the wall, pale and panting.

"A good night's work!" remarked Chaffey, the constable, as he possessed himself of the musket, pistol-belt, and hunting-knife. "I guess this pitcher won't go to the well any more."

"We'll see," Sandy exclaimed, with a sneer. "You've got me, not through any pluck o' your'n, but through black, underhanded treachery. You'd better double chain and handcuff me, or I may be too much for you yet!"

"I guess you'll do," said the constable, examining the cords by the light of a lantern which his assistant had in the meantime fetched from without. "I'll even untie your knees, for you've to walk over the hill to the next farmhouse, where we'll find a wagon to carry you to Chester jail. I promise you more comfortable quarters than these, by daylight."

The constable then turned to Deb. Smith, who had neither moved or spoken.

"You needn't come with us without you want to," he said. "You can get your share of the money at any time; but you must remember to be ready to appear and testify, when Court meets."

"Must I do that?" she gasped.

"Why, to be sure! It's a reg'lar part of the trial, and can't be left out, though there's enough to hang the fellow ten times over, without you."

The two unbound Sandy Flash's knees and placed themselves on each side of him, the constable holding a cocked pistol in his right hand.

"March is the word, is it?" said the highwayman. "Well, I'm ready. Potter was right, after all; he said there'd be a curse on the money, and there is; but I never guessed the curse 'd come upon me through *you*, Deb.!"

"Oh, Sandy!" she cried, starting forward, "you druv me to it! The curse was o' your own makin'—and I gev you a last chance tonight, but you throwed it from you!"

"Very well, Deb," he answered, "if I've got my curse, don't think you'll not have your'n! Go down to Chester and git your blood money, and see what'll come of it, and what'll come to you!"

He turned towards her as he spoke, and the expression of his face seemed so frightful that she shuddered and covered her eyes. The next moment, the old cabin door creaked open, fell back with a crash, and she was alone.

She stared around at the dreary walls. The sound of their footsteps had died away, and only the winter night-wind wailed through the crannies of the hut. Accustomed as she was to solitary life and rudest shelter, and to the companionship of her superstitious fancies, she had never before felt such fearful loneliness, such overpowering dread. She heaped sticks upon the fire, sat down before it, and drank from the jug. Its mouth was still wet from his lips, and it seemed that she was already drinking down the commencement of the curse.

Her face worked, and hard, painful groans burst from her lips. She threw herself upon the floor and grovelled there, until the woman's relief which she had almost unlearned forced its forgotten way, through cramps and agonies, to her eyes. In the violent passion of her weeping and moaning, God saw and pitied, that night, the struggles of a dumb, ignorant, yet not wholly darkened nature.

Two hours afterwards she arose, sad, stern, and determined, packed together the things she had brought with her, quenched the fire (never again to be relighted) upon the hearth, and took her way, through cold and darkness, down the valley.

CHAPTER 25

Two Attempts

The news of Sandy Flash's capture ran like wildfire through the county. As the details became more correctly known, there was great rejoicing but greater surprise, for Deb. Smith's relation to the robber, though possibly surmised by a few, was unsuspected by the community at large. In spite of the service which she had rendered by betraying her paramour into the hands of justice, a bitter feeling of hostility towards her was developed among the people, and she was generally looked upon as an accomplice to Sandy Flash's crimes, who had turned upon him only when she had ceased to profit by them.

The public attention was thus suddenly drawn away from Gilbert Potter, and he was left to struggle, as he best might, against the difficulties entailed by his loss. He had corresponded with Mr. Trainer, the conveyancer in Chester, and had learned that the money still due must not only be forthcoming on the first of April, but that it probably could not be obtained there. The excitement for buying lands along the Allegheny, Ohio, and Beaver rivers in western Pennsylvania had seized upon the few capitalists of the place, and Gilbert's creditor had already been subjected to inconvenience and possible loss, as one result of the robbery. Mr. Trainer therefore suggested that he should make a new loan in his own neighborhood, where the spirit of speculation had not yet reached.

The advice was prudent and not unfriendly, although of a kind more easy to give than to carry into execution. Mark's money-belt had been restored, greatly against the will of the good-hearted fellow (who would have cheerfully lent Gilbert the whole amount had he possessed it), and there was enough grain yet to be threshed and sold, to yield something more than a hundred dollars; but this was all which Gilbert could count upon

from his own resources. He might sell the wagon and one span
of horses, reducing by their value the sum which he would be
obliged to borrow; yet his hope of recovering the money in
another year could only be realized by retaining them, to continue, from time to time, his occupation of hauling flour.

Although the sympathy felt for him was general and very
hearty, it never took the practical form of an offer of assistance,
and he was far too proud to accept that plan of relief which a
farmer, whose barn had been struck by lightning and consumed,
had adopted, the previous year—going about the neighborhood
with a subscription-list, and soliciting contributions. His nearest
friends were as poor as, or poorer than, himself, and those able
to aid him felt no call to tender their services.

Martha Deane knew of this approaching trouble, not from
Gilbert's own lips, for she had seen him but once and very
briefly since his return from the chase of Sandy Flash. It was
her cousin Mark, who, having entered into an alliance, offensive
and defensive, with her lover, betrayed (considering that the end
sanctioned the means) the confidence reposed in him.

The thought that her own coming fortune lay idle, while Gilbert might be saved by the use of a twentieth part of it, gave
Martha Deane no peace. The whole belonged to him prospec-
tively, yet would probably be of less service when it should be
legally her own to give, than the fragment which now would lift
him above anxiety and humiliation. The money had been be-
queathed to her by a maternal aunt, whose name she bore, and
the provisions by which the bequest was accompanied, so light
and reasonable before, now seemed harsh and unkind.

The payment of the whole sum, or any part of it, she saw,
could not be anticipated. But she imagined there must be a way
to obtain a loan of the necessary amount, with the bequest as
security. With her ignorance of business matters, she felt the
need of counsel in this emergency; yet her father was her guardian, and there seemed to be no one else to whom she could
properly apply. Not Gilbert, for she fancied he might reject the
assistance she designed, and therefore she meant to pay the debt
before it became due, without his knowledge; nor Mark, nor
Farmer Fairthorn. Betsy Lavender, when appealed to, shook her
head, and remarked,

"Lord bless you, child! a wuss snarl than ever. I'm gittin' a
bit skeary when you talk o' law and money matters, and that's

the fact. Not that I find fault with your wishin' to do it, but the contràry, and there might be ways, as you say, only I'm not lawyer enough to find 'em, and as to advisin' where I don't see my way clear, Defend me from it!"

Thus thrown back upon herself, Martha was forced to take the alternative which she would gladly have avoided, and from which, indeed, she hoped nothing—an appeal to her father. Gilbert Potter's name had not again been mentioned between them. She, for her part, had striven to maintain her usual gentle, cheerful demeanor, and it is probable that Dr. Deane made a similar attempt; but he could not conceal a certain coldness and stiffness, which made an uncomfortable atmosphere in their little household.

"Well, Betsy," Martha said (they were in her room, upstairs), "Father has just come in from the stable, I see. Since there is no other way, I will go down and ask his advice."

"You don't mean it, child!" cried the spinster.

Martha left the room, without answer.

"She's got *that* from him, anyhow," Miss Betsy remarked, "and which o' the two is stubbornest, I couldn't undertake to say. If he's dead-set on the wrong side, why, she's jist as dead-set on the right side, and that makes a mortal difference. I don't see why I should be all of a trimble, that only sets here and waits, while she's stickin' her head into the lion's mouth; but so it is! Isn't about time for *you* to be doin' somethin', Betsy Lavender!"

Martha Deane entered the front sitting room with a grave, deliberate step. The Doctor sat at his desk, with a pair of heavy silver-rimmed spectacles on his nose, looking over an antiquated "Materia Medica." His upper lip seemed to have become harder and thinner, at the expense of the under one, which pouted in a way that expressed vexation and ill-temper. He was, in fact, more annoyed than he would have confessed to any human being. Alfred Barton's visits had discontinued, and he could easily guess the reason. Moreover, a suspicion of Gilbert Potter's relation to his daughter was slowly beginning to permeate the neighborhood; and more than once, within the last few days, all his peculiar diplomacy had been required to parry a direct question. He foresaw that the subject would soon come to the notice of his elder brethren among the Friends, who felt self-privileged to rebuke and remonstrate, even in family matters of so delicate a nature.

It was useless, the Doctor knew, to attempt coercion with Martha. If any measure could succeed in averting the threatened shame, it must be kindly persuasion, coupled with a calm, dispassionate appeal to her understanding. The quiet, gentle way in which she had met his anger, he now saw, had left the advantage of the first encounter on her side. His male nature and long habit of rule made an equal self-control very difficult on his part, and he resolved to postpone a recurrence to the subject until he should feel able to meet his daughter with her own weapons. Probably some reflection of the kind then occupied his mind, in spite of the "Materia Medica" before him.

"Father," said Martha, seating herself with a bit of sewing in her hand, "I want to ask thee a few questions about business matters."

The Doctor looked at her. "Well, thee's taking a new turn," he remarked. "Is it anything very important?"

"Very important," she answered; "it's about my own fortune."

"I thought thee understood, Martha, that that matter was all fixed and settled, until thee's twenty-five, unless—unless—"

Here the Doctor hesitated. He did not wish to introduce the sore subject of his daughter's marriage.

"I know what thee means, Father. Unless I should sooner marry, with thy consent. But I do not expect to marry now, and therefore do not ask thy permission. What I want to know is whether I could not obtain a loan of a small sum of money, on the security of the legacy?"

"That depends on circumstances," said the Doctor, slowly, and after a long pause, during which he endeavored to guess his daughter's design. "It might be—yes, it might be; but, Martha, surely thee doesn't want for money? Why should thee borrow?"

"Couldn't thee suppose, Father, that I need it for some good purpose? I've always had plenty, it is true; but I don't think thee can say I ever squandered it foolishly or thoughtlessly. This is a case where I wish to make an investment—a permanent investment."

"Ah, indeed? I always fancied thee cared less for money than a prudent woman ought. How much might this investment be?"

"About six hundred dollars," she answered.

"Six hundred!" exclaimed the Doctor; "that's a large sum to venture, a large sum! Since thee can only raise it with my help, thee'll certainly admit my right, as thy legal guardian, if not as thy father, to ask where, how, and on what security the money will be invested?"

Martha hesitated only long enough to reflect that her father's assertion was probably true, and without his aid she could do nothing. "Father," she then said, "*I* am the security."

"I don't understand thee, child."

"I mean that my whole legacy will be responsible to the lender for its repayment in three years from this time. The security *I* ask, I have in advance; it is the happiness of my life!"

"Martha! thee doesn't mean to say that thee would—"

Dr. Deane could get no further. Martha, with a sorrowful half-smile, took up his word.

"Yes, Father, I would. Lest thee should not have understood me right, I repeat that I would, and will, lift the mortgage on Gilbert Potter's farm. He has been very unfortunate, and there is a call for help which nobody heeds as he deserves. If I give it now, I simply give a part in advance. The whole will be given afterwards."

Dr. Deane's face grew white, and his lip trembled, in spite of himself. It was a minute or two before he ventured to say, in a tolerably steady voice,

"Thee still sets up thy right (as thee calls it) against mine, but mine is older built and will stand. To help thee to this money would only be to encourage thy wicked fancy for the man. Of course, I can't do it; I wonder thee should expect it of me. I wonder, indeed, thee should think of taking as a husband one who borrows money of thee almost as soon as he has spoken his mind!"

For an instant Martha Deane's eyes flashed. "Father!" she cried, "it is not so! Gilbert doesn't even know my desire to help him. I must ask this of thee, to speak no evil of him in my hearing. It would only give me unnecessary pain, not shake my faith in his honesty and goodness. I see thee will not assist me, and so I must endeavor to find whether the thing cannot be done without thy assistance. In three years more the legacy will be mine; I shall go to Chester, and consult a lawyer, whether my own note for that time could not be accepted!"

"I can spare thee the trouble," the Doctor said. "In case of thy death before the three years are out, who is to pay the note? Half the money falls to me, and half to thy uncle Richard. Thy aunt Martha was wise. It truly seems as if she had foreseen just what has happened, and meant to balk thy present rashness. Thee may go to Chester, and welcome, if thee doubts my word; but unless thee can give positive assurance that thee will be alive in three years' time, I don't know of anyone foolish enough to advance the money."

The Doctor's words were cruel enough; he might have spared his triumphant, mocking smile. Martha's heart sank within her, as she recognized her utter helplessness. Not yet, however, would she give up the sweet hope of bringing aid; for Gilbert's sake she would make another appeal.

"I won't charge thee, Father, with being intentionally unkind. It would almost seem, from thy words, that thee is rather glad than otherwise, because my life is uncertain. If I *should* die, would thee not care enough for my memory to pay a debt, the incurring of which brought me peace and happiness during life? *Then*, surely, thee would forgive; thy heart is not so hard as thee would have me believe; thee wishes me happiness, I cannot doubt, but thinks it will come in *thy* way, not in mine. It is not possible to grant me this—only this—and leave everything else to time?"

Dr. Deane was touched and softened by his daughter's words. Perhaps he might even have yielded to her entreaty at once, had not a harsh and selfish condition presented itself in a very tempting form to his mind.

"Martha," he said, "I fancy that thee looks upon this matter of the loan in the light of a duty, and will allow that thy motives may be weighty to thy own mind. I ask thee to calm thyself, and consider things clearly. If I grant thy request, I do so against my own judgment, yea—since it concerns thy interests—against my own conscience. This is not a thing to be lightly done, and if I should yield, I might reasonably expect some little sacrifice of present inclination—yet all for thy future good—on thy part. I would cheerfully borrow the six hundred dollars for thee, or make it up from my own means, if need be, to know that the prospect of thy disgrace was averted. Thee sees no disgrace, I am aware, and pity that it is so; but if thy feeling for the young man is entirely pure and unselfish, it should be enough to know that thee had saved him from ruin, without considering thyself bound to him for life."

The Doctor sharply watched his daughter's face while he spoke. She looked up, at first, with an eager, wondering light of hope in her eyes—a light that soon died away, and gave place to a cloudy, troubled expression. Then the blood rose to her cheeks, and her lips assumed the clear, firm curve which always reflected the decisions of her mind.

"Father," she said, "I see thee has learned how to tempt, as well as threaten. For the sake of doing a present good, thee would have me bind myself to do a lifelong injustice. Thee would have me take an external duty to balance a violation of the most sacred conscience of my heart. How little thee knows me! It is not alone that I am necessary to Gilbert Potter's happiness, but also that he is necessary to mine. Perhaps it is the will of heaven that so great a bounty should not come to me too easily, and I must bear, without murmuring, that my own father is set against me. Thee may try me, if thee desires, for the coming three years, but I can tell thee as well, now, what the end will be. Why not rather tempt me by offering the money Gilbert needs, on the condition of my giving up the rest of the legacy to thee? That would be a temptation, I confess."

"No!" he exclaimed, with rising exasperation, "if thee has hardened thy heart against all my counsels for thy good, I will at least keep my own conscience free. I will not help thee by so much as the moving of a finger. All I can do is to pray that thy stubborn mind may be bent, and gradually led back to the Light!"

He put away the book, took his cane and broad-brimmed hat, and turned to leave the room. Martha rose, with a sad but resolute face, and went upstairs to her chamber.

Miss Betsy Lavender, when she learned all that had been said on both sides, was thrown into a state of great agitation and perplexity of mind. She stared at Martha Deane without seeming to see her, and muttered from time to time such fragmentary phrases as, "If I was right-down sure," or "It'd only be another weepon tried and throwed away, at the wust."

"What are you thinking of, Betsy?" Martha finally asked.

"Thinkin' of? Well, I can't rightly tell you. It's a bit o' knowledge that come in my way, once't upon a time, never meanin' to make use of it in all my born days, and I wouldn't now, only for your two sakes; not that it concerns you a mite; but never mind, there's ten thousand ways o' workin' on men's minds, and I can't do no more than try my way."

Thereupon Miss Lavender arose, and would have descended to the encounter at once, had not Martha wisely entreated her to wait a day or two, until the irritation arising from her own interview had had time to subside in her father's mind.

"It's puttin' me on nettles, now that I mean fast and firm to do it; but you're quite right, Martha," the spinster said.

Three or four days afterwards she judged the proper time had arrived, and boldly entered the Doctor's awful presence. "Doctor," she began, "I've come to have a little talk, and it's no use beatin' about the bush, plainness o' speech bein' one o' my ways; not that folks always thinks it a virtue, but oftentimes the contràry, and so may you, maybe; but when there's a worry in a house, it's better, whatsoever and whosoever, to have it come to a head than go on achin' and achin', like a blind bile!"

"H'm," snorted the Doctor, "I see what thee's driving at, and I may as well tell thee at once, that if thee comes to me from Martha, I've heard enough from her, and more than enough."

"More'n enough," repeated Miss Lavender. "But you're wrong. I come neither from Martha, nor yet from Gilbert Potter; but I've been thinkin' that you and me, bein' old—in a measure, that is—and not so direckly concerned, might talk the thing over betwixt and between us, and maybe come to a better understandin' for both sides."

Dr. Deane was not altogether disinclined to accept this proposition. Although Miss Lavender sometimes annoyed him, as she rightly conjectured, by her plainness of speech, he had great respect for her shrewdness and her practical wisdom. If he could but even partially win her to his views, she would be a most valuable ally.

"Then say thy say, Betsy," he assented.

"Thy say, Betsy. Well, first and foremost, I guess we may look upon Alf. Barton's courtin' o' Martha as broke off for good, the fact bein' that he never wanted to have her, as he's told me since with his own mouth."

"What?" Dr. Deane exclaimed.

"With his own mouth," Miss Lavender repeated. "And as to his reasons for lettin' on, I don't know 'em. Maybe you can guess 'em, as you seem to ha' had everything cut and dried betwixt and between you; but that's neither here nor there—Alf. Barton bein' out o' the way, why, the coast's clear, and so Gilbert's case is to be considered by itself; and let's come to the p'int, namely, what you've got ag'in him?"

"I wonder thee can ask, Betsy! He's poor, he's baseborn, without position or influence in the neighborhood—in no way a husband for Martha Deane! If her head's turned because he has been robbed, and marvelously saved, and talked about, I suppose I must wait till she comes to her right senses."

"I rather expect," Miss Lavender gravely remarked, "that they were bespoke before all that happened, and it's not a case o' suddent fancy, but somethin' bred in the bone and not to be cured by plasters. We won't talk o' that now, but come back to Gilbert Potter, and I dunno as you're quite right in any way about his bein's and doin's. With that farm o' his'n, he can't be called poor, and I shouldn't wonder, though I can't give no proofs, but never mind, wait awhile and you'll see, that he's not baseborn, after all; and as for respect in the neighborhood, there's not a man more respected nor looked up to—so the last p'int's settled, and we'll take the t'other two; and I s'pose you mean his farm isn't enough?"

"Thee's right," Dr. Deane said. "As Martha's guardian, I am bound to watch over her interests, and every prudent man will agree with me that her husband ought at least to be as well off as herself."

"Well, all I've got to say, is, it's lucky for you that Naomi Blake didn't think as you do when she married you. What's sass for the goose ought to be sass for the gander (meanin' you and Gilbert), and every prudent man will agree with me."

This was a home-thrust which Dr. Deane was not able to parry. Miss Lavender had full knowledge whereof she affirmed, and the Doctor knew it.

"I admit that there might be other advantages," he said, rather pompously, covering his annoyance with a pinch of snuff —"advantages which partly balance the want of property. Perhaps Naomi Blake thought so too. But here, I think, it would be hard for thee to find such. Or does thee mean that the man's disgraceful birth is a recommendation?"

"Recommendation? No!" Miss Lavender curtly replied.

"We need go no further, then. Admitting thee's right in all other respects, here is cause enough for me. I put it to thee, as a sensible woman, whether I would not cover both myself and Martha with shame, by allowing her marriage with Gilbert Potter?"

Miss Lavender sat silently in her chair and appeared to meditate.

"Thee doesn't answer," the Doctor remarked, after a pause.

"I dunno how it come about," she said, lifting her head and fixing her dull eyes on vacancy; "I was thinkin' o' the time I was up at Strasburg, while your brother was livin', more'n twenty year ago.

With all his habitual self-control and gravity of deportment, Dr. Deane could not repress a violent start of surprise. He darted a keen, fierce glance at Miss Betsy's face, but she was staring at the opposite wall, apparently unconscious of the effect of her words.

"I don't see what that has to do with Gilbert Potter," he presently said, collecting himself with an effort.

"Nor I, neither," Miss Lavender absently replied, "only it happened that I knowed Eliza Little—her that used to live at the Gap, you know—and just afore she died, that fall the fever was so bad, and I nussin' her, and not another soul awake in the house, she told me a secret about your brother's boy, and I must say few men would ha' acted as Henry done, and there's more'n one mighty beholden to him."

Dr. Deane stretched out his hand as if he would close her mouth. His face was like fire, and a wild expression of fear and pain shot from his eyes.

"Betsy Lavender," he said, in a hollow voice, "thee is a terrible woman. Thee forces even the secrets of the dying from them, and brings up knowledge that should be hidden forever. What can all this avail thee? Why does thee threaten me with appearances that cannot now be explained, all the witnesses being dead?"

"Witnesses bein' dead," she repeated. "Are you sorry for that?"

He stared at her in silent consternation.

"Doctor," she said, turning towards him for the first time, "there's no livin' soul that knows, except you and me, and if I seem hard, I'm no harder than the knowledge in your own heart. What's the difference, in the sight o' the Lord, between the one that has a bad name and the one that has a good name?

Come, you set yourself up for a Chris'en, and so I ask you whether you're the one that ought to fling the first stone; whether repentance—and there's that, of course, for you a'n't a nateral bad man, Doctor, but rather the contràry—oughtn't to be showed in deeds, to be wuth much! You're set ag'in Martha, and your pride's touched, which I can't say as I wonder at, all folks havin' pride, me among the rest, not that I've much to be proud of, goodness knows; but never mind, don't you talk about Gilbert Potter in that style, leastways before me!"

During this speech, Dr. Deane had time to reflect. Although aghast at the unexpected revelation, he had not wholly lost his cunning. It was easy to perceive what Miss Lavender intended to do with the weapon in her hands, and his aim was to render it powerless.

"Betsy," he said, "there's one thing thee won't deny—that, if there was a fault, (which I don't allow), it has been expiated. To make known thy suspicions would bring sorrow and trouble upon two persons for whom thee professes to feel some attachment; if thee could prove what thee thinks, it would be a still greater misfortune for them than for me. They are young, and my time is nearly spent. We all have serious burdens which we must bear alone, and thee mustn't forget that the same consideration for the opinion of men which keeps thee silent, keeps me from consenting to Martha's marriage with Gilbert Potter. We are bound alike."

"We're not!" she cried, rising from her seat. "But I see it's no use to talk any more, now. Perhaps since you know that there's a window in you, and me lookin' in, you'll try and keep th' inside o' your house in better order. Whether I'll act accordin' to my knowledge or not depends on how things turns out, and so sufficient unto the day is the evil thereof, or however it goes!"

With these words she left the room, though foiled, not entirely hopeless.

"It's like buttin' over an old stone-wall," she said to Martha. "The first hit with a rammer seems to come back onto you, and jars y'r own bones, and maybe the next, and the next; and then little stones git out o' place, and then the wall shakes, and comes down—and so we've been a-doin'. I guess I made a crack today, but we'll see."

CHAPTER 26

The Last of Sandy Flash

The winter crept on, February was drawing to a close, and still Gilbert Potter had not ascertained whence the money was to be drawn which would relieve him from embarrassment. The few applications he had made were failures; some of the persons really had no money to invest, and others were too cautious to trust a man who, as everybody knew, had been unfortunate. In five weeks more the sum must be made up, or the mortgage would be foreclosed.

Both Mary Potter and her son, in this emergency, seemed to have adopted, by accident or sympathy, the same policy towards each other—to cheer and encourage, in every possible way. Gilbert carefully concealed his humiliation on returning home from an unsuccessful appeal for a loan, and his mother veiled her renewed sinking of the heart, as she heard of his failure, under a cheerful hope of final success which she did not feel. Both had, in fact, one great consolation to fall back upon—she, that he had been mercifully saved to her, he, that he was beloved by a noble woman.

All the grain that could be spared and sold placed but little more than a hundred dollars in Gilbert's hands, and he began seriously to consider whether he should not be obliged to sell his wagon and team. He had been offered a hundred and fifty dollars (a very large sum, in those days) for Roger, but he would as soon have sold his own right arm. Not even to save the farm would he have parted with the faithful animal. Mark Deane persisted in increasing his seventy-five dollars to a hundred, and forcing the loan upon his friend; so one third of the amount was secure, and there was still hope for the rest.

It is not precisely true that there had been no offer of assistance. There was *one*, which Gilbert half-suspected had been instigated by Betsy Lavender. On a Saturday afternoon, as he visited Kennett Square to have Roger's forefeet shod, he encountered Alfred Barton at the blacksmith's shop, on the same errand.

"The man I wanted to see!" cried the latter, as Gilbert dismounted. "Ferris was in Chester last week, and he saw Chaffey, the constable, you know, that helped catch Sandy; and Chaffey told him he was sure, from something Sandy let fall, that Deb. Smith had betrayed him out of revenge, because he robbed you. I want to know how it all hangs together."

Gilbert suddenly recalled Deb. Smith's words, on the day after his escape from the inundation, and a suspicion of the truth entered his mind for the first time.

"It must have been so!" he exclaimed. "She has been a better friend to me than many people of better name."

Barton noticed the bitterness of the remark, and possibly drew his own inference from it. He looked annoyed for a moment, but presently beckoned Gilbert to one side, and said,

"I don't know whether you've given up your foolish suspicions about me and Sandy; but the trial comes off next week, and you'll have to be there as a witness, of course, and can satisfy yourself, if you please, that my explanation was nothing but the truth. I've not felt so jolly in twenty years, as when I heard that the fellow was really in the jug!"

"I told you I believed your words," Gilbert answered, "and that settles the matter. Perhaps I shall find out how Sandy learned what you said to me that evening on the back-porch of the Unicorn, and if so, I am bound to let you know it."

"See here, Gilbert!" Barton resumed. "Folks say you must borrow the money you lost, or the mortgage on your farm will be foreclosed. Is that so? and how much money might it be, altogether, if you don't mind telling?"

"Not so much, if those who have it to lend had a little faith in me—some four or five hundred dollars."

"That ought to be got, without trouble," said Barton. "If I had it by me, I'd lend it to you in a minute; but you know I borrowed from Ferris myself, and all o' my own is so tied up that I couldn't move it without the old man getting on my track. I'll tell you what I'll do, though; I'll endorse your note for a year, if it can be kept a matter between ourselves and the lender. On account of the old man, you understand."

The offer was evidently made in good faith, and Gilbert hesitated, reluctant to accept it, and yet unwilling to reject it in a manner that might seem unfriendly.

"Barton," he said at last, "I've never yet failed to meet a money obligation. All my debts, except this last, have been paid on the day I promised, and it seems a little hard that my own name, alone, shouldn't be good for as much as I need. Old Fairthorn would give me his endorsement, but I won't ask for it; and I mean no offense when I say that I'd rather get along without yours, if I can. It's kind in you to make the offer, and to show that I'm not ungrateful, I'll beg you to look round among your rich friends and help me to find the loan."

"You're a mighty independent fellow, Gilbert, but I can't say as I blame you for it. Yes, I'll look round in a few days, and maybe I'll stumble on the right man by the time I see you again."

When Gilbert returned home, he communicated this slight prospect of relief to his mother. "Perhaps I am a little too proud," he said; "but you've always taught me, Mother, to be beholden to no man, if I could help it; and I should feel more uneasy under an obligation to Barton than to most other men. You know I must go to Chester in a few days, and must wait till I'm called to testify. There will then be time to look around, and perhaps Mr. Trainer may help me yet."

"You're right, boy!" Mary Potter cried, with flashing eyes. "Keep your pride; it's not of the mean kind! Don't ask for or take any man's endorsement!"

Two days before the time when Gilbert was summoned to Chester, Deb. Smith made her appearance at the farm. She entered the barn early one morning with a bundle in her hand, and dispatched Sam, whom she found in the stables, to summon his master. She looked old, weather-beaten, and haggard, and her defiant show of strength was gone.

In betraying Sandy Flash into the hands of justice, she had acted from a fierce impulse, without reflecting upon the inevitable consequences of the step. Perhaps she did not suspect that she was also betraying herself, and more than confirming all the worst rumors in regard to her character. In the universal execration which followed the knowledge of her lawless connection with Sandy Flash, and her presumed complicity in his crimes, the merit of her service to the county was lost. The popular

mind, knowing nothing of her temptations, struggles, and sufferings, was harsh, cold, and cruel, and she felt the weight of its
verdict as never before. A few persons of her own ignorant class,
who admired her strength and courage in their coarse way, advised her to hide until the first fury of the storm should be
blown over. Thus she exaggerated the danger, and even felt uncertain of her reception by the very man for whose sake she had
done the deed and accepted the curse.

Gilbert, however, when he saw her worn, anxious face, the
eyes, like those of a dumb animal, lifted to his with an appeal
which she knew not how to speak, felt a pang of compassionate
sympathy.

"Deborah!" he said, "you don't look well; come into the
house and warm yourself!"

"No!" she cried, "I won't darken your door till you've heerd
what I've got to say. Go 'way, Sam; I want to speak to Mr.
Gilbert, alone."

Gilbert made a sign, and Sam sprang down the ladder to the
stables under the threshing-floor.

"Mayhap you've heerd already," she said. "A blotch on a
body's name spreads fast and far. Mine was black enough before,
God knows, but they've blackened it more."

"If all I hear is true," Gilbert exclaimed, "You've blackened it
for my sake, Deborah. I'm afraid you thought I blamed you in
some way for not preventing my loss; but I'm sure you did what
you could to save me from it!"

"Ay, lad, that I did! But the devil seemed to ha' got into
him. Awful words passed between us, and then—the devil got
into *me*, and—you know what follered. He wouldn't believe the
money was your'n, or I don't think he'd ha' took it; he wasn't a
bad man at heart, Sandy wasn't, only stubborn at the wrong
times, and brung it onto himself by that. But you know what
folks says about me?"

"I don't care what they say, Deborah!" Gilbert cried. "I
know that you are a true and faithful friend to me, and I've not
had so many such in my life that I'm likely to forget what
you've tried to do!"

Her hard, melancholy face became at once eager and tender.
She stepped forward, put her hand on Gilbert's arm, and said, in
a hoarse, earnest, excited whisper,

"Then maybe you'll take it? I was almost afeard to ax you—I

thought you might push me away, like the rest of 'em; but you'll take it, and that'll seem like a liftin' of the curse! You won't mind how it was got, will you? I had to git it in that way, because no other was left to me!"

"What do you mean, Deborah?"

"The money, Mr. Gilbert! They allowed me half, though the constables was for thirds, but the Judge said I'd arned the full half—God knows, ten thousand times wouldn't pay me!—and I've got it here, tied up safe. It's your'n, you know, and maybe there a'n't quite enough, but as fur as it goes; and I'll work out the amount o' the rest, from time to time, if you'll let me come onto your place!"

Gilbert was powerfully and yet painfully moved. He forgot his detestation of the relation in which Deb. Smith had stood to the highwayman, in his gratitude for her devotion to himself. He felt an invincible repugnance towards accepting her share of the reward, even as a loan; it was "blood money," and to touch it in any way was to be stained with its color; yet how should he put aside her kindness without inflicting pain upon her rude nature, made sensitive at last by abuse, persecution, and remorse?

His face spoke in advance of his lips, and she read its language with wonderful quickness.

"Ah!" she cried, "I mistrusted how it'd be; you don't want to say it right out, but I'll say it for you! You think the money'd bring you no luck—maybe a downright curse—how can I say it won't? Ha'n't it cursed me? Sandy said it would, even as your'n follered him. What's it good for, then? It burns my hands, and them that's clean, won't touch it. There, you damned devil's-bait— my arm's sore, and my heart's sore, wi' the weight o' you!"

With these words she flung the cloth, with its bunch of hard silver coins, upon the threshing-floor. It clashed like the sound of chains. Gilbert saw that she was sorely hurt. Tears of disappointment, which she vainly strove to hold back, rose to her eyes, as she grimly folded her arms, and facing him, said,

"Now, what am I to do?"

"Stay here for the present, Deborah," she answered.

"Eh? A'n't I summonsed? The job I undertook isn't done yet; the wust part's to come! Maybe they'll let me off from puttin' the rope round his neck, but I a'n't sure o' that!"

"Then come to me afterwards," she said, gently, striving to allay her fierce, self-accusing mood. "Remember that you always have a home and a shelter with me, whenever you need them. And I'll take your money," he added, picking it up from the floor, "take it in trust for you, until the time shall come when you will be willing to use it. Now go in to my mother."

The woman was softened and consoled by his words. But she still hesitated.

"Maybe she won't—she won't—"

"She will!" Gilbert exclaimed. "But if you doubt, wait here until I come back."

Mary Potter earnestly approved of his decision to take charge of the money, without making use of it. A strong, semi-superstitious influence had so entwined itself with her fate, that she even shrank from help unless it came in an obviously pure and honorable form. She measured the fullness of her coming justification by the strict integrity of the means whereby she sought to deserve it. Deb. Smith, in her new light, was no welcome guest, and with all her coarse male strength, she was still woman enough to guess the fact; but Mary Potter resolved to think only that her son had been served and befriended. Keeping that service steadily before her eyes, she was able to take the outcast's hand, to give her shelter and food, and, better still, to soothe her with that sweet, unobtrusive consolation which only a woman can bestow—which steals by avenues of benevolent cunning into a nature that would repel a direct expression of sympathy.

The next morning, however, Deb. Smith left the house, saying to Gilbert, "You won't see me ag'in, without it may be in Court, till after all's over; and then I may have to ask you to hide me for awhile. Don't mind what I've said; I've no larnin', and can't always make out the rights o' things—and sometimes it seems there's two Sandys, a good 'un and a bad 'un, and meanin' to punish one, I've ruined 'em both!"

When Gilbert reached Chester, the trial was just about to commence. The little old town on the Delaware was crowded with curious strangers, not only from all parts of the county, but even from Philadelphia and the opposite New Jersey shore. Every one who had been summoned to testify was beset by an inquisitive circle, and none more so than himself. The court-house was packed to suffocation; and the sheriff, heavily armed, could with difficulty force a way through the mass. When the clanking of the prisoner's irons was heard, all the pushing, struggling, murmuring sounds ceased until the redoutable highwayman stood in the dock.

He looked around the courtroom with his usual defiant air, and no one observed any change of expression as his eyes passed rapidly over Deb. Smith's face or Gilbert Potter's. His hard red complexion was already beginning to fade in confinement, and his thick hair, formerly close-cropped for the convenience of disguises, had grown out in not ungraceful locks. He was decidedly a handsome man, and his bearing seemed to show that he was conscious of the fact.

The trial commenced. To the astonishment of all, and as it was afterwards reported, against the advice of his counsel, the prisoner plead guilty to some of the specifications of the indictment, while he denied others. The Collectors whom he had plundered were then called to the witness stand, but the public seemed to manifest less interest in the loss of its own money, than in the few cases where private individuals had suffered, and waited impatiently for the latter.

Deb. Smith had so long borne the curious gaze of hundreds of eyes, whenever she lifted her head, that when her turn came, she was able to rise and walk forward without betraying any emotion. Only when she was confronted with Sandy Flash, and he met her with a wonderfully strange, serious smile, did she shudder for a moment and hastily turn away. She gave her testimony in a hard, firm voice, making her statements as brief as possible and volunteering nothing beyond what was demanded.

On being dismissed from the stand, she appeared to hesitate. Her eyes wandered over the faces of the lawyers, the judges, and the jurymen, as if with a dumb appeal, but she did not speak. Then she turned towards the prisoner, and some words passed between them which, in the general movement of curiosity, were only heard by the two or three persons who stood nearest.

"Sandy!" she was reported to have said, "I couldn't help myself; take the curse off o' me!"

"Deb., it's too late," he answered. "It's begun to work, and it'll work itself out!"

Gilbert noticed the feeling of hostility with which Deb. Smith was regarded by the spectators—a feeling that threatened to manifest itself in some violent way, when the restraints of the place should be removed. He therefore took advantage of the

great interest with which his own testimony was heard, to present her character in the light which her services to him shed
upon it. This was a new phase of the story, and produced a
general movement of surprise. Sandy Flash, it was noticed, sitting with his fettered hands upon the rail before him, leaned
forward and listened intently, while an unusual flush deepened
upon his cheeks.

The statements, though not strictly in evidence, were permitted by the court, and they produced the effect which Gilbert
intended. The excitement reached its height when Deb. Smith,
ignorant of rule, suddenly rose and cried out,

"It's true as Gospel, every word of it! Sandy, do you hear?"

She was removed by the constable, but the people, as they
made way, uttered no word of threat or insult. On the contrary,
many eyes rested on her hard, violent, wretched face with an
expression of very genuine compassion.

The trial took its course, and terminated with the result
which everybody—even the prisoner himself—knew to be inevitable. He was pronounced guilty, and duly sentenced to be
hanged by the neck until he was dead.

Gilbert employed the time which he could spare from his
attendance at the court in endeavoring to make a new loan, but
with no positive success. The most he accomplished was an
agreement, on the part of his creditor, that the foreclosure
might be delayed two or three weeks, provided there was a good
prospect of the money being obtained. In ordinary times he
would have had no difficulty; but, as Mr. Trainer had written,
the speculation in western lands had seized upon capitalists, and
the amount of money for permanent investment was already
greatly diminished.

He was preparing to return home when Chaffey, the constable, came to him with a message from Sandy Flash. The latter
begged for an interview, and both judge and sheriff were anxious
that Gilbert should comply with his wishes, in the hope that a
full and complete confession might be obtained. It was evident
that the highwayman had accomplices, but he steadfastly refused
to name them, even with the prospect of having his sentence
commuted to imprisonment for life.

Gilbert did not hesitate a moment. There were doubts of his
own to be solved—questions to be asked, which Sandy Flash
could alone answer. He followed the constable to the gloomy,

high-walled jail-building, and was promptly admitted by the sheriff into the low, dark, heavily barred cell, wherein the prisoner sat upon a wooden stool, the links of his leg-fetters passed through a ring in the floor.

Sandy Flash lifted his face to the light and grinned, but not with his old, mocking expression. He stretched out his hand which Gilbert took—hard and cold as the rattling chain at his wrist. Then, seating himself with a clash upon the floor, he pushed the stool towards his visitor, and said,

"Set down, Potter. Limited accommodations, you see. Sheriff, you needn't wait; it's private business."

The sheriff locked the iron door behind him, and they were alone.

"Potter," the highwayman began, "you see I'm trapped and done for, and all, it seems, on account o' that little affair of your'n. You won't think it means much, now, when I say I was in the wrong there; but I swear I was! I had no particular spite ag'in Barton, but he's a swell, and I like to take such fellows down; and I was dead sure you were carryin' his money, as you promised to."

"Tell me one thing," Gilbert interrupted; "how did you know I promised to take money for him?"

"I knowed it, that's enough; I can give you, word for word, what both o' you said, if you doubt me."

"Then, as I thought, it was Barton himself!" Gilbert cried.

Sandy Flash burst into a roaring laugh. "*Him!* Ah-ha! you think we go snacks,* eh? Do I look like a fool? Barton'd give his eyeteeth to put the halter round my neck with his own hands! No, no, young man; I have ways and ways o' learnin' things that you nor him'll never guess."

His manner, even more than his words, convinced Gilbert. Barton was absolved, but the mystery remained. "You won't deny that you have friends?" he said.

"Maybe," Sandy replied, in a short, rough tone. "That's nothin' to you," he continued; "but what I've got to say is, whether or no you're a friend to Deb., she thinks you are. Do you mean to look after her, once't in a while, or are you one o' them that forgits a good turn?"

"I have told her," said Gilbert, "that she shall always have a

*Divide profits (ed.).

home and a shelter in my house. If it's any satisfaction to you, here's my hand on it!"

"I believe you, Potter. Deb.'s done ill by me; she shouldn't ha' bullied me when I was sore and tetchy, and fagged out with *your* curst huntin' of me up and down! But I'll do that much for her and for you. Here; bend your head down; I've got to whisper."

Gilbert leaned his ear to the highwayman's mouth.

"You'll only tell *her*, you understand?"

Gilbert assented.

"Say to her these words—don't forgit a single one of 'em!— Thirty steps from the place she knowed about, behind the two big chestnut-trees, goin' towards the first cedar, and a forked sassyfrack growin' right over it. What she finds is your'n."

"Sandy!" Gilbert exclaimed, starting from his listening posture.

"Hush, I say! You know what I mean her to do—give you your money back. I took a curse with it, as you said. Maybe that's off o' me, now!"

"It is!" said Gilbert, in a low tone, "and forgiveness—mine and my mother's—in the place of it. Have you any"—he hesitated to say the words—"any last messages, to her or anybody else, or anything you would like to have done?"

"Thank ye, no!—unless Deb. can find my black hair and whiskers. Then you may give 'em to Barton, with my dutiful service."

He laughed at the idea until his chains rattled.

Gilbert's mind was haunted with the other and darker doubt, and he resolved, in his last interview, to secure himself against its recurrence. In such an hour he could trust the prisoner's words.

"Sandy," he asked, "have you any children?"

"Not to my knowledge; and I'm glad of it."

"You must know," Gilbert continued, "what the people say about my birth. My mother is bound from telling me who my father was, and I dare not ask her any questions. Did you ever happen to know her, in your younger days, or can you remember anything that will help me to discover his name?"

The highwayman sat silent, meditating, and Gilbert felt that his heart was beginning to beat painfully fast, as he waited for the answer.

"Yes," said Sandy, at last, "I did know Mary Potter when I was a boy, and she knowed me, under another name. I may say I liked her, too, in a boy's way, but she was older by three or four years, and never thought o' lookin' at me. But I can't remember anything more; if I was out o' this, I'd soon find out for you!"

He looked up with an eager, questioning glance, which Gilbert totally misunderstood.

"What was your other name?" he asked, in a barely aduible voice.

"I dunno as I need tell it," Sandy answered; "what'd be the good? There's some yet livin', o' the same name, and they wouldn't thank me."

"Sandy!" Gilbert cried desperately, "answer this one question —don't go out of the world with a false word in your mouth!— You are not my father?"

The highwayman looked at him a moment, in blank amazement. "No, so help me God!" he then said.

Gilbert's face brightened so suddenly and vividly that Sandy muttered to himself, "I never thought I was that bad."

"I hear the sheriff at the outside gate," he whispered again. "Don't forgit—thirty steps from the place she knowed about— behind the two big chestnut-trees, goin' towards the first cedar— and a forked sassyfrack growin' right over it! Good-bye, and good-luck to the whole o' your life!"

The two clasped hands with a warmth and earnestness which surprised the sheriff. Then Gilbert went out from his old antagonist.

That night Sandy Flash made an attempt to escape from the jail, and very nearly succeeded. It appeared, from some mysteri-· ous words which he afterwards let fall, and which Gilbert alone could have understood, that he had a superstitious belief that something he had done would bring him a new turn of fortune. The only result of the attempt was to hasten his execution. Within ten days from that time he was transformed from a living terror into a romantic name.

CHAPTER 27

Gilbert Independent

Gilbert Potter felt such an implicit trust in Sandy Flash's promise of restitution that, before leaving Chester, he announced the forthcoming payment of the mortgage to its holder. His homeward ride was like a triumphal march, to which his heart beat the music. The chill March winds turned into May breezes as they touched him; the brown meadows were quick with ambushed bloom. Within three or four months his life had touched such extremes of experience that the fate yet to come seemed to evolve itself speedily and naturally from that which was over and gone. Only one obstacle yet remained in his path—his mother's secret. Towards that he was powerless; to meet all others he was brimming with strength and courage.

Mary Potter recognized, even more keenly and with profounder faith than her son, the guidance of some inscrutable power. She did not dare to express so uncertain a hope, but something in her heart whispered that the day of her own deliverance was not far off, and she took strength from it.

It was nearly a week before Deb. Smith made her appearance. Gilbert, in the meantime, had visited her cabin on the Woodrow farm, to find it deserted, and he was burning with impatience to secure, through her, the restoration of his independence. He would not announce his changed prospects, even to Martha Deane, until they were put beyond further risk. The money once in his hands, he determined to carry it to Chester without loss of time.

When Deb. arrived, she had a weary, hunted look, but she was unusually grave and silent, and avoided further reference to the late tragical episode in her life. Nevertheless, Gilbert led her aside and narrated to her the particulars of his interview with Sandy Flash. Perhaps he softened, with pardonable equivocation, the latter's words in regard to her; perhaps he conveyed a sense of forgiveness which had not been expressed; for Deb. more than once drew the corners of her hard palms across her eyes. When he gave the marks by which she was to recognize a certain spot, she exclaimed,

"It was hid the night I dreamt of him! I knowed he must ha' been nigh, by that token. O, Mr. Gilbert, he said true! I know the place; it's not so far away; this very night you'll have y'r money back!"

After it was dark she set out, with a spade upon her shoulder, forbidding him to follow, or even to look after her. Both mother and son were too excited to sleep. They sat by the kitchen fire, with one absorbing thought in their minds, and speech presently became easier than silence.

"Mother," said Gilbert, "when—I mean *if*—she brings the money, all that has happened will have been for good. It has proved to us that we have true friends (and I count my Roger among them), and I think that our independence will be worth all the more, since we came so nigh losing it again."

"Ay, my boy," she replied; "I was over-hasty, and have been lessoned. When I bend my mind to submit, I make more headway than when I try to take the Lord's work into my own hands. I'm fearsome still, but it seems there's a light coming from somewhere—I don't know where."

"Do you feel that way, Mother?" he exclaimed. "Do you think—let me mention it this once!—that the day is near when you will be free to speak? Will there be anything more you can tell me, when we stand free upon our own property?"

Mary Potter looked upon his bright, wistful, anxious face, and sighed. "I can't tell—I can't tell," she said. "Ah, my boy, you would understand it, if I dared say one thing, but that might lead you to guess what mustn't be told; and I will be faithful to the spirit as well as the letter. It must come soon, but nothing you or I can do would hasten it a minute."

"One word more, Mother," he persisted, "will our independence be no help to you?"

"A great help," she answered, "or, maybe, a great comfort would be the true word. Without it, I might be tempted to—but see, Gilbert, how can I talk? Everything you say pulls at the one thing that cuts my mouth like a knife, because it's shut tight on it! And the more because I owe it to you—because I'm held back from my duty to my child—maybe every day putting a fresh sorrow into his heart! Oh, it's not easy, Gilbert; it don't grow lighter from use, only my faith is the stronger and surer, and that helps me to bear it."

"Mother, I meant never to have spoken of this again," he said. "But you're mistaken; it is no sorrow; I never knew what it was to have a light heart, until you told me your trouble, and the question came to my mouth tonight because I shall soon feel strong in my own right as a man, and able to do more than you might guess. If, as you say, no man can help you, I will wait and be patient with you."

"That's all we can do now, my child. I wasn't reproaching you for speaking, for you've held your peace a long while, when I know you've been fretting; but this isn't one of the troubles that's lightened by speech, because all talking must go around the outside, and never touch the thing itself."

"I understand," he said, and gazed for a long time into the fire, without speaking.

Mary Potter watched his face, in the wavering light of the flame. She marked the growing decision of the features, the forward, fearless glance of the large, deep-set eye, the fuller firmness and sweetness of the mouth, and the general expression, not only of self-reliance, but of authority, which was spread over the entire countenance. Both her pride in her son, and her respect for him, increased as she gazed. Heretofore, she had rather considered her secret as her own property, her right to which he should not question; but now it seemed as if she were forced to withhold something that of right belonged to him. Yet no thought that the mysterous obligation might be broken even entered her mind.

Gilbert was thinking of Martha Deane. He had passed that first timidity of love which shrinks from the knowledge of others, and longed to tell his mother what noble fidelity and courage Martha had exhibited. Only the recollection of the fearful swoon into which she had fallen bound his tongue; he felt that the first return to the subject must come from her. She lay back in her chair and seemed to sleep; he rose from time to time, went out into the lane and listened—and so the hours passed away.

Towards midnight a heavy step was heard, and Deb. Smith, hot, panting, her arms daubed with earth, and a wild light in her eyes, entered the kitchen. With one hand she grasped the ends of her strong tow-linen apron, with the other she still shouldered the spade. She knelt upon the floor between the two, set the apron in the light of the fire, unrolled the end of a leathern saddlebag, and disclosed the recovered treasure.

"See if it's all right!" she said.

Mary Potter and Gilbert bent over the rolls and counted them. It was the entire sum, untouched.

"Have you got a sup o' whiskey, Mr. Gilbert?" Deb. Smith asked. "Ugh! I'm hot and out o' breath, and yet I feel mortal cold. There was a screech-owl hootin' in the cedar; and I dunno how 't is, but there always seems to be things around, where money's buried. You can't see 'em, but you hear 'em. I thought I'd ha' dropped when I turned up the sassyfrack bush, and got hold on it; and all the way back I feared a big arm 'd come out o' every fence-corner, and snatch it from me!"*

Mary Potter set the kettle on the fire, and Deb. Smith was soon refreshed with a glass of hot grog. Then she lighted her pipe and watched the two as they made preparations for the journey to Chester on the morrow, now and then nodding her head with an expression which chased away the haggard sorrow from her features.

This time the journey was performed without incident. The road was safe, the skies were propitious, and Gilbert Potter returned from Chester an independent man, with the redeemed mortgage in his pocket. His first care was to assure his mother of the joyous fact; his next to seek Martha Deane, and consult with her about their brightening future.

On the way to Kennett Square, he fell in with Mark, who was radiant with the promise of Richard Rudd's new house, secured to him by the shrewd assistance of Miss Betsy Lavender.

"I tell you what it is, Gilbert," said he; "don't you think I might as well speak to Daddy Fairthorn about Sally? I'm gettin' into good business now, and I guess th' old folks might spare her pretty soon."

"The sooner, Mark, the better for you; and you can buy the

---

*It does not seem to have been generally known in the neighborhood that the money was unearthed. A tradition of that and other treasure buried by Sandy Flash is still kept alive; and during the past ten years two midnight attempts have been made to find it, within a hundred yards of the spot indicated in the narrative.

wedding suit at once, for I have your hundred dollars ready."

"You don't mean that you won't use it, Gilbert?"

Who so delighted as Mark, when he heard Gilbert's unexpected story? "Oh, glory!" he exclaimed; "the tide's turnin', old fellow! What'll you bet you're not married before I am? It's got all over the country that you and Martha are engaged, and that the Doctor's full o' gall and wormwood about it; I hear it wherever I go, and there's more for you than there is against you, I tell you that!"

The fact was as Mark had stated. No one was positively known to have spread the rumor, but it was afloat and generally believed. The result was to invest Gilbert with a fresh interest. His courage in confronting Sandy Flash, his robbery, his wonderful preservation from death, and his singular connection, through Deb. Smith, with Sandy Flash's capture, had thrown a romantic halo around his name, which was now softly brightened by the report of his love. The stain of his birth and the uncertainty of his parentage did not lessen his interest, but rather increased it; and as any man who is much talked about in a country community will speedily find two parties created, one enthusiastically admiring, the other contemptuously depreciating him, so now it happened in this case.

The admirers, however, were in a large majority, and they possessed a great advantage over the detractors, being supported by a multitude of facts, while the latter were unable to point to any act of Gilbert Potter's life that was not upright and honorable. Even his love of Martha Deane was shorn of its presumption by her reciprocal affection. The rumor that she had openly defied her father's will created great sympathy, for herself and for Gilbert, among the young people of both sexes—a sympathy which frequently was made manifest to Dr. Deane, and annoyed him not a little. His stubborn opposition to his daughter's attachment increased, in proportion as his power to prevent it diminished.

We may therefore conceive his sensations when Gilbert Potter himself boldly entered his presence. The latter, after Mark's description, very imperfect though it was, of Martha's courageous assertion of the rights of her heart, had swiftly made up his mind to stand beside her in the struggle, with equal firmness and equal pride. He would openly seek an interview with her, and if he should find her father at home, as was probable at that hour, would frankly and respectfully acknowledge his love, and defend it against any attack.

On entering the room, he quietly stepped forward with extended hand, and saluted the Doctor, who was so taken by surprise that he mechanically answered the greeting before he could reflect what manner to adopt towards the unwelcome visitor.

"What might be thy business with me?" he asked, stiffly, recovering from the first shock.

"I called to see Martha," Gilbert answered. "I have some news which she will be glad to hear."

"Young man," said the Doctor, with his sternest face and voice, "I may as well come to the point with thee, at once. If thee had had decency enough to apply to me before speaking thy mind to Martha, it would have saved us all a great deal of trouble. I could have told thee then, as I tell thee now, that I will never consent to her marriage with thee. Thee must give up all thought of such a thing."

"I will do so," Gilbert replied, "when Martha tells me with her own mouth that such is her will. I am not one of the men who manage their hearts according to circumstances. I wish, indeed, I were more worthy of Martha; but I am trying to deserve her, and I know no better way than to be faithful as she is faithful. I mean no disrespect to you, Dr. Deane. You are her father; you have every right to care for her happiness, and I will admit that you honestly think I am not the man who could make her happy. All I ask is, that you should wait a little and know me better. Martha and I have both decided that we must wait, and there is time enough for you to watch my conduct, examine my character, and perhaps come to a more favorable judgment of me."

Dr. Deane saw that it would be harder to deal with Gilbert Potter than he had imagined. The young man stood before him so honestly and fearlessly, meeting his angry gaze with such calm, frank eyes, and braving his despotic will with such a modest, respectful opposal, that he was forced to withdraw from his haughty position, and to set forth the same reasons which he had presented to his daughter.

"I see," he said, with a tone slightly less arrogant, "that thee is sensible, in some respects, and therefore I put the case to thy understanding. It's too plain to be argued. Martha is a rich bait for a poor man, and perhaps I oughtn't to wonder—knowing the heart of man as I do—that thee was tempted to turn her head to favor thee; but the money is not yet hers, and I, as her father, can never allow that thy poverty shall stand for three years between her and some honorable man to whom her money would be no temptation! Why, if all I hear be true, thee hasn't even any certain roof to shelter a wife; thy property, such as it is, may be taken out of thy hands!"

Gilbert could not calmly hear these insinuations. All his independent pride of character was aroused; a dark flush came into his face, the blood was pulsing hotly through his veins, and indignant speech was rising to his lips, when the inner door unexpectedly opened, and Martha entered the room.

She instantly guessed what was taking place, and summoned up all her self-possession to stand by Gilbert without increasing her father's exasperation. To the former, her apparition was like oil on troubled waters. His quick blood struck into warm channels of joy as he met her glowing eyes and felt the throb of her soft, elastic palm against his own. Dr. Deane set his teeth, drew up his underlip, and handled his cane with restless fingers.

"Father," said Martha, "if you are talking of me, it is better that I should be present. I am sure there is nothing that either thee or Gilbert would wish to conceal from me."

"No, Martha!" Gilbert exclaimed; "I came to bring you good news. The mortgage on my farm is lifted, and I am an independent man!"

"Without my help! Does thee hear that, Father?"

Gilbert did not understand her remark; without heeding it, he continued,

"Sandy Flash, after his sentence, sent for me and told me where the money he took from me was to be found. I carried it to Chester, and have paid off all my remaining debt. Martha, your father has just charged me with being tempted by your property. I say to you, in his presence, put it beyond my reach —give it away, forfeit the conditions of the legacy—let me show truly whether I ever thought of money in seeking you!"

"Gilbert," she said, gently, "Father doesn't yet know you as I do. Others will no doubt say the same thing, and we must both make up our minds to have it said; yet I cannot, for that, relinquish what is mine of right. We are not called upon to sacrifice to the mistaken opinions of men; your life and mine will show, and manifest to others in time, whether it is a selfish tie that binds us together."

"Martha!" Dr. Deane exclaimed, feeling that he should lose ground, unless this turn of the conversation were interrupted; "thee compels me to show thee how impossible the thing is, even if this man were of the richest. Admitting that he is able to support a family, admitting that thee waits three years, comes into thy property, and is still of a mind to marry him against my will, can thee forget—or has he so little consideration for thee as to forget—that he bears his mother's name?"

"Father!"

"Let me speak, Martha," said Gilbert, lifting his head, which had drooped for a moment. His voice was earnest and sorrowful, yet firm. "It is true that I bear my mother's name. It is the name of a good, an honest, an honorable, and a God-fearing woman. I wish I could be certain that the name which legally belongs to me will be as honorable and as welcome. But Martha knows, and you, her father, have a right to know, that I shall have another. I have not been inconsiderate. I trampled down my love for her, as long as I believed it would bring disgrace. I will not say that now, knowing her as I do, I could ever give her up, even if the disgrace was not removed—"

"Thank you, Gilbert!" Martha interrupted.

"But there is none, Dr. Deane," he continued, "and when the time comes, my birth will be shown to be as honorable as your own, or Mark's."

Dr. Deane was strangely excited at these words. His face colored, and he darted a piercing, suspicious glance at Gilbert. The latter, however, stood quietly before him, too possessed by what he had said to notice the Doctor's peculiar expression; but it returned to his memory afterwards.

"Why," the Doctor at last stammered, "I never heard of this before!"

"No," Gilbert answered, "and I must ask of you not to mention it further, at present. I must beg you to be patient until my mother is able to declare the truth."

"What keeps her from it?"

"I don't know," Gilbert sadly replied.

"Come!" cried the Doctor, as sternly as ever, "this is rather a likely story! If Potter isn't thy name, what is?"

"I don't know," Gilbert repeated.

"No; nor no one else! How dare thee address my daughter—talk of marriage with her—when thee don't know thy real name? What name would thee offer to her in exchange for her own? Young man, I don't believe thee!"

"I do," said Martha, rising and moving to Gilbert's side.

"Martha, go to thy room!" the Doctor cried. "And as for thee, Gilbert Potter, or Gilbert Anything, I tell thee, once and for all, never speak of this thing again—at least, until thee can show a legal name and an honorable birth! Thee has not prejudiced me in thy favor by thy devices, and it stands to reason that I should forbid thee to see my daughter—to enter my doors!"

"Dr. Deane," said Gilbert, with sad yet inflexible dignity, "it is impossible, after what you have said, that I should seek to enter your door, until my words are proved true and I am justified in your eyes. The day may come sooner than you think. But I will do nothing secretly; I won't promise anything to you that I can't promise to myself; and so I tell you, honestly and aboveboard, that while I shall not ask Martha to share my life until I can offer her my true name, I must see her from time to time. I'm not fairly called upon to give up that."

"No, Gilbert," said Martha, who had not yet moved from her place by his side, "it is as necessary to my happiness as to yours. I will not ask you to come here again; you cannot, and must not, even for my sake; but when I need your counsel and your sympathy, and there is no other way left, I will go to you."

"Martha!" Dr. Deane exclaimed; but the word conveys no idea of his wrath and amazement.

"Father," she said, "this is thy house, and it is for thee to direct, here. Within its walls, I will conduct myself according to thy wishes; I will receive no guest whom thee forbids, and will even respect thy views in regard to my intercourse with our friends; but unless thee wants to deprive me of all liberty, and set aside every right of mine as an accountable being, thee must allow me sometimes to do what both my heart and my conscience command!"

"Is it a woman's place," he angrily asked, "to visit a man?"

"When the two have need of each other, and God has joined their hearts in love and in truth, and the man is held back from reaching the woman, then it is her place to go to him!"

Never before had Dr. Deane beheld upon his daughter's sweet, gentle face such an expression of lofty spiritual authority. While her determination really outraged his conventional nature, he felt that it came from a higher source than his prohibition. He knew that nothing which he could urge at that moment would have the slightest weight in her mind, and moreover, that the liberal, independent customs of the neighborhood, as well as the respect of his sect for professed spiritual guidance, withheld him from any harsh attempt at coercion. He was powerless, but still inflexible.

As for Martha, what she had said was simply included in what she was resolved to do; the greater embraced the less. It was a defiance of her father's authority, very painful from the necessity of its assertion, but rendered inevitable by his course. She knew with what tenacity he would seize and hold every inch of relinquished ground; she felt, as keenly as Gilbert himself, the implied insult which he could not resent; and her pride, her sense of justice, and the strong fidelity of her woman's heart, alike impelled her to stand firm.

"Good-bye, Martha!" Gilbert said, taking her hand. "I must wait."

"We wait together, Gilbert!"

CHAPTER 28

Miss Lavender Makes a Guess

There were signs of spring all over the land, and Gilbert resumed his farm-work with the fresh zest which the sense of complete ownership gave. He found a purchaser for his wagon, sold one span of horses, and thus had money in hand for all the coming expenses of the year. His days of hauling, of anxiety, of painful economy, were over; he rejoiced in his fully developed and recognized manhood, and was cheered by the respect and kindly sympathy of his neighbors.

Meanwhile, the gossip, not only of Kennett, but of Marlborough, Pennsbury, and New-Garden, was as busy as ever. No subject of country talk equalled in interest the loves of Gilbert Potter and Martha Deane. Mark, too open-hearted to be entrusted with any secret, was drawn upon wherever he went, and he revealed more (although he was by no means Martha's confidant) than the public had any right to know. The idlers at the Unicorn had seen Gilbert enter Dr. Deane's house, watched his return therefrom, made shrewd notes of the Doctor's manner when he came forth that evening, and guessed the result of the interview almost as well as if they had been present.

The restoration of Gilbert's plundered money, and his hardly acquired* independence as a landholder, greatly strengthened the hands of his friends. There is no logic so convincing as that of good luck; in proportion as a man is fortunate (so seems to run the law of the world), he attracts fortune to him. A good deed would not have helped Gilbert so much in popular estimation as this sudden and unexpected release from his threatened difficulties. The blot upon his name was already growing fainter, and a careful moral arithmetician might have calculated the point of prosperity at which it would cease to be seen.

*Acquired with difficulty (ed.).

Nowhere was the subject discussed with greater interest and excitement than in the Fairthorn household. Sally, when she first heard the news, loudly protested her unbelief; why, the two would scarcely speak to each other, she said; she had seen Gilbert turn his back on Martha as if he couldn't bear the sight of her; it ought to be, and she would be glad if it was, but is wasn't!

When, therefore, Mark confirmed the report, and was led on, by degrees, to repeat Gilbert's own words, Sally rushed out into the kitchen with a vehemence which left half her apron hanging on the door-handle, torn off from top to bottom in her whirling flight, and announced the fact to her mother.

Joe, who was present, immediately cried out,

"O, Sally! now I may tell about Mark, mayn't I?"

Sally seized him by the collar, and pitched him out the kitchen door. Her face was the color of fire.

"My gracious, Sally!" exclaimed Mother Fairthorn, in amazement; "what's that for?"

But Sally had already disappeared, and was relating her trouble to Mark, who roared with wicked laughter, whereupon she nearly cried with vexation.

"Never mind," said he; "the boy's right. I told Gilbert this very afternoon that it was about time to speak to the old man; and he allowed it was. Come out with me and don't be afeard— I'll do the talkin'."

Hand in hand they went into the kitchen, Sally blushing and hanging back a little. Farmer Fairthorn had just come in from the barn, and was warming his hands at the fire. Mother Fairthorn might have had her suspicions, but it was her nature to wait cheerfully, and say nothing.

"See here, Daddy and Mammy!" said Mark, "have either o' you any objections to Sally and me bein' a pair?"

Farmer Fairthorn smiled, rubbed his hands together, and turning to his wife, asked, "What has Mammy to say to it?"

She looked up at Mark with her kindly eyes, in which twinkled something like a tear, and said, "I was guessin' it might turn out so between you two, and if I'd had anything against you, Mark, I wouldn't ha' let it run on. Be a steady boy, and you'll make Sally a steady woman. She's had pretty much her own way."

Thereupon Farmer Fairthorn, still rubbing his hands, ventured to remark, "The girl might ha' done worse." This was equivalent to a hearty commendation of the match, and Mark so understood it. Sally kissed her mother, cried a little, caught her gown on a corner of the kitchen table, and thus the betrothal was accepted as a family fact. Joe and Jake somewhat disturbed the bliss of the evening, it is true, by bursting into the room from time to time, staring significantly at the lovers, and then rushing out again with loud whoops and laughter.

Sally could scarcely await the coming of the next day to visit Martha Deane. At first she felt a little piqued that she had not received the news from Martha's own lips, but this feeling speedily vanished in the sympathy with her friend's trials. She was therefore all the more astonished at the quiet, composed bearing of the latter. The tears she had expected to shed were not once drawn upon.

"O, Martha!" she cried, after the first impetuous outburst of feeling, "to think that it has all turned out just as I wanted! No, I don't quite mean that; you know I couldn't wish you to have crosses; but about Gilbert! And it's too bad—Mark has told me dreadful things, but I hope they're not all true; you don't look like it; and I'm so glad, you can't think!"

Martha smiled, readily untangling Sally's thoughts, and said, "I mustn't complain, Sally. Nothing has come to pass that I had not prepared my mind to meet. We will only have to wait a little longer than you and Mark."

"No you won't!" Sally exclaimed, "I'll make Mark wait, too! And everything must be set right—somebody must do something! Where's Betsy Lavender?"

"Here!" answered the veritable voice of the spinster, through the open door of the small adjoining room.

"Gracious, how you frightened me!" cried Sally. "But Betsy, you seem to be able to help everybody; why can't you do something for Martha and Gilbert?"

"Martha and Gilbert. That's what I ask myself, nigh onto a hundred times a day, child. But there's things that takes the finest kind o' wit to see through, and you can't make a bead purse out of a sow's ear, neither jerk Time by the forelock, when there a'n't a hair, as you can see, to hang on to. I dunno as you'll rightly take my meanin'; but never mind, all the same, I'm flummuxed, and it's the longest and hardest flummux o' my life!"

Miss Betsy Lavender, it must here be explained, was more profoundly worried than she was willing to admit. Towards Martha she concealed the real trouble of her mind under the garb of her quaint, jocular speech, which meant much or little, as one might take it. She had just returned from one of her social pilgrimages, during which she had heard nothing but the absorbing subjects of gossip. She had been questioned and cross-questioned, entreated by many, as Sally had done, to do something (for all had great faith in her powers), and warned by a few not to meddle with what did not concern her. Thus she had come back that morning, annoyed, discomposed, and more dissatisfied with herself than ever before, to hear Martha's recital of what had taken place during her absence.

In spite of Martha's steady patience and cheerfulness, Miss Lavender knew that the painful relation in which she stood to her father would not be assuaged by the lapse of time. She understood Dr. Deane's nature quite as well as his daughter, and was convinced that, for the present, neither threats nor persuasions would move his stubborn resistance. According to the judgment of the world (the older part of it, at least), he had still right on his side. Facts were wanted; or, rather, the *one* fact upon which resistance was based must be removed.

With all this trouble, Miss Lavender had a presentiment that there was work for her to do, if she could only discover what it was. Her faith in her own powers of assistance was somewhat shaken, and she therefore resolved to say nothing, promise nothing, until she had both hit upon a plan and carried it into execution.

Two or three days after Sally's visit, on a mild, sunny morning in the beginning of April, she suddenly announced her intention of visiting the Potter farmhouse.

"I ha'n't seen Mary since last fall, you know, Martha," she said; "and I've a mortal longin' to wish Gilbert joy o' his good luck, and maybe say a word to keep him in good heart about you. Have you got no message to send by me?"

"Only my love," Martha answered; "and tell him how you left me. He knows I will keep my word; when I need his counsel, I will go to him."

"If more girls talked and thought that way, us women 'd have fairer shakes," Miss Lavender remarked, as she put on her cloak and pattens.

When she reached the top of the hill overlooking the glen, she noticed fresh furrows in the field on her left. Clambering through the fence, she waited until the heads of a pair of horses made their appearance, rising over the verge of the hill. As she conjectured, Gilbert Potter was behind them, guiding the plow-handle. He was heartily glad to see her, and halted his team at the corner of the "land."

"I didn't know as you'd speak to me," said she, with assumed grimness. "Maybe you wouldn't, if I didn't come direct from *her*. Ah, you needn't look wild, it's only her love, and what's the use, for you had it already; but never mind, lovyers is never satisfied; and she's chipper and peart enough, seein' what she has to bear for your sake, but she don't mind that, on the contràry, quite the reverse, and I'm sure you don't deserve it!"

"Did she tell you what passed between us, the last time?" Gilbert asked.

"The last time. Yes. And jokin' aside, which often means the contràry in my crooked ways o' talkin', a'n't it about time somethin' was done?"

"What can be done?"

"I dunno," said Miss Lavender, gravely. "You know as well as I do what's in the way, or rather none of us knows *what* it is, only *where* it is; and a thing unbeknown may be big or little; who can tell? And latterly I've thought, Gilbert, that maybe your mother is in the fix of a man I've heerd tell on, that fell into a pit, and ketched by the last bush, and hung on, and hung on, till he could hold on no longer; so he gev himself up to death, shet his eyes and let go, and lo and behold! the bottom was a matter o' six inches under his feet! Leastways, everything p'ints to a sort o' skeary fancy bein' mixed up with it, not a thing to laugh at, I can tell you, but as earnest as sin, for I've seen the likes, and maybe easy to make straight if you could only look into it yourself; but you think there's no chance o' that?"

"No," said Gilbert. "I've tried once too often, already; I shall not try again."

"Try again," Miss Lavender repeated. "Then, why not?"—but here she paused, and seemed to meditate. The fact was, she had been tempted to ask Gilbert's advice in regard to the plan she was revolving in her brain. The tone of his voice, however, was discouraging; she saw that he had taken a firm and gloomy resolution to be silent—his uneasy air hinted that he desired to avoid further talk on this point. So, with a mental reprimand of the indiscretion into which her sympathy with him had nearly betrayed her, she shut her teeth and slightly bit her tongue.

"Well, well," she said; "I hope it'll come out before you're both old and sour with waitin', that's all! I don't want such true love as your'n to be like firkin-butter at th' end; for as fresh, and firm, and well-kep' as you please, it ha'n't got the taste o' the clover and the sweet-grass; but who knows? I may dance at your weddin', after all, sooner'n I mistrust; and so I'm goin' down to spend the day with y'r mother!"

She strode over the furrow and across the weedy sod, and Gilbert resumed his plowing. As she approached the house, Miss Lavender noticed that the secured ownership of the property was beginning to express itself in various slight improvements and adornments. The space in front of the porch was enlarged, and new flower-borders set along the garden paling; the barn had received a fresh coat of whitewash, as well as the trunks of the apple trees, which shone like white pillars; and there was a bench with bright straw beehives under the lilac bush. Mary Potter was at work in the garden, sowing her early seeds.

"Well, I do declare!" exclaimed Miss Lavender, after the first cordial greetings were over. "Seems almost like a different place, things is so snugged up and put to rights."

"Yes," said Mary Potter; "I had hardly the heart, before, to make it everything that we wanted; and you can't think what a satisfaction I have in it now."

"Yes, I can! Give me the redishes, while you stick in them beets. I've got a good forefinger for plantin' 'em—long and stiff; and I can't stand by and see you workin' alone, without fidgets."

Miss Lavender threw off her cloak and worked with a will. When the gardening was finished, she continued her assistance with the house, and fully earned her dinner before she sat down to it. Then she insisted on Mary Potter bringing out her sewing, and giving her something more to do; it was one of her working days, she said; she had spent rather an idle winter; and moreover, she was in such spirits at Gilbert's good fortune, that she couldn't be satisfied without doing something for him, and to sew up the seams of his new breeches was the very thing! Never had she been so kind, so cheerful, and so helpful, and Mary

Potter's nature warmed into happy content in her society.

No one should rashly accuse Miss Lavender if there was a little design in this. The task she had set herself to attempt was both difficult and delicate. She had divided it into two portions, requiring very different tactics, and was shrewd enough to mask in every possible way the one from which she had most hopes of obtaining a result. She made no reference, at first, to Gilbert's attachment to Martha Deane, but seemed to be wholly absorbed in the subject of the farm; then, taking wide sweeps through all varieties of random gossip, preserving a careless, thoughtless, rattling manner, she stealthily laid her pitfalls for the unsuspecting prey.

"I was over 't Warren's t'other day," she said, biting off a thread, "and Becky had jist come home from Phildelphy. There's new-fashioned bonnets comin' up, she says. She stayed with Allen's, but who they are I don't know. Laws! now I think on it, Mary, you stayed at Allen's, too, when you were there!"

"No," said Mary Potter, "it was at—Treadwell's."

"Treadwell's? I thought you told me Allen's. All the same to me, Allen or Treadwell; I don't know either of 'em. It's a long while since I've been in Phildelphy, and never likely to go ag'in. I don't fancy trampin' over them hard bricks, though, to be sure, a body sees the fashions; but what with boxes tumbled in and out o' the stores, and bar'ls rollin', and carts always goin' by, you're never sure o' y'r neck; and I was sewin' for Clarissa Lee, Jackson that was, that married a dry goods man, the noisiest place that ever was; you could hardly hear yourself talk; but a body gets used to it, in Second Street, close't to Market, and were you anywheres near there?"

"I was in Fourth Street," Mary Potter answered, with a little hesitation. Miss Lavender secretly noticed her uneasiness, which, she also remarked, arose not from suspicion but from memory.

"What kind o' buttons are you goin' to have, Mary?" she asked. "Horn splits, and brass cuts the stuff, and mother o' pearl wears to eternity, but they're so awful dear. Fourth Street, you said? One street's like another to me, after you get past the corners. I'd always know Second, though, by the tobacco shop, with the wild Injun at the door, liftin' his tommyhawk to skulp you—ugh!—but never mind, all the same, skulp away for what I care, for I a'n't likely ever to lay eyes on you ag'in!"

Having thus, with perhaps more volubility than was required, covered up the traces of her design, Miss Lavender cast about how to commence the second and more hopeless attack. It was but scant intelligence which she had gained, but in that direction she dared not venture further. What she now proposed to do required more courage and less cunning.

Her manner gradually changed; she allowed lapses of silence to occur, and restricted her gossip to a much narrower sweep. She dwelt, finally, upon the singular circumstances of Sandy Flash's robbery of Gilbert, and the restoration of the money.

"Talkin' o' Deb. Smith," she then said, "Mary, do you mind when I was here last harvest, and the talk we had about Gilbert? I've often thought on it since, and how I guessed right for once't, for I know the ways o' men, if I am an old maid, and so it's come out as I said, and a finer couple than they'll make can't be found in the county!"

Mary Potter looked up, with a shadow of the old trouble on her face. "You know all about it, Betsy, then?" she asked.

"Bless your soul, Mary, everybody knows about it! There's been nothin' else talked about in the neighborhood for the last three weeks; why, ha'n't Gilbert told you o' what passed between him and Dr. Deane, and how Martha stood by him as no woman ever stood by a man?"

An expression of painful curiosity, such as shrinks from the knowledge it craves, came into Mary Potter's eyes. "Gilbert has told me nothing," she said, "since—since that time."

"That time. I won't ask you *what* time; it's neither here nor there; but you ought to know the run o' things, when it's common talk." And therewith Miss Lavender began at the beginning, and never ceased until she had brought the history, in all its particulars, down to that very day. She did not fail to enlarge on the lively and universal interest in the fortunes of the lovers which was manifested by the whole community. Mary Potter's face grew paler and paler as she spoke, but the tears which some parts of the recital called forth were quenched again, as it seemed, by flashes of aroused pride.

"Now," Miss Lavender concluded, "you see just how the matter stands. I'm not hard on you, savin' and exceptin' the facts is hard, which they sometimes are, I don't deny; but here we're all alone with our two selves, and you'll grant I'm a friend, though I may have queer ways o' showin' it; and why shouldn't I say that all the trouble comes o' Gilbert bearin' your name?"

"Don't I know it!" Mary Potter cried. "Isn't my load heaped up heavier as it comes towards the end? What can I do but wait till the day when I can give Gilbert his father's name?"

"His father's name! Then you can do it, someday? I suspicioned as much. And you've been bound up from doin' it, all this while—and that's what's been layin' so heavy on your mind, wasn't it?"

"Betsy," said Mary Potter, with sudden energy, "I'll say as much as I dare, so that I may keep my senses. I fear, sometimes, I'll break altogether for want of a friend like you, to steady me while I walk the last steps of my hard road. Gilbert was born in wedlock; I'm not bound to deny that; but I committed a sin—not the sin people charge me with—and the one that persuaded me to it has to answer for more than I have. I bound myself not to tell the name of Gilbert's father—not to say where or when I was married, not to do or say anything to put others on the track, until—but there's the sin and the trouble and the punishment all in one. If I told that, you might guess the rest. You know what a name I've had to bear, but I've taken my cross and fought my way, and put up with all things, that might deserve the fullest justification the Lord has in His hands. If I had known all beforehand, Betsy—but I expected the release in a month or two, and it hasn't come in twenty-five years!"

"Twenty-five years!" repeated Miss Lavender, heedless of the drops running down her thin face. "If there was a sin, Mary, even as big as a yearlin' calf, you've worked off the cost of it, years ago! If you break your word now, you'll stand justified in the sight o' the Lord, and of all men, and even if you think a scrimption of it's left, remember your dooty to Gilbert, and take a less justification for his sake!"

"I've been tempted that way, Betsy, but the end I wanted has been set in my mind so long I can't get it out. I've seen the Lord's hand so manifest in these past days, that I'm fearsome to hurry His judgments. And then, though I try not to, I'm waiting from day to day—almost from hour to hour—and it seems that if I was to give up and break my vow, He would break it for me the next minute afterwards, to punish my impatience!"

"Why," Miss Lavender exclaimed, "it must be your husband's death you're waitin' for!"

Mary Potter started up with a wild look of alarm. "No—no—not his death!" she cried. "I should want him to—be living! Ask me no more questions; forget what I've said, if it don't incline you to encourage me! That's why I've told you so much!"

Miss Lavender instantly desisted from further appeal. She rose, put her arm around Mary Potter's waist, and said, "I didn't mean to frighten or to worry you, deary. I may think your conscience has worked on itself, like, till it's ground a bit too sharp; but I see just how you're fixed, and won't say another word, without it's to give comfort. An open confession's good for the soul, they say, and half a loaf's better than no bread, and you haven't violated your word a bit, and so let it do you good!"

In fact, when Mary Potter grew calm, she was conscious of a relief the more welcome because it was so rare in her experience. Miss Lavender, moreover, hastened to place Gilbert's position in a more cheerful light, and the same story, repeated for a different purpose, now assumed quite another aspect. She succeeded so well that she left behind her only gratitude for the visit.

Late in the afternoon she came forth from the farmhouse, and commenced slowly ascending the hill. She stopped frequently and looked about her; her narrow forehead was wrinkled, and the base of her long nose was set between two deep furrows. Her lips were twisted in a pucker of great perplexity, and her eyes were nearly closed in a desperate endeavor to solve some haunting, puzzling question.

"It's queer," she muttered to herself, when she had nearly reached the top of the hill—"it's mortal queer! Like a whippoorwill on a moonlight night: you hear it whistlin' on the next fence-rail, it doesn't seem a yard off; you step up to ketch it, and there's nothin' there; then you step back ag'in, and 'whippoor-will! whip-poor-will!' whistles louder 'n ever—and so on, the whole night, and some folks say they can throw their voices outside o' their bodies, but that's neither here nor there.

"Now why can't I ketch hold o' this thing? It isn't a yard off me, I'll be snaked! And I dunno what ever she said that makes me think so, but I feel it in my bones, and no use o' callin' up words; it's one o' them things that comes without callin', when they come at all, and I'm so near guessin' I'll have no peace day or night."

With many similar observations she resumed her walk, and presently reached the border of the plowed land. Gilbert's back was towards her; he was on the descending furrow. She looked at him, started, suddenly lost her breath, and stood with open mouth and wide, fixed eyes.

"Ha-ha-a! Ha-ha-a-a!'"

Loud and shrill her cry rang across the valley. It was like the yell of a war-horse, scenting the battle afar off. All the force of her lungs and muscles expended itself in the sound.

The next instant she dropped upon the moist, plowed earth, and sat there, regardless of gown and petticoat. "Good Lord!" she repeated to herself, over and over again. Then, seeing Gilbert approaching, startled by the cry, she slowly arose to her feet.

"A good guess," she said to herself, "and what's more, there's ways o' provin' it. He's comin', and he mustn't know; you're a fool, Betsy Lavender, not to keep your wits better about you, and go rousin' up the whole neighborhood; good [luck] that your face is crooked and don't show much o' what's goin' on inside!"

"What's the matter, Betsy?" asked Gilbert.

"Nothin'—one o' my crazy notions," she said. "I used to holler like a killdeer when I was a girl and got out on the Brandywine hills alone, and I s'pose I must ha' thought about it, and the yell sort o' come of itself, for it just jerked me off o' my feet; but you needn't tell anybody that I cut such capers in my old days, not that folks'd much wonder, but the contràry, for they're used to me."

Gilbert laughed heartily, but he hardly seemed satisfied with the explanation. "You're all of a tremble," he said.

"Am I? Well, it's likely—and my gownd all over mud; but there's one favor I want to ask o' you, and no common one, neither, namely, the loan of a horse for a week or so."

"A horse?" Gilbert repeated.

"A horse. Not Roger, by no means; I couldn't ask that, and he don't know me, anyhow; but the least rough-pacin' o' them two, for I've got considerable ridin' over the country to do, and I wouldn't ask you, but it's a busy time o' year, and all folks isn't so friendly."

"You shall have whatever you want, Betsy," he said. "But you've heard nothing?"

"Nothin' o' one sort or t'other. Make yourself easy, lad."

Gilbert, however, had been haunted by new surmises in regard to Dr. Deane. Certain trifles had returned to his memory since the interview, and rather than be longer annoyed with them, he now opened his heart to Miss Lavender.

A curious expression came over her face. "You've got sharp eyes and ears, Gilbert," she said. "Now supposin' I wanted your horse o' purpose to clear up your doubts in a way to satisfy you, would you mind lettin' me have it?"

"Take even Roger!" he exclaimed.

"No, that bay'll do. Keep thinkin' *that's* what I'm after, and ask me no more questions."

She crossed the plowed land, crept through the fence, and trudged up the road. When a clump of bushes on the bank had hid Gilbert from her sight, she stopped, took breath, and chuckled with luxurious satisfaction.

"Betsy Lavender," she said, with marked approval, "you're a cuter old thing than I took you to be!"

CHAPTER 29

Mysterious Movements

The next morning Sam took Gilbert's bay horse to Kennett Square and hitched him in front of Dr. Deane's door. Miss Lavender, who was on the lookout, summoned the boy into the house, to bring her own sidesaddle down from the garret, and then proceeded to pack a small valise, with straps corresponding to certain buckles behind the saddle. Martha Deane looked on with some surprise at this proceeding, but as Miss Lavender continued silent, she asked no questions.

"There!" exclaimed the spinster, when everything was ready, "now I'm good for a week's travel, if need be! You want to know where I'm goin', child, I see, and you might as well out with the words, though not much use, for I hardly know myself."

"Betsy," said Martha, "you seem so strange, so unlike yourself, ever since you came home last evening. What is it?"

"I remembered somethin', on the way up; my head's been so bothered that I forgot things, never mind what, for I must have some business o' my own or I wouldn't seem to belong to myself, and so I've got to traipse round considerable—money matters and the likes—and folks a'n't always ready for you to the minute; therefore count on more time than what's needful, say I."

"And you can't guess when you will be back?" Martha asked.

"Hardly under a week. I want to finish up everything and come home for a good long spell."

With these words she descended to the road, valise in hand, buckled it to the saddle, and mounted the horse. Then she said good-bye to Martha, and rode briskly away, down the Philadelphia road.

Several days passed and nothing was heard of her. Gilbert

Potter remained on his farm, busy with the labor of the opening spring; Mark Deane was absent, taking measurements and making estimates for the new house, and Sally Fairthorn spent all her spare time in spinning flax for a store of sheets and tablecloths, to be marked "S. A. F." in red silk, when duly woven, hemmed, and bleached.

One afternoon during Miss Lavender's absence, Dr. Deane was again called upon to attend Old Man Barton. It was not an agreeable duty, for the Doctor suspected that something more than medical advice was in question. He had not visited the farmhouse since his discovery of Martha's attachment to Gilbert Potter—had even avoided intercourse with Alfred Barton, towards whom his manner became cold and constrained. It was a sore subject in his thoughts, and both the Bartons seemed to be, in some manner, accessory to his disappointment.

The old man complained of an attack of "buzzing in the head," which molested him at times, and for which bleeding was the Doctor's usual remedy. His face had a flushed, congested, purple hue, and there was an unnatural glare in his eyes; but the blood flowed thickly and sluggishly from his skinny arm, and a much longer time than usual elapsed before he felt relieved.

"Gad, Doctor!" he said, when the vein had been closed, "the spring weather brings me as much fullness as a young buck o' twenty. I'd be frisky yet, if 't wasn't for them legs. Set down, there; you've news to tell me!"

"I think, Friend Barton," Dr. Deane answered, "thee'd better be quiet a spell. Talking isn't exactly good for thee."

"Eh?" the old man growled; "maybe you'd like to think so, Doctor. If I am house-bound, I pick up some things as they go around. And I know why you let our little matter drop so sudden."

He broke off with a short, malicious laugh, which excited the Doctor's ire. The latter seated himself, smoothed his garments and his face, became odorous of bergamot and wintergreen, and secretly determined to repay the old man for this thrust.

"I don't know what thee may have heard, Friend Barton," he remarked, in his blandest voice. "There is always plenty of gossip in this neighborhood, and some persons, no doubt, have been too free with my name—mine and my daughter's, I may say. But I want thee to know that that has nothing to do with the relinquishment of my visits to thee. If thee's curious to learn the reason, perhaps thy son Alfred may be able to give it more circumstantially than I can."

"What, what, what!" exclaimed the old man. "The boy told you not to come, eh?"

"Not in so many words, mind thee; but he made in unnecessary—quite unnecessary. In the first place, he gave me no legal evidence of any property, and until that was done, my hands were tied. Further, he seemed very loath to address Martha at all, which was not so singular, considering that he never took any steps, from the first, to gain her favor; and then he deceived me into imagining that she wanted time, after she had positively refused his addresses. He is mistaken, and thee too, if you think that I am very anxious to have a man of no spirit and little property for my son-in-law!"

The Doctor's words expressed more than he intended. They not only stung, but betrayed his own sting. Old Man Barton crooked his claws around his hickory staff, and shook with senile anger; while his small, keen eyes glared on his antagonist's face. Yet he had force enough to wait until the first heat of his feeling subsided.

"Doctor," he then said, "mayhap my boy's better than a man o' no name and no property. He's worth, anyways, what I choose to make him worth. Have you made up y'r mind to take the t'other, that you've begun to run him down, eh?"

They were equally matched, this time. The color came into Dr. Deane's face, and then faded, leaving him slightly livid about the mouth. He preserved his external calmness, by a strong effort, but there was a barely perceptible tremor in his voice, as he replied,

"It is not pleasant to a man of my years to be made a tool of, as I have every reason to believe thy son has attempted. If I had yielded to his persuasions, I should have spent much time—all to no purpose, I doubt not—in endeavoring to ascertain what thee means to do for him in thy will. It was, indeed, the only thing he seemed to think or care much about. If he has so much money of his own, as thee says, it is certainly not creditable that he should be so anxious for thy decease."

The Doctor had been watching the old man as he spoke, and the increasing effect of his words was so perceptible that he succeeded in closing with an agreeable smile and a most luxurious pinch of snuff. He had not intended to say so much, at the commencement of the conversation, but he had been sorely provoked, and the temptation was irresistible.

The effect was greater than he had imagined. Old Barton's face was so convulsed that, for a few minutes, the Doctor feared an attack of complete paralysis. He became the physician again, undid his work as much as possible, and called Miss Ann into the room, to prevent any renewal of the discussion. He produced his stores of entertaining gossip, and prolonged his stay until all threatening symptoms of the excitement seemed to be allayed. The old man returned to his ordinary mood, and listened, and made his gruff comments, but with temporary fits of abstraction. After the Doctor's departure, he scarcely spoke at all, for the remainder of the evening.

A day or two afterwards, when Alfred Barton returned in the evening from a sale in the neighborhood, he was aware of a peculiar change in his father's manner. His first impression was that the old man, contrary to Dr. Deane's orders, had resumed his rations of brandy and exceeded the usual allowance. There was a vivid color on his flabby cheeks; he was alert, talkative, and frequently chuckled to himself, shifting the hickory staff from hand to hand, or rubbing his gums backward and forward on its rounded end.

He suddenly asked, as Alfred was smoking his pipe before the fire,

"Know what I've been thinkin' of, today, boy?"

"No, Daddy; anything about the crops?"

"Ha! ha! a pretty good crop for somebody it'll be! nearly time for me to make my will, eh? I'm so old and weak—no life left in me—can't last many days!"

He laughed with a hideous irony, as he pronounced these words. His son stared at him, and the fire died out in the pipe between his teeth. Was the old man getting childish? he asked himself. But no; he had never looked more diabolically cunning and watchful.

"Why, Daddy," Alfred said at last, "I thought—I fancied, at least, you'd done that long ago."

"Maybe I have, boy; but maybe I want to change it. I had a talk with the Doctor when he came down to bleed me, and since there's to be no match between you and the girl—"

He paused, keeping his eyes on his son's face, which lengthened and grew vacant with a vague alarm.

"Why, then," he presently resumed, *"you're* so much poorer by the amount o' her money. Would it be fair, do you think, if I was to put that much to what I might ha' meant for you before? Don't you allow you ought to have a little more, on account o' your disapp'intment?

"If you think so, Dad, it's all right," said the son, relighting his pipe. "I don't know, though, what Elisha 'd say to it; but then, he's no right to complain, for he married full as much as I'd ha' got."

"That he did, boy; and when all's said and done, the money's my own to do with it what I please. There's no law o' the oldest takin' all. Yes, yes, I'll have to make a new will!"

A serene joy diffused itself through Alfred Barton's breast. He became frank, affectionate, and confidential.

"To tell you the truth, Dad," he said, "I was mighty afraid you'd play the deuce with me, because all's over between me and Martha Deane. You seemed so set on it."

"So I was—so I was," croaked the old man, "but I've got over it since I saw the Doctor. After all I've heerd, she's not the wife for you; it's better as it is. You'd rayther have the money without her, tell the truth now, you dog, ha! ha!"

"Damme, Dad, you've guessed it!" Alfred cried, joining in the laugh. "She's too high-flown for me. I never fancied a woman that's ready to take you down, every other word you say; and I'll tell you now, that I hadn't much stomach for the match, at any time; but you wanted it, you know, and I've done what I could, to please you."

"You're a good boy, Alfred—a mighty good boy."

There was nothing very amusing in this opinion, but the old man laughed over it, by fits and starts, for a long time.

"Take a drop o' brandy, boy!" he said. "You may as well have my share, till I'm ready to begin ag'in."

This was the very climax of favor. Alfred arose with a broad beam of triumph on his face, filled the glass, and saying, "Here's long life to you, Dad!" turned it into his mouth.

"Long life?" the old man muttered. "It's pretty long as it is—eighty-six and over; but it may be ninety-six, or a hundred and six; who knows? Anyhow, boy, long or short, I'll make a new will!"

Giles was now summoned to wheel him into the adjoining room and put him to bed. Alfred Barton took a second glass of brandy (after the door was closed), lighted a fresh pipe, and seated himself again before the embers to enjoy the surprise and exultation of his fortune. To think that he had worried himself so long for that which finally came of itself! Half his fear of the old man, he reflected, had been needless; in many things he had acted like the veriest fool! Well, it was a consolation to know that all his anxieties were over. The day that should make him a rich and important man might be delayed (his father's strength and vitality were marvellous), but it was certain to come.

Another day or two passed by, and the old man's quick, garrulous, cheerful mood continued, although he made no further reference to the subject of the will. Alfred Barton deliberated whether he should suggest sending for Lawyer Stacy, but finally decided not to hazard his prospects by a show of impatience. He was therefore not a little surprised when his sister Ann suddenly made her appearance in the barn, where he and Giles were mending some dilapidated plow-harness, and announced that the lawyer was even then closeted with their father. Moreover, for the first time in his knowledge, Ann herself had been banished from the house. She clambered into the haymow, sat down in a comfortable spot, and deliberately plied her knitting-needles.

Ann seemed to take the matter as coolly as if it were an everyday occurrence, but Alfred could not easily recover from his astonishment. There was more than accident here, he surmised. Mr. Stacy had made his usual visit not a fortnight before; his father's determination had evidently been the result of his conversation with Dr. Deane; and in the meantime no messenger had been sent to Chester; neither was there time for a letter to reach there. Unless Dr. Deane himself were concerned in secretly bringing about the visit—a most unlikely circumstance—Alfred Barton could not understand how it happened.

"How did th' old man seem, when you left the house?" he asked.

" 'Pears to me I ha'n't seen him so chipper these twenty years," said Ann.

"And how long are they to be left alone?"

"No tellin'," she answered, rattling her needles. "Mr. Stacy'll come, when all's done; and not a soul is to go any nearder the house till he gives the word."

Two hours, three hours, four hours passed away, before the

summons came. Alfred Barton found himself so curiously ex-cited that he was fain to leave the harness to Giles, and quiet himself with a pipe or two in the meadow. He would have gone up to the Unicorn for a little stronger refreshment, but did not dare to venture out of sight of the house. Miss Ann was the perfect image of Patience in a haymow, smiling at his anxiety. The motion of her needles never ceased, except when she counted the stitches in narrowing.

Towards sunset, Mr. Stacy made his appearance at the barn door, but his face was a sealed book.

On the morning of that very day, another mysterious incident occurred. Jake Fairthorn had been sent to Carson's on the old gray mare on some farm-errand—perhaps to borrow a pickaxe or a post-spade. He had returned as far as the Philadelphia road and was entering the thick wood on the level before descending to Redley Creek, when he perceived Betsy Lavender leading Gilbert Potter's bay horse through a gap in the fence, after which she commenced putting up the rails behind her.

"Why, Miss Betsy! what are you doin'?" cried Jake, spurring up to the spot.

"Boys should speak when they're spoken to, and not come where they're not wanted," she answered, in a savage tone. "Maybe I'm goin' to hunt bears."

"Oh, please, let me go along!" eagerly cried Jake, who be-lieved in bears.

"Go along! Yes, and be eat up." Miss Lavender looked very much annoyed. Presently, however, her face became amiable; she took a buckskin purse out of her pocket, selected a small silver coin, and leaning over the fence, held it out to Jake.

"Here!" she said, "here's a 'levenpenny-bit for you, if you'll be a good boy, and do exackly as I bid you. Can you keep from gabblin', for two days? Can you hold your tongue and not tell anybody till day after tomorrow that you seen me here, goin' into the woods?"

"Why, that's easy as nothin'!" cried Jake, pocketing the coin. Miss Lavender, leading the horse, disappeared among the trees.

But it was not quite so easy as Jake supposed. He had not been at home ten minutes, before the precious piece of silver, transferred back and forth between his pocket and his hand in the restless ecstasy of possession, was perceived by Joe. Then, as

Jake stoutly refused to tell where it came from, Joe rushed into the kitchen, exclaiming,

"Mammy, Jake's stole a levy!"

"She'll take it from me ag'in, if I tell," he whimpered.

"She? Who?" cried both at once, their curiosity now fully excited; and the end of it was that Jake told the whole story, and was made wretched.

"Well!" Sally exclaimed, "this beats all! Gilbert Potter's bay horse, too! What ever could she be after? I'll have no peace till I tell Martha, and so I may as well go up at once, for there's something in the wind, and if she don't know already, she ought to!"

Thereupon Sally put on her bonnet, leaving her pewters half scoured, and ran rather than walked to the village. Martha Deane could give no explanation of the circumstance, but endeavored, for Miss Lavender's sake, to conceal her extreme surprise.

"We shall know what it means," she said, "when Betsy comes home, and if it's anything that concerns me, I promise, Sally, to tell you. It may, however, relate to some business of her own, and so I think we had better quietly wait and say nothing about it."

Nevertheless, after Sally's departure, Martha meditated long and uneasily upon what she had heard. The fact that Miss Lavender had come back from the Potter farmhouse, and set forth on some mysterious errand, had already disquieted her. More than the predicted week of absence had passed, and now Miss Lavender, instead of returning home, appeared to be hiding in the woods, anxious that her presence in the neighborhood should not be made known. Moreover she had been seen by the landlord of the Unicorn, three days before, near Logtown, riding towards Kennett Square.

These mysterious movements filled Martha Deane with a sense of anxious foreboding. She felt sure that they were connected in some way with Gilbert's interests, and Miss Lavender's reticence now seemed to indicate a coming misfortune which she was endeavoring to avert. If these fears were correct, Gilbert needed her help also. He could not come to her; was she not called upon to go to him?

Her resolution was soon taken, and she only waited until her father had left on a visit to two or three patients along the

Street Road. His questions, she knew, would bring on another painful conflict of will, and she would save her strength for Gilbert's necessities. To avoid the inferences of the tavern loungers, she chose the longer way, eastward out of the village to the crossroad running past the Carson place.

All the sweet, faint tokens of spring cheered her eyes and calmed the unrest of her heart, as she rode. Among the dead leaves of the woods, the snowy blossoms of the bloodroot had already burst forth in starry clusters; the anemones trembled between the sheltering knees of the old oaks, and here and there a single buttercup dropped its gold on the meadows. These things were so many presentiments of brighter days in nature, and they awoke a corresponding faith in her own heart.

As she approached the Potter farm she slackened her horse's pace, and deliberated whether she should ride directly to the house or seek for Gilbert in the fields. She had not seen Mary Potter since that eventful Sunday the previous summer, and felt that Gilbert ought to be consulted before a visit which might possibly give pain. Her doubts were suddenly terminated by his appearance, with Sam and an ox-cart, in the road before her.

Gilbert could with difficulty wait until the slow oxen had removed Sam out of hearing.

"Martha! were you coming to me?" he asked.

"As I promised, Gilbert," she said. "But do not look so anxious. If there really is any trouble, I must learn it of you."

She then related to him what she had noticed in Miss Lavender's manner, and learned of her movements. He stood before her, listening, with his hand on the mane of her horse, and his eyes intently fixed on her face. She saw the agitation her words produced, and her own vague fears returned.

"Can you guess her business, Gilbert?" she asked.

"Martha," he answered, "I only know that there is something in her mind, and I believe it concerns me. I am afraid to guess anything more, because I have only my own wild fancies to go upon, and it won't do to give 'em play!"

"What are those fancies, Gilbert? May I not know?"

"Can you trust me a little, Martha?" he implored. "Whatever I know, you shall know; but if I sometimes seek useless trouble for myself, why should I seek it for you? I'll tell you now one fear I've kept from you, and you'll see what I mean."

He related to her his dread that Sandy Flash might prove to

be his father, and the solution of it in the highwayman's cell. "Have I not done right?" he asked.

"I am not sure, Gilbert," she replied, with a brave smile; "you might have tested my truth once more if you had spoken your fears."

"I need no test, Martha; and you won't press me for another, now. I'll only say, and you'll be satisfied with it, that Betsy seemed to guess what was in my mind, and promised, or rather expected, to come back with good news."

"Then," said Martha, "I must wait until she makes her appearance."

She had hardly spoken the words, before a figure became visible between the shock-headed willows, where the road crosses the stream. A bay horse—and then Betsy Lavender herself!

Martha turned her horse's head, and Gilbert hastened forward with her, both silent and keenly excited.

"Well!" exclaimed Miss Betsy, "what are you two a-doin' here?"

There was news in her face, both saw; yet they also remarked that the meeting did not seem to be entirely welcome to her.

"I came," said Martha, "to see whether Gilbert could tell me why you were hiding in the woods, instead of coming home."

"It's that—that good-for-nothin' serpent, Jake Fairthorn!" cried Miss Lavender. "I see it all now. Much Gilbert could tell you, howsever, or you him, o' *my* business, and haven't I a right to it, as well as other folks; but never mind, fine as it's spun it'll come to the sun, as they say o' flax and sinful doin's; not that such is mine, but you may think so if you like, and you'll know in a day or two, anyhow!"

Martha saw that Miss Lavender's lean hands were trembling, and guessed that her news must be of vital importance. "Betsy," she said, "I see you don't mean to tell us; but one word you can't refuse—is it good or bad?"

"Good or bad?" Miss Lavender repeated, growing more and more nervous, as she looked at the two anxious faces. "Well, it isn't bad, so peart yourselves up, and ask me no more questions, this day, nor yet tomorrow, maybe; because if you do, I'll just screech with all my might; I'll holler, Gilbert, wuss 'n you heerd, and much good that'll do you, givin' me a crazy name all over the country. I'm in dead earnest; if you try to worm anything more out o' me, I'll screech; and so I was goin' to bring your horse home, Gilbert, and have a talk with your mother, but you've made me mortal weak betwixt and between you; and I'll ride back with Martha, by your leave, and you may send Sam right away for the horse. No; let Sam come now, and walk alongside, to save me from Martha's cur'osity."

Miss Lavender would not rest until this arrangement was made. The two ladies then rode away through the pale, hazy sunset, leaving Gilbert Potter in a fever of impatience, dread, and hope.

CHAPTER 30

The Funeral

The next morning, at daybreak, Dr. Deane was summoned in haste to the Barton farmhouse. Miss Betsy Lavender, whose secrets, whatever they were, had interfered with her sleep, heard Giles's first knock, and thrust her nightcap out of the window before he could repeat it. The old man, so Giles announced, had a bad spell—a 'plectic fit, Lawyer Stacy called it, and they didn't know as he'd live from one hour to another.

Miss Lavender aroused the Doctor, then dressed herself in haste, and prepared to accompany him. Martha, awakened by the noise, came into the spinster's room in her nightdress.

"Must you go, Betsy?" she asked.

"Child, it's a matter o' life and death, more likely death; and Ann's a dooless critter at best, hardly ever off the place, and need o' Chris'en help, if there ever was such; so don't ask me to stay, for I won't, and all the better for me, for I daresn't open my lips to livin' soul till I've spoke with Mary Potter!"

Miss Lavender took the footpath across the fields, accompanied by Giles who gave up his saddled horse to Dr. Deane. The dawn was brightening in the sky as they reached the farmhouse, where they found Alfred Barton restlessly walking backwards and forwards in the kitchen, while Ann and Mr. Stacy were endeavoring to apply such scanty restoratives—consisting principally of lavender and hot bricks—as the place afforded.

An examination of the eyes and the pulse, and a last abortive attempt at phlebotomy, convinced Dr. Deane that his services were no longer needed. Death, which so many years before had lamed half the body, now asserted his claim to the whole. A wonderfully persistent principle of vitality struggled against the clogged functions for two or three hours, then yielded, and the small fragment of soul in the old man was cast adrift, with little

315

chance of finding a comfortable lodging in any other world.

Ann wandered about the kitchen in a dazed state, dropping tears everywhere, and now and then moaning, "O Betsy, how'll I ever get up the funeral dinner?" while Alfred, after emptying the square bottle of brandy, threw himself upon the settle and went to sleep. Mr. Stacy and Miss Lavender, who seemed to know each other thoroughly at the first sight, took charge of all the necessary arrangements; and as Alfred had said, "*I* can't look after anything; do as you two like, and don't spare expense!" they ordered the coffin, dispatched messengers to the relatives and neighbors, and soothed Ann's unquiet soul by selecting the material for the dinner, and engaging the Unicorn's cook.

When all was done, late in the day, Miss Lavender called Giles and said, "Saddle me a horse, and if no sidesaddle, a man's 'll do, for go I must; it's business o' my own, Mr. Stacy, and won't wait for me; not that I want to do more this day than what I've done, goodness knows; but I'll have a fit myself if I don't!"

She reached the Potter farmhouse at dark, and both mother and son were struck with her flushed, excited, and yet weary air. Their supper was over, but she refused to take anything more than a cup of tea; her speech was forced, and more rambling and disconnected than ever. When Mary Potter left the kitchen to bring some fresh cream from the springhouse, Miss Lavender hastily approached Gilbert, laid her hand on his shoulder, and said,

"Lad, be good this once't, and do what I tell you. Make a reason for goin' to bed as soon as you can; for I've been workin' in your interest all this while, only I've got that to tell your mother, first of all, which you mustn't hear; and you may hope as much as you please, for the news isn't bad, as 'll soon be made manifest!"

Gilbert was strangely impressed by her solemn, earnest manner, and promised to obey. He guessed, and yet feared to believe, that the long release of which his mother had spoken had come at last; how else, he asked himself, should Miss Lavender become possessed of knowledge which seemed so important? As early as possible he went up to his bedroom, leaving the two women alone. The sound of voices, now high and hurried, now, apparently, low and broken, came to his ears. He resisted the temptation to listen, smothered his head in the pillow to further muffle the sounds, and after a long, restless struggle with his own mind, fell asleep. Deep in the night he was awakened by the noise of a shutting door, and then all was still.

It was very evident, in the morning, that he had not miscalculated the importance of Miss Lavender's communication. Was this woman, whose face shone with such a mingled light of awe and triumph, his mother? Were these features, where the deep lines of patience were softened into curves of rejoicing, the dark, smouldering gleam of sorrow kindled into a flashing light of pride, those he had known from childhood? As he looked at her in wonder, renewed with every one of her movements and glances, she took him by the hand and said,

"Gilbert, wait a little!"

Miss Lavender insisted on having breakfast by sunrise, and as soon as the meal was over demanded her horse. Then first she announced the fact of Old Man Barton's death, and that the funeral was to be on the following day.

"Mary, you must be sure and come," she said, as she took leave; "I know Ann expects it of you. Ten o'clock, remember!"

Gilbert noticed that his mother laid aside her sewing and when the ordinary household labor had been performed, seated herself near the window with a small old Bible, which he had never before seen in her hands. There was a strange fixedness in her gaze, as if only her eyes, not her thoughts, were directed upon its pages. The new expression of her face remained; it seemed already to have acquired as permanent a stamp as the old. Against his will he was infected by its power, and moved about in barn and field all day with a sense of the unreality of things, which was very painful to his strong, practical nature.

The day of the old man's funeral came. Sam led up the horses, and waited at the gate with them to receive his master's parting instructions. Gilbert remarked with surprise that his mother placed a folded paper between the leaves of the Bible, tied the book carefully in a linen handkerchief, and carried it with her. She was ready, but still hesitated, looking around the kitchen with the manner of one who had forgotten something. Then she returned to her own room, and after some minutes came forth, paler than before, but proud, composed, and firm.

"Gilbert," she said, almost in a whisper, "I have tried you sorely, and you have been wonderfully kind and patient. I have no right to ask anything more; I *could* tell you everything now, but this is not the place nor the time I had thought of, for so many years past. Will you let me finish the work in the way pointed out to me?"

"Mother," he answered, "I cannot judge in this matter, knowing nothing. I must be led by you; but, pray, do not let it be long?"

"It will not be long, my boy, or I wouldn't ask it. I have one more duty to perform, to myself, to you, and to the Lord, and it must be done in the sight of men. Will you stand by me, not question my words, not interfere with my actions, however strange they may seem, but simply believe and obey?"

"I will, Mother," he said, "because you make me feel that I must."

They mounted, and side by side rode up the glen. Mary Potter was silent; now and then her lips moved, not, as once, in some desperate appeal of the heart for pity and help, but as with a thanksgiving so profound that it must needs to be constantly renewed to be credited.

After passing Carson's, they took the shorter way across the fields, and approached the Barton farmhouse from below. A large concourse of people was already assembled; and the rude black hearse, awaiting its burden in the lane, spread the awe and the gloom of death over the scene. The visitors were grouped around the doors, silent or speaking cautiously in subdued tones; and all newcomers passed into the house to take their last look at the face of the dead.

The best room, in which the corpse lay, was scarcely used once in a year, and many of the neighbors had never before had occasion to enter it. The shabby, antiquated furniture looked cold and dreary from disuse, and the smell of camphor in the air hardly kept down the musty, mouldy odors which exhaled from the walls. The head and foot of the coffin rested on two chairs placed in the center of the room; and several women, one of whom was Miss Betsy Lavender, conducted the visitors back and forth, as they came. The members of the bereaved family were stiffly ranged around the walls, the chief mourners consisting of the old man's eldest son, Elisha, with his wife and three married sons, Alfred, and Ann.

Mary Potter took her son's arm, and they passed through the throng at the door, and entered the house. Gilbert silently returned the nods of greeting; his mother neither met nor avoided the eyes of others. Her step was firm, her head erect, her bearing full of pride and decision. Miss Lavender, who met her with a questioning glance at the door, walked beside her to the room of death, and then—what was remarkable in her—became very pale.

They stood by the coffin. It was not a peaceful, solemn sight, that yellow face, with its wrinkles and creases and dark blotches of congealed blood, made more pronounced and ugly by the white shroud and cravat, yet a tear rolled down Mary Potter's cheek as she gazed upon it. Other visitors came, and Gilbert gently drew her away, to leave the room; but with a quick pressure upon his arm, as if to remind him of his promise, she quietly took her seat near the mourners, and by a slight motion indicated that he should seat himself at her side.

It was an unexpected and painful position; but her face, firm and calm, shamed his own embarrassment. He saw, nevertheless, that the grief of the mourners was not so profound as to suppress the surprise, if not indignation, which the act called forth. The women had their handkerchiefs to their eyes, and were weeping in a slow, silent, mechanical way; the men had handkerchiefs in their hands, but their faces were hard, apathetic, and constrained.

By and by the visitors ceased; the attending women exchanged glances with each other and with the mourners, and one of the former stepped up to Mary Potter and said gently,

"It is only the family, now."

This was according to custom, which required that just before the coffin was closed, the members of the family of the deceased should be left alone with him for a few minutes, and take their farewell of his face undisturbed by other eyes. Gilbert would have risen, but his mother, with her hand on his arm, quietly replied,

"We belong to the family."

The woman withdrew, though with apparent doubt and hesitation, and they were left alone with the mourners.

Gilbert could scarcely trust his senses. A swift suspicion of his mother's insanity crossed his mind; but when he looked around the room and beheld Alfred Barton gazing upon her with a face more livid than that of the dead man, this suspicion was followed by another, no less overwhelming. For a few minutes everything seemed to whirl and spin before his eyes; a light broke upon him, but so unexpected, so incredible, that it came with the force of a blow.

The undertaker entered the room and screwed down the lid of the coffin; the pallbearers followed and carried it to the hearse. Then the mourners rose and prepared to set forth, in the order of their relation to the deceased. Elisha Barton led the way, with his wife; then Ann, clad in her Sunday black, stepped forward to take Alfred's arm.

"Ann," said Mary Potter, in a low voice, which yet was heard by every person in the room, "that is my place."

She left Gilbert and moved to Alfred Barton's side. Then, slightly turning, she said, "Gilbert, give your arm to your aunt."

For a full minute no other word was said. Alfred Barton stood motionless, with Mary Potter's hand on his arm. A fiery flush succeeded to his pallor; his jaw fell, and his eyes were fixed upon the floor. Ann took Gilbert's arm in a helpless, bewildered way.

"Alfred, what does all this mean?" Elisha finally asked.

He said nothing; Mary Potter answered for him, "It is right that he should walk with his wife rather than his sister."

The horses and chairs were waiting in the lane, and helping neighbors were at the door; but the solemn occasion was forgotten in the shock produced by this announcement. Gilbert started and almost reeled; Ann clung to him with helpless terror; and only Elisha, whose face grew dark and threatening, answered.

"Woman," he said, "you are out of your senses! Leave us; you have no business here!"

She met him with a proud, a serene and steady countenance. "Elisha," she answered, "we are here to bury your father and my father-in-law. Let be until the grave has closed over him; then ask Alfred whether I could dare to take my rightful place before today."

The solemn decision of her face and voice struck him dumb. His wife whispered a few words in his ear, and he turned away with her, to take his place in the funeral procession.

It was Alfred Barton's duty to follow, and if it was not grief which impelled him to bury his face in his handkerchief as they issued from the door, it was a torture keener than was ever mingled with grief—the torture of a mean nature pilloried in its meanest aspect for the public gaze. Mary (we must not call her Potter, and cannot yet call her Barton) rather led him than was led by him, and lifted her face to the eyes of men. The shame which she might have felt as his wife was lost in the one over-powering sense of the justification for which she had so long waited and suffered.

When the pair appeared in the yard, and Gilbert followed with Miss Ann Barton on his arm, most of the funeral guests looked on in stupid wonder, unable to conceive the reason of the two thus appearing among the mourners. But when they had mounted and were moving off, a rumor of the startling truth ran from lip to lip. The proper order of the procession was forgotten; some untied their horses in haste and pushed forward to convince themselves of the astonishing fact; others gathered into groups and discussed it earnestly. Some had suspected a relation of the kind, all along, so they said; others scouted at the story, and were ready with explanations of their own. But not a soul had another thought to spare for Old Man Barton that day.

Dr. Deane and Martha heard what had happened as they were mounting their horses. When they took their places in the line, the singular companionship behind the hearse was plainly visible. Neither spoke a word, but Martha felt that her heart was beating fast, and that her thoughts were unsteady.

Presently Miss Lavender rode up and took her place at her side. Tears were streaming from her eyes, and she was using her handkerchief freely. It was some time before she could command her feelings enough to say, in a husky whisper,

"I never thought to ha' had a hand in such wonderful doin's, and how I held up through it, I can't tell. Glory to the Lord, the end has come; but, no—not yet—not quite; only enough for one day, Martha; isn't it?"

"Betsy," said Martha, "please ride a little closer, and explain to me how it came about. Give me one or two points for my mind to rest on, for I don't seem to believe even what I see."

"What I see. No wonder, who could? Well, it's enough that Mary was married to Alf. Barton a matter o' twenty-six year ago, and that he swore her to keep it secret till th' old man died, and he's been her husband all this while, and knowed it!"

"Father!" Martha exclaimed in a low, solemn voice, turning to Dr. Deane, "think, now, what it was thee would have had me do!"

The Doctor was already aware of his terrible mistake. "Thee was led, child," he answered. "thee was led! It was a merciful Providence."

"Then might thee not also admit that I have been led in that other respect, which has been so great a trial to thee?"

He made no reply.

The road to Old Kennett never seemed so long; never was a corpse so impatiently followed. A sense of decency restrained those who were not relatives from pushing in advance of those who were; yet it was very tantalizing to look upon the backs of Alfred Barton and Mary, Gilbert and Ann, when their faces must be such a sight to see!

These four, however, rode in silence. Each, it may be guessed, was sufficiently occupied with his or her own sensations—except, perhaps, Ann Barton, who had been thrown so violently out of her quiet, passive round of life by her father's death, that she was incapable of any great surprise. Her thoughts were more occupied with the funeral dinner yet to come, than with the relationship of the young man at her side.

Gilbert slowly admitted the fact into his mind, but he was so unprepared for it by anything in his mother's life or his own intercourse with Alfred Barton, that he was lost in a maze of baffled conjectures. While this confusion lasted, he scarcely thought of his restoration to honor, or the breaking down of that fatal barrier between him and Martha Deane. His first sensation was one of humiliation and disappointment. How often had he been disgusted with Alfred Barton's meanness and swagger! How much superior, in many of the qualities of manhood, was even the highwayman, whose paternity he had so feared! As he looked at the broad, heavy form before him, in which even the lines of the back expressed cowardice and abject shame, he almost doubted whether his former disgrace was not preferable to his present claim to respect.

Then his eyes turned to his mother's figure, and a sweet, proud joy swept away the previous emotion. Whatever the acknowledged relationship might be to him, to her it was honor —yea, more than honor; for by so much and so cruelly as she had fallen below the rights of her pure name as a woman, the higher would she now be set, not only in respect, but in the reverence earned by her saintly patience and self-denial. The wonderful transformation of her face showed him what this day was to her life, and he resolved that no disappointment of his own should come between her and her triumph.

To Gilbert the way was not too long, nor the progress too

slow. It gave him time to grow familiar, not only with the fact, but with his duty. He forcibly postponed his wandering conjectures, and compelled his mind to dwell upon that which lay immediately before him.

It was nearly noon before the hearse reached Old Kennett meetinghouse. The people of the neighborhood, who had collected to await its arrival, came forward and assisted the mourners to alight. Alfred Barton mechanically took his place beside his wife, but again buried his face in his handkerchief. As the wondering, impatient crowd gathered around, Gilbert felt that all was known, and that all eyes were fixed upon himself and his mother, and his face reflected her own firmness and strength. From neither could the spectators guess what might be passing in their hearts. They were both paler than usual, and their resemblance to each other became very striking. Gilbert, in fact, seemed to have nothing of his father except the peculiar turn of his shoulders and the strong build of his chest.

They walked over the grassy, briery, unmarked mounds of old graves to the spot where a pile of yellow earth denoted Old Barton's resting-place. When the coffin had been lowered, his children, in accordance with custom, drew near, one after the other, to bend over and look into the narrow pit. Gilbert led up his trembling aunt, who might have fallen in had he not carefully supported her. As he was withdrawing, his eyes suddenly encountered those of Martha Deane, who was standing opposite, in the circle of hushed spectators. In spite of himself a light color shot into his face, and his lips trembled. The eager gossips, who had not missed even the wink of an eyelid, saw this fleeting touch of emotion, and whence it came. Thenceforth Martha shared their inspection; but from the sweet gravity of her face, the untroubled calm of her eyes, they learned nothing more.

When the grave had been filled, and the yellow mound ridged and patted with the spade, the family returned to the grassy space in front of the meetinghouse, and now their more familiar acquaintances, and many who were not, gathered around to greet them and offer words of condolence. An overpowering feeling of curiosity was visible upon every face; those who did not venture to use their tongues used their eyes the more.

Alfred Barton was forced to remove the handkerchief from his face, and its haggard wretchedness (which no one atrributed to grief for his father's death) could no longer be hidden. He appeared to have suddenly become an old man, with deeper wrinkles, slacker muscles, and a helpless, tottering air of weakness. The corners of his mouth drooped, hollowing his cheeks, and his eyes seemed unable to bear up the weight of the lids; they darted rapidly from side to side, or sought the ground, not daring to encounter, for more than an instant, those of others.

There was no very delicate sense of propriety among the people, and very soon an inquisitive old Quaker remarked,

"Why, Mary, is this true that I hear? Are you two man and wife?"

"We are," she said.

"Bless us! how did it happen?"

The bystanders became still as death, and all ears were stretched to catch the answer. But she, with proud, impenetrable calmness, replied,

"It will be made known."

And with these words the people were forced, that day, to be satisfied.

CHAPTER 31

The Will

During the homeward journey from the grave, Gilbert and his mother were still the central figures of interest. That the members of the Barton family were annoyed and humiliated was evident to all eyes; but it was a pitiful, undignified position, which drew no sympathy towards them, while the proud, composed gravity of the former commanded respect. The young men and women, especially, were unanimously of the opinion that Gilbert had conducted himself like a man. They were disappointed, it was true, that he and Martha Deane had not met, in the sight of all. It was impossible to guess whether she had been already aware of the secret, or how the knowledge of it would affect their romantic relation to each other.

Could the hearts of the lovers have been laid bare, the people would have seen that never had each felt such need of the other never had they been possessed with such restless yearning. To the very last, Gilbert's eyes wandered from time to time towards the slender figure in the cavalcade before him, hoping for the chance of a word or look; but Martha's finer instinct told her that she must yet hold herself aloof. She appreciated the solemnity of the revelation, saw that much was yet unexplained, and could have guessed, even without Miss Lavender's mysterious hints, that the day would bring forth other and more important disclosures.

As the procession drew nearer Kennett Square, the curiosity of the funeral guests, balked and yet constantly stimulated, began to grow disorderly. Sally Fairthorn was in such a flutter that she scarcely knew what she said or did; Mark's authority alone prevented her from dashing up to Gilbert, regardless of appearances. The old men, especially those in plain coats and broad-brimmed hats, took every opportunity to press near the mourners; and but for Miss Betsy Lavender, who hovered around the latter like a watchful dragon, both Gilbert and his mother would have been seriously annoyed. Finally the gate at the lane-end closed upon them, and the discomfited public rode on to the village, tormented by keen envy of the few who had been bidden to the funeral dinner.

When Mary alighted from her horse, the old lawyer approached her.

"My name is Stacy, Mrs. Barton," he said, "and Miss Lavender will have told you who I am. Will you let me have a word with you in private?"

She slightly started at the name he had given her; it was the first symptom of agitation she had exhibited. He took her aside, and began talking earnestly in a low tone. Elisha Barton looked on with an amazed, troubled air, and presently turned to his brother.

"Alfred," he said, "it is quite time all this was explained."

But Miss Lavender interfered.

"It's your right, Mr. Elisha, no denyin' that, and the right of all the fam'ly; so we've agreed to have it done afore all together, in the lawful way, Mr. Stacy bein' a lawyer; but dinner first, if you please, for eatin's good both for grief and cur'osity, and it's hard tellin' which is uppermost in this case. Gilbert, come here!"

He was standing alone, beside the paling. He obeyed her call.

"Gilbert, shake hands with your uncle and aunt. Mr. Elisha, this is your nephew, Gilbert Barton, Mr. Alfred's son."

They looked at each other for a moment. There was that in Gilbert's face which enforced respect. Contrasted with his father, who stood on one side, darting stealthy glances at the group from the corners of his eyes, his bearing was doubly brave and noble. He offered his hand in silence, and both Elisha Barton and his wife felt themselves compelled to take it. Then the three sons, who knew the name of Gilbert Potter, and were more astonished than shocked at the new relationship, came up and greeted their cousin in a grave but not unfriendly way.

"That's right!" exclaimed Miss Lavender. "And now come in to dinner, all o' ye! I gev orders to have the meats dished as soon as the first horse was seen over the rise o' the hill, and it'll all be smokin' on the table."

Though the meal was such as no one had ever before seen in the Barton farmhouse, it was enjoyed by very few of the company. The sense of something to come after it made them silent and uncomfortable. Mr. Stacy, Miss Lavender, and the sons of Elisha Barton, with their wives, carried on a scattering, forced conversation, and there was a general feeling of relief when the pies, marmalade, and cheese had been consumed, and the knives and forks laid crosswise over the plates.

When they arose from the table, Mr. Stacy led the way into the parlor. A fire, in the meantime, had been made in the chill, open fireplace, but it scarcely relieved the dreary, frosty aspect of the apartment. The presence of the corpse seemed to linger there, attaching itself with ghastly distinctness to the chair and hickory staff in a corner.

The few dinner guests who were not relatives understood that this meeting excluded them, and Elisha Barton was therefore surprised to notice, after they had taken their seats, that Miss Lavender was one of the company.

"I thought," he said, with a significant look, "that it was to be the family only."

"Miss Lavender is one of the witnesses to the will," Mr. Stacy answered, "and her presence is necessary, moreover, as an important testimony in regard to some of its provisions."

Alfred Barton and Gilbert both started at these words, but from very different feelings. The former, released from public scrutiny, already experienced a comparative degree of comfort, and held up his head with an air of courage; yet now the lawyer's announcement threw him into an agitation which it was not possible to conceal. Miss Lavender looked around the circle, coolly nodded her head to Elisha Barton, and said nothing.

Mr. Stacy arose, unlocked a small niche let into the wall of the house, and produced the heavy oaken casket in which the old man kept the documents relating to his property. This he placed upon a small table beside his chair, opened it, and took out the topmost paper. He was completely master of the situation, and the deliberation with which he surveyed the circle of the excited faces around him seemed to indicate that he enjoyed the fact.

"The last will and testament of Abiah Barton, made the day before his death," he said, "revokes all former wills, which were destroyed by his order, in the presence of myself and Miss Elizabeth Lavender."

All eyes were turned upon the spinster, who again nodded, with a face of preternatural solemnity.

"In order that you, his children and grandchildren," Mr. Stacy continued, "may rightly understand the deceased's intention in making this last will, when the time comes for me to read it, I must first inform you that he was acquainted with the fact of his son Alfred's marriage with Mary Potter."

Alfred Barton half sprang from his seat, and then fell back with the same startled, livid face, which Gilbert already knew. The others held their breath in suspense—except Mary, who sat near the lawyer, firm, cold, and unmoved.

"The marriage of Alfred Barton and Mary Potter must therefore be established, to *your* satisfaction," Mr. Stacy resumed, turning towards Elisha. "Alfred Barton, I ask you to declare whether this woman is your lawfully wedded wife?"

A sound almost like a groan came from his throat, but it formed the syllable, "Yes."

"Further, I ask you to declare whether Gilbert Barton, who has until this day borne his mother's name of Potter, is your lawfully begotten son?"

"Yes."

"To complete the evidence," said the lawyer, "Mary Barton, give me the paper in your hands."

She untied the handkerchief, opened the Bible, and handed Mr. Stacy the slip of paper which Gilbert had seen her place between the leaves that morning. The lawyer gave it to Elisha Barton, with the request that he would read it aloud.

It was the certificate of a magistrate at Burlington, in the Colony of New Jersey, setting forth that he had united in wedlock Alfred Barton and Mary Potter. The date was in the month of June, 1771.

"This paper," said Elisha, when he had finished reading, "appears to be genuine. The evidence must have been satisfactory to you, Mr. Stacy, and to my father, since it appears to have been the cause of his making a new will; but as this new will probably concerns me and my children, I demand to know why, if the marriage was legal, it has been kept secret so long? The fact of the marriage does not explain what has happened today."

Mr. Stacy turned towards Gilbert's mother, and made a sign.

"Shall I explain it in my way, Alfred?" she asked, "or will you, in yours?"

"There's but one story," he answered, "and I guess it falls to your place to tell it."

"It does!" she exclaimed. "You, Elisha and Ann, and you, Gilbert, my child, take notice that every word of what I shall say is the plain God's truth. Twenty-seven years ago, when I was a young woman of twenty, I came to this farm to help Ann with the housework. You remember it, Ann; it was just after your mother's death. I was poor; I had neither father nor mother, but I was as proud as the proudest, and the people called me good-looking. You were vexed with me, Ann, because the young men came now and then, of a Sunday afternoon; but I put up with your hard words. You did not know that I understood what Alfred's eyes meant when he looked at me; I put up with you because I believed I could be mistress of the house, in your place. You have had your revenge of me since, if you felt the want of it—so let that rest!"

She paused. Ann, with her handkerchief to her eyes, sobbed out, "Mary, I always liked you better 'n you thought."

"I can believe it," she continued, "for I have been forced to look into my heart and learn how vain and mistaken I then was. But I liked Alfred, in those days; he was a gay young man, and accounted good-looking, and there were merry times just before the war, and he used to dress bravely, and was talked about as likely to marry this girl or that. My head was full of him, and I believed my heart was. I let him see from the first that it must be honest love between us, or not at all; and the more I held back, the more eager was he, till others began to notice, and the matter was brought to his father's ears."

"I remember that!" cried Elisha, suddenly.

"Yet it was kept close," she resumed. "Alfred told me that the old man had threatened to cut him out of his will if he should marry me, and I saw that I must leave the farm; but I gave out that I was tired of the country, and wanted to find service in Philadelphia. I believed that Alfred would follow me in a week or two, and he did. He brought news I didn't expect, and it turned my head upside down. His father had had a paralytic stroke, and nobody believed he'd live more than a few weeks. It was in the beginning of June, and the doctors said he couldn't get over the hot weather. Alfred said to me, Why wait? —you'll be taking up with some city-fellow, and I want you to be my wife at once. On my side I thought, Let him be made rich and free by his father's death, and wives will be thrown in his way; he'll lose his liking for me, by little and little, and somebody else will be mistress of the farm. So I agreed, and we went to Burlington together, as being more out of the way and easier to be kept secret; but just before we came to the Squire's, he seemed to grow fearsome all at once, lest it should be found out, and he bought a Bible and swore me by my soul's salvation never to say I was married to him until after his father died. Here's the Bible, Alfred! Do you remember it? Here, here's the place where I kissed it when I took the oath!"

She rose from her seat, and held it towards him. No one could doubt the solemn truth of her words. He nodded his head mechanically, unable to speak. Still standing, she turned towards Elisha Barton, and exclaimed,

"*He* took the same oath, but what did it mean to him! What does it mean to a man? I was young and vain; I thought only of holding fast to my good luck! I never thought of—of"—(here her faced flushed, and her voice began to tremble)—"of *you*, Gilbert! I fed my pride by hoping for a man's death, and never dreamed I was bringing a curse on a life that was yet to come! Perhaps he didn't then, either; the Lord pardon me if I judge him too hard. What I charge him with, is that he held me to my oath, when—when the fall went by and the winter, and his father lived, and his son was to be born! It was always the same—Wait a little, a month or so, maybe; the old man couldn't live, and it was the difference between riches and poverty for us. Then I begged for poverty and my good name, and after that he kept away from me. Before Gilbert was born, I hoped I might die in giving him life; then I felt that I must live for his sake. I saw my sin, and what punishment the Lord had measured out to me, and that I must earn His forgiveness; and He mercifully hid from my sight the long path that leads to this day; for if the release hadn't seemed so near, I never could have borne to wait!"

All the past agony of her life seemed to discharge itself in these words. They saw what the woman had suffered, what wonderful virtues of patience and faith had been developed from the vice of her pride, and there was no heart in the company so stubborn as to refuse her honor. Gilbert's eyes were fixed on her face with an absorbing expression of reverence; he neither knew nor heeded that there were tears on his cheeks. The women wept in genuine emotion, and even the old lawyer was obliged to wipe his dimmed spectacles.

Elisha rose, and approaching Alfred, asked, in a voice which he strove to make steady, "Is all this true?"

Alfred sank his head; his reply was barely audible,

"She has said no more than the truth."

"Then," said Elisha, taking her hand, "I accept you, Mary Barton, and acknowledge your place in our family."

Elisha's wife followed, and embraced her with many tears, and lastly Ann, who hung totteringly upon her shoulder as she cried,

"Indeed, Mary, indeed I always liked you; I never wished you any harm!"

Thus encouraged, Alfred Barton made a powerful effort. There seemed but one course for him to take; it was a hard one, but he took it.

"Mary," he said, "you have full right and justice on your side. I've acted meanly towards you—meaner, I'm afraid, than any man before ever acted towards his wife. Not only to you, but to Gilbert; but I always meant to do my duty in the end. I waited from month to month, and year to year, as you did; and then things got set in their way, and it was harder and harder to let out the truth. I comforted myself—that wasn't right, either, I know—but I conforted myself with the thought that you were doing well; I never lost sight of you, and I've been proud of Gilbert, though I didn't dare show it, and always wanted to lend him a helping hand, if he'd let me."

She drew herself up and faced him with flashing eyes.

"How did you mean to do your duty by me? How did you mean to lend Gilbert a helping hand? Was it by trying to take a second wife during my lifetime, and that wife the girl whom Gilbert loves?"

Her questions cut to the quick, and the shallow protestations he would have set up were stripped off in a moment, leaving bare every cowardly shift of his life. Nothing was left but the amplest confession.

"You won't believe me, Mary," he stammered, feebly weeping with pity of his own miserable plight, "and I can't ask you to—but it's the truth! Give me your Bible! I'll kiss the place you kissed, and swear before God that I never meant to marry Martha

Deane! I let the old man think so, because he hinted it'd make a difference in his will, and he drove me—he and Dr. Deane together—to speak to her. I was a coward and a fool that I let myself to be driven that far, but I couldn't and wouldn't have married her!"

"The whole snarl's comin' undone," interrupted Miss Lavender. "I see the end on 't. Do you mind that day, Alf. Barton, when I come upon you suddent, settin' on the log and sayin' 'I can't see the way,'—the very day, I'll be snaked, that you spoke to the Doctor about Martha Deane!—and then *you* so mortal glad that she wouldn't have you! You *have* acted meaner 'n dirt; I don't excuse him, Mary; but never mind, justice is justice, and he's told the truth this once't."

"Sit down, friends!" said Mr. Stacy. "Before the will is read, I want Miss Lavender to relate how it was that Abiah Barton and myself became acquainted with the fact of the marriage."

The reading of the will had been almost forgotten in the powerful interest excited by Mary Barton's narrative. The curiosity to know its contents instantly revived, but was still subordinate to that which the lawyer's statement occasioned. The whole story was so singular that it seemed as yet but half explained.

"Well, to begin at the beginnin'," said Miss Lavender, "it all come o' my wishin' to help two true-lovyers, and maybe you'll think I'm as foolish as I'm old, but never mind, I'll allow that; and I saw that nothin' could be done till Gilbert got his lawful name, and how to get it was the trouble, bein' as Mary was swore to keep secret. The long and the short of it is, I tried to worm it out o' her, but no use; she set her teeth as tight as sin, and all I did learn was, that when she was in Phildelphy—I knowed Gilbert was born there, but didn't let on—she lived at Treadwell's, in Fourth Street. Then turnin' over everything in my mind, I suspicioned that she must be waitin' for somebody to die, and that's what held her bound; it seemed to me I *must* guess right away, but I couldn't and couldn't, and so goin' up the hill, nigh puzzled to death, Gilbert ploughin' away from me, bendin' his head for'ard a little—there! turn round, Gilbert! turn round, Alf. Barton! Look at them two sets o' shoulders!"

Miss Lavender's words were scarcely comprehensible, but all saw the resemblance between father and son, in the outline of the shoulders, and managed to guess her meaning.

"Well," she continued, "it struck me then and there, like a streak o' lightnin'; I screeched and tumbled like a shot hawk, and so betwixt the saddle and the ground, as the sayin' is, it come to me—not mercy, but knowledge, all the same, you know what I mean; and I saw them was Alf. Barton's shoulders, and I remembered the old man was struck with palsy the year afore Gilbert was born, and I dunno how many other things come to me all of a heap; and now you know, Gilbert, what made me holler. I borrowed the loan o' his bay horse and put off for Phildelphy the very next day, and a mortal job it was; what with bar'ls and boxes pitched hither and yon, and people laughin' at y'r odd looks—don't talk o' Phildelphy manners to me, for I've had enough of 'em!—and old Treadwell dead when I did find him, and the daughter married to Greenfield in the brass and tinware business, it's a mercy I ever found out anything."

"Come to the point, Betsy," said Elisha, impatiently.

"The point, Betsy. The p'int's this: I made out from the Greenfield woman that the man who used to come to see Mary Potter was the perfect pictur' o' young Alf. Barton; then to where she went next, away down to the t'other end o' Third Street, boardin', he payin' the board till just afore Gilbert was born—and that's enough, thinks I, let me get out o' this rackety place. So home I posted, but not all the way, for no use to tell Mary Potter, and why not go right to Old Man Barton, and let him know who his daughter-in-law and son is, and see what'll come of it? Th' old man, you must know, always could abide me better 'n most women, and I wasn't a bit afeard of him, not lookin' for legacies, and wouldn't have 'em at any such price; but never mind. I hid my horse in the woods and sneaked into the house across the fields, the back way, and good luck that nobody was at home but Ann, here; and so I up and told the old man the whole story."

"The devil!" Alfred Barton could not help exclaiming, as he recalled his father's singular manner on the evening of the day in question.

"Devil!" Miss Lavender repeated. "More like an angel put it into my head. But I see Mr. Elisha's fidgetty, so I'll make short work o' the rest. He curst and swore awful, callin' Mr. Alfred a mean pup, and I dunno what all, but he hadn't so much to say ag'in Mary Potter; he allowed she was a smart lass, and he'd heerd o' Gilbert's doin's, and the lad had grit in him. 'Then,' says I, 'here's a mighty wrong been done, and it's for you to set it right afore you die, and if you manage as I tell you, you can be even with Mr. Alfred;' and he perks up his head and asks how, and says I 'This way'—but what I said'll be made manifest by Mr. Stacy, without my jumpin' ahead o' the proper time. The end of it was, he wound up by sayin', 'Gad, if Stacy was only here!' 'I'll bring him!' says I, and it was fixed betwixt and between us two, Ann knowin' nothin' o' the matter; and off I traipsed back to Chester, and brung Mr. Stacy, and if that good-for-nothin' Jake Fairthorn hadn't ha' seen me—"

"That will do, Miss Lavender," said Mr. Stacy, interrupting her. "I have only to add that Abiah Barton was so well convinced of the truth of the marriage, that his new will only requires the proof which has today been furnished, in order to express his intentions fully and completely. It was his wish that I should visit Mary Barton on the very morning afterwards; but his sudden death prevented it, and Miss Lavender ascertained, the same evening, that Mary, in view of the neglect and disgrace which she had suffered, demanded to take her justification into her own hands. My opinion coincided with that of Miss Lavender, that she alone had the right to decide in the matter, and that we must give no explanation until she had asserted, in her own way, her release from a most shameful and cruel bond."

It was a proud moment of Miss Lavender's life when, in addition to her services, the full extent of which would presently be known, a lawyer of Mr. Stacy's reputation so respectfully acknowledged the wisdom of her judgment.

"If further information upon any point is required," observed the lawyer, "it may be asked for now; otherwise, I will proceed to the reading of the will."

"Was—was my father of sound mind—that is, competent to dispose of his property?" asked Elisha Barton, with a little hesitation.

"I hope the question will not be raised," said Mr. Stacy, gravely; "but if it is I must testify that he was in as full possession of his faculties as at any time since his first attack twenty-six years ago."

He then read the will, amid the breathless silence of the company. The old man first devised to his elder son, Elisha Barton, the sum of twenty thousand dollars, investments secured by mortgages on real estate; an equal amount to his daughter-in-law, Mary, provided she was able to furnish legal proof of her marriage to his son, Alfred Barton; five thousand dollars each to his four grandchildren, the three sons of Elisha, and Gilbert Barton; ten thousand dollars to his daughter Ann; and to his son Alfred the occupancy and use of the farm during his life, the property, at his death, to pass into the hands of Gilbert Barton. There was also a small bequest to Giles, and the reversions of the estate were to be divided equally among all the heirs. The witnesses to the will were James Stacy and Elizabeth Lavender.

Gilbert and his mother now recognized, for the first time, what they owed to the latter. A sense of propriety kept them silent; the fortune which had thus unexpectedly fallen into their hands was the least and poorest part of their justification. Miss Lavender, also, was held to silence, but it went hard with her. The reading of the will gave her such an exquisite sense of enjoyment that she felt quite choked in the hush which followed it.

"As the marriage is now proven," Mr. Stacy said, folding up the paper, "there is nothing to prevent the will from being carried into effect."

"No, I suppose not," said Elisha; "it is as fair as could be expected."

"Mother, what do you say?" asked Gilbert, suddenly.

"Your grandfather wanted to do me justice, my boy," said she. "Twenty thousand dollars will not pay me for twenty-five years of shame; no money could; but it was the only payment he had to offer. I accept this as I accepted my trials. The Lord sees fit to make my worldly path smooth to my feet, and I have learned neither to reject mercy nor wrath."

She was not elated; she would not, on that solemn day, even express gratification in the legacy for her son's sake. Though her exalted mood was but dimly understood by the others, they felt its influence. If any thought of disputing the will, on the ground of his father's incompetency, had ever entered Elisha Barton's mind, he did not dare, then or afterwards, to express it.

The day was drawing to a close, and Elisha Barton with his sons, who lived in the adjoining township of Pennsbury, made preparations to leave. They promised soon to visit Gilbert and his mother. Miss Lavender, taking Gilbert aside, announced that she was going to return to Dr. Deane's.

"I s'pose I may tell her," she said, trying to hide her feelings under a veil of clumsy irony, "that it's all up betwixt and between you, now you're a rich man; and of course as she wouldn't have the father, she can't think o' takin' the son."

"Betsy," he whispered, "tell her that I never yet needed her love so much as now, and that I shall come to her tomorrow."

"Well, you know the door stands open, even accordin' to the Doctor's words."

As Gilbert went forth to look after the horses, Alfred Barton followed him. The two had not spoken directly to each other during the whole day.

"Gilbert," said the father, putting his hand on the son's shoulder, "you know, now, why it always cut me to have you think ill of me. I deserve it, for I've been no father to you; and after what you've heard today, I may never have a chance to be one. But if you *could* give me a chance—if you could—"

Here his voice seemed to fail. Gilbert quietly withdrew his shoulder from the hand, hesitated a moment, and then said, "Don't ask me anything now, if you please. I can only think of my mother today."

Alfred Barton walked to the garden fence, leaned his arms upon it, and his head upon them. He was still leaning there, when mother and son rode by in the twilight, on their way home.

CHAPTER 32

The Lovers

Both mother and son made the homeward ride in silence. A wide space, a deep gulf of time, separated them from the morning. The events of the day had been so startling, so pregnant with compressed fate, the emotions they had undergone had been so profound, so mixed of the keenest elements of wonder, pain, and pride, that a feeling of exhaustion succeeded. The old basis of their lives seemed to have shifted, and the new foundations were not yet firm under their feet.

Yet, as they sat together before the hearth-fire that evening, and the stern, proud calm of Gilbert's face slowly melted into a gentler and tenderer expression, his mother was moved to speak.

"This has been *my* day," she said; "it was appointed and set apart for me from the first; it belonged to me, and I have used it, in my right, from sun to sun. But I feel now, that it was not my own strength alone that held me up. I am weak and weary, and it almost seems that I fail in thanksgiving. Is it, Gilbert, because you do not rejoice as I had hoped you would?"

"Mother," he answered, "whatever may happen in my life, I can never feel so proud of myself, as I felt today to be your son. I do rejoice for your sake, as I shall for my own, no doubt, when I get better used to the truth. You could not expect me, at once, to be satisfied with a father who has not only acted so cruelly towards you, but whom I have suspected of being my own rival and enemy. I don't think I shall ever like the new name as well as the old, but it is enough for me that the name brings honor and independence to you!"

"Perhaps I ought to ha' told you this morning, Gilbert. I thought only of the justification, not of the trial; and it seemed easier to speak in actions, to you and to all men at once, as I did, than to tell the story quietly to you alone. I feared it might take away my strength if I didn't follow step by step, the course marked out for me."

"You were right, Mother!" he exclaimed. "What trial had I, compared with yours? What tale had I to tell—what pain to feel, except that if I had not been born, you would have been saved twenty-five years of suffering!"

"No, Gilbert!—never say, never think that! I see already the suffering and the sorrow dying away as if they'd never been, and you left to me for the rest of life the Lord grants; to me a son has been more than a husband!"

"Then," he asked in an anxious, hesitating tone, "would you consider that I was not quite so much a son—that any part of my duty to you was lost—if I wished to bring you a daughter, also?"

"I know what you mean, Gilbert. Betsy Lavender has told me all. I am glad you spoke of it, this day; it will put the right feeling of thanksgiving into my heart and yours. Martha Deane never stood between us, my boy; it was I that stood between you and her!"

"Mother!" he cried, a joyous light shining from his face, "you love her? You are willing that she should be my wife?"

"Ay, Gilbert; willing, and thankful, and proud."

"But the very name of her struck you down! You fell into a deadly faint when I told you I had spoken my mind to her!"

"I see, my boy," she said; "I see now why you never mentioned her name from that time. It was not Martha Deane, but the name of the one you thought wanted to win her away from you—your father's name, Gilbert—that seemed to put a stop to my life. The last trial was the hardest of all, but don't you see it was only the bit of darkness that comes before the daylight?"

While this new happiness brought the coveted sense of thanksgiving to mother and son, and spread an unexpected warmth and peace over the close of the fateful day, there was the liveliest excitement in Kennett Square, over Miss Lavender's intelligence. That lady had been waylaid by a dozen impatient questioners before she could reach the shelter of Dr. Deane's roof; and could only purchase release by a hurried statement of the main facts, in which Alfred Barton's cruelty, and his wife's wonderful fidelity to her oath, and the justice done to her and Gilbert by the old man's will, were set forth with an energy that multiplied itself as the gossip spread.

In the adjoining townships, it was reported and believed, the very next day, that Alfred Barton had tried to murder his wife and poison his father—that Mary had saved the latter, and inherited, as her reward, the entire property.

Once safely housed, Miss Lavender enjoyed another triumph. She related the whole story, in every particular, to Martha Deane, in the Doctor's presence, taking especial care not to omit Alfred's words in relation to his enforced wooing.

"And there's one thing I mustn't forgit, Martha," she declared, at the close of her narrative. "Gilbert sends word to you that he needs your true-love more'n ever, and he's comin' up to see you tomorrow; and says I to him, The door's open, even accordin' to the Doctor's words; and so it is, for he's got his true name, and free to come. You're a man o' your word, Doctor, and nothin's been said or done, thank goodness, that can't be easy mended!"

What impression this announcement made upon Dr. Deane could not be guessed by either of the women. He rose, went to the window, looked into the night for a long time without saying a word, and finally betook himself to his bed.

The next morning, although there were no dangerous cases on his hands, he rode away, remarking that he should not be home again until the evening. Martha knew what this meant, and also what Miss Lavender meant in hurrying down to Fairthorn's, soon after the Doctor's departure. She became restless with tender expectation; her cheeks burned, and her fingers trembled so that she was forced to lay aside her needlework. It seemed very long since she had even seen Gilbert; it was a long time (in the calendar of lovers) since the two had spoken to each other. She tried to compare the man he had been with the man he now was—Gilbert poor, disgraced and in trouble, with Gilbert rich and honorably born; and it almost seemed as if the latter had impoverished her heart by taking from it the need of that faithful, passionate sympathy which she had bestowed upon the former.

The long hour of waiting came to an end. Roger was once more tethered at the gate, and Gilbert was in the room. It was not danger, this time, beyond the brink of which they met, but rather a sudden visitation of security; yet both were deeply and powerfully agitated. Martha was the first to recover her composure. Withdrawing herself from Gilbert's arms, she said,

"It was not right that the tests should be all on my side. Now it is my turn to try you, Gilbert!"

Even her arch, happy smile did not enlighten him. "How, Martha?" he asked.

"Since you don't know, you are already tested. But how grave you look! Have I not yet learned all of this wonderful, wonderful history? Did Betsy Lavender keep something back?"

"Martha!" he cried, "you shame me out of the words I had meant to say. But they were doubts of my own position, not of you. Is my new name better or worse in your ears, than my old one?"

"To me you are only Gilbert," she answered, "as I am Martha to you. What does it matter whether we write Potter or Barton? Either is good in itself, and so would any other name be; but Barton means something, as the world goes, and therefore we will take it. Gilbert, I have put myself in your place, since I learned the whole truth. I guessed you would come to me with a strange, uncertain feeling—not a doubt, but rather a wonder; and I endeavored to make your new circumstances clear to my mind. Our duty to your mother is plain, she is a woman beside whom all other women we know seem weak and insignificant. It is not that which troubled you, I am sure, when you thought of me. Let me say, then, that so far as our relation to your father is concerned, I will be guided entirely by your wishes."

"Martha," he said "that *is* my trouble—or, rather, my disappointment—that with my true name I must bring to you and fasten upon you the whole mean and shameful story! One parent must always be honored at the expense of the other, and my name still belongs to the one that is disgraced."

"I foresaw your feeling, Gilbert. You were on the point of making another test for me; that is not fair. The truth has come too suddenly—the waters of your life have been stirred too deeply; you must wait until they clear. Leave that to Alfred Barton and your mother. To me, I confess, he seems very weak rather than very bad. I can now understand the pains which his addresses to me must have cost him. If I ever saw fear on a man's face, it was on his when he thought I might take him at his word. But, to a man like you, a mean nature is no better than a bad one. Perhaps I feel your disappointment as deeply as you can; yet it is our duty to keep this feeling to ourselves. For your mother's sake, Gilbert, you must not let the value of her justification be lessened in her eyes. She deserves all the happiness you and I can give her, and if she is willing to receive me, some day, as a daughter—"

Gilbert interrupted her words by clasping her in his arms. "Martha!" he exclaimed, "your heart points out the true way because it is true to the core! In these things a woman sees clearer than a man; when I am with you only, I seem to have proper courage and independence—I am twice myself! Won't you let me claim you—take you—soon? My mother loves you; she will welcome you as my wife, and will your father still stand between us?"

Martha smiled. "My father is a man of strong will," she said, "and it is hard for him to admit that his judgment was wrong. We must give him a little time—not urge, not seem to triumph, spare his pride, and trust to his returning sense of what is right. You might claim reparation, Gilbert, for his cruel words; I could not forbid you; but after so much strife let there be peace, if possible."

"It is at least beyond his power," Gilbert replied, "to accuse me of sordid motives. As I said before, Martha, give up your legacy, if need be, but come to me!"

"As *I* said before, Gilbert, the legacy is honestly mine, and I will come to you with it in my hands."

Then they both began to smile, but it was a conflict of purpose which drew them nearer together, in both senses—an emulation of unselfish love, which was compromised by clasping arms and silent lips.

There was a sudden noise in the back part of the house. A shrill voice was heard, exclaiming, "I will—I will! don't hold me!"—the door burst open, and Sally Fairthorn whirled into the room, with the skirt of her gown torn loose on one side from the body. Behind her followed Miss Lavender, in a state of mingled amusement and anger.

Sally kissed Martha, then Gilbert, then threw an arm around the neck of each, crying and laughing hysterically: "O Martha! O Gilbert! you'll be married first—I said it—but Mark and I must be your bridesmaids; don't laugh, you know what I mean; and Betsy wouldn't have me break in upon you; but I waited half an hour, and then off, up here, she after me, and we're both out o' breath! Did ever, ever such a thing happen!"

"You crazy thing!" cried Miss Lavender. "No, such a thing

never happened, and wouldn't ha' happened this time, if I'd ha' been a little quicker on my legs; but never mind, it serves me right; you two are to blame, for why need I trouble my head furder about ye? There's cases, they say, where two's company, and three's overmuch; but you may fix it for yourselves next time, and welcome; and there's one bit o' wisdom I've got by it—foller true-lovyers, and they'll wear your feet off, and then want you to go on the stumps!"

"We won't relieve you yet, Betsy," said Gilbert; "will we, Martha? The good work you've done for us isn't finished."

"Isn't finished. Well, you'll gi' me time to make my will, first. How long d' ye expect me to last, at this rate? Is my bones brass and my flesh locus'-wood? Am I like a tortle, that goes around the fields a hundred years?"

"No," Gilbert answered, "but you shall be like an angel, dressed all in white, with roses in your hair. Sally and Mark, you know, want to be the first bridesmaids—"

Sally interrupted him with a slap, but it was not very violent, and he did not even attempt to dodge it.

"Do you hear, Betsy?" said Martha. "It must be as Gilbert says."

"A pretty fool you'd make o' me," Miss Lavender remarked, screwing up her face to conceal her happy emotion.

Gilbert soon afterwards left for home, but returned towards evening, determined, before all things, to ascertain his present standing with Dr. Deane. He did not anticipate that the task had been made easy for him; but this was really the case. Wherever Dr. Deane had been that day, whoever he had seen, the current talk all ran one way. When the first surprise of the news had been exhausted, and the Doctor had corrected various monstrous rumors from his own sources of positive knowledge, one inference was sure to follow—that now there could be no objection to his daughter becoming Gilbert Barton's wife. He was sounded, urged, almost threatened, and finally returned home with the conviction that any further opposition must result in an immense sacrifice of popularity.

Still, he was not ready to act upon that conviction at once. He met Gilbert with a bland condescension, and when the latter, after the first greeting, asked,

"Have I now the right to enter your house?"

The Doctor answered,

"Certainly. Thee has kept thy word, and I will willingly admit that I did thee wrong in suspecting thee of unworthy devices. I may say, also, that so far as I was able to judge, I approved of thy behavior on the day of thy grandfather's funeral. In all that has happened heretofore, I have endeavored to act cautiously and prudently; and thee will grant, I doubt not, that thy family history is so very far out of the common way, as that no man could be called upon to believe it without the strongest evidence. Of course, all that I brought forward against thee now falls to the ground."

"I trust, then," Gilbert said, "that you have no further cause to forbid my engagement with Martha. My mother has given her consent, and we both hope for yours."

Dr. Deane appeared to reflect, leaning back in his chair, with his cane across his knees. "It is a very serious thing," he said, at last, "very serious, indeed. Not a subject for hasty decision. Thee offered, if I remember rightly, to give me time to know thee better; therefore thee cannot complain if I were now disposed to accept thy offer."

Gilbert fortunately remembered Martha's words, and restrained his impatience.

"I will readily give you time, Dr. Deane," he replied, "provided you will give me opportunities. You are free to question all who know me, of course, and I suppose you have done so. I will not ask you to take the trouble to come to me, in order that we may become better acquainted, but only that you will allow me to come to you."

"It would hardly be fair to deny thee that much," said the Doctor.

"I will ask no more now. I never meant, from the first, to question your interest in Martha's happiness, or your right to advise her. It may be too soon to expect your consent, but at least you'll hold back your refusal?"

"Thee's a reasonable young man, Gilbert," the Doctor remarked, after a pause which was quite unnecessary. "I like that in thee. We are both agreed, then, that while I shall be glad to see thee in my house, and am willing to allow to Martha and thee the intercourse proper to a young man and woman, it is not yet to be taken for granted that I sanction your desired marriage. Remember me kindly to thy mother, and say, if thee pleases, that I shall soon call to see her."

Gilbert had scarcely reached home that evening before Deb. Smith, who had left the farmhouse on the day following the recovery of the money, suddenly made her appearance. She slipped into the kitchen without knocking, and crouched down in a corner of the wide chimney-place, before she spoke. Both mother and son were struck by the singular mixture of shyness and fear in her manner.

"I heerd all about it, today," she presently said, "and I wouldn't ha' come here, if I'd ha' knowed where else to go to. They're after me this time, Sandy's friends, in dead earnest; they'll have my blood if they can git it; but you said once't you'd shelter me, Mr. Gilbert!"

"So I will, Deborah!" he exclaimed; "do you doubt my word?"

"No, I don't; but I dunno how 'tis—you're rich now, and as wellborn as the best of 'em, and Mary's lawful-married and got her lawful name; and you both seem to be set among the folks that can't feel for a body like me; not that your hearts is changed, only it comes different to me, somehow."

"Stay here, Deborah, until you feel sure you're safe," said Mary. "If Gilbert or I should refuse to protect you, your blood would be upon our heads. I won't blame you for doubting us; I know how easy it is to lose faith in others; but if you think I was a friend to you while my name was disgraced, you must also remember that I knew the truth then as well as the world knows it now."

"Bless you for sayin' that, Mary! There wasn't much o' my name at any time; but what little I might ha' had is clean gone—nothin' o' me left but the strong arm! I'm not a coward, as you know, Mr. Gilbert; I'll meet any man, face to face, in a fair and open fight. Let 'em come in broad day, and on the high road!—not lay in wait in bushes and behind fences to shoot me down unawares."

They strove to quiet her fears, and little by little she grew composed. The desperate recklessness of her mood contrasted strangely with her morbid fear of an ambushed enemy. Gilbert suspected that it might be a temporary insanity, growing out of her remorse for having betrayed Sandy Flash. When she had been fed and had smoked a pipe or two, she seemed quite to forget it, and was almost her own self when she went up to her bed in the western room.

The moon, three quarters full, was hanging over the barn, and made a peaceful, snowy light about the house. She went to the window, opened it, and breathed the cool air of the April night. The "herring-frogs" were keeping up an incessant, birdlike chirp down the glen, and nearer at hand the plunging water of the millrace made a soothing noise. It really seemed that the poor creature had found a quiet refuge at last.

Suddenly, something rustled and moved behind the mass of budding lilacs at the farther corner of the garden-paling. She leaned forward; the next moment there was a flash, the crack of a musket rang sharp and loud through the dell, followed by a whiz and thud at her very ear. A thin drift of smoke rose above the bushes, and she saw a man's figure springing to the cover of the nearest apple-tree. In another minute, Gilbert made his appearance, gun in hand.

"Shoot him, Gilbert!" cried Deb. Smith; "it's Dougherty!"

Whoever it was, the man escaped; but by a singular coincidence, the Irish ostler disappeared that night from the Unicorn tavern, and was never again seen in the neighborhood.

The bullet had buried itself in the window-frame, after having passed within an inch or two of Deb. Smith's head.* To Gilbert's surprise, all her fear was gone; she was again fierce and defiant, and boldly came and went, from that night forth, saying that no bullet was or would be cast, to take her life.

Therein she was right; but it was a dreary life and a miserable death which awaited her. For twenty-five years she wandered about the neighborhood, achieving wonders in spinning, reaping and threshing, by the undiminished force of her arm, though her face grew haggard and her hair gray; sometimes plunging into wild drinking-bouts with the rough male companions of her younger days; sometimes telling a new generation, with weeping and violent self-accusation, the story of her treachery; but always with the fearful conviction of a yet unfulfilled curse hanging over her life. Whether it was ever made manifest, no man could tell; but when she was found lying dead on the floor of her lonely cabin on the Woodrow farm, with staring, stony eyes, and the lines of unspeakable horror on her white face, there were those who recalled her own superstitious forebodings, and believed them.

---

*The hole made by the bullet still remains in the window-frame of the old farm-house.

CHAPTER 33

Husband and Wife

It may readily be guessed that such extraordinary develop-ments as those revealed in the preceding chapters produced more than a superficial impression upon a quiet community like that of Kennett and the adjoining townships. People secluded from the active movements of the world are drawn to take the greater interest in their own little family histories—a feeling which by and by amounts to a partial sense of ownership, justifying not only any degree of advice or comment, but sometimes even actual interference.

The Quakers, who formed a majority of the population, and generally controlled public sentiment in domestic matters through the purity of their own domestic life, at once pro-nounced in favor of Mary Barton. The fact of her having taken an oath was a slight stumbling block to some; but her patience, her fortitude, her submission to what she felt to be the Divine Will, and the solemn strength which had upborne her on the last trying day, were qualities which none could better appreciate. The fresh, warm sympathies of the younger people, already given to Gilbert and Martha, now also embraced her; far and wide went the wonderful story, carrying with it a wave of pity and respect for her, of contempt and denunciation for her hus-band.

The old Friends and their wives came to visit her, in their stately chairs; almost daily, for a week or two, the quiet of the farm was invaded, either by them, or by the few friends who had not forsaken her in her long disgrace, and were doubly welcome now. She received them all with the same grave, simple dignity of manner, gratefully accepting their expressions of sympathy, and quietly turning aside the inconsiderate questions that would have probed too deeply and painfully.

To an aged Friend—a preacher of the sect—who plumply asked her what course she intended to pursue towards her husband, she replied,

"I will not trouble my season of thanksgiving. What is right for me to do will be made manifest when the occasion comes."

This reply was so entirely in the Quaker spirit that the old man was silenced. Dr. Deane, who was present, looked upon her with admiration.

Whatever conjectures Alfred Barton might have made in advance of the consequences which would follow the disclosure of his secret marriage, they could have borne no resemblance to the reality. It was not in his nature to imagine the changes which the years had produced in his wife. He looked forward to wealth, to importance in the community, and probably supposed that she would only be too glad to share the proud position with him. There would be a little embarrassment at first, of course; but his money would soon make everything smooth.

Now, he was utterly defeated, crushed, overwhelmed. The public judgment, so much the more terrible where there is no escape from it, rolled down upon him. Avoided or coldly ignored by the staid, respectable farmers, openly insulted by his swaggering comrades of the fox-hunt and the barroom, jeered at and tortured by the poor and idle hangers-on of the community, who took a malicious pleasure in thus repaying him for his former haughtiness and their own humility, he found himself a moral outcast. His situation became intolerable. He no longer dared to show himself in the village, or upon the highways, but slunk about the house and farm, cursing himself, his father, and the miserable luck of his life.

When, finally, Giles begged to know how soon his legacy would be paid, and hinted that he couldn't stay any longer than to get possession of the money, for, hard as it might be to leave an old home, he must stop going to the mill, or getting the horses shod, or sitting in the Unicorn barroom of a Saturday night, and a man might as well be in jail at once, and be done with it—when Alfred Barton heard all this, he deliberated, for a few minutes, whether it would not be a good thing to cut his own throat.

Either that, or beg for mercy; no other course was left.

That evening he stole up to the village, fearful at every step of being seen and recognized, and knocked timidly at Dr.

Deane's door. Martha and her father were sitting together, when he came into the room, and they were equally startled at his appearance. His large frame seemed to have fallen in, his head was bent, and his bushy whiskers had become quite gray; deep wrinkles seamed his face; his eyes were hollow, and the corners of his mouth drooped with an expression of intolerable misery.

"I wanted to say a word to Miss Martha, if she'll let me," he said, looking from one to the other.

"I allowed thee to speak to my daughter once too often," Dr. Deane sternly replied. "What thee has to say now must be said in my presence."

He hesitated a moment, then took a chair and sat down, turning towards Martha. "It's come to this," he said, "that I must have a little mercy, or lay hands on my own life. I haven't a word to say for myself; I deserve it all. I'll do anything that's wanted of me—whatever Mary says, or people think is her right that she hasn't yet got, if it's mine to give. You said you wished me well, Miss Martha, even at the time I acted so shamefully; I remember that, and so I ask you to help me"

She saw that he spoke truth, at last, and all her contempt and disgust could not keep down the quick sensation of pity which his wretchedness inspired. But she was unprepared for his appeal, and uncertain how to answer it.

"What would you have me do?" she asked.

"Go to Mary on my behalf! Ask her to pardon me, if she can, or say what I can do to earn her pardon—that the people may know it. They won't be so hard on me, if they know she's done that. Everything depends on her, and if it's true, as they say, that she's going to sue for a divorce and take back her own name for herself and Gilbert, and cut loose from me forever, why, it'll just—"

He paused, and buried his face in his hands.

"I have not heard of that," said Martha.

"Haven't you?" he asked. "But it's too likely to be true."

"Why not go directly to Mary, yourself?"

"I will, Miss Martha, if you'll go with me, and maybe say a kind word now and then—that is, if you think it isn't too soon for mercy!"

"It is never too soon to *ask* for mercy," she said, coming to a sudden decision. "I will go with you; let it be tomorrow."

"Martha," warned Dr. Deane, "isn't thee a little hasty?"

"Father, I decide nothing. It is in Mary's hands. He thinks my presence will give him courage, and that I cannot refuse."

The next morning, the people of Kennett Square were again startled out of their proprieties by the sight of Alfred Barton, pale, agitated, and avoiding the gaze of everyone, waiting at Dr. Deane's gate, and then riding side by side with Martha down the Wilmington road. An hour before, she had dispatched Joe Fairthorn with a note to Gilbert, informing him of the inpending visit. Once on the way, she feared lest she had ventured too far; it might be, as her father had said, too hasty; and the coming meeting with Gilbert and his mother disquieted her not a little. It was a silent, anxious ride for both.

When they reached the gate, Gilbert was on hand to receive them. His face always brightened at the sight of Martha, and his hands lifted her as tenderly as ever from the saddle. "Have I done right?" she anxiously whispered.

"It is for Mother to say," he whispered back.

Alfred Barton advanced, offering his hand. Gilbert looked upon his father's haggard, imploring face, a moment; a recollection of his own disgrace shot into his heart, to soften, not to exasperate; and he accepted the hand. Then he led the way into the house.

Mary Barton had simply said to her son, "I felt that he would come, sooner or later, and that I must give him a hearing—better now, perhaps, since you and Martha will be with me."

They found her awaiting them, pale and resolute.

Gilbert and Martha moved a little to one side, leaving the husband and wife facing each other. Alfred Barton was too desperately moved to shrink from Mary's eyes; he strove to read something in her face which might spare him the pain of words; but it was a strange face he looked upon. Not that of the black-eyed, bright-cheeked girl, with the proud carriage of her head and the charming scorn of her red lip, who had mocked, fascinated, and bewildered him. The eyes were there, but they had sunk into the shade of the brows, and looked upon him with an impenetrable expression; the cheeks were pale, the mouth firm and rigid, and out of the beauty which seduced had grown a power to resist and command.

"Will you shake hands with me, Mary?" he faltered.

She said nothing, but moved her right hand slightly towards him. It lay in his own a moment, cold and passive.

"Mary!" he cried, falling on his knees at her feet, "I'm a ruined, wretched man! No one speaks to me but to curse; I've no friend left in the world; the very farm-hand leaves me! I don't know what'll become of me, unless you feel a little pity— not that I deserve any, but I ask it of you, in the name of God!"

Martha clung to Gilbert's arm, trembling, and more deeply moved than she was willing to show. Mary Barton's face was convulsed by some passing struggle, and when she spoke, her voice was hoarse and broken.

"You know what it is, then," she said, "to be disgraced in the eyes of the world. If you have suffered so much in these two weeks, you may guess what I have borne for twenty-five years!"

"I see it now, Mary!" he cried, "as I never saw it before. Try me! Tell me what to do!"

"The Lord has done it, already; there is nothing left."

He groaned; his head dropped hopelessly upon his breast.

Gilbert felt that Martha's agitation ceased. She quietly released her hold of his arm, lifted her head, and spoke,

"Mother, forgive me if I speak when I should hold my peace; I would only remind you that there is yet one thing left. It is true, as you say; the Lord has justified you in His own way, and at His own time, and has revenged the wrong done to you by branding the sin committed towards Himself. Now He leaves the rest to your own heart. Think that He holds back and waits for the words that shall declare whether you understand the spirit in which He deals towards His children!"

"Martha, my dear child!" Mary Barton exclaimed, "what can I do?"

"It is not for me to advise you, Mother. You, who put my impatient pride to shame, and make my love for Gilbert seem selfish by contrast with your long self-sacrifice! What right have I, who have done nothing, to speak to you, who have done so much that we never can reckon it? But, remember that in the Lord's government of the world pardon follows repentance, and it is not for us to exact like for like, to the uttermost farthing!"

Mary Barton sank into a chair, covered her face with her hands, and wept aloud.

There were tears in Martha's eyes; her voice trembled, and her words came with a softness and tenderness that soothed while they pierced:

"Mother, I am a woman like yourself; and, as a woman, I feel the terrible wrong that has been done to you. It may be as hard for you now to forget, as then to bear; but it is certainly greater and nobler to forgive than to await justice! Because I reverence you as a strong and pure and great-hearted woman—because I want to see the last and best and sweetest grace of our sex added to your name—and lastly, for Gilbert's sake, who can feel nothing but pain in seeing his father execrated and shunned—I ask your forgiveness for your husband!"

"Mary!" Alfred Barton cried, lifting up his head in a last appeal, "Mary, this much, at least! Don't go to the courts for a divorce! Don't get back your own name for yourself and Gilbert! Keep mine, and make it more respectable for me! And I won't ask you to pardon me, for I see you can't!"

"It is all clear to me, at last!" said Mary Barton. "I thank you, Martha, my child, for putting me in the right path. Alfred, don't kneel to me; if the Lord can pardon, who am I that I should be unforgiving? I fear me I was nigh to forfeit His mercy. Gilbert, yours was half the shame; yours is half the wrong; can you join me in pardoning your father and my husband?"

Gilbert was powerfully moved by the conflict of equally balanced emotions, and but for the indication which Martha had given, he might not at once have been able to decide. But it seemed now that his course was also clear. He said,

"Mother, since you have asked the question, I know how it should be answered. If you forgive your husband, I forgive my my father."

He stepped forward, seized Alfred Barton gently by the shoulder, and raised him to his feet. Mary Barton then took her husband's hand in hers, and said, in a solemn voice.

"I forgive you, Alfred, and will try to forget. I know not what you may have heard said, but I never meant to go before the court for a divorce. Your name is part of my right, a part of Gilbert's—our son's—right; it is true that you have debased the name, but we will keep it and make it honorable! We will not do that to the name of Barton which you have done to the name of Potter!"

It was very evident that though she had forgiven, she had not yet forgotten. The settled endurance of years could not be unlearned in a moment. Alfred Barton felt that her forgiveness implied no returning tenderness, not even an increase of respect; but it was more than he had dared to hope, and he felt humbly grateful. He saw that a consideration for Gilbert's position had been the chief element to which he owed his wife's relenting mood, and this knowledge was perhaps his greatest encouragement.

"Mary," he said, "you are kinder than I deserve. I wish I could make you and Gilbert understand all that I have felt. Don't think my place was easy; it wasn't. It was a hell of another kind. I have been punished in my way, and will be now to the end o' my life, while you two will be looked up to, and respected beyond any in the neighborhood; and if I'm not treated like a dog, it'll only be for your sakes! Will you let me say to the people that you have pardoned me? Will you say it yourselves?"

Martha, and perhaps Gilbert also, felt that it was the reflected image of Alfred Barton's meanness, as it came back to him in the treatment he had experienced, rather than his own internal consciousness of it, which occasioned his misery. But his words were true thus far; his life was branded by it, and the pardon of those he had wronged could not make that life more than tolerable.

"Why not?" said Gilbert, replying to him. "There has been enough of secrets. I am not ashamed of forgiveness—my shame is, that foregiveness is necessary."

Alfred Barton looked from mother to son with a singular, wistful expression. He seemed uncertain whether to speak or how to select his words. His vain, arrogant spirit was completely broken, but no finer moral instinct came in its place to guide him; his impulses were still coarse, and took, from habit, the selfish color of his nature. There are some persons whom even humiliation clothes with a certain dignity; but he was not one of them. There are others whose tact, in such emergencies, assumes the features of principle, and sets up a feeble claim to respect; but this quality is a result of culture, which he did not possess. He simply saw what would relieve him from the insupportable load of obloquy under which he groaned, and awkwardly hazarded the pity he had excited, in asking for it.

"Mary," he stammered, "I—I hardly know how to say the words, but you'll understand me; I want to make good to you all the wrong I did, and there seems no way but this—if you'll let me care for you, slave for you, anything you please; you shall have your own say in house and farm; Ann'll give up everything to you. She always liked you, she says, and she's lonely since th' old man died and nobody comes near us—not just at once, I mean, but after awhile, when you've had time to think of it, and Gilbert's married. You're independent in your own right, I know, and needn't do it; but, see! it'd give me a chance, and maybe Gilbert wouldn't feel quite so hard towards me, and—"

He stopped, chilled by the increasing coldness of his wife's face. She did not immediately reply; to Martha's eye she seemed to be battling with some proud, vindictive instinct. But she spoke at last, and calmly:

"Alfred, you should not have gone so far. I have pardoned you, and that means more than the words. It means that I must try to overcome the bitterness of my recollections, that I must curb the tongues of others when they are raised against you, must greet you when we meet, and in all proper ways show the truth of my forgiveness to the world. Anger and reproach may be taken from the heart, and yet love be as far off as ever. If anything ever could lead me back to you it would not be love, but duty to my son, and his desire; but I cannot see the duty now. I may never see it. Do not propose this thing again. I will only say, if it be any comfort to you, that if you try to show your repentance as I my pardon, try to clean your name from the stain you have cast upon it, my respect shall keep pace with that of your neighbors, and I shall in this way, and in no other, be drawn nearer to you!"

"Gilbert," said Alfred Barton, "I never knew your mother before today. What she says gives me some hope, and yet it makes me afraid. I'll try to bring her nearer, I will, indeed; but I've been governed so long by th' old man that I don't seem to have any right strength o' my own. I must have some help, and you're the only one I can ask it of; will you come and see me sometimes? I've been so proud of you, all to myself, my boy! and if I thought you could once call me 'father' before I die—"

Gilbert was not proof against these words and the honest tears by which they were accompanied. Many shy, hesitating tokens of affection in his former intercourse with Alfred Barton suddenly recurred to his mind, with their true interpretation. His load had been light, compared to his mother's; he had only learned the true wrong in the hour of reparation; and moreover, in assuming his father's name he became sensitive to the prominence of its shame.

"Father," he answered, "if you have forfeited a son's obedience, you have still a man's claim to be helped. Mother is right;

it is in your power to come nearer to us. She must stand aside and wait; but I can cross the line which separates you, and from this time on I shall never cross it to remind you of what is past and pardoned, but to help you, and all of us, to forget it!"

Martha laid her hand upon Gilbert's shoulder, leaned up and kissed him upon the cheek.

"Rest here!" she said. "Let a good word close the subject! Gilbert, take your father out and show him your farm. Mother, it is near dinner-time; I will help you set the table. After dinner, Mr. Barton, you and I will ride home together."

Her words were obeyed; each one felt that no more should be said at that time. Gilbert showed the barn, the stables, the cattle in the meadow, and the fields rejoicing in the soft May weather; Martha busied herself in kitchen and cellar, filling up the pauses of her labor with cheerful talk; and when the four met at the table, so much of the constraint in their relation to each other had been conquered, that a stranger would never have dreamed of the gulf which had separated them a few hours before. Martha shrewdly judged that when Alfred Barton had eaten at his wife's table, they would both meet more easily in the future. She did not expect that the breach could ever be quite filled; but she wished, for Gilbert's sake, to make it as narrow as possible.

After dinner, while the horses were being saddled, the lovers walked down the garden-path, between the borders of blue iris and mountain-pink.

"Gilbert," said Martha, "are you satisfied with what has happened?"

"Yes," he answered, "but it has shown to me that something more must be done."

"What?"

"Martha, are these the only two who should be brought nearer?"

She looked at him with a puzzled face. There was a laughing light in his eyes, which brought a new luster to hers, and a delicate blush to her fair cheeks.

"Is it not too soon for me to come?" she whispered.

"You *have* come," he answered; "you were in your place; and it will be empty—the house will be lonely, the farm without its mistress—until you return to us!"

CHAPTER 34

The Wedding

The neighborhood had decreed it. There was but one just, proper, and satisfactory conclusion to all these events. The decision of Kennett was unanimous that its story should be speedily completed. New-Garden, Marlborough, and Pennsbury, so far as heard from, gave their hearty consent; and the people would have been seriously disappointed—the tide of sympathy might even have been checked—had not Gilbert Barton and Martha Deane prepared to fulfill the parts assigned to them.

Dr. Deane, of course, floated with the current. He was too shrewd to stand forth as a conspicuous obstacle to the consummation of the proper sense of justice. He gave, at once, his full consent to the nuptials, and took the necessary steps, in advance, for the transfer of his daughter's fortune into her own hands. In short, as Miss Lavender observed, there was an end of snarls. The lives of the lovers were taken up, as by a skillful hand, and evenly reeled together.

Gilbert now might have satisfied his ambition (and the people, under the peculiar circumstances of the case, would have sanctioned it) by buying the finest farm in the neighborhood; but Martha had said,

"No other farm can be so much *yours*, and none so welcome a home to me. Let us be satisfied with it, at least for the first years."

And therein she spoke wisely.

It was now the middle of May, and the land was clothed in tender green and filled with the sweet breath of sap and bud and blossom. The vivid emerald of the willow-trees, the blush of orchards, and the cones of snowy bloom along the wood-sides, shone through and illumined even the days of rain. The month of marriage wooed them in every sunny morning, in every twilight fading under the torch of the lovers' star.

In spite of Miss Lavender's outcries, and Martha's grave doubts, a fortnight's delay was all that Gilbert would allow. He would have dispensed with bridal costumes and merrymakings— so little do men understand of these matters—but he was hooted down, overruled, ignored, and made to feel his proper insignificance. Martha almost disappeared from his sight during the interval. She was sitting upstairs in a confusion of lutestring, whalebone, silk, and cambric; and when she came down to him for a moment, the kiss had scarcely left her lips before she began to speak of the make of his new coat, and the fashion of the articles he was still expected to furnish.

If he visited Fairthorn's, it was even worse. The sight of him threw Sally into such a flutter that she sewed the right side of one breadth to the wrong side of another, attempted to clear-starch a woollen stocking, or even, on one occasion, put a fowl into the pot unpicked and undressed. It was known all over the country that Sally and Mark Deane were to be bridesmaid and groomsman, and they both determined to make a brave appearance.

But there was another feature of the coming nuptials which the people did not know. Gilbert and Martha had determined that Miss Betsy Lavender should be second bridesmaid, and Martha had sent to Wilmington for a purple silk and a stomacher of the finest cambric in which to array her. A groomsman of her age was not so easy to find; but young Pratt, who had stood so faithfully by Gilbert during the chase of Sandy Flash, merrily avowed his willingness to play the part; and so it was settled without Miss Lavender's knowledge.

The appointed morning came, bringing a fair sky, mottled with gentle, lingering clouds, and a light wind from the west. The wedding company were to meet at Kennett Square, and then ride to Squire Sinclair's, where the ceremony would be performed by that magistrate; and before ten o'clock, the hour appointed for starting, all the surrounding neighborhood poured into the village. The hitching-bar in front of the Unicorn, and every post of fence or garden-paling, was occupied by the tethered horses. The wedding guests, comprising some ten or fifteen persons, assembled at Dr. Deane's, and each couple, as they arrived, produced an increasing excitement among the spectators.

The fact that Alfred Barton had been formally pardoned by

his wife and son, did not lessen the feeling with which he was regarded, but it produced a certain amoung of forbearance. The people were curious to know whether he had been bidden to the wedding, and the conviction was general that he had no business to be there. The truth is, it had been left free to him whether to come or not, and he had very prudently chosen to be absent.

Dr. Deane had set up a "chair," which was to be used for the first time on this occasion. It was a ponderous machine, with drab body and wheels, and curtains of drab camlet looped up under its stately canopy. When it appeared at the gate, the Doctor came forth, spotless in attire, bland, smiling, a figure of sober gloss and agreeable odors. He led Mary Barton by the hand; and her steel-colored silk and white crepe shawl so well harmonized with his appearance that the two might have been taken for man and wife. Her face was calm, serene, and full of quiet gratitude. They took their places in the chair, the lines were handed to the Doctor, and he drove away, nodding right and left to the crowd.

Now the horses were brought up in pairs and the younger guests began to mount. The people gathered closer and closer; and when Sam appeared, leading the well-known and beloved Roger, there was a murmur which in a more demonstrative community would have been a cheer. Somebody had arranged a wreath of lilac and snowy viburnum, and fastened it around Roger's forehead; and he seemed to wear it consciously and proudly. Many a hand was stretched forth to pat and stroke the noble animal, and everybody smiled when he laid his head caressingly over the neck of Martha's gray.

Finally only six horses remained unmounted; then there seemed to be a little delay indoors. It was explained when young Pratt appeared, bold and bright, leading the reluctant Miss Lavender, rustling in purple splendor, and blushing—actually blushing—as she encountered the eyes of the crowd. The latter were delighted. There was no irony in the voice that cried, "Hurrah for Betsy Lavender!" and the cheer that followed was the expression of a downright, hearty good will. She looked around from her saddle, blushing, smiling, and on the point of bursting into tears; and it was a godsend, as she afterwards remarked, that Mark Deane and Sally Fairthorn appeared at that moment.

Mark, in sky-blue coat and breeches, suggested, with his rosy face and yellow locks, a son of the morning; while Sally's white muslin and cherry-colored scarf heightened the rich beauty of her dark hair and eyes, and her full, pouting lips. They were a buxom* pair, and both were too happy in each other and in the occasion to conceal the least expression of it.

There now only remained our hero and heroine, who immediately followed. No cheer greeted them, for the wonderful chain of circumstances which had finally brought them together made the joy of the day solemn, and the sympathy of the people reverential. Mark and Sally represented the delight of betrothal; these two the earnest sanctity of wedlock.

Gilbert was plainly yet richly dressed in a bottle-green coat, with white waistcoat and breeches; his ruffles, gloves, hat and boots were irreproachable. So manly looking a bridegroom had not been seen in Kennett for many a day. Martha's dress of heavy pearl-gray satin was looped up over a petticoat of white dimity, and she wore a short cloak of white crepe. Her hat, of the latest style, was adorned with a bunch of roses and a white, drooping feather. In the saddle, she was charming; and as the bridal pair slowly rode forward, followed by their attendants in the proper order, a murmur of admiration, in which there was no envy and no ill-natured qualification, went after them.

A soft glitter of sunshine, crossed by the shadows of slow-moving clouds, lay upon the landscape. Westward, the valley opened in quiet beauty, the wooded hills on either side sheltering, like protecting arms, the white farmhouses, the gardens, and rosy orchards scattered along its floor. On their left, the tall grove rang with the music of birds, and was gay, through all its light-green depths, with the pink blossoms of the wild azalea. The hedges, on either side, were purple with young sprays, and a bright, breathing mass of sweetbrier and wild grape crowned the overhanging banks, between which the road ascended the hill beyond.

At first the company were silent; but the enlivening motion of the horses, the joy of the coming summer, the affectionate sympathy of nature soon disposed them to a lighter mood. At Hallowell's, the men left their hoes in the corn-field, and the women their household duties, to greet them by the roadside. Mark looked up at the new barn, and exclaimed,

*Blithe (ed.).

"Not quite a year ago! Do you mind it, Gilbert?"

Martha pointed to the green turf in front of the house, and said with an arch voice,

"Gilbert, do you remember the question you put to me, that evening?"

And finally Sally burst out, in mock indignation,

"Gilbert, there's where you snapped me up, because I wanted you to dance with Martha; what do you think of yourself now?"

"You all forget," he answered, "that you are speaking of somebody else."

"How? somebody else?" asked Sally.

"Yes; I mean Gilbert Potter."

"Not a bad turn-off," remarked Miss Lavender. "He's too much for you. But I'm glad, anyhow, you've got your tongues, for it was too much like a buryin' before, and me fixed up like King Solomon, what for, I'd like to know? and the day made o' purpose for a weddin', and true-love all right for once't—I'd like just to holler and sing and make merry to my heart's content, with a nice young man alongside o' me, too, a thing that don't often happen!"

They were heartily, but not boisterously, merry after this; but as they reached the New-Garden road, there came a wild yell from the rear, and the noise of galloping hoofs. Before the first shock of surprise had subsided, the Fairthorn gray mare thundered up, with Joe and Jake upon her back, the scarlet lining of their blue cloaks flying to the wind, their breeches covered with white hair from the mare's hide, and their faces wild with delight. They yelled again as they drew rein at the head of the procession.

"Why, what upon earth—" began Sally; but Joe saved her the necessity of a question.

"Daddy said we shouldn't go!" he cried. "But we *would*—we got Bonnie out o' the field, and put off! Cousin Martha, you'll let us go along and see you get married; won't you, now? Maybe we'll never have another chance!"

This incident produced great amusement. The boys received the permission they coveted, but were ordered to the rear, Mark reminding them that as he was soon to be their uncle, they must learn, betimes, to give heed to his authority.

"Be quiet, Mark!" exclaimed Sally, with a gentle slap.

"Well, I don't begrudge it to 'em," said Miss Lavender. "It's somethin' for 'em to remember when they're men-grown; and they belong to the fam'ly, which I don't; but never mind, all the same, no more do you, Mr. Pratt; and I wish I was younger, to do credit to you!"

Merrily trotted the horses along the bit of level upland; and then, as the land began to fall towards the western branch of Redley Creek, they saw the Squire's house on a green knoll to the north, and Dr. Deane's new chair already resting in the shade of the gigantic sycamore at the door. The lane-gates were open, the Squire's parlor was arranged for their reception; and after the ladies had put themselves to rights in the upper rooms, the company gathered together for the ceremony.

Sunshine, and hum of bees, and murmur of winds, and scent of flowers, came in through the open windows, and the bridal pair seemed to stand in the heart of the perfect springtime. Yet tears were shed by all the women except the bride; and Sally Fairthorn was so absorbed by the rush of her emotions, that she came within an ace of saying "I will!" when the Squire put the question to Martha. The ceremony was brief and plain, but the previous history of the parties made it very impressive. When they had been pronounced man and wife, and the certificate of marriage had been duly signed and witnessed by all present, Mary Barton stepped forward and kissed her son and daughter with a solemn tenderness. Then the pent-up feelings of all the others broke loose, and the amount of embracing which followed was something quite unusual for Kennett. Betsy Lavender was not cheated out of her due share; on the contrary, it was ever afterwards reported that she received more salutes than even the bride. She was kissed by Gilbert, by Mark, by her young partner, by Dr. Deane, and lastly by the jolly Squire himself—to say nothing of the feminine kisses, which, indeed, being very imperfect gifts, hardly deserve to be recorded.

"Well!" she exclaimed, pushing her ruffled hair behind her ears, and smoothing down her purple skirt, "to think o' my bein' kissed by so many men, in my old days!—but why not?—it may be my last chance, as Joe Fairthorn says, and laugh if you please, I've got the best of it; and I don't belie my natur', for twistin' your head away and screechin' is only make-believe, and the more some screeches the more they want to be kissed; but fair and square, say I—if you want it, take it, and that's just what I've done!"

There was a fresh rush for Miss Lavender after this, and she stood her ground with commendable patience, until Mark ventured to fold her in a good-natured hug, when she pushed him away, saying,

"For the Lord's sake, don't spile my new things! There—go 'way, now! I've had enough to last me ten year!"

Dr. Deane soon set out with Mary Barton, in the chair, and the rest of the company mounted their horses, to ride back to Kennett square by the other road, past the quarries and across Tuffkenamon.

As they halted in the broad, shallow bed of the creek, letting their horses drink from the sparkling water, while the wind rollicked among the meadow bloom of golden saxifrage and scarlet painted-cup and blue spiderwort before them, the only accident of the day occurred; but it was not of a character to disturb their joyous mood.

The old Fairthorn mare stretched her neck to its utmost length before she bent it to drink, obliging Joe to lean forwards over her shoulder, to retain his hold of the short rein. Jake, holding on to Joe, leaned with him, and they waited in this painful posture till the mare slowly filled herself from the stream. Finally she seemed to be satisfied; she paused, snorted, and then, with wide nostrils, drank an equal amount of air. Her old sides swelled; the saddle-girth, broken into two places long before, and mended with tow-strings, suddenly parted, and Joe, Jake, saddle and all, tumbled down her neck into the water. They scrambled out in a lamentable plight, soused and dripping, amid the endless laughter of the company, and were glad to keep to the rear for the remainder of the ride.

In Dr. Deane's house, meanwhile, there were great preparations for the wedding dinner. A cook had been brought from Wilmington at an unheard-of expense, and the village was filled with rumors of the marvellous dishes she was to produce. There were pippins encased in orange peel and baked; a roasted peacock, with tail spread; a stuffed rockfish; a whole ham enveloped in dough, like a loaf of bread, and set in the oven; and a wilderness of the richest and rarest pies, tarts, and custards.

Whether all these rumors were justified by the dinner, we will not undertake to say; it is certain that the meal, which was spread in the large sitting room, was most bountiful. No one was then shocked by the decanters of port and canary wine upon the sideboard, or refused to partake of the glasses of foamy eggnog offered to them from time to time, through the afternoon. The bride-cake was considered a miracle of art, and the fact that Martha divided it with a steady hand, making the neatest and cleanest of cuts, was considered a good omen for her married life. Bits of the cake were afterwards in great demand throughout the neighborhood, not so much to eat, as to dream upon.

The afternoon passed away rapidly, with mirth and noise, in the adjoining parlor. Sally Fairthorn found a peculiar pleasure in calling her friend "Martha Barton!" whereupon Mark said,

"Wait a bit, Martha, and you can pay her back. Daddy Fairthorn promised this morning to give me a buildin' lot off the field back o' the corner, and just as soon as Rudd's house is up, I'm goin' to work at mine."

"Mark, do hush!" Sally exclaimed, reddening, "and before everybody!"

Miss Lavender sat in the midst, stately, purple, and so transformed that she professed she no longer knew her own self. She was, nevertheless, the life of the company; the sense of what she had done to bring on the marriage was a continual source of inspiration. Therefore, when songs were proposed and sung, and Mark finally called upon her, uproariously seconded by all the rest, she was moved, for the last time in her life, to comply.

"I dunno what you mean, expectin' such a thing o' me," she said. " 'Pears to me I'm fool enough already, settin' here in purple and fine linen, like the Queen o' Rome—not that I don't like singin', but the contrary, quite the reverse; but with me it'd be a squawk and nothin' else; and fine feathers may make fine birds for what I care, more like a poll-parrot than a nightingale, and they say you must stick thorns into 'em to make 'em sing; but I guess it'll be t' other way, and my singin'll stick thorns into you!"

They would take no denial; she could and must sing them a song. She held out until Martha said, "for my wedding day, Betsy!" and Gilbert added, "and mine, too." Then she declared, "Well, if I must, I s'pose I must. But as for weddin'-songs, such as I've heerd in my younger days, I dunno one of 'em, and my head's pretty much cleared o' such things, savin' and exceptin' one that might be a sort o' warnin' for Mark Deane, who knows?—not that there's sea-farin' men about these parts; but never mind, all the same; if you don't like it, Mark, you've brung it onto yourself!"

Thereupon, after shaking herself, gravely composing her face, and clearing her throat, she began, in a high, shrill, piercing voice, rocking her head to the peculiar lilt of the words, and interpolating short explanatory remarks, to sing—

THE BALLAD OF THE HOUSE-CARPENTÈR

" 'Well-met, well-met, my own true-love!'

"*She* says,

> 'Well-met, well-met, cried *he*;
> For 't is I have returned from the salt, salt sea,
> And it's all for the love of thee!'

" 'It's I might ha' married a king's daughter fair,'

"*He* goes on sayin',

> 'And fain would she ha' married me,
> But it's I have refusèd those crowns of gold,
> And it's all for the love of thee!'

"Then *she*,

> " 'If you might ha' married a king's daughter fair,'
> I think you are for to blame;
> For it's I have married a house-carpentèr,
> And I think he's a fine young man!'

"So look out, Mark! and remember, all o' you, that they're talkin' turn about; and he begins—

> " 'If you'll forsake your house-carpentèr
> And go along with me,
> I'll take you to where the grass grows green
> On the banks of the sweet Wil-lee!'

> " 'If I forsake my house-carpentèr,
> And go along with thee,
> It's what have you got for to maintain me upon,
> And to keep me from slave-ree?'

" 'It's I have sixteen ships at sea,
　　All sailing for dry land,
　　And four-and-twenty sailors all on board
　　　Shall be at your command!'

"She then took up her lovely little babe,
　　And she gave it kisses three;
　　'Lie still, lie still, my lovely little babe,
　　　And keep thy father compa-nee!'

"She dressed herself in rich array,
　　And she walked in high degree,
　　And the four-and-twenty sailors took 'em on board,
　　　And they sailed for the open sea!

"They had not been at sea two weeks,
　　And I'm sure it was not three,
　　Before this maid she began for to weep,
　　　And she wept most bitter-lee.

" 'It's do you weep for your gold?' cries he;
　　'Or do you weep for your store,
　　Or do you weep for your house-carpentèr
　　　You never shall see any more?'

" 'I do not weep for my gold,' cries she,
　　'Nor I do not weep for my store,
　　But it's I do weep for my lovely little babe,
　　　I never shall see any more!"

"They had not been at sea three weeks,
　　And I'm sure it was not four,
　　When the vessel it did spring a leak,
　　　And it sank to rise no more!"

"Now, Mark, here comes the moral:

　　"Oh, cruel be ye, sea-farin' men,
　　　Oh, cruel be your lives,—
　　A-robbing of the house-carpentèrs,
　　　And a-taking of their wives!"

The shouts and laughter which greeted the conclusion of Miss Lavender's song brought Dr. Deane into the room. He was a little alarmed lest his standing in the Society might be damaged by so much and such unrestrained merriment under his roof. Still he had scarcely the courage to reprimand the bright, joyous faces before him; he only smiled, shook his head, and turned to leave.

"I'm a-goin', too," said Miss Lavender, rising. "The sun's not an hour high, and the Doctor, or somebody, must take Mary Barton home; and it's about time the rest o' you was makin' ready; though they've gone on with the supper, there's enough to do when you get there!"

The chair rolled away again, and the bridal party remounted their horses in the warm, level light of the sinking sun. They were all in their saddles except Gilbert and Martha.

"Go on!" he cried, in answer to their calls; "we will follow."

"It won't be half a homecomin', without you're along," said Mark; "but I see you want it so. Come on, boys and girls!"

Gilbert returned to the house and met Martha, descending the stairs in her plain riding-dress. She descended into his open arms, and rested there, silent, peaceful, filled with happy rest.

"My wife at last, and forever!" he whispered.

They mounted and rode out of the village. The fields were already beginning to grow gray under the rosy amber of the western sky. The breeze had died away, but the odors it had winnowed from orchard and meadow still hung in the air. Faint cheeps and chirps of nestling life came from the hedges and grassy nooks of bank and thicket, but they deepened, not disturbed, the delicious repose settling upon the land. Husband and wife rode slowly, and their friendly horses pressed nearer to each other, and there was none to see how their eyes grew deeper and darker with perfect tenderness, their lips more sweetly soft and warm, with the unspoken, because unspeakable, fortune of love. In the breath of that happy twilight all the pangs of the past melted away; disgrace, danger, poverty, trial, were behind them; and before them, nestling yet unseen in the green dell which divided the glimmering landscape, lay the peace, the shelter, the lifelong blessing of home.